ALEXANDER WILSON was a writer, spy and secret service officer. He served in the First World War before moving to India to teach as a Professor of English Literature and eventually became Principal of Islamia College at the University of Punjab in Lahore. He began writing spy novels whilst in India and he enjoyed great success in the 1930s with reviews in the *Telegraph*, *Observer* and the *Times Literary Supplement* amongst others. Wilson also worked as an intelligence agent and his characters are based on his own fascinating and largely unknown career in the Secret Intelligence Service. He passed away in 1963.

By Alexander Wilson

The Mystery of Tunnel 51
The Devil's Cocktail
Wallace of the Secret Service
Get Wallace!
His Excellency, Governor Wallace
Microbes of Power
Wallace at Bay
Wallace Intervenes
Chronicles of the Secret Service

His Excellency, Governor Wallace

ALEXANDER WILSON

Allison & Busby Limited
12 Fitzroy Mews
London W1T 6DW
allisonandbusby.com

First published in 1936.
This edition published by Allison & Busby in 2015.

A CIP catalogue record for this book is available from
the British Library.

10 9 8 7 6 5 4 3 2 1

Paperback ISBN 978-0-7490-1825-2

Typeset in 10.25/15.5 pt Adobe Garamond Pro by
Allison & Busby Ltd.

The paper used for this Allison & Busby publication
has been produced from trees that have been legally sourced
from well-managed and credibly certified forests.

Printed and bound by
CPI Group (UK) Ltd, Croydon, CR0 4YY

CONTENTS

CHAPTER ONE

A Cabinet Meeting

Sir Leonard Wallace sank back into the comfortable depths of his well-upholstered chair, and gave vent to a deep sigh of satisfaction. The great oak desk before him was piled high with decoded reports from his numerous agents abroad, and for three hours he had been engaged in reading them with the utmost care, bringing to bear on every document that power of thoughtful concentration which enables him to grapple with the most difficult and delicate problems. Innumerable marginal notes pencilled in in his small but easily read calligraphy gave promise of much work in the near future for that branch of his staff which dealt exclusively with records and reports relative to international intrigue. Not that that was an unusual state of affairs. Of all Government departments the Intelligence Service is the hardest worked, and day and night, year in and year out, its activities continue quietly, efficiently, thoroughly. It is the eye of Empire, ever watching, ever searching, never for one moment sleeping, or even relaxing, for on its vigilance depends the well-being of Great Britain, her dominions and dependencies.

In repose Sir Leonard rather gives the impression that he is of indolent, lackadaisical character. He seldom permits a hint of the dynamic driving power that is in him to show on the surface. But those who are intimately acquainted with him, who work with him and under him, know the force that lies behind that cool, unruffled exterior, the imagination and quick perception of that brilliant brain. His amazing self-control and unexcitable temperament have, on numerous occasions, brought him triumphant through situations in which more nervous or ebullient men would have gone under.

He is a slightly built man of middle height, with an attractive, good-humoured face. Quick to see the amusing side of anything, his intense, steel-grey eyes yet seem often to belie the humorous curves of his mouth. During the Great War he lost his left arm, but, with the aid of an artificial limb, has overcome the handicap in surprising fashion. With his right hand he accomplishes much for which any other man would require two. The counterfeit member is invariably covered by a glove, and kept unobtrusively in a pocket, but at times is brought into action very cleverly. He used it now as he lay back in his chair, and filled his pipe from a large bowl on the desk. But directly the tobacco was burning to his satisfaction, the artificial hand was returned to its pocket. He pressed one of the buttons under the ledge of the desk, and almost at once, after a preliminary knock, a small, grey-haired man with extremely sharp eyes entered the room. Sir Leonard waved his hand towards the mass of reports.

'A nice little job that will keep your fellows going all night, Maddison,' he commented. 'A good many – those marked "Immediate" of course – must be dealt with without the slightest delay. By the way, Gottfried seems to be having as much work as he can cope with over that German–Czecho-Slovakian border affair. Is Cartright available?'

'Yes, sir.'

'Then tell him to join Gottfried at Zwickau. He'd better leave tonight. There's a pharmaceutical conference on and, as he's an expert in drugs, can easily pass himself off as a chemist and the representative of one of our big houses. Major Brien will furnish him with his credentials. Cartright will know how to get in touch with Gottfried.'

He smiled a trifle grimly, and an answering smile appeared fleetingly on the lips of the other, as he turned towards the door, his arms loaded with the documents he had lifted from the desk.

'Oh – er – Maddison, just a minute,' called Sir Leonard. 'Have we received any information concerning that Hong Kong scandal?'

The small, grey-haired man succeeded in getting one eye focused on Sir Leonard round the corner of his bundle.

'Nothing officially, sir,' he replied, 'but I think we'll soon be drawn in. As you know, there's a very hush-hush sort of Cabinet meeting at number ten this afternoon, and I believe it is being held to discuss the Hong Kong affair. It commenced at three, and was still on ten minutes ago.'

Wallace glanced at the clock on the mantelpiece, and smiled.

'Two and a half hours solid talk, and nothing accomplished

for a bet,' he remarked. 'Oh, well, if they can't come to a decision, we'll be asked to suggest something – perhaps to take the affair in hand. Tell Shannon and Carter to stand by. They may have a trip to Hong Kong before them.'

Maddison departed with his load. Sir Leonard rose, strolled into the adjoining lavatory where he washed his hand, and prepared to leave for home. While he was thus engaged, the low hum of the buzzer on one of the telephones with which his desk was adorned reached his ears. He returned to the office, and eyed the instrument somewhat quizzically.

'I thought so,' he murmured, as he lifted the receiver to his ear. 'Wallace speaking,' he announced.

'Can you come to Downing Street, Sir Leonard?' asked an urgent voice, which he recognised as that of the Premier's private secretary. 'An emergency meeting of the Cabinet is being held here, and the Prime Minister wishes me to inform you that a point has arisen about which it is necessary to consult you.'

'I'll be there in five minutes,' replied Wallace.

He replaced the receiver, knocked out the ashes of his pipe, and put on his hat.

'So I am to face the whole Cabinet,' he murmured. 'How nice for me! But they must be perturbed.'

Five minutes later exactly he was admitted to the historic precincts of 10 Downing Street, and ushered into the chamber where the conference was being held. A dozen pairs of eyes regarded his advent with interest not unmixed, in most cases, with relief. At the head of a long, highly-polished table sat the Prime Minister, his clean-shaven, ruddy countenance giving him the appearance of a sporting squire. There was no indication whatever in his physiognomy that he possessed any particular intellectual gifts, statesmanlike or otherwise. One could imagine him, attired in riding apparel, jogging round a country estate or following hounds. As head of the Government, presiding over a meeting of the Cabinet, he looked peculiarly out of place. On either side of the table, ranged according to precedence, sat the ministers of state. Sir Leonard was quick to note that, though there were a few absentees, all the most important members of the Cabinet were present. The Prime Minister greeted him courteously, inviting him to take a chair at the other end of the table.

'It was good of you to respond so promptly to my request to join us, Sir Leonard,' he acknowledged in a bluff, hearty voice, and continued: 'It is, as you are aware, rather unusual for anyone but a member of the Government to be present at a meeting of this nature. You, however, hold a privileged, I might add, unique position, and I believe I am correct in saying that this is not the first time you have been called into consultation at a conference of the Cabinet.'

Wallace felt inclined to ask him to come to the point, but tactfully made no comment. Verbosity, he well knew, was a disease which afflicted most members of Parliament. The Premier sat back in his chair, and folded his arms. He cleared his throat, as though about to launch into a lengthy oration.

'We have met today,' he went on, 'to discuss a very serious matter. My Right Honourable friend, the Secretary of State for the Colonies, has been the recipient of news of a most alarming nature from Hong Kong. For some time he has been receiving reports which caused him a great deal of unease, but only last night was he put in full possession of the startling facts. Sir Stanley Ferguson, His Majesty's representative in the colony, has sent a very full and exhaustive statement. It is not my intention to read it to you – you will have full access to that and all other documents relative to the subject. I will content myself by giving you the bare outlines.' He cleared his throat again, and Sir Leonard moved a little restlessly. 'It is generally regarded,' declared the leader of the Government, 'that your activities are mostly bound up in affairs under the purview of the Foreign Office, but—'

'Pardon me, sir,' interrupted Wallace; 'that is a misapprehension. It is true that most of the work accomplished by my department is in connection with foreign affairs and, therefore, I am in closer touch generally with the Foreign Secretary than with most other gentlemen of your Cabinet. May I remind you, however, that the Intelligence Service exists for the benefit of Great Britain not only in alien countries but at home, in the dominions, and the colonies as well. Some years ago there was a misunderstanding of that nature, as a result of which the functions of my department were clearly and succinctly outlined in a confidential memorandum to the heads of all Government offices.'

'Quite so! Quite so!' responded the Premier, smiling slightly as he turned his eyes momentarily in the direction of the Foreign Secretary. 'Nevertheless, one or two of my Right Honourable friends were not quite clear on that point. Your statement, Sir Leonard, will have done much to remove the possibility of future misapprehensions.'

'At the same time,' interposed the Foreign Secretary, it must be understood that my department is entitled to priority.'

In consequence of his remark, a debate on the subject threatened to develop, but Sir Leonard had no intention of sitting there a mute listener of a controversy that had no actual bearing on the business in hand. He startled the Right Honourable gentlemen, scandalised some, by interrupting.

'Gentlemen,' he protested, 'such a discussion is hardly relevant, if I am to be made acquainted with the matter for which I was summoned here. I have agents and assistants enough to undertake whatever duties are required, even if all of you were involved. It is only rarely that the exigencies of the service leave me in any way short-handed. At the moment, having heard something of the trouble in Hong Kong, I have given instructions for two of my most reliable men to hold themselves in readiness to proceed to China at a moment's notice.'

'You don't quite understand the situation yet, Sir Leonard,' observed the Foreign Secretary drily. 'The suggestion is that you be asked to go to Hong Kong yourself for a period of at least six months.'

If he had expected to see Wallace show his surprise, he was disappointed, but probably because he knew the Chief of the Secret Service well, and had had more dealings with him than any of the others, he anticipated nothing of the sort. Sir Leonard merely leant a little forward, and addressed the Prime Minister.

'Perhaps you will be good enough to give me the bare outlines of this Hong Kong affair, sir, as you intimated you were about to do.'

'Certainly,' was the reply, 'but, before I proceed, it may save time, if you tell me how much you already know. You mentioned a moment ago that you had heard something of the trouble in Hong Kong.'

'My knowledge amounts to little more than a rumour, sir, to the effect that there has been a serious embezzlement of funds, and that the secret of certain fortifications is known to Japan.'

The Premier inclined his head gravely.

'That is the gist of our information,' he admitted. 'It appears that for some years the Government of Hong Kong has been systematically defrauded of large sums of money, the total amount of which is believed to be in the neighbourhood of a hundred million dollars – that is ten million pounds. Cleverly forged government bonds were responsible for the greater part of the leakage, but false contracts, fictitious loans, and various other criminal activities have also played their part. Some months ago it was brought to Sir Stanley Ferguson's notice by the then Senior Assistant Treasurer, who, on the resignation of the Colonial Treasurer, took the latter's place, that all was not well. He instituted an enquiry, as a result of which it was discovered that expenditure since the war had increased by two hundred per cent, when on paper only fifty per cent, a reasonable increase, had been shown. Various officials were suspended, and are awaiting trial, but it is obvious that they are merely catspaws. Everything pointed to the belief that a powerful organisation was manipulating the finances. It sounds incredible, but there can be little doubt that such was the case.

'Sir Stanley ordered the most rigid investigation, and at last it was discovered that a wealthy Macanese, by name of Mathos, was involved. His arrest was immediately ordered, but when the police arrived to apprehend him he was found to have committed suicide. Certain papers were seized and, although no names were mentioned in these, they proved beyond doubt that there are certain members of the Legislative Council implicated. As you will see from a perusal of Sir Stanley's report, various incidents, presumably having a bearing on the conspiracy, have taken place in rapid succession. A magistrate in Shanghai, who telegraphed that important information had come into his hands, was asked to repair to Hong Kong. On the voyage he disappeared over the side of the steamer, and was drowned. A Chinese banker who declared that he knew a great deal was found dead in bed. He had been poisoned. You will gather, therefore, how urgent it is that the truth must be discovered and the guilty unmasked. Absolute disaster looms ahead, unless the conspiracy is quickly and definitely crushed. The latest information includes the news that a Japanese merchant found in prohibited territory, and arrested, boasted that the Hong Kong fortifications were as an open book to the government of his country. He refused to say more, however. It appears likely that the betrayal of our military secrets is connected with the other affair, but of that, I understand, there is no absolute proof.

'The police seem helpless; Sir Stanley Ferguson has done his utmost, but is on the verge of a nervous breakdown. This is a matter, Sir Leonard, which we feel can only be dealt with by you. Experts sent out by you may accomplish much, but affairs are in such an extremely serious state that we are agreed that it is necessary for you to be on the spot with full executive power in your hands.'

He paused, and regarded Wallace earnestly.

'You mean—' began the latter.

'I mean that my Right Honourable colleague, the Secretary of State for the Colonies, proposes, with our full sanction, to give Sir Stanley Ferguson six months' leave of absence, to be extended if necessary, to enable him to recover fully his health, his place, while he is away, to be filled by you.'

As he finished speaking, all eyes in that famous apartment were turned on Sir Leonard; there fell an almost heavy silence as though everyone was endeavouring to breathe as quietly as possible. The Secretary of State for the Colonies, a man whose expression was habitually solemn, made no attempt to hide his anxiety. Several others were there who appeared just as concerned. The Foreign Secretary sat erect, a frown upon his ascetic countenance. He was torn between two emotions; the feeling that Sir Leonard's absence in the Far East for such a long period might place activities nearer home at a serious disadvantage, and the knowledge that he was the only man at all likely to save the situation in Hong Kong and unmask the conspirators. Wallace himself sat calmly turning over the proposition in his mind. Presently a smile curved his lips.

'I have never,' he declared, 'felt the slightest ambition to be governor of a colony.'

'That is well known,' returned the Colonial Secretary drily. 'My predecessor took some time to recover from the shock of your point blank refusal, when you were offered Ceylon some two or three years ago. But,' he added eagerly, 'this is a different proposition. It will be only a temporary appointment. We realise that in asking you to abandon your headquarters for seven or eight months we are more or less jeopardising other national interests, but you can always keep in touch with the man you leave in charge in case of emergency.'

Again Sir Leonard smiled.

'I am not worrying about that,' he remarked. 'I am not indispensable by any means. There are two or three men capable of taking my place. I am quite prepared to go to Hong Kong, but I am not convinced yet that it is necessary for me to go out as governor. I would prefer to undertake the mission without any official designation.'

'We feel,' the Prime Minister assured him, 'that it is necessary you should have full executive power. Without it you may be gravely handicapped.'

Sir Leonard rose from his chair.

'If you will let me have all documents relative to the conspiracy, sir,' he observed, 'I will study them tonight, and consider thoroughly my own position as possible investigator from every angle.'

'They will be sent to you by special messenger within half an hour,' promised the Premier.

'If I accept, will I be given absolute *carte blanche*?'

'You will.'

'I presume the affair is to be kept as secret as possible? Nothing more than is absolutely necessary should be allowed to reach the press.'

'Every precaution will be taken to ensure that,' was the reply. 'And when can I expect to hear from you, Sir Leonard?'

'You will have my decision at ten o'clock tomorrow morning.'

Wallace bowed courteously, and walked from the room.

CHAPTER TWO

Wallace Accepts the Appointment

Sir Leonard retired to bed at a very late hour that night. It was the height of the London season, and he attended one or two functions with Lady Wallace before he felt himself at liberty to seek the seclusion of the study of his house in Piccadilly. There eventually, he removed his dress coat, donned an old smoking jacket and, having filled and lit a pipe, settled down to a careful perusal of the reports sent from Sir Stanley Ferguson, the Governor of Hong Kong, to the Colonial Secretary. Although of a lengthy nature they were distinctly discursive and prolix, and he learnt little more from them than he already knew. There was not the slightest doubt, however, that an exceedingly grave situation had arisen in the Far East, and it was not long before he decided that, if he were to cope with the conspiracy at all successfully, it was necessary for him to be on the spot himself. Whether it was politic that he should go out as Acting-Governor was a different matter, and he sat considering the point until well in to the small hours. Apart from his own dislike of holding a position in which he would necessarily be almost continually in the limelight, he felt at first that being so much in the public eye would be a distinct obstacle to his activities. On the other hand it would certainly be a definite advantage to possess full executive power, while it should be possible to shed the limelight on occasions if essential. Carefully he weighed up all the pros and cons and, at last, locking away the documents in his safe, went off to bed with his mind made up. He had decided to accept the Premier's offer.

He told Lady Wallace at breakfast that he had been asked to act as Governor of Hong Kong while Sir Stanley Ferguson was on leave. She was astonished, especially when he went on to inform her that, on consideration, he had resolved to take the post. Molly longed ardently for the day to come when her husband would retire from his position as Chief of the Intelligence Service, and either accept an appointment of less danger, or settle down to the life of a country gentleman. Always when he left her on his hazardous missions, she suffered the most acute anxiety, and a good deal of her life, in consequence, was an ordeal of nerve-racking apprehension. She did her utmost to hide her solicitude from him, knowing that her duty as his wife lay in doing all she could to assist, and not interfere with or hinder him in his work. Her nobility of character was to be expected in a woman whose family had ever been noted for its intense patriotism, but that did not prevent her from suffering. Sir Leonard fully realised what she endured, but never commented. His pride in her was perhaps even greater than her pride in him. Theirs was a great devotion and a perfect understanding. That he should be prepared to accept what, at least on the surface, appeared to be an innocuous appointment, even if it were only for six months or thereabouts, gave her a good deal of surprise as well as unqualified delight. Of course, she understood that behind it must lie some urgent necessity for his presence in Hong Kong, but she argued to herself that a public appointment of such a nature would, at least, be assured of comparative freedom from the dangers he usually faced.

Without going very deeply into the circumstances that had led to such an appointment being offered to him, he told her there had been malpractices in the control of finance in the colony and certain other leakages, and that he would be required to investigate. She felt a glow of pleasure, when he went on with a smile to talk of the success she would undoubtedly prove as 'The Governor's Lady'. He impressed upon her the necessity of making her preparations for the voyage at once in order that they could sail at the earliest possible moment. Afterwards he gave instructions to Batty, his manservant, which caused that worthy to beam with hearty approval. During his career as a sailor, Batty had been stationed in Hong Kong for two years on HMS *Tamar*, which had then been the guardship. The prospect of returning to the Far East appealed to him immensely. A gentleman who viewed the imminent departure of his chief with less complacence was Major Brien. He did not relish being left in charge at headquarters for so long a period.

'It will take you five weeks to go out and five weeks to return, on top of a sojourn out there of six months or more,' he complained. 'Hang it all, Leonard! You'll be away for at least eight months.'

'Well, what does that matter?' asked Wallace. 'I have perfect confidence in your ability to carry on.'

'I haven't. Suppose something requiring the brains and ingenuity that only you can provide turns up, what then?'

'Your trouble, Bill, is that you suffer from an inferiority complex. You have become so used to leaving things to me that you're afraid to rely upon yourself. But I rely upon you, so remember that. One of these days I may decide to retire. Then you would find yourself in charge permanently.'

'God forbid!' murmured Brien fervently. 'When you go I go also.'

'Nonsense! But reverting to the present situation: you have a splendid man in Maddison to support you, and several others, and you can always keep in touch with me in an emergency. Ten or twelve thousand miles means nothing in these days of wireless.'

Brien had perforce to be content with that but, as the time drew near for Sir Leonard's departure, the frown upon his second in command's brow grew more portentous, his fair hair seemed to become permanently ruffled. The Prime Minister had received Sir Leonard's decision at the time promised, and had made no attempt to hide the satisfaction it gave him. The appointment duly appeared in the *Gazette*, and Sir Leonard had the honour of being received by the King at Buckingham Palace. His Majesty once again showed his great interest in the work of the Intelligence Service, and expressed the hope that, in his forthcoming investigations, Wallace would be as successful as he had been in the past.

Sir Leonard left nothing to chance. Thorough in everything he did, he took care to ensure that, as far as possible, Major Brien should have no reason to complain that any instructions or advice that could be of assistance to him, while left in charge, should be neglected. With that meticulous regard for detail and power of anticipation that had always been the admiration of his lifelong friend, he made easy the path the latter would have to tread during his absence abroad. Carter, one of his ablest assistants, a young man who had graduated to the Secret Service by way of the Criminal Investigation Department, was to accompany him ostensibly as secretary. Another man, perhaps the most brilliant of his agents, had a prolonged interview with him, as a result of which Mr Gerald Cousins, travelling under an assumed name, left London very hurriedly by airliner one bright morning for the East. At last, a couple of days before he and Lady Wallace were due to embark at Marseilles, satisfied that he had neglected nothing, Sir Leonard allowed himself to relax. It was then that he received a typewritten missive dated from the Charing Cross Hotel.

Sir,
You will be well advised to abandon your intention of proceeding to Hong Kong. It will be realised by certain people in that colony that you have accepted the appointment of Governor for reasons not unconnected with their nefarious activities. Those people will not stick at murder to safeguard themselves.
I am, Sir,
Your obedient servant,
John Baxter

The receipt of such a document naturally had no effect on Sir Leonard's plans, but it afforded him a certain amount of elation. Here, he reflected, was one who perhaps could give him very important information. He and Maddison promptly visited the Charing Cross Hotel, and asked to see Mr Baxter. When the latter learnt who they were, he appeared terrified. He looked like a man on the verge of a nervous breakdown. Escorting them to his bedroom, and taking care to bolt the door, he declared that by accident he had discovered that a very prominent individual was concerned in the Hong Kong conspiracy. Since then he had gone in fear for his life. He had narrowly escaped assassination on several occasions, and eventually, giving up an important post that he had held for years, had left Hong Kong, and returned to England. Even then, he asserted, he was not safe. Only that morning he had discovered that the rooms on either side of his had been engaged by three Phillipinos, thought to be brothers – two being in one, and the third occupying the other apartment alone. Their name – Gochuico – was unfamiliar to him, but that meant nothing. The significant fact was that the important individual, of whose connection with the scandal he was aware, had Philippinos in his service.

He was extremely reluctant to divulge the name of the man, but, urged by Sir Leonard, he was about to do so when, from the direction of the window, came the sharp report of a revolver, followed by a groan as Baxter collapsed. Maddison at once sprang to his side, and bent over him. He was dead, a small hole in the centre of his forehead testifying to the accuracy of the shot that had been fired at him.

Heedless of his own danger, Wallace had darted across to

the window. As far as he could see there was no one outside, but he quickly discovered how the assassin had come – and gone. The rooms below possessed bay windows, and thus extended some feet farther out than those of the floor above, forming a kind of balcony. The murderer had simply stepped out of the window of a neighbouring room, no doubt had listened to the conversation and, at the crucial moment, had killed Baxter, afterwards diving back from whence he had come. Shouting to Maddison to send for the manager, and telephone Scotland Yard, Sir Leonard tore across to the door, and stepped out into the corridor. He was just in time to observe three men hurry into an elevator. One glanced back. He was a small fellow with black hair, sallow complexion, and dark, almond-shaped eyes. The others were a little taller, but he could not see their faces. His shouts to the lift attendant were not heard, whereupon he raced desperately down the stairs. He was too late, of course, to intercept them, but he learnt the direction the men had taken.

For a long time, aided by the station police and several porters, Sir Leonard searched the neighbourhood without success. The Philippinos had vanished completely. He gave up the quest at last, returning to the hotel. Except in the neighbourhood of Baxter's room, there appeared no excitement. Residents and members of the staff had either not heard the shot, or had mistaken it for something less thrilling. Inspector Graham of Scotland Yard was in charge; had already searched the adjoining rooms, finding several indications of a hurried flight. There was little doubt that the Gochuico brothers had followed Baxter to England, and that it was one of them who had murdered him.

The suitcases belonging to the Philippinos were opened, and carefully searched by Maddison and Wallace, but nothing was found to give a clue in any way to the identity of the man who had ordered Baxter's death; nothing, in fact, of any help whatever. The dead man's belongings proved equally negative. In the numerous letters and notebooks found in his trunk there was no mention at all of the Hong Kong scandal, and certainly of no one likely to be involved in it. Somewhat disappointed, Sir Leonard eventually gave up the search, and, as the police surgeon had arrived with another inspector, he and Maddison departed, leaving the police to take charge. He telephoned Scotland Yard for news that night after dinner. He was told that the three Gochuico brothers were still at large, and no clue to their whereabouts had been obtained. A description of them had been circulated, and all ports warned, but, as Sir Leonard remarked, there was not much hope. Men who had committed a crime so daring would be certain to have taken steps to ensure their getting away safely from England.

He felt that he had been robbed of an opportunity of obtaining some valuable information. However, the knowledge he possessed might be of great assistance in his efforts to unmask the Hong Kong conspirators. Whether or not the three men who had tracked Baxter to England were really brothers and their name Gochuico, it should not prove a very difficult task to discover what prominent citizen of Hong Kong employed men of their race. Wallace had not anticipated an easy task in Hong Kong, or one free from danger. Events would now cause him to be doubly cautious. He had had ample proof of the lengths to which the conspirators would go.

It was necessary, of course, that certain aspects of the murder of Baxter should be hushed up; that no mention of the Secret Service being interested should be permitted to come out at the inquest. The police handled the matter satisfactorily enough from Sir Leonard's point of view. They furnished the press with the story of a vendetta which had ended in Baxter being traced to London and assassinated. The manager of the hotel was sworn to secrecy regarding the presence on the scene of the Chief of the Intelligence Corps and his assistant, Maddison. As the name of his hotel was not divulged, he was somewhat relieved. It is no advertisement for a hotel to be known as the scene of a murder.

Leaving Major Brien and Maddison to watch events, with instructions to learn all they could from the Gochuicos, in the event of the latter being captured, Wallace left London with his wife by the P&O special train. Their son, Adrian, remained in England at school, to his great disgust. Lady Wallace had been inclined to persuade her husband to allow the little fellow to accompany them, but he had pointed out that Adrian was getting on so well at school that it would have been a great pity to have interrupted his progress for so long a period as eight months. At the back of his mind was the feeling that, if danger arose in Hong Kong, it would be better if Adrian were not in the colony. He was not too happy about Molly accompanying him, but, short of telling her his fears, he was unable to furnish her with any reason why she should remain in England.

They had their first taste of the formality of the life of a governor of a British Colony, when they were officially received at Marseilles by the captain of the ship on which they were to travel. They embarked at once; Carter, who was to act as Sir Leonard's secretary, following them up the gangway, leaving Batty and Lady Wallace's maid to see to the disposal of the luggage. The captain entertained them in his cabin for half an hour before the *Rawalpindi* sailed, and Sir Leonard impressed on him that the less formality there was on the boat the better he would be pleased. Captain Taylor smiled with a good deal of relief.

'I am glad to hear you insist on that, Sir Leonard,' he admitted with bluff heartiness. 'We get so many bigwigs – I beg your pardon,' he interrupted himself with a grin, 'I meant important people – travelling to and fro who insist on the strictest punctilio that it is a comfort to know you want none of it.'

When Lady Wallace had gone to her cabin to get settled in, as she put it, Captain Taylor became grave.

'It's none of my business, of course, Sir Leonard,' he observed, 'but, knowing who you are and something of affairs in Hong Kong, it doesn't require a great deal of acumen to guess why you are going there as governor. If I may presume to give you a word of warning, I advise you to be continually on the *qui vive* from the moment you set foot on the island.'

'What do you know?' questioned Wallace sharply.

'Nothing. That is, nothing of any help to you. There is a gigantic conspiracy going on, aimed, it is believed, chiefly at Britain's power in the Far East. It won't cease because that wholesale embezzlement of government funds has been discovered. My knowledge merely amounts to what I have been told in the clubs, the office, and by the compradors who come aboard full of tales, and I suppose your official information is infinitely greater and more reliable than mine.'

'I'm not so sure,' commented Sir Leonard. 'A Chinese comprador very often possesses a fund of private intelligence that is far more valuable than any amount of official information.'

Captain Taylor smiled.

'Ah! You know the breed?'

'Well enough to feel interested in anything you can repeat that has been told to you by them about affairs in Hong Kong.'

'I'll do my best, sir, to remember all I have been told during the voyage, and place it at your disposal.'

'Thanks.'

There came a knock at the door; a young officer looked in.

'Pilot's aboard, sir,' he announced, 'and all's ready for casting off.'

The captain nodded, and dismissed him with a wave of his hand. He and Sir Leonard rose from their chairs.

'Tell me,' invited the latter; 'why did you think it necessary to warn me to be on my guard in Hong Kong?'

Taylor shrugged his shoulders.

'Your reputation is well-known all over the world,' he replied, 'and if it is so evident to me why you, of all men, should accept an appointment of such a nature, it is hardly likely that the men you are after will overlook the reason. They will fear your coming, Sir Leonard, and I'm afraid will do their utmost to – to—'

He hesitated.

'Put me out of the way,' supplied Wallace with a smile. 'Perhaps you are right, Taylor, but for heaven's sake keep your fears to yourself when my wife is about.'

'Of course,' returned the other, a suspicion of indignation in his tone. 'I shall be glad,' he went on, 'if you and Lady Wallace will do me the honour of taking coffee with me up here after dinner, sir.'

'We shall be delighted,' responded Wallace, 'if you'll remember to refrain from being so confoundedly formal.'

The captain chuckled, and went up to the bridge. Descending to the promenade deck, Sir Leonard stood with the chattering throng watching the hawsers being cast off, as the tugs got into position, and began to warp the *Rawalpindi* from the P&O dock. The throb of the engines, the hoarse commands from the bridge, the excitable shouting of the French dockhands on the quay below gave him a sense of thrill. Lady Wallace found him, and they stood together watching the panorama of Marseilles, as the ship drew out from the docks and headed for the open sea. The great statue of the Virgin surmounting the belfry of Notre Dame de la Garde sparkled in the sunshine; every detail was visible. A funicular car could be seen clearly, as it made its way up the mountainside to the church which probably holds the most commanding position of any place of worship in the world. Several of their fellow passengers, the majority men, also stayed in the neighbourhood, but they had no eyes for the charms of the land they were rapidly leaving. Unobtrusively they were looking at and admiring the beautiful woman so close to them. Sir Leonard knew it, and smiled to himself. He was quite used to the sight of approving men and envious women studying the glorious chestnut hair waving so attractively round the shapely head, the deep blue eyes, perfectly formed lips, dainty nose, and clear unspoilt complexion of his wife. He felt no resentment; rather he approved. He was generous enough and humble enough to feel that he had no right to monopolise such beauty.

It was not until the Château d'If in its rocky fastness, and with its memories of Edmond Dantes, was left far astern that he and his wife moved. Lady Wallace went below, while Sir Leonard strolled along to the smoking room. There he found Carter, and invited that young man to have a drink with him. One or two of the girls on board had already noticed the tall, well-knit, good-looking man with the bronzed complexion, wavy brown hair and patrician features; had probably decided that he would be a distinct acquisition as companion and playmate to help pass away the tedious hours of the voyage. Carter, catching sight of the inviting smile on the lips of one young siren, had promptly retired to the safety of the smoke room.

'You know, sir,' he said in reply to a remark of Sir Leonard's, 'there's something about a boat which makes it dangerous for a mere man who puts his job before everything else. Women seem to acquire some sort of enchantment that is hard to resist. If I ever get married – which the Lord forbid – it will be because of the atmosphere on board ship.'

Wallace laughed.

'I'm afraid I cannot allow you to become romantic on this trip, Carter,' he declared, 'there is too much depending on it. I want a secretary with all his wits about him.'

The happy-go-lucky nature of Tommy Carter came to the rescue. He grinned broadly.

'You can depend on me, sir,' he proclaimed. 'Can't think what made me talk such rot.'

Sir Leonard watched the men thronging the smoke room, and calling loudly for drinks. Most of them, tanned by years spent under tropic suns, were easy to place. Members of the Indian Civil Service with their bored air of superiority, keen-eyed engineers, cheery soldiers were all among those present. Others there were whose occupations were more difficult to guess at, including specimens of that peculiar type of individual, so common in the East, who always seems to have plenty of money, is seen everywhere, yet has no definite employment as far as can be ascertained. Wallace finds a fascination in studying his fellow men. It is certain that he learns more about them in a casual glance than the majority of human beings would discover on fairly intimate acquaintance. Idly now he watched them as they sat at the small tables or crowded round the bar, waited upon by stewards or attended to by the barman and his mate.

Suddenly he stiffened. A man had entered the saloon, stood looking round somewhat self-consciously as though he had come to seek somebody, but was not in his own part of the ship. He was of medium height, thin, and sallow, with almond-shaped eyes, and black shiny hair. He bore a remarkable resemblance to the little Philippino of whom Wallace had obtained a glimpse in the Charing Cross Hotel, though taller and slimmer. Sir Leonard felt certain that this man was one of the Gochuico brothers, and a feeling of satisfaction shot through him. The newcomer presently caught sight of the man for whom he was searching; edged his way towards a stout, prosperous-looking Chinaman dressed in perfectly fitting European clothes. But before he reached the latter he was turned back by a peremptory shake of the head. Wallace, watching without appearing to do so, saw the Philippino disappear from the smoking saloon, observed the Chinaman quickly follow him, and noted the covert glance that the latter shot in his direction, before he, too, went out. Carter suddenly became aware of the curious smile on his chief's lips.

'Has anything happened, sir?' he asked eagerly.

'We are just entering upon the second act of our little play,' was the quiet response.

CHAPTER THREE

Enter Wun Cheng Lo

Glorious weather favoured the *Rawalpindi* on her run to Port Said. The Mediterranean was at its calmest and bluest and, though the late August sun shone with fierce intensity, its heat was tempered by a slight head wind, strong enough and fresh enough to keep everybody comfortable and in good spirits. Deck games were quickly in full swing and, before long, Sir Leonard, mixing freely with his fellow passengers, and entering wholeheartedly into their pastimes, had proved himself extremely difficult to beat at deck tennis and quoits. He and Carter frequently partnered each other at doubles in the former game, and became known as the invincibles.

Captain Taylor and the Chief of the Intelligence Service became very good friends. The former spent as much time as he could spare with Sir Leonard, though never obtruding. He repeated all the information he had obtained of affairs in Hong Kong to Wallace, none of it, unfortunately, adding very materially to the knowledge the latter already possessed. It became the usual thing for them to take coffee together in the captain's cabin after dinner at night, when they would discuss the conspiracy that, like a canker, was eating away the security of Great Britain in the Far East. Sometimes Lady Wallace would sit with them, but was generally too much in demand on the promenade deck, where dancing was indulged in nightly. Both men took care never to refer to the subject uppermost in their thoughts in her presence.

Inquiries elicited the fact that the stout Chinaman, who had roused Sir Leonard's interest on the first day of the voyage, was a wealthy merchant of Kowloon. As far as could be ascertained, he was a man of unimpeachable character and integrity who, in many ways, had accomplished much of value in the social and economic life of the colony. But his behaviour in the smoking saloon and intimacy with a second class passenger, whom Wallace was convinced was one of the Gochuico brothers, made him suspect. Observation of the little happenings had, more than once, enabled the Secret Service man to discover events of far-reaching importance. From the moment that he had followed the presumed Philippino from the smoking room, the Chinaman was under observation. Acting on Sir Leonard's instructions, Carter, in the most casual manner, began to cultivate his acquaintance. The Kowloon merchant, under the impression that it was he who had sought Carter's company, would have been surprised to know the truth. In the same manner, though less subtly, Batty struck up a fair amount of intimacy with the Philippino in the second class. The latter's name was down on the passenger list as Feodoro, he admitted to his nationality, and there were certainly no others of his breed on the boat. Nevertheless, Wallace felt certain he was one of the three who had been residents of the Charing Cross Hotel.

It was while the ship was running at reduced speed through the Straits of Messina that Wallace first had any conversation with the Chinaman. The beauty of that delectable spot was somewhat marred by a slight mist, but the passengers crowded the decks, eager to drink to the full the charm of one of the loveliest panoramas in the world. Etna was completely obscured, but the neighbouring hills, with Messina itself nestling coyly at the base, were plainly visible. The gentle slopes of Calabria on the other side, with the white walls of Reggio appearing to descend until they were embraced by the softly lapping waves, were at times shrouded in the filmy vapour, at others glistening in the sunshine. Men and women, sitting precariously in small boats rocked by the swell caused by the passing of the liner, waved handkerchiefs, and smiled happily up at the crowded decks. An Italian ship, the *Genova*, bound from Bombay to Naples and Genoa, passed, it seemed, within a stone's throw. A white-clad figure flourished his arms from the bridge. Captain Taylor waved back. He informed Sir Leonard afterwards that the man he had saluted was Captain Ferrara, one of the most genial and best liked skippers who had ever sailed east of Suez.

Wallace noticed the exchange of friendly greetings, and focused his glasses on the bridge of the other vessel. He saw a stocky figure with fair hair and moustache whose round face was beaming with delight. A thoroughly good fellow, he decided, and turned away, little guessing that he was to meet the Italian under very different circumstances. The ferry was passing some distance ahead, and he was about to look at the long low boat carrying a train across the Straits, when his elbow hit a stanchion, and he dropped the glasses. At once a man close by stooped, picked them up, and handed them to him with a low bow. It was the Chinaman.

'Permit, your Excellency,' he said in perfect though somewhat flowery English, 'this low-born hand to return the binoculars to your honourable keeping.'

'Thank you,' nodded Wallace. He was about to turn away, but changed his mind. The man obviously was eager to have speech with him. Sir Leonard decided to give him the opportunity.

'I presume you are destined for China?' he smiled. 'Is it Hong Kong or Shanghai?'

'Hong Kong, your Excellency,' was the reply. 'I have the privilege of being an insignificant merchant of that jewel of the sublime British Crown. It is my humble desire to be of service to your Excellency.'

'That is very nice of you, Mr—'

'Wun Cheng Lo is the name bestowed on their unimportant son by his honourable parents, illustrious sir.'

'Well, in what way do you think you can be of service to me, Mr Wun Cheng Lo?'

'In Hong Kong the times are inauspicious for a change of executive. I know, of course, that the present high-born and eminent Governor, Sir Stanley Ferguson, is ill—'

'Oh, and how did you know that?'

The Chinaman shrugged his broad shoulders.

'Even the humblest of your servants is acquainted with

news that is common to all interested in Hong Kong.'

'I see,' commented Wallace. 'I did not know that knowledge of Sir Stanley's ill health was so universal.'

'Your Excellency will pardon me, if I presume to remind you that, had the exalted Sir Stanley been in good health, there would have been no need for him to be relieved by your noble self.'

His face remained entirely impassive as he spoke, but Sir Leonard caught a gleam that looked distinctly cynical in his eyes.

'That is quite true,' agreed the Chief of the Secret Service. 'But in what way are the times inauspicious for a change of governors?'

Again came a shrug of the shoulders.

'Events are happening which it is unwise for a man of inquiring mind to investigate. Your magnificent reputation, your Excellency, will be known to the base dogs who live only for their own advancement to the detriment of the honourable nation they are supposed to serve. They will fear you, and with fear will go murderous designs.'

'Look here,' exclaimed Wallace sharply, 'are you warning me against some imaginary danger?'

'Not imaginary, your Excellency,' Wun Cheng Lo shook his head solemnly. 'I am afraid there are low-born wretches in Hong Kong who will seek your death to prevent your discovering their evil plots.'

'Who are these people?'

The Chinaman shook his head.

'That valuable knowledge is withheld from me. But I return to Hong Kong hoping that I shall be able to put my humble service at your disposal. It is my desire to seek until I can uncover these vile plotters who are making the colony stink with iniquity. I fear for you, illustrious Sir Leonard, therefore I go to aid you as far as in this poor insignificant body and brain lies.'

'Do you actually mean to say that you are going back to Hong Kong especially for that purpose?'

'That is so, your Excellency.'

'But why?'

'Because, though humble and of no account, I am not without influence, and am a loyal subject of the majestic might of Britain. It is my duty to do what I can.'

'You must know something of importance.'

'I know nothing, most honourable sir, but that which is known to all. But I have means by which it is possible I may glean information. My wretched servants are many, my lowly operations widespread. Everything I possess will be at your honourable disposal. In order to do my poor best for you, I make but one request.'

'What is that?'

'When in Hong Kong, I beg that I may have access to you at all hours – day or night. It may be necessary, your Excellency, if I am to be of real service to you.'

So that was what was behind all the assurances of loyalty and flowery protestation! Wun Cheng Lo wished to have access to Government House; to be able to come and go without question. He seemed to be rather transparent for a Chinaman. Yet, wondered Sir Leonard, would he have had any suspicions of the man, if he had not seen the incident in the smoking saloon? The expression on the Englishman's face gave no indication of his thoughts; not a flicker of suspicion appeared in his eyes.

'I appreciate your desire to be of help to me in the event, which I doubt, of help being necessary, Wun Cheng Lo,' he observed. 'But what you ask is rather unusual. Not being a member of my staff, it would seem hardly desirable that you should have access to me at any time. Then again what guarantees have I of your good faith?'

'My name and reputation stand high,' replied Wun Cheng Lo, forgetting to be flowery in his apparent earnestness. 'Apart from that, your Excellency, I will always be alone, and members of your staff can be present when I have the honour of an interview with you.'

'And you really think the position in Hong Kong is such that I shall require assistance from people who are as loyal as you?'

'I know it, though my poverty-stricken mind has yet failed to suspect the direction from which danger will threaten your Excellency.'

'Very well, Wun Cheng Lo, I will consider your offer. I am grateful to you for making it, and am disposed to accept. We will speak again.'

The Chinaman, despite his bulky proportions, bowed almost to the ground, and departed. A little later Wallace repeated the conversation he had had to Carter.

'If I do get assassinated,' he chuckled, 'it will only be my fault with all the warnings I am getting.'

'But if, as you think, sir,' commented Carter, 'Wun Cheng Lo is on the other side of the fence, I can't see why he should give away his party's fears and suspicions concerning you.

After all, he is putting you on your guard, and that seems to me the very thing he would refrain from doing, if he is antagonistic to you.'

'Not a bit of it,' disagreed Sir Leonard. 'He knows very well – they all know – that I am not merely replacing Ferguson because he is ill. He realises that, with all the information concerning the situation in Hong Kong that must have been placed at my disposal, I am already as suspicious and on my guard as I am ever likely to be. If I am not very much mistaken, he also knows that I was present at the tragedy in the Charing Cross Hotel, and that I learnt a lot there. Therefore, he is not doing anything subversive to the interests of his fellow conspirators. On the contrary, by obtaining my trust and confidence, he is going a long way towards helping them. He will think that by warning me, and offering his services, I am bound to think he is loyal and above suspicion. He will argue that I should never suspect a man who did his utmost to put me on my guard. Then, if I accept the offer of his services as a kind of spy, he is in the unique position of being persona grata in Government House itself, and able to carry out any mischief his confederates care to hatch.'

'What do you intend to do, sir?'

'Accept his offer. If Mr Wun Cheng Lo is in the pay of the organisation that is wrecking Hong Kong – and I feel certain he is – he should be very useful to us. We'll let him think that we have the most touching faith in him. As time goes on, we'll even take him into our confidence, and tell him that I have really become Governor in order to investigate and smash the conspiracy.'

Carter grinned cheerfully. He loved this chief of his who

played the great game as though, in very truth, it were a game. He himself had been unable to find out anything of importance from the Chinaman. The latter had, however, cunningly attempted to pump Carter, much to that young man's amusement. That had been the only cause for suspicion he had given, though at the time, Carter was disposed to look upon it as idle curiosity and nothing more.

'Do you think he is likely to be a very important member of the organisation, sir?' he asked.

Wallace shook his head.

'No; but I believe he is the henchman of an important member, if not of the head himself. We're rather lucky, Carter. We don't altogether start with our eyes shut. Mr Wun Cheng Lo and the Philippino on board between them ought to give us considerable assistance, though they won't know they're doing it.'

'They must have kept in pretty close touch with their principal or principals in China.'

'Of course,' nodded Wallace. 'And I suspect that, now the Chinaman has left England, there will be no further cables of instructions. His job there has been accomplished. Every cable from Hong Kong since the murder of Baxter has been copied and sent to headquarters for examination to ascertain if it was in code. As there has been no wireless message from Maddison since we sailed, I presume nobody has been left behind for any reason. If there has, and instructions are sent to him, we'll be told – Maddison will see to that.'

The weather continued fine after leaving Suez, but it was appallingly hot in the Red Sea. Deck games and sports were confined to the evenings, and then only indulged in by the younger and hardier among the passengers. The majority lay about in deck chairs on any part of the deck where a breath of air could be obtained. Iced drinks were in constant demand, and the swimming bath became quite the most popular part of the ship. A general sigh of relief went up once Aden had been left behind, for it was much cooler in the Arabian Sea.

Considerably more than half of the passengers disembarked at Bombay, while there were only a few fresh arrivals. In consequence, the ship appeared almost empty when she sailed for Colombo. There the Governor-elect of Hong Kong and his wife were given an official reception, and a tour of the district had been arranged for their benefit. They would have preferred to have done their sightseeing in a less formal manner. Sir Leonard, in fact, although appreciating the thought underlying the reception, felt distinctly bored at times, especially during a garden party held in the afternoon under the auspices of the legislative council. A drive in the evening through the avenues of beautiful trees, where the scent of the cinnamon was at times almost overpowering, to Mount Lavinia was, both to him and Molly, the most enjoyable event of the day. As the *Rawalpindi* was not sailing until the next morning, they stayed the night as guests of the Governor at Government House. A number of additional passengers embarked at Colombo. They were scrutinised carefully by Carter, and information respecting them obtained as far as possible from the purser, especially concerning those bound for Hong Kong. None of them seemed to be other than perfectly harmless travellers.

Since his initial talk with Wun Cheng Lo, Sir Leonard had had occasional conversations with the Chinaman, without, however, referring more than casually to the subject which had originally come under discussion. Wun Cheng Lo, although his face maintained the unemotional, impassive expression common to most Chinamen, was undoubtedly burning to receive a satisfactory answer to the request he had made to the Englishman. Sir Leonard once or twice caught the eager light in his eyes when his offer to be of service was mentioned, and smiled to himself. He knew the Kowloon merchant was unwilling to repeat the suggestion that he should have access at all times to the new Governor of Hong Kong for fear of giving himself away by appearing too anxious.

At last, it was on the evening prior to the arrival of the ship in Singapore, the Chief of the Intelligence Department intimated to Wun Cheng Lo that he had thought matters over, and had decided to accept the latter's offer. He added that the Chinaman would be regarded as an unofficial and secret member of his staff, and orders would be given in Hong Kong that he was to be allowed to come and go without hindrance, on the strict understanding that his movements were to be very guarded in order to avoid giving suspicion to the opposition – if indeed the latter existed. Wun Cheng Lo bowed almost to the ground, thus preventing Wallace from noting the expression on his face. With a good deal of flowery declamation, he declared that henceforth he and all in his service would work for the sole purpose of confounding the enemies of the British State and protecting the life of the new Governor.

Inwardly longing to kick the fellow, Sir Leonard accepted his protestations with gratified dignity. Thereupon he proceeded to take Wun Cheng Lo into his confidence, admitting that his main object in accepting the appointment in Hong Kong was to be able to investigate the conspiracy, and unmask the conspirators. He confessed that he was very much in the dark, and would be compelled to rely to a great extent on his new ally. Wun Cheng Lo appeared almost overcome at the proof that such trust was to be placed in him, and reiterated his assertion of absolute devotion. Late that night, he despatched a wireless message to an address in Kowloon. The senior operator, who had been warned, handed a copy to the captain. The latter passed it on to Wallace, as they sat drinking their after-dinner coffee. It was in English, obviously without guile, for all the world to read, merely stating that negotiations had been successful, and that plans for undertaking the control of the new agency were to be put in hand at once. Sir Leonard chuckled softly to himself as he put the slip of paper into his pocket.

'Quite clever,' he commented. 'Our friend has informed those interested in Hong Kong that he has succeeded in following out their instructions, and has wormed his way into my confidence. He further advises that plans must be made immediately for my subjection in the light of the information now in their possession.'

Captain Taylor looked sharply at him.

'Do you really believe that?' he asked anxiously.

'There is just one chance in a thousand,' replied Wallace, 'that I am mistaken, and have misjudged Mr Wun Cheng Lo. But I am prepared to stake my life that I am right. To my mind, what I have to go on is pretty conclusive evidence. First, Cheng Lo meets the Philippino, and obviously does not want me to witness the meeting, to judge from the manner he signed to the other to leave the smoking room, and the glance he threw in my direction before following him. Second, he does his best to obtain my confidence and get me to accept him as a kind of protector, spy, and general agent. Third, when he apparently succeeds, he immediately sends a wireless message to Hong Kong, which, though outwardly perfectly innocuous, fits in admirably with what I calculate he really intends to convey. Fourth, my man Batty has reported that he has held several secret conversations late at night in a quiet part of the second class deck with the man who calls himself Feodoro. Batty was unable to get close enough to hear what was said. I don't suppose it would have been much good in any case, as they probably spoke in Chinese. You see, therefore, that I have really quite a lot to go on. As evidence in a court of law it would mean nothing, but to me it means a lot.'

'What are you going to do?' asked the captain. 'Will you have Wun Cheng Lo and the Philippino arrested on arrival in Hong Kong?'

'Good Lord, no! Through them I hope to find out who are behind the embezzlement of funds and leakage of State secrets in the colony. They don't know they are under suspicion; the Chinaman believes he has obtained my confidence. They'll be given as much rope as they want, but either I or one of my men will always be holding on to the other end.'

Captain Taylor shook his head doubtfully.

'Take care, Sir Leonard,' he warned once again. 'I don't think you realise what you are up against.'

'Do you?'

'No; but I am convinced it is something pretty big. An organisation probably with vast resources in men and money.'

'We know it has money,' commented Wallace drily, 'to judge from the amount that has percolated from the coffers of the treasury during the past few years.'

The Governor of the Straits Settlements was away on tour, when the *Rawalpindi* arrived at Singapore. He sent a message to Sir Leonard apologising for his absence, which certain unsettled conditions up-country had made necessary. Sir Leonard's anticipations of escaping an official reception were not altogether fulfilled, however. He found that he was expected to receive prominent officials, merchants, and other important people, and attend a luncheon to be held in his and his wife's honour at the club. Once that was over, however, he and Molly were allowed more or less to follow their inclinations. As the *Rawalpindi* was not sailing until late at night, there was plenty of time to inspect the city and its surroundings in fairly leisurely fashion. They took tea at Raffles Hotel, and later returned there for dinner to which Sir Leonard had invited a few guests of whom Captain Taylor was one.

Singapore by night is a fascinating spectacle, and Wallace with Taylor and the officer in command of troops sat on the veranda lazily smoking, and gazing at the myriad lights on the ships reflected dazzlingly from the water, while the other members of the party danced below. A large Chinese junk, looking grotesque and ghostly in the moonlight, languidly entered the harbour, her curiously shaped sails flapping idly against the mast. From somewhere came the plaintive melody of a native instrument. A woman's shrill voice raised in anger rose suddenly from a sampan, followed by the wail of a child. The three men, puffing contentedly at their cigars, felt thoroughly at peace with the world as they sat there. Unfortunately their contentment was not destined to last long. They heard the sound of running feet, a white clad figure, breathing rapidly, appeared on the veranda, which, being unlighted, made it difficult for him to distinguish between the trio.

'Captain Taylor?' he gasped questioningly.

'Here,' replied the commander of the *Rawalpindi*; then recognising the other as one of his own officers: 'What's the matter, Morrison?'

'There's been a murder, sir,' came the reply in agitated tones.

Taylor sat up suddenly.

'Murder!' he exclaimed. 'Not on the ship?'

'Yes, sir. A Chinese deck passenger who embarked today was found knifed. Mr Ramsay sent me to tell you.'

'Good Lord!' cried the perturbed skipper, rising hastily to his feet. 'I'll have to go at once. Excuse me, gentlemen.'

He hurried off, accompanied by his third officer. Sir Leonard and the general discussed the affair, and hazarded various conjectures without feeling a great deal of concern. A murder was not exactly a rare occurrence in that part of the world, though the fact that it had taken place on the P&O mail boat caused it to be of more interest to the two men. They came to the conclusion that the victim had been trying to escape from some vengeance, had been followed aboard by his enemy, or enemies, and assassinated.

'Poor beggar!' commented the general, 'but perhaps he deserved it. He'd probably stolen another man's wife.'

A soft-footed Malay servant appeared on the veranda, and informed him that he was wanted on the telephone. Excusing himself, he strolled away, leaving Sir Leonard alone. Hardly a minute had passed, when three figures crept, without the suspicion of a sound, towards the unconscious man. When they were within a yard or so of him, some sixth sense warned him of his danger, but too late. He sprang to his feet, but, at the same time, they flung themselves on him. A cloth saturated with the sickly, sweet-smelling fumes of chloroform enveloped his head. He strove to cry out, struggled feebly; then sank into their arms. As silently as they had come, they departed, carrying their burden with them.

A few minutes later the general returned to the veranda fuming with indignation. There had been no telephone call, and the man who had delivered the message had disappeared. It was certain he had not been an employee of the hotel.

'Can't understand it,' he began. 'Some sort of mistake I suppose, but a damn silly one. I'd like to—'

He became aware that Sir Leonard Wallace was absent. Never for a moment did he connect the two incidents. Throwing himself into his chair, and growling angrily, he sat waiting for the Governor-elect of Hong Kong to return.

CHAPTER FOUR

Batty Goes Ashore

Sir Leonard's manservant, Batty, once a naval seaman, now and for many years past the confidential servant of the Chief of the Secret Service, had enjoyed every moment of the voyage from Marseilles. It was very rarely that Sir Leonard went anywhere without the man who served him so well. Not only did the short, stout ex-sailor look after his employer's domestic and physical comfort, but on innumerable occasions had aided him in his investigations until he had come to be regarded, and certainly regarded himself, as an unofficial member of the Secret Service. He had accompanied Sir Leonard to most parts of the world, travelling with him in train, aeroplane, or ship, but it was only to be expected that he regarded the sea as his natural element, and was never so happy as when he felt the deck of a stout ship beneath his feet, and drew in great lung-expanding gusts of the good sea air. His cup of joy had been filled to overflowing by the prospect of visiting Hong Kong for a short spell. During his service on the China station, he had had a gloriously happy time, and ever since had hankered to revisit the land of such blissful memories.

He had become a favourite with the European quartermasters and other white members of the crew of the *Rawalpindi*. Even the Lascars, possibly recognising in him a son of the sea like themselves, had formed an affection for him, and were always eager to perform little services for him. Often, when his duties permitted, he was to be found yarning in the foc's'le, where the European members of the crew had their quarters, or sunning himself among them on the well deck. Nevertheless, he did not neglect what he considered his duty towards his fellow passengers of the second saloon. He became the life and soul of the happy company in that part of the ship. His twinkling blue eyes, round red face, and amusing little snub nose always were certain of bringing joy and laughter wherever he took them.

Religiously he went ashore at every port, having previously ascertained whether or not his employer had need of his services. At first, feeling in honour bound, he took Lady Wallace's maid with him, but as soon as she had formed friendships of her own, and he felt that he could safely leave her to the protection of her little circle, he took his shore leave, as he called it, with cronies of his own temperament and inclinations. At Port Said, he had spent a considerable sum of money at the emporium of Simon Arzt, had been called Mr McPherson by vendors of Turkish delight and would-be sellers of obscene postcards, and had had scraggy little chickens extracted from his nasal organ by the 'gulli, gulli' men. At

Aden he had taken his friends to see the so-called mermaids, visited the famous tanks, and imbibed tepid beer at enormous cost in a fly-blown restaurant. In Ceylon he had seriously contemplated a trip to Trincomali, which he remembered as a charming spot often visited by his ship when he had been on the East Indian station. But time and his obligations to Sir Leonard precluded this, and he satisfied himself with guiding a party round Colombo, most of the members of which knew it as well as he, but deferred to the superior knowledge his seafaring experience was supposed to have given him.

Despite all these relaxations, Batty never neglected his duty in the slightest degree. He was always on hand when required; it was never necessary to send for him. He has what may appear to some people the uncanny faculty of turning up when his employer is thinking that he may want him, but this is really the result of the perfect understanding between master and man. When told to keep his eye on the Philippino Feodora, and find out all he could about the man without making his intentions conspicuous, he set to work with such excessive zeal and caution that he almost defeated his own purpose. However, Carter was always within call, ready to give him advice. The Philippino proved very uncommunicative, probably because he knew of Batty's associations with Sir Leonard, but one item of information he did let drop, perhaps inadvertently, the night before the ship reached Singapore. It was to the effect that he had two brothers, whom he stated were in Hong Kong. The coincidence was too good to be overlooked. Sir Leonard felt that he now possessed another link in what he liked to call his chain of evidence.

Batty stood by while Sir Leonard and Lady Wallace were receiving their visitors on arrival in Singapore, but as soon as they had gone ashore for luncheon, he joined his friends, who were loyally, though somewhat impatiently, awaiting his coming. By that time it was close on twelve-thirty, the hour at which passengers in the second saloon partook of their midday meal. It was decided – the suggestion came from a Scotch engineer – to lunch on board before going ashore to sample the delights of Singapore. Afterwards, motor cars driven by Malays in gaily coloured sarongs took the overheated though boisterously happy party for a tour round the city and its neighbourhood. It was dusk when they arrived back at the docks, and, sad to relate, all but three, of whom Batty was one, had fallen by the wayside. The delinquents had insisted on sampling native spirits at the wayside drinking houses, at first more for the fun of the thing than for any other reason, but, as the potent liquid took possession of their senses, they had insisted, despite the indignant protests of Batty and the other two, in indulging in a regular drinking bout.

The ex-sailor and his companions, although helpless to get them to discontinue their orgy, remained with them for fear that harm might overtake them, knowing perfectly well that most natives would consider them fair prey if left to their own resources, and strip them of all they possessed. To their relief, they got them back to the docks much sooner than they had anticipated, principally because the offenders by that time were in too helpless a condition to protest. They were almost carried aboard, and deposited in their bunks, whereupon Batty delivered himself of an indignant protest.

'If I ever step ashore again,' he growled, 'with drunken lubbers what don't know 'ow to behave like Christian men an' drop anchor when they've taken enough aboard, I'll – I'll be in me second childhood.'

'Man, they were no' drunk when they stepped ashore,' the Scotch engineer, one of the sober stalwarts, reminded him.

'I think Batty means to say that he's not going to risk going ashore with them any more,' the third man, a sergeant in the Hong Kong police force, remarked.

'You're right, I'm not,' declared the ex-sailor. 'They behaved disgraceful. Why, what in 'caven's name d'you think my governor would say, if 'e knew that I was sailing in such company. I'm not goin' ashore with 'em again – no; not if they goes on their bended knees.'

'It's no verra likely ye wull,' put in the Scotsman drily, 'since ye disembark at Hong Kong, and Hong Kong is the next stop.'

Batty looked at him as though he had propounded a great and startling truth.

'Swab my decks!' he exclaimed picturesquely, 'you're right. I'd forgot that. It's a pity they went an' made 'ogs o' theirselves like that,' he added regretfully; 'they ain't bad coves.'

'Well, it can't be helped now,' put in the sergeant. 'They've rather spoilt things, but I propose we three go ashore, have a quiet little dinner somewhere, and enjoy the rest of the evening on our own.'

'Man,' protested the engineer, 'why spend gude siller on a dinner ashore, when a better one is provided here for which we ha' already paid? Let us eat here. Afterwards we can go across to Raffles, ha' a few wee drinks, and go to the pictures.'

The other two laughingly agreed.

It is a striking commentary on the irony of life that, if Batty's companions in disgrace had not indulged in a carouse and become thoroughly and hopelessly inebriated, the chances are that the career of Sir Leonard Wallace would have ended that night, that he would never have taken the oath as Governor of Hong Kong – to put it bluntly, that he would in all probability have been assassinated.

Still feeling somewhat aggrieved at the conduct of their erstwhile comrades, one or two of them had by then begun to regret bitterly their foolish indulgence in the raw, fiery poison brewed by the Malays, the sober three went ashore again half an hour or so after dinner, and wandered along to Raffles Hotel. As they approached the side entrance, making a circuit to avoid the gardens, where men and women sat in evening dress at little round tables, waited upon by Malay waiters, Batty happened to glance up. At that moment, Sir Leonard Wallace, Captain Taylor, and a tall, lean, military-looking man appeared on the veranda, and sank into chairs, which a servant had placed in position for them. Acting apparently under orders, the man then switched off the electric current, leaving the three in a kind of half-light. But Batty had observed that his master was in evening dress and, under his breath, he bitterly reproached himself. In the annoyance caused by the debacle of the afternoon and early evening, it had quite slipped his mind that Sir Leonard would want to dress for dinner. It is true that he had told Batty he would not require him any more that day, when he had first gone ashore, obviously intending to fend for himself. But the ex-sailor always made it a point of honour, whether off duty or not, to turn up in the evening to help his employer dress, unless he had been definitely told that Sir Leonard did not intend to change, or, as sometimes happened, Lady Wallace informed him that she would assist her husband. Although remarkably expert in the use of one hand, Sir Leonard was not entirely able to cope with the intricacies of evening dress. Tying a bow, for instance, beat him completely. Batty felt that, for almost the first time since he had been in the service of the Chief of the Intelligence Department, he had let him down.

'The swabs!' he muttered, blaming the drunken quartette who had taken up so much of his time and attention. 'The perishing swabs!'

His companions heard him, and inquired into the reason of his fresh outburst. When he explained, they merely laughed, being quite unable to understand his point of view. But he continued to feel annoyed with himself; even the drinks he consumed, the music of an excellent band, and the bustle and glitter of the bar altogether failing to cure the depression his lapse had cast upon his spirits. Before accompanying his companions to the pictures, he decided that he would have to see Sir Leonard and explain. He told the others of his intentions and, although still expressing their amusement, they assured him they would wait for him.

'I might 'ave to sail about in the offing for a bit before I get a chance of a word with him,' he said.

'Well, don't sail about too long,' returned the sergeant jovially.

Batty asked his way to the veranda, where he had caught a

glimpse of Sir Leonard and, after satisfying the under-manager, to whom he spoke, of his *bona fides*, received the necessary directions. He was about to walk up the stairs, when he saw Captain Taylor, accompanied by a ship's officer, emerge from a lift, and hurry through the lounge. Wondering idly what had happened to cause the commander of the *Rawalpindi* to look so stern and to move in such a precipitate manner, the ex-sailor went on his way. He lost himself twice, but eventually got in the right direction. He came to a semi-lighted room in which he met four natives laboriously carrying a roll of carpet. They hurried by at sight of him, and he caught a whiff of some odour which was vaguely familiar. The veranda opened out from the room and, after hesitating a moment or two, he peered out. To his surprise there was nobody there. At first he thought he had come to the wrong place, but the sight of the three chairs, and a glance at the gardens below, convinced him that he had not made a mistake. He walked on to the veranda, wondering where his employer had gone. The sight of a half-smoked cigar smouldering away on the floor surprised him. He picked it up, and examined it. It was a Henry Clay, a brand Sir Leonard usually smoked; then a faint aroma of the perfume he had so recently noticed reached his nostrils. Suddenly he remembered what it was, and a dreadful suspicion assailed him. His face went white under the tan, and, without a moment's hesitation, he dashed from the veranda, across the room, bent on finding the men carrying the carpet, and demanding that they should unroll it.

Two ladies, fanning themselves vigorously, met him in a corridor, and stood astounded as he tore by. A waiter hurried round a corner carrying a tray. Batty grabbed him fiercely, upsetting the glasses in his charge, almost shouting at him as he asked if he had seen four men carrying a roll of carpet. Fortunately the waiter understood English. In trembling tones, he related that he had seen them going down the service staircase. They had told him they were taking the carpet to be cleaned. Shouting that he did not want to know what they had told him, Batty, in his agitation, shook the man until his teeth rattled; demanded to know in which direction were the service stairs. Having obtained the information, the ex-sailor released the now thoroughly frightened Chinaman, and tore off in the direction indicated. He found them without difficulty; descended in headlong fashion. At the bottom, passages, into which opened numerous apartments, seemed to run in every direction. For a moment Batty stood irresolute, wondering which way to turn. There was nobody about to ask. Then he heard the throb of a motor engine, the sound came from straight ahead, and without further hesitation he hastened on. He quickly reached a doorway and, tearing through, found himself at the back of the premises in a large compound. A van stood, the engine running, a few yards away, and he caught a glimpse of the carpet as it was finally being stowed inside.

Three men, standing by the door at the back, saw him coming, sprang into the interior of the vehicle, at the same time yelling to the driver. The latter immediately slipped in his clutch, and the car started to move as Batty reached the door. He made a frantic grab, but a savage blow, catching him on the side of the head, sent him reeling to the ground. If he had had any doubts before, he was convinced now that he was on the right track; that the body of Sir Leonard was

inside the roll of carpet. Feeling sick and dizzy he staggered
to his feet, and set off in pursuit of the van which was now
beginning to get up speed. It swung out of the compound
daringly, the driver risking a collision with anything passing
in the busy road beyond. He was lucky in one sense,
unlucky in another. Although there was no obstruction
to his reckless progress, a water cart had recently gone by
leaving the macadam of the road wet and slippery. The van
skidded, turned completely round, and came to rest with
a dull, crunching sound, as a wing was buckled, against a
lamp post. By that time, Batty's cries and general behaviour
had naturally drawn attention to the van, and were causing
a good deal of curiosity. Servants of the hotel followed
him from the compound, people gathered in the street, a
couple of policemen hurried up. The van rapidly drew back
from the lamp post, and darted off just as the ex-sailor was
within a yard or two of it again. To his joy, however, a taxi
arrived on the scene, as a feeling of despair began to take
possession of the little man. Promptly he jumped on the
running board, shouting to the driver to follow the van,
which was drawing away in the distance. Luckily the man
understood, and nodded. Batty pulled open the door, flung
himself inside, but almost at once he had it open again,
and was yelling to the driver to slow down. Two figures,
recognisable as his friends of the boat, had come strolling
round the corner of the hotel.

'Jump in!' he roared and, noticing him for the first time,
they stood and stared.

'Come on,' he almost screamed. 'Don't stand there like a
pair of windjammers in the doldrums.'

'What the hell—' began the police sergeant, but he got in, followed by his surprised companion. 'What's got you?' he demanded, 'and how'd you get all that blood on your face?'

Batty was engaged in giving the driver directions to overtake the van, which could be still seen in the distance, and make it pull up by getting in front. The Malay chauffeur grinned his understanding. Apparently he regarded the affair as an amusing adventure. The ex-sailor sank back into a seat, tenderly feeling his head. He made a grimace as he saw the blood on his hand. The other two were regarding him curiously with anxiety in their eyes. Punctuating his narrative with full-blooded, deep sea oaths, which showed the depth of his feeling, for Batty rarely used anything but the mildest language, he rapidly told them what had happened.

'Good God!' breathed the police sergeant in astounded tones.

The engineer made no comment, but the look in his eyes spoke volumes. Thereafter, the three of them sat forward, grimly staring straight ahead. Their driver drove with great skill. Several times they lost their quarry as it turned corners, but always picked it up again, the well-lighted streets enabling them to keep it in view. It was obviously making for the open country and, as soon as Batty realised that, he grew more anxious than ever. He knew that once away from the lamps and brilliantly illumined shop windows, it would not be a very difficult matter for the kidnappers to elude their pursuers. But luck was with the latter. The vehicle ahead was twice forced to slow down, while their own car made uninterrupted progress, with the result that when the outskirts of Singapore were reached they were less than twenty yards away.

With the houses left behind, and a fine open road before them, there took place a grim race, the taxi slowly but surely gaining on the vehicle ahead. At last it drew almost level, whereupon the doors at the back of the van opened, and a man, hanging precariously on to one of them, shouted something to the driver. The latter shook his head, yelling something in reply. The other man then produced a long, thin-bladed knife which he shook threateningly, but again the driver of the taxi shook his head. Batty leant out of the window towards the latter.

'What is he saying?' he yelled.

Back on the rushing air came the taxi man's reply.

'Tuan, him say I stop, he give me much money. I no stop, then I get killed. I no stop,' he added simply.

'Good for you,' shouted back Batty. 'You won't regret it. God! We're going ahead. That's the stuff.'

It was true. The taxi had drawn alongside and, for a little while, the two cars ran abreast. A motor with brilliant headlights tore by in the other direction, being forced almost off the road owing to nearly all the available space being taken up by the others. Back on the air came momentarily the sound of a voice raised in execration, lost almost at once in the distance. Gradually the taxi began to forge ahead. Then Batty noticed that the driving seat of the van was not closed in, and a daring plan came into his head. He flung open the door and, stepping out on to the running board, reached across to the other vehicle. Twice his fingers missed contact, but the third time they touched, and grasped the framework of the windscreen. At once he swung himself across, accomplishing a daredevil feat that few but sailors could achieve. The driver, hanging grimly to the steering wheel with one hand, tried to dislodge him with the other, but Batty, having succeeded in getting both feet planted in the van, steadied himself; then hit the fellow a full-blooded punch straight between the eyes. The Malay, momentarily stunned, sagged over sideways, his nerveless fingers slipping from the wheel. It looked as though a disaster was imminent, the van, left without a controlling hand, swerving violently towards the undergrowth at the side of the road. The ex-sailor, however, succeeded only just in time in keeping it to the road, and, as the driver's foot was no longer on the accelerator, it began to slow down. It was fortunate for Batty that there was no communication between the driving cab and the interior of the van, otherwise he would have been stabbed by the occupants. He found and pulled on the brake with such force that the engine ceased functioning, and the vehicle stopped with a jerk. Then he sprang to the ground to find that the other three Malays had descended from the back, and, with knives raised menacingly, viciously, were bearing down upon him.

The lights of Singapore had been left far behind, and the moonlight only filtered fitfully through the waving foliage of the great trees lining the road and meeting almost overhead. There was quite enough light to fight by, though, reflected Batty grimly, as unarmed he awaited the attack. His antagonists hesitated, however, probably thinking he possessed a revolver. Their indecision proved their undoing, for it gave time to the other white men to reach their comrade. The taxi had pulled up some distance ahead, the two had at once tumbled out, and sprinted back. They reached him as the Malays sprang. Immediately there was a fierce rough and tumble. Batty caught the wrist of the first man as he struck downward, and they toppled over fighting desperately for the upper hand, one to stab, the other to make his adversary drop the knife. The sergeant, with a bull-like roar, tackled another fellow in rugby fashion, bringing him down with such force that the breath was knocked out of his body and the weapon fell from his grip. The Englishman dragged him to his feet, and knocked him unconscious with a powerful and scientifically delivered upper cut. He then went to Batty's assistance. The engineer, finding himself opposed to the third and most powerful native, was not having matters his own way. He narrowly missed being stabbed, the knife tearing through his jacket and grazing his shoulder. He got in a pretty hefty punch in the fellow's solar plexus, however, before they both went to ground. Here again it developed into a fight for possession of the knife. The Scotsman fought like a wild cat, but the Malay succeeded in getting on top. Gradually he overcame the white man's resistance, the knife slowly but relentlessly being forced down towards the latter's throat. It was within an inch or two when there sounded a dull thwack. The Malay collapsed on top of his opponent, and lay still. The engineer thrust him aside, struggled to his feet. Standing by, grinning with delight, was the taxi driver, a large spanner in his hand.

'Him gone sleep,' he remarked in a tone of great satisfaction.

'Laddie,' observed the Scotsman solemnly, 'ye saved my life.'

Between them Batty and the sergeant had overcome the ex-sailor's antagonist, and the fight was over. As they turned to ask the engineer if he were all right, however, the fellow, left momentarily unguarded, slipped away among the trees. They made no attempt to pursue him, being content to let him go. The driver, they found, had acted also on the principle that discretion is the better part of valour. When they went to collect him, he had disappeared. Batty turned eagerly to the rear of the van, and pulled up dead. Standing there, leaning somewhat dizzily against the vehicle, his shirt front crumpled, looking quite unlike his usual immaculately-groomed self, was Sir Leonard Wallace.

CHAPTER FIVE

The Intercepted Wireless Messages

'Quite an interesting fight,' he remarked shakily, but nevertheless cheerfully. 'To whom am I indebted for my rescue? Oh, is that you, Batty? I thought I heard your voice.'

The ex-sailor hurried up to him.

'Are you badly 'urt, sir?' he inquired solicitously.

'Not hurt at all,' was the reassuring reply. 'I was chloroformed, and that has left me feeling slightly dazed and sick. Otherwise I am all right.'

'A wee spot of this will do ye gude, sir,' put in the Scotsman, producing a flask from his hip pocket.

Sir Leonard accepted it gratefully, drank sparingly of the brandy within, and declared himself quite fit again. On request, Batty introduced the two without whom he knew he would never have effected the rescue. Sir Leonard thanked them warmly. He also had a word of praise for the driver of the taxi, who grinned with delight.

'Now, if you're ready,' Wallace suggested, 'we'll be getting back. I'm afraid my disappearance will be causing a certain amount of fuss. You can drive that van, Batty, can't you? I'd like to take these two back with us.'

He nodded at the recumbent natives. They were promptly and unceremoniously dumped into the van. The man whom the sergeant had laid out was beginning to recover consciousness; the other showed no signs of life. The sergeant assured himself that they had no other weapons concealed about them, and volunteered to ride with them to Singapore, a precaution which Sir Leonard agreed would be necessary to prevent them from escaping. An alteration in the suggested arrangement was made, the Scotsman driving the van, while Batty travelled in the taxi with his master. On the way he related how his suspicions of foul play had been roused and the manner in which the van had been tracked. He was highly commended for his conduct, but it was typical of Batty that he still insisted on apologising for his lack of attention in being absent when Wallace was dressing for dinner.

Twenty minutes later the two cars drew up behind Raffles Hotel, no further attempt at molestation having been made. The taxi driver was rewarded in a manner that almost caused his eyes to bulge from his head. He declared that he would be always ready to drive them on any further adventurous undertakings they contemplated, and departed most regretfully, when he was told they were bound for Hong Kong, and would not require his services again. The sergeant and engineer were left in charge of the captives, while Sir Leonard, accompanied by Batty, made his way as unobtrusively as possible to the manager's office. There, in addition to the manager himself, they found General Harrington, Captain Taylor, and the Commissioner of Police, all looking exceedingly worried. A general cry of relief greeted their appearance, and questions poured in a torrent from the lips of the four men.

'One at a time, please,' smiled Wallace.

He sank into a chair, and gave a rapid account of what had happened. His audience was horrified, but Batty came in for a good deal of congratulation, which caused that genial ex-mariner a lot of embarrassment. He shuffled his feet uneasily, and hung his head like a schoolboy caught committing an offence.

A whisky and soda was handed to Sir Leonard, another to Batty. The former was greatly relieved to hear that no hint of his disappearance had been allowed to reach the ears of his wife. Carter had taken it upon himself to tell her that he was engaged in a conference that might last some time, and to remain near her in case she began to show any anxiety at her husband's prolonged absence.

'By gad!' exclaimed the general, 'it's the most daring outrage I've ever heard of. What was the object of it?'

'My assassination, I suppose,' returned Wallace grimly. 'If they had attempted to murder me on the veranda, I might have had time to cry out before I died; my body might have been discovered, and have caused a hue and cry before my assailants had an opportunity to get away. Chloroforming me, and removing me as they did, left no trace. They assumed that I would not be missed for some time. Meanwhile they would have taken me well out into the country, and murdered me at their leisure.'

'It's diabolical!' cried the manager. 'And to think that it should have taken place in my hotel. The cunning of it! The wicked cunning of it! You see, we are engaged in a carpet cleaning campaign, but in order not to disturb the guests too much, we had arranged that they should be taken away at night, cleaned, and returned early in the morning. The men who abducted you must have learnt that; they entered the service door, said they had come for the carpet in the upper lounge, and nobody disputed their right. When your absence began to cause anxiety, Sir Leonard, I made inquiries, was told about the carpet, which rather surprised me, for the cleaning firm does not generally collect before midnight, was even annoyed, but I never thought of connecting it with your disappearance.'

'That is natural enough,' Wallace assured him. 'They certainly were fiendishly clever. The manner in which they worked the whole affair was most ingenious: it must have been decided upon very suddenly, too.' He eyed Captain Taylor and General Harrington. 'They got you away by a simple enough trick, Harrington, but to go to the length of murdering a Chinese passenger to cause you to return to the ship, Taylor, is about the most cold-blooded idea I've heard of for a long time. I suppose he was killed?'

'Dead as a doornail,' nodded the captain. 'Somebody climbed aboard, I think, stabbed the first deck passenger he came to – there are only half a dozen – without a sound, and went over the side again.'

'What I don't understand, sir,' interposed the Commissioner of Police, 'is how these devils could have possibly known that you, Captain Taylor, and General

Harrington would be sitting alone on the veranda after dinner.'

'They took a chance, I suppose,' replied Sir Leonard; then: 'Good Lord! No, they didn't,' he exclaimed. 'Do you remember at dinner one of the ladies asked me if I were going to dance?' The general and Captain Taylor nodded. 'Well, my reply was, "No; it is too warm. I shall take Captain Taylor and General Harrington on to that secluded part of the veranda above the dining room, and we'll yarn while you dance".'

'By Jove! So you did,' cried Harrington, while the captain nodded.

'There was somebody there in the pay of these people,' went on Wallace. 'He reported what I had said, they were looking for their opportunity, and there you are.'

'Who can the scoundrels be behind all this?' came in exasperated tones from the commissioner.

'That's for you to find out, if you can,' returned Wallace drily. 'We'll have the two captives in presently, and see if we can get anything out of them. Of course they're only tools, but they may be able to give us some information, if they will speak. What did you do when you found I was missing?'

'The hotel was searched first,' replied Harrington; 'then, when we were certain you were not on the premises, we got hold of the commissioner here. The police are searching the whole city. We couldn't get a clue of any sort.'

'They might be recalled now, I think,' remarked Wallace, 'since I happen to be here. It is extraordinary that nobody mentioned the incident of the van and Batty's attempts to catch it. There must have been a good deal of commotion, and his agitation must have been remarked by certain people in the hotel.'

'Up to now, nobody has come forward,' replied the police chief, as he turned to the telephone. 'You see, sir, you had been barely missing an hour, and investigations only started about half an hour before you returned.'

'Of course,' nodded Wallace. 'I was forgetting. It seems hours to me.'

'The assistant manager told me that Mr Batty had been inquiring for you, Sir Leonard,' put in the manager. 'That delayed our investigations a little longer, because we took it for granted you had gone somewhere with him, possibly back to the ship. It was only when Captain Taylor returned, and expressed anxiety about your absence that we began to feel really perturbed.'

'And I, like a fool,' grunted Harrington, 'was sitting on the veranda waiting for you.'

Sir Leonard smiled.

'You lack the keen sense of smell that Batty possesses, general,' he observed. 'It was the whiff of chloroform on the veranda that first started him on my track.'

'Well, we all haven't the advantage,' commented Harrington, 'of serving under you, Sir Leonard, and learning from you how to use our senses to the best advantage.'

Wallace smiled.

'I haven't come out of this affair with any honours,' he remarked. 'I should have been more on my guard. In fact I consider I was caught like the veriest tyro.'

'I can't agree with that,' observed the commissioner, who had returned from the telephone after giving orders for the search to be called off. 'A Malay can move more silently than any creature, human or otherwise, that I know. You hadn't a chance, sir. Shall we have those prisoners of yours in now, and see what we can get out of them?'

'Let me tidy myself up a bit first, and show myself to my wife and guests for a minute or two,' replied Wallace; 'then we'll put them through it.'

The manager promptly proved the efficiency of his hotel by taking Sir Leonard into a private dressing room and, with the help of a valet, turning him out in five minutes in spotless linen without the suspicion of a crease or mark of any kind on his clothing. Batty's head was dressed, the nasty cut he had received being neatly plastered. His clothes, which had not been improved by their contact with the ground during the fight, also underwent the attentions of the valet, all traces of the rough treatment to which they had been subjected being removed.

Sir Leonard found most of his guests still dancing, wondered a little at their hardihood in continuing in such heat, though it is true their gyrations were performed under a host of rapidly whirling fans. The men in dark evening clothes looked cooler than those in white, while none of the ladies showed any signs of fatigue or of being overheated. Molly was reclining on a long chair in the garden, with a colonel of a British infantry regiment sitting on one side of her, and Carter on the other. It says a lot for the latter's training that he showed not a flicker of emotion of any sort as his eyes fell on his chief, though his relief must have been vast, for he had been gnawed with anxiety. Molly smiled up at her husband.

'I was beginning to grow anxious about you, Leonard,'

she remarked lightly. 'Fancy deserting your guests for so long in this barefaced manner.'

'Rather important business kept me,' he explained, 'which is not quite concluded. I shall have to leave you again for a little while.'

He stayed chatting for a few minutes; then strolled away again. He returned to the manager's office, where the others awaited his coming somewhat impatiently. At once the commissioner went off accompanied by two policemen, who had been standing by for orders, to bring in the prisoners. They were gone for some time; then the commissioner returned alone, his eyes hard and grim, his lips drawn together in a tight line.

'They haven't escaped?' snapped Sir Leonard, noting the expression on his face.

'They're dead – both of them,' came the astounding reply.

There was complete silence for a few seconds, a muttered oath from the general being the first sound to cut into the profound hush that had fallen on the room at the police chief's words.

'Any idea how it happened?' questioned Sir Leonard at length.

The other nodded.

'You had better hear the story of the men you left in charge, Sir Leonard,' he said. 'I brought them along with me.'

He went to the door, and called the sergeant and engineer into the room. They both looked thoroughly startled. Wallace noticed at once that the latter had received a cut on the shoulder, and suggested that it should be dressed.

'It's no' much, sir,' protested the Scotchman, 'just a wee scratch. It's no' giving me verra much trouble.'

Sir Leonard insisted, and the wound was at once attended to.

'When did you get it?' he asked.

'During the bit scrap we had, sir,' he was told. 'I might ha' been far worse off, if yon taxi driver had no' been so handy wi' a spanner.'

The sergeant acted as spokesman. He related that soon after Sir Leonard and Batty had left him and his companion in charge of the van, two men dressed in European clothes had arrived. They announced that they were police officers, and had been sent to handcuff the prisoners. The sergeant, being a policeman himself, had asked to see their credentials, and had been shown regulation police cards. After that, he put no obstacle in their way. He certainly rather wondered at their request to him and the Scotsman to stand back, but thought it was only rather cheap officiousness on their part. They entered the van, closing themselves in. Three or four minutes passed; then they emerged, and locked the doors. The engineer asked them where they had obtained the key, but they merely smiled at him in a superior sort of fashion. Their attitude annoyed the sergeant, and he felt a wish that he could have them under him in Hong Kong for a while. They told him and his companion that they need not wait; that they themselves would be back in a few minutes. Nevertheless, the sergeant decided to remain where he was, not feeling altogether easy in his mind. The engineer agreed to stay with him.

'That's really all I can tell you, sir,' concluded the alert-looking police officer.

'I'll continue,' put in the commissioner. 'As soon as I reached the van, I ordered my men to bring the prisoners out. I was very much surprised when I was told by this man of the handcuffing and locking of the doors by supposed police officers, and naturally my suspicions were aroused, especially as I felt fairly certain that nobody but we knew of the Malays in the van. I sent to the police station adjacent to find if the orders had emanated from there and, if so, to procure the keys. As I suspected, the officer in charge knew nothing about it. Without further ado we broke the doors in. Inside both men were stretched out dead. Each had been stabbed to the heart.'

Sir Leonard paced the room for several minutes in deep thought. Presently he took the commissioner by the arm; led him from the room.

'The tentacles of the Hong Kong conspiracy seem to reach to all parts of the world,' he murmured. 'The real villains of the piece are in Hong Kong, not here. Nevertheless, I ask you to spare no pains to run the men who have organised today's little show to earth. It may help in certain investigations I intend to pursue in Hong Kong.'

'I guessed that you were not merely taking Sir Stanley Ferguson's place for the benefit of your health – or his,' observed the commissioner. 'But do you really think tonight's affair was inspired by the man or men behind the Hong Kong scandal, sir?'

'I am convinced of it. They seem to be utterly callous and unscrupulous whoever they are. Those poor devils of Malays were murdered to prevent their speaking. I don't suppose they knew much, if anything, but this organisation takes no risks.'

'How could they possibly have known they were in the van?'

'A first-class espionage system. They must have eyes everywhere. Well, you've an interesting job before you, but if you find out anything that is likely to be of the slightest assistance to me, wireless me to the boat or Hong Kong at once. You have three murders to solve, these Malays and the Chinese deck passenger. What has been done about him, by the way?'

'His body has been removed to the mortuary, and all the other deck passengers taken ashore and held, pending inquiries. I don't suppose that any of them killed him, though.'

'No; you might as well let them go. He was merely offered up as a sacrifice, because he happened to be most conveniently placed for killing. Like a lazy farm wife choosing the chicken nearest the gate of the run to save her the trouble of going right in. Good God! What a parcel of fiends!'

He re-entered the office, told the manager to see that Batty and his two friends were entertained at his expense, and invited Captain Taylor and General Harrington to accompany him back to his guests. The Commissioner of Police hurried off to set in motion the machinery of the law for the apprehension of the men behind the kidnapping of Sir Leonard and the murder of the natives, but he went with rather a hopeless expression on his face. The only clue was a motor van, which had probably been stolen. The descriptions he obtained of the murderers who had declared themselves to be police officers might help, but he did not feel very optimistic about it, while those of the actual kidnappers and the man who had given General Harrington the false telephone message were too vague to be of any assistance at all. It may as well be recorded here that none of them was ever traced and no clue to their identity or the identity of their employers discovered. The abduction of Sir Leonard and the murders went down into the limbo of unsolved crimes.

The *Rawalpindi* continued on her way to Hong Kong without delay, for ships, particularly those carrying His Majesty's mail, must proceed on their lawful occasions no matter what outrages may be perpetrated by or occur to those aboard them. Batty's friends were sworn to secrecy, and nobody but those actually concerned knew anything of the attempted abduction of the temporary Governor of Hong Kong. No suspicion or hint of the outrage reached the ears of Molly, and she continued to enjoy the voyage, and looked forward to a pleasant, if socially busy, sojourn in the Far Eastern colony.

When Carter learnt the full story of what had occurred, his feelings can be better imagined than described. There and then he made up his mind never to let his chief out of his sight more than he could possibly help. He realised that Sir Leonard's life would be in hourly danger, and that those threatening it were about the most unscrupulous and fiendishly ingenious scoundrels it were possible to imagine. He gave no thought to the probability that his own life would very likely be equally in peril. That was a risk he always had to face as a member of Great Britain's Secret Service, but he felt it became an additional duty of his to guard the safety of the man whose existence was so valuable to England.

The attitude of Wun Cheng Lo was somewhat of a puzzle

to Sir Leonard. The man showed as impassive a face as ever, but the Chief of the Intelligence Corps sensed that he was labouring under a feeling of indignation. The question was, why? He thought the matter over very carefully, and reached the conclusion that the affair in Singapore had been engineered without the Chinaman being enlightened. Despite the fact that the latter had informed his principals of his success in worming his way into the confidence of the new governor, and consequently preparing the way for the dénouement in Hong Kong, they had made arrangements without advising or consulting him to end the career of the man, whose coming they seemed to fear, in Singapore. Sir Leonard felt fairly certain that Wun Cheng Lo knew what had taken place, which argued that he had met the agent or agents of his employers in the port from which the *Rawalpindi* had so recently sailed. Acting on his pretence of putting full trust in the Chinaman, he decided to speak of the narrow escape he had had. He was promenading the deck on the afternoon following the ship's departure from Singapore, and came upon the Chinaman dozing in a chair. There was nobody else in the vicinity. He stopped, whereupon Wun Cheng Lo sprang to his feet with remarkable agility for one of his bulk, and bowed low.

'You missed a chance of proving your words in Singapore,' Wallace remarked jokingly.

The Chinaman's face remained unchanged, but his eyes showed concern.

'Are you suggesting, Your Excellency,' he asked with a similitude of anxiety, 'that your contemptible servant has in some manner failed your worshipful self?'

'No, Wun Cheng Lo; you were not to know that I was in danger.'

Thereupon he proceeded to tell him of the outrage. The Chinaman listened attentively, giving vent occasionally to exclamations expressive of horror. At the end of the recital, he again bowed low, speaking with abject repentance and humility, and blaming himself with much flowery verbosity, because he had not been on hand.

'I did not suspect, worm that I am,' he concluded, 'that an attempt might he made to dim the light of your noble countenance so far from your destination. Never again, while your illustrious Excellency is Governor of Hong Kong, will these low-born eyes cease watching lest harm threaten you.'

Sir Leonard said a few words reiterating his confidence in the man, and walked away.

'Pshaw!' he muttered to himself in disgust. 'The fellow is nauseating with his unctuous hypocrisy.'

Carter, a broad smile on his face, came to him in his cabin a little later, and handed him a slip of paper. It was a copy of a wireless message which had been despatched by Wun Cheng Lo that morning to the same address in Kowloon as before. It stated that a mistake had been made in attempting to open the agency in any place but Hong Kong, adding that the sender, having obtained the confidence of the party concerned, was the only fit person to make arrangements.

'Our friend is peeved,' chuckled Carter. 'At least it looks like it, if this means what we think it does.'

'I'm certain of it,' returned Wallace; 'more certain, in fact, than I was before we reached Singapore.'

'Do you think Wun Cheng Lo had anything to do with the murder of that Chinese deck passenger, sir?'

Wallace shook his head.

'No. If he had, it would have meant that he was fully cognisant of the attempt to kidnap me!'

'What about the Philippino, Feodoro?'

'Batty has ascertained for me that he was with a party of second-class passengers all the afternoon and evening. No; neither of them was in any way concerned with the business. Arrangements had probably been made long before the ship reached Singapore, and were not altered when Wun Cheng Lo's message was received, either because there was not time, or because the instigators thought that I might as well be murdered in Singapore as elsewhere.'

Late that night a wireless message reached the ship for Wun Cheng Lo. A copy was sent down to Wallace without delay, although he had already retired to bed, but he had asked the captain to instruct the senior operator to allow no fear of disturbing him to influence him in postponing the delivery of any message of that kind. Sir Leonard sat up in bed, when the door had closed on the messenger, switched on the reading lamp, and tore open the sealed envelope. He read the communication with every appearance of satisfaction.

'At last,' he murmured to himself. 'A real clue.'

Yet the message seemed innocent enough. It stated that the sender agreed that Wun Cheng Lo was the fit person to make arrangements, that a bad blunder had taken place in attempting to extend the agency beyond Hong Kong without his knowledge, and that his associates were highly gratified at the success of his negotiations. But it was the last part of the message which caused Sir Leonard's exclamation. A meeting of the board, it was asserted, would be held to discuss the situation at seven in the evening of the sixteenth of the month at Sales. There was no signature.

'Whatever and wherever Sales is,' reflected Wallace, 'it should not be difficult to discover it. We are due in on the fifteenth – they are losing no time. If, as I am convinced, I am correct in substituting conspirators for board, it will be a queer thing if I don't know who they are by the night of September the sixteenth.'

He pushed the paper and envelope under his pillow, switched off the light, and sank further down into the bed. But some hours passed before he fell asleep; his brain was too busy planning to enable him to seek slumber at once.

The wonderful weather which the *Rawalpindi* had experienced during most of the voyage deserted her early the following morning. Quite suddenly she was caught by the tail end of a typhoon and, for six hours, struggled through mountainous seas. The wind howled with devilish ferocity, as though all the demons in hell had combined to hurl hatred and venom at the liner and her passengers, while the rain fell in torrents; pitilessly, uninterruptedly. Life lines were secured round the decks, but few ventured up; they felt the risk was too great. Not many of the passengers were taken ill, a great number were too scared, for at times the ship rolled or pitched to such a degree that it seemed that she would never be able to right herself. A large junk swept past with the speed of a racehorse, her mast gone, her crew clinging to anything they could lay their hands on, but nothing could be done to help them. A lot of the top hamper of the *Rawalpindi* was carried away, several seamen were injured, three or four had narrow escapes from being washed overboard. Then, as suddenly as it had come, the storm passed, the great lashing waves subsided into a long, oily swell, the leaden clouds broke, disclosing the blue sky behind.

While the typhoon was at its height, Sir Leonard Wallace sat in the smoking saloon in deep discussion with Carter. The room was practically deserted and, for once in a way, they were able to talk there without fear of being overheard. Their conversation centred principally round the word 'Sales' in the wireless message to Wun Cheng Lo. They had no method of discovering whether it referred to the name of a person or place. Captain Taylor and Batty's police sergeant friend were unable to supply the required information when cautiously consulted. As a result of their colloquy, a wireless message in code was later despatched to London to be at once, relayed to a certain small individual, who, a little over a week before, had informed Wallace by wireless that he had arrived in Hong Kong on a coasting boat. He had taken up his residence in one of the smaller and not very savoury hotels there. Sir Leonard had opened his campaign in earnest.

CHAPTER SIX

A Couple of Beachcombers

At about the same time that the *Rawalpindi* was lying in Colombo harbour, a small coasting vessel from Saigon wallowed her way into Hong Kong. She was old and dirty, what remained of her paintwork showing in patches amidst the prevailing rust; her engines had passed their best days years before, and groaned in decrepit protest when in action. Apparently the skipper and his crew had long given up any idea of keeping the ship tidy, for, from bows to stern, above deck and below, she was an eyesore. It would seem hardly conceivable that such a boat carried European passengers, nevertheless she did and, on the trip in question, landed no less than four in Hong Kong, while three others were continuing on to Shanghai. It is true, none of them looked as though they could rub two pennies together. With perhaps the exception of a couple who seemed still to retain a certain amount of respect for their personal appearance, they were of the beachcombing fraternity, those hobos of the sea who wander from port to port out East, eking out some sort of existence, living mostly for what they can get to drink, until death, through the medium of his close friend delirium tremens, takes them for his own.

The two who still clung to some measure of respectability, though the veneer was obviously wearing very thin, were utterly dissimilar in appearance. They had, however, two tastes in common; one was an intense liking for spirits, particularly brandy; the other, strangely enough, was a love for music and poetry. The tall, lean individual with hooked nose, thin lips, and eyes that once must have been very fine indeed, accidentally let out the information that he was an engineer by profession. He had built bridges over some of the mighty rivers of India, had been acclaimed brilliant until drink had taken hold of him, and caused him to lose job after job. Eventually he had wandered aimlessly farther east to add one more unit to that pile of human flotsam and jetsam that drifted about among the islands of the Malay archipelago, up to Hong Kong and Shanghai, and back again.

The other was harder to place. He seldom, if ever, spoke of himself, but his general knowledge must have been almost unique. Whether drunk, or on the rare occasions when he was sober, he seemed able to discuss any subject under the sun. The arts, particularly poetry and, to a lesser extent, music, for, as he declared, music and poetry always went together, were a passion with him. He had a habit of finding suitable quotations for almost any subject. Where he came from nobody knew, and probably cared less – who bothers where those white failures, seen so frequently in the Orient, emanate from? He was obviously an Englishman and, when very intoxicated, spoke sometimes in maudlin tones of an old mother at home. He was barely five feet in height, with the slim figure of a boy, but his age might have been anything from thirty-five to fifty. His face was most surprisingly and amusingly wrinkled and, when he smiled, it became a mass of creases, all conveying such a sense of merriment, that people looking at him were unable to forbear from smiling also. He called himself George Collins, but, as the engineer, when he first heard it, remarked, 'Don' sh'posc tha's your name 'tall, but we're all 'like on thish lil hooker. Mine's not James Kenton, but tha's what I call m'self!'

The once-famous engineer was quite correct. George Collins was not the real name of the man who claimed it. It was, in fact, the fourth alias he had given himself since he had left London at the behest of Sir Leonard Wallace, for his real name was Gerald Cousins, and he had adopted the role of semi-beachcomber not from necessity, but to cloak the identity of one of Great Britain's cleverest Secret Service men. He had travelled from Croydon to Karachi by airliner as Sidney Sharp. Unobtrusively he had crossed India to Calcutta as William Duncan. Monsieur Pierre Chambertin, a representative of the famous Parisian firm of *Lalère et Cie*, had travelled from Calcutta to Cochin China by French air liner. The very few people who met him in the French dependency heard casually a couple of days afterwards that he had been compelled to return to France in a hurry on receipt of an important cable. But there arrived in Saigon docks a small, rather disreputable figure, by name George

Collins, whose soiled and crumpled ducks, down-at-heel shoes, dented topee, battered suitcase, and general air of decreptitude signalled him out as merely one of the white derelicts of the East. He took passage for Hong Kong on a boat that, like himself, was very much the worse for wear, and found himself one of a small party of his own kidney.

He had struck up a curious sort of friendship with the man calling himself James Kenton and, during the voyage, they had had little to do with the other five, for even among beachcombers there is a pathetic kind of social distinction. Kenton and Collins went ashore together at Victoria, and found unsavoury accommodation in a dingy building on Robinson Road which gave itself the high-sounding name of Hotel Paris. Though quite a third of the way up the Peak and, therefore, some considerable distance from the water front, this establishment was much frequented by members of the society to which Kenton and Collins belonged. They were followed in by a young Chinaman, excessively slant-eyed, but of far more animated and cheerful countenance than is usual with sons of what had once been the Celestial Empire. This young man, hardly taller than Cousins himself, had flatly declined to allow the latter to go ashore without him. He had been the cook's mate on the steamer. One day, when the ugly little vessel had been rolling and pitching even more than usual, he had fallen overboard, while engaged in emptying a bucket of slops. The skipper had not been unduly perturbed by the accident – one Chinaman the less among his crew would not upset his philosophy of life, though he regretted the bucket – but Cousins had witnessed the mishap, and, with great promptitude, had flung overboard two lifebuoys, and dived in himself. Thereupon, using strange and fearsome epithets, the captain had stopped the ship and lowered a boat, not so much because he felt his disreputable passenger was any more worth saving than the Chinese boy, as from a desire to recover the buoys, for they represented half the number the boat possessed.

Cousins and the cook's mate were picked up, and thereafter the latter swore by all his gods that nothing but death itself should separate him from the man who had risked his life for him. Cousins did his best to discourage him, but it was useless. He might just as well have spoken to a table or a chair; the Chinaman simply listened with bland countenance, but when Cousins went ashore, he went also.

At the Hotel Paris, Kenton suggested that he and his friend should share a room, but Cousins declined. He had his own reasons for desiring to be alone. Kenton – he was almost sober at the time – chose to take offence at that, and threatened to go elsewhere, but, when Cousins made no objection, he decided to remain. The slatternly woman, who received them in a poky little dining room reeking of garlic, demanded, not unreasonably, a deposit before she would agree to their staying in her house. With a show of reluctance, Cousins handed her a ten dollar note, whereupon she welcomed them with great volubility. She informed them that she was a poor widow woman of pure Portuguese descent – an obvious untruth, as everything about her spoke of the mixed breeding which the island of Macao has indulged in for so long, the results of which are spread in great numbers round southern China. However, neither Cousins nor his companion disputed her assertion. They knew that Macanese, like all or most

Eurasians, are always eager to make believe that their blood is of the purest. They waited patiently while she spoke of the hardships life had brought her, especially after her husband had, with great inconsideration, departed this mortal coil and thrown up a good post. Eventually, still talking, she led them to their rooms, and only departed when Kenton closed the door of his rudely but firmly in her face. Cousins shuddered slightly when he looked round the apartment that had been allotted to him. It was redolent of bad cooking and musty furniture. The bedding looked unhealthy; the mosquito curtain was a joke, with its numerous tears and slits, through which whole battalions of the insects could fly at the same time; the matting suggested centipedes and other crawling dangers. However, the veranda running along outside the window hinted to Cousins that he would be more comfortable sleeping on a couple of chairs out there, even though it overlooked the servants' quarters, and collected another variety of odours. Apparently Kenton thought the same. He walked along the veranda from his room, and poked his head in at the window.

'Don't think much of the quarters,' he observed. 'I'm going to sleep out here – when I sleep in this pigsty at all.'

'What are you going to do other times?' asked Cousins.

The ex-engineer grinned.

'Acting innocent, aren't you?' he scoffed. 'Now I ask you: what happens when we get dead drunk in some joint or other, and fall asleep? We stay put, don't we? Or get thrown out and sleep where we land. Not that they let you lie about in Hong Kong. They're devilish nasty to bums like you and me here, if we don't mind our *p*'s and *q*'s. Hell! I've a devil of a thirst on me.'

'Have you any money?' asked Cousins.

'Enough to get blotto on, and, when that's gone, it's easy enough to get more.' He winked his eye profoundly. 'You learn a thing or two when you touch bottom, boy, don't you?'

Cousins grinned and nodded, his face creasing into hundreds of little puckers that caused the other to smile broadly. He had heard of the means employed by the drifting wasters of the Orient to raise money, and a feeling of repugnance overcame him. He liked Kenton, knew his history, and he felt it a terrible pity that a man of such ability should sink so low.

'Why don't you cut it out, Jim?' he asked seriously.

'Cut what out?' queried the other, raising his eyebrows in surprise.

'The drink! Cut it out, and make an effort to get back to where you belong.'

Kenton stared at him in silence for a few seconds; then burst into a roar of laughter that seemed to shake the room.

'Lord! What a joke!' he chuckled. 'That from you! Why, I'd begin to think you were a missionary in disguise, if I hadn't seen you put it away even better than I can myself. What's got you? Have you come all over virtuous, or is that your idea of a joke?'

Cousins laughed. His advice hardly fitted in with the character he was playing, still he felt sorry for the other man; wished he could help, and save him from the loathsome finale.

'No; it wasn't a joke,' he declared. 'You know how it is – you're a decent sort of fellow; I realise it more than ever now I see you sober for about the first time. You've done things, been something. It's a darn shame to let yourself go like you are. I'm different, nothing matters. I've nothing to cling to. You have: respectability, achievement, name. If I were in your place, I'd cling hard enough to pull myself back to where I once was.'

Kenton eyed him with a frown, his words had touched a chord that, for a moment, caused him to think and regret. But his drink-sodden mind was not capable of holding to a thought of that nature for long.

'Out on you for a scurvy knave,' he returned half-jokingly, half angrily. 'You preach like a blasted parson. I've been holding on to the shreds of respectability for a long time. But shreds aren't reliable; they give way under pressure. Quit playing the fool, George. I'll drink when I like, where I like, how I like. It's a darned rotten world, and the best way I know of enjoying life is to get drunk, so I'll keep on doing it.'

Cousins shrugged his shoulders.

'"*Dum vivimus vivamus*",' he murmured. 'I see you are intent on accompanying me to perdition, so I'll say no more.'

'Thank the Lord for that. When you're ready we'll start on a binge. There's a joint here that – well, you'll find out for yourself. It's run by a bloke called Tavares – greatest scoundrel unhung, but he knows what's what.'

'I seem to have heard the name,' murmured Cousins.

'Of course you have, if you've been wandering round the East for the number of years you say you have. Strange that you should never have reached Hong Kong before,' he added reflectively.

'Not so strange,' returned Cousins, 'when you remember that I've hardly handled a couple of dollars at a time for God knows how long, and only an unexpected remittance has given me this chance of stretching my legs so to speak.'

Kenton nodded.

'You must have a certain amount of simplicity about you,' he observed. 'When you first told me about that remittance on the boat, I thought you were spinning a yarn. One doesn't generally talk about remittances in our circle, too likely to be an accident. Anyhow, the least there is to fear is that you'll be touched until all your coin is touched out of you.'

'I guessed you were pretty square,' smiled Cousins. 'I didn't tell the others.'

'You wouldn't be here now, if you had,' was the grim reply. 'Is there any of it left?'

The little man nodded.

'About twenty pounds.'

Kenton whistled ecstatically.

'We can get gloriously drunk on that,' he exclaimed; then grinned almost boyishly. 'That's touching you by suggestion.'

'We're in this together,' Cousins assured him.

'What's mine's yours, sort of thing. Bully for you, George. When it's gone I'll do my handwalking stunt – the Chinks love it; it brings in quite a lot sometimes. I'd better bill it as my renowned act. Spectacle of well-educated Englishman, once respectable, crawling round like an animal or balancing himself on his hands – as performed before all the pot-bellied Chinks in China.'

Cousins shuddered.

'What were you saying about Tavares?' he asked.

'Dunno. Oh, yes I do, though. He used to be a sort of confidential butler-cum-valet chap to that bloke who shot himself, when things got so hot – Mathos I mean.' Cousins

metaphorically pricked up his ears. Mathos was the name of
the swindler round whom the Hong Kong financial scandal
centred, and who had committed suicide to avoid arrest.
'Tavares already had the dive he now owns,' went on Kenton,
'when he was in service, but since Mathos died, he has made
no end of a big thing out of it. Of course no respectable
people go there; at least not openly, so we'll be all right,' he
added cynically. 'He only escaped arrest himself by the skin
of his teeth when the showdown came – evidence insufficient
or something. I bet he owns a pot of money.'

Cousins was thinking rapidly. One of his intentions, as
soon as he had settled down in Hong Kong, had been to
become a habitué of the dancing hall and drinking house
run by this Tavares. As Kenton knew the place, he decided
to commence activities at once. The man's name had been
mentioned to him by Sir Leonard Wallace in London, and he
already knew most of what Kenton had told him. Sir Leonard
had urged him to become as familiar as he could with the
fellow, there being a chance that by so doing he might learn
quite a lot about the conspiracy. At all events he might as
well commence his investigations there as elsewhere. Kenton
had given him a lead, and he resolved to take it.

'Let us go,' he suggested. 'My tongue is beginning to
feel like a lime-kiln, and I gather there's only water to drink
in this dump. As the wag remarked when he parodied the
bishop's saying about beer, "Those that drink water will
think water".'

'Very true too,' commented Kenton approvingly. 'What
was the bishop's saying?'

'Those that drink beer will think beer.'

'And not a bad thing to drink and think, when there's no whisky or brandy about.' He nodded his head. 'It's pretty certain that I spend most of my life in thinking brandy.'

They walked from the room to find the Chinese boy, who had insisted on following Cousins, squatting on the mat outside. The little man regarded him with each wrinkle on his face expressing perplexity.

'So you're still hanging about,' he sighed. 'What am I to do with you?'

The boy regarded him with a bland smile.

'Where master go me go,' he proclaimed with an air of finality.

'Wait for me down below, Jim,' suggested Cousins to his companion, 'while I have a chat with this fellow.'

'Don't be long then,' replied the other. 'I've been sober far too long. Can't think how I allowed myself to get into such a reprehensible state.'

He wandered away, and Cousins re-entered his shabby room, bidding the Chinaman follow him.

'Now, look here,' he began. 'It's not a bit of good your hanging on to me in this manner. I can't afford a servant, and I don't want one.'

'Me no savvy,' replied the boy still smiling. 'Master him fetchum me outee water, me stopee always with master.'

'That's all very well, and I appreciate the sentiments. I suppose I'd better speak to you in your own pidgin English. Now listen! No got money, no can pay, savvy?'

The smile became broader than ever.

'Me no wantchee money. Me wantchee work for master because master my good fliend.'

'But there's no work.'

'Me makee too muchee work. You looksee bimeby.'

'Oh, you will, will you?' Cousins sighed in exasperation. 'If I have no money,' he asked, 'how will you get food?'

'Master catchee money, me catchee food; master no catchee money, me no catchee food.'

'You're the limit,' groaned Cousins.

The Chinaman nodded his head brightly.

'Me plenty limit,' he agreed, 'too muchee limit.'

'You certainly are.' Considering the situation for a few minutes, he decided that apparently he had no choice. The fellow would remain with him whatever he said. And, after all, it might prove a great advantage to possess a servant who was likely to be as faithful as this young man. 'All right,' he decided at last; 'you can stay.'

An ecstatic look came into the boy's eyes. He said something rapidly in Chinese that sounded like a prayer; then reverted to his pidgin English.

'Me allo time too muchee good servant belong you, master,' he declared earnestly, 'me no bobbely, allo time velly good work, allo time fightee.'

Cousins frowned in perplexity.

'Fight whom?' he demanded. 'I don't want you to fight anybody.'

'No fight, fightee,' explained the boy, 'go plenty too muchee quick.'

'Oh, I see. Well, you'll do I daresay. As Shakespeare has it, "He must needs go that the Devil drives". You certainly gave me no choice but to engage you.'

'Me no debbil, master.'

'I hope you aren't. What is your name?'

'Me Ho Fang Ho, master.'

'Two ho's! A fellow of infinite jest, I presume. Well, you'd better go, and find yourself quarters. Here's some money to get food and anything else you want.'

Fang Ho stared at the three dollars placed in his hand.

'Me tinkee you no gotee money,' he exclaimed.

'Sometimes I have, sometimes I have not,' explained Cousins patiently.

'When you have got,' smiled the boy, 'you get too muchee dlunk, when you no have got no can get dlunk.'

'You saucy young scoundrel!'

'Me no sarcy, master, me talkee tlue. Allo samee you velly good man dlunk, no dlunk.'

He was gone, rattling the coins in his hand. Cousins stared after him.

'Well, I'm hanged!' he exclaimed.

He joined Kenton, who was awaiting him below, looking thoroughly exasperated. They started forth together, presenting a rather amusing contrast. Once Kenton looked down at his companion, and grinned.

'Jove! Aren't you tiny?' he ejaculated. 'You remind me of "Tich" Freeman. He is about your height.' A faraway look came into his eyes, and for a moment his whole expression changed. 'God!' he muttered softly, almost to himself, 'What wouldn't I give to see Frank Woolley knocking up one of his glorious centuries again, and little Freeman diddling them out.' His mood altered abruptly. 'Darn it! I'm getting maudlin, and I'm as sober as a judge. Must have a touch of the sun.'

Cousins said nothing, but he made a resolve to save this man, if he could, and take him home to England, when his work was finished. He felt somewhat guilty at the thought that he was accompanying him to a drinking bout which would end in his becoming thoroughly and hopelessly drunk. A quick and almost imperceptible shrug of his shoulders put finis to such thoughts. He had his duty to do. He wished to become known in the colony as a drink-sodden waster, and there was no better way of acquiring that reputation than in the company of one who was already well-known as a complete and irredeemable drunkard.

They walked along together without saying much. One was thinking of the carouse to come; the craving for brandy was eating into his brain, hastening his steps, causing an intense gleam of anticipation to appear in his eyes; the other's thoughts were very far from such sordid considerations. He was thinking of the tremendous task Sir Leonard Wallace had undertaken and his own part in it.

The sun was setting and, in a few minutes, darkness would fall with the suddenness peculiar to that belt of the earth lying between the tropics of Cancer and Capricorn. Nevertheless, the harbour still presented a busy spectacle, as they walked along by the seafront. A beautiful Canadian Pacific liner lay surrounded by a host of sampans, like a swan mothering a large brood of ugly ducklings; several cargo boats were taking in or discharging merchandise, great arc lamps beginning to glow on the lighters tied up to them; an intermediate P&O boat was leaving her anchorage; a British India vessel had recently arrived. Over by the Kowloon side a large barque, her masts and shrouds looking spidery in the rapidly failing light, lay alongside a wharf. She presented a great contrast to an essentially modern Japanese cruiser anchored close by. The strains of a band came clearly across the water from the naval guardship, as the ensign was hauled down. Involuntarily Cousins raised his dilapidated topee. He and his companion stopped for a while to watch the noisy disembarkation of Chinese passengers from a river boat just in from Canton. The spectacle greatly interested Cousins, but the craving for drink was too strong in Kenton to allow him to dally. Impatiently he turned away, drawing the little man with him.

They came at length to a block of tall houses situated in that part of the town where the Chinese quarter proper begins and the European district ends. Exactly in the centre was one, which by its exterior arrangement loudly proclaimed its purpose. A group of small round tables and chairs outside under an awning were reminiscent of the continental cafés. Verandas on each storey also contained their quota of the same furnishings. There were very few vacant tables, the chairs being occupied by a laughing, chatting assemblage of polyglot humanity. From within came the blare of an over-saxophoned band playing an untuneful dance number. High up in great gilt letters, floodlit from a balcony below, was the name TAVARES – nothing else. Cousins observed that the house on one side was apparently a Turkish bath establishment; on the other was a private dwelling.

'The people living there,' he commented, nodding towards the place, 'can't obtain much peace and quietness. Tavares seems popular, to judge from the number of patrons already present.'

'He's popular all right,' returned Kenton. 'Come along. This isn't the spot for us.'

He led the way through the chatting throng into the interior of the building. Cousins found himself in a large, garishly furnished hall. Tables and chairs, very few of them vacant, lined the walls; in the centre a dozen couples were dancing, all of them, with one exception, Macanese, or, as they would no doubt have designated themselves, Portuguese. A broad staircase ran up to a gallery above also crowded with people. In the background on a rostrum sat the bandsmen playing as though in a frenzy, the strident strains of the untuneful foxtrot grating on the ear in cacophonous jangle. Skirting the dancers, Kenton, followed closely by his companion, walked to the rear of the hall until he reached a curtained doorway to the left of the platform. He was about to pull the portière aside, when a figure came striding through, stopped abruptly as he saw them, looked them up and down. He was a stout, swarthy, greasy-looking man of medium height arrayed in white evening attire. Round his protuberant middle was a black cummerbund into which was stuck a scarlet silk handkerchief. His thick black hair, oiled until it shone again, was brushed back from his forehead. He possessed a large bulbous nose, thick sensual lips, an indeterminate chin that seemed to recede into the fleshy coarseness of his neck, small black eyes set close together under heavy black eyebrows, and an unkempt moustache. His expression, as he surveyed them, changed from that of interest to contempt.

'What you doing here?' he demanded in harsh tones. 'You don't belong in this part of my house.'

'We were about to find our way to the other,' Kenton told him airily.

'There is a back door for people like you. Keep to it.'

'How very rude!' murmured Cousins. 'Who is this person, Jim?'

With a flourish of his arm, and a mocking bow, Kenton performed the introduction.

'This, my dear George,' he proclaimed, 'is Mr José Tavares, our genial, gentlemanly, and captivating host.'

CHAPTER SEVEN

The Genial José Tavares

Cousins eyed the proprietor with interest, wondering how much he could tell about the circumstances leading up to the suicide of his late employer, Mathos, if he were disposed to talk. Quickly the Secret Service man weighed up the other, and came to the conclusion that he was an unscrupulous, crafty, and cruel voluptuary, a man who would stoop to almost any deed that was likely to be of unholy pleasure or profit to him. Tavares' air of disdain increased. With pointed insolence, he gazed at the worn shoes that had once been white buckskin, the soiled and crumpled suit, the decrepit topee held in a hand, the unsteadiness of which proclaimed the owner's failing, and addressed himself to the little man.

'I do not seem to remember you. I know most of the damn fool derelicts who come to my house, but you – no.' He turned to Kenton. 'You I have seen before. What cesspool were you in when you came across this microbe?'

Cousins' eyes glinted. He began to feel a yearning to lay unfriendly hands on Mr José Tavares. Kenton remained unaffected.

'Not yours, as you gather,' he replied with calm impudence. 'I had rather a difficulty in getting Mr Collins to come here with me. He's apt to be particular.'

Tavares frowned heavily.

'Don't come through this way again,' he growled. 'I will not have my respectable patrons contaminated.' He waved his hand airily. 'That is all; you may go, but remember!'

'Just a minute, you!' Cousins stayed him with uplifted hand. 'I've drunk in most dives east of Suez, and I've never been spoken to like that before. My money's as good as anybody else's who comes here, and, if I care to honour your rotten old house with my presence, I'll come in whichever way I like, so put that in your fat head, and keep it there as a reminder.'

Tavares' little eyes flashed.

'How you dare speak like me to that!' he snarled, becoming a little mixed in his excitement. 'If I say one word, you go out on your nose.'

'Oh, yeah!' returned Cousins in true film style. In his hand appeared like lightning a long thin-bladed knife, the point of which he proceeded to tap against the bulging shirt front of the now thoroughly alarmed Macanese. 'Listen, friend, I may be small, but, like most little men, I know how to look after myself. I've been jugged more often than I like to remember for beating up fellows like you who got my goat. And I've made an art of knife sticking so as to lay a man on his back yelling with agony without actually killing him.'

He looked round, appearing to be searching for something, Tavares following his eyes as though fascinated. Kenton had been listening with the air of one overcome by a feeling of amazed incredulity. There was a lull in the dancing; members of the band were staring down at the scene below the rostrum with great interest; some of the patrons had approached, and were looking on. Cousins espied an ornate picture hanging on the wall eighteen or twenty yards away.

'See the cord that monstrosity is hanging by?' he asked. 'Well, watch!'

Holding his knife by the point, he suddenly threw it. Glittering in malevolent fashion, under the brilliant lights above, it sped with unerring aim, cutting completely through the string to stick quivering in the wall. The picture swung drunkenly to one side, seemed to hang in that position for a second; then crashed to the floor. A gasp of wonder broke from the spectators of this amazing feat of accuracy. Tavares found it necessary to wipe a few beads of perspiration away from his forehead. Cousins looked up at him, his lips curved in a smile that somehow seemed to suggest a rascally mind. He almost swaggered as he crossed the room to recover the weapon. Back in front of Tavares, he again tapped that gentleman on his shirt front.

'That's just to show you I'm not to be insulted,' he declared. 'Treat me right, and you'll find I'm as peaceful as a dove. As Pepys says: "With peace and honour I am willing to spare anything so as to keep all ends together". Come on, Jim, that drink's long overdue, or shall we go somewhere else where we are treated more civilly?'

Tavares seemed to waken from a stupor.

'Please do not go,' he pleaded, catching Cousins by the arm. 'I only made the joke – yes. It will be an honour to have you in my premises.'

The little man winked at his companion. Arm in arm they swept the curtain aside, and disappeared into the room beyond. Tavares signalled angrily to the orchestra to play; bowed the interested guests back to their tables. He went from one group to another exchanging pleasantries, but all the time his manner was a trifle distrait, his little pig-like eyes held a look of pensiveness in them. A man who could throw a knife like that, a ne'er-do-well, one who, by his own confession, had spent a considerable amount of his life in gaol, might perhaps be useful. Besides, had not Tavares seen the rogue look in his eye, and Tavares could always tell. Decidedly a man to conciliate.

The room into which Kenton and Cousins had gone was neither so large nor so flamboyantly showy. Half a dozen curtained alcoves, each containing a table and two chairs, were on one side, while a bar ran the whole length of the wall opposite. Behind this, Chinese boys in blue smocks, overlooked by two Macanese in white jackets, served drinks to the men and women crowding by the counter or sitting at the numerous little tables. The floor, unlike the polished teak of the dance hall, was rough and ill-swept. The walls were distempered a pale green, which, in the strong light of the numerous barely shaded electric globes, had rather a sickly effect. A row of gaming machines, along the farther side of the room on either side of a door, was almost as well patronised as the counter. A staircase behind the bar, against the wall separating the saloon from the dance hall, was the only visible connection with the upper regions of the house. Cousins ascertained that spittoons were in abundance, and he and Kenton found a vacant table in one of the alcoves provided with two. Spittoons or flowerpots, it may as well be explained, were a necessary adjunct to Cousins' drinking bouts. He called for a bottle of brandy and two glasses, which were quickly forthcoming. As the Chinese waiter put the bottle on the table, Kenton grabbed it with a great sigh of relief. His eyes shone feverishly, his hands trembled with a dreadful eagerness. Into his glass he poured a very liberal dose and, without waiting for Cousins to help himself, drank it off at one gulp, never turning a hair.

'Ah!' he breathed, 'that's better. God how I wanted it!' His speech had already thickened slightly, as though its natural timbre had been thinned by his unwonted abstention, and was now returning to its proper quality. He waited until Cousins had filled his glass; then, replenishing his own; 'Here's to my little friend the fire-eater!' he toasted. 'Say, George, you certainly gave me a surprise tonight. Who would ever have thought that you were such a dangerous little blighter. Tavares' face, when you threw that knife, was a study in six different sorts of fear. I'm sure, as he watched it quivering in the wall, he could almost feel it in his black body. Hell! That's a long speech for me.' He drained his glass, followed the action with a loud hiccough, and apologised gravely. 'But you haven't done all you told him, have you? I mean to say, beaten up men, and stuck knives in 'em.'

'I have, Jim,' declared Cousins. 'When I get roused, I see red, and nothing rouses me more than to be insulted. But I don't kill; at least I don't think I've killed anyone yet.'

Thereupon he told Kenton a series of lurid yarns about entirely imaginary episodes of his past life. The other, drinking deep the while, listened to him with an expression in which respect and repugnance seemed surprisingly to mingle. It was all done with a purpose. Cousins had quickly taken the measure of Tavares, and had decided that if the Macanese took him for an unscrupulous, stop-at-nothing kind of ruffian with a marked ability at throwing a knife, he might quite likely consider it would be useful to cultivate him and, at the moment, there was nothing Cousins desired more than to become intimate, or at least on familiar terms with Tavares. He felt that by so doing he would be going a long way towards obtaining some of the information for which he had come to Hong Kong as advance agent of Sir Leonard Wallace. Tavares would, no doubt, question Kenton about him, which was the reason the Secret Service man was filling his friend's mind with tales of the kind calculated to cause Tavares to rise to the bait.

By the time Cousins' fictitious reminiscing was finished, so was the brandy, and Kenton was in the bemused state usual with him. He had not appeared to notice that Cousins had hardly touched the bottle, which was just as well. The little man disliked pouring so much of the liquor away, not because he had any particular liking for it, but because it was an extravagance, though an unavoidable one. As a matter of fact, he was beginning to detest the stuff, for, though so much was spilt into handy receptacles during the bouts he pretended to have, of necessity a considerable amount found its way down his throat. Kenton eyed him with drunken solemnity.

'I'm glad you don' kill,' he observed. 'I don' b'lieve in killing myself. Of course some people deserve to be done in. But be careful; don' throw th' knife 'bout too much might go in wrong place some day.' He gazed at Cousins as he might at something unique. 'Fancy,' he mused, 'fancy George being such bloodthirsty lil beggar. Oh, you naughty lil man. Still won't make 'ny difference to my friendship. I promise you that, my boy. I like you, an' when I like 'nybody I stick to 'em – tha's what I do; stick to 'em. Besides you got lotta good in you. I know I'm good judge.' He waggled his finger impressively; then noticed the empty bottle. 'Boy,' he shouted, '*apportez-moi* – no, tha' won't do, it's French. Bring 'nother bottle brandy. Fightee!'

The bottle was brought at once, and the drinking continued. It was noticeable that, as time went on, Collins, otherwise Cousins, degenerated into very much the same state as his companion, but whereas Kenton was quiet in his cups and inclined to be maudlin, the other grew somewhat noisy, and gave the impression that it would take little to cause him to become aggressive. The place was packed with a motley collection of individuals of both sexes, most of whom were not very far removed from the condition of the two men in the alcove. Tavares made no objection to the amount his patrons drank so long as they caused no trouble. If anything of that nature threatened, the offenders were promptly put out by two hefty gentlemen, who had the appearance of retired prize-fighters, and peace was at once restored.

A number of the men present were sailors from the boats with a good sprinkling of the nondescript, seedy-looking individuals found in every port, whose mode of existence is a complete mystery to everybody. There were also, of course, others, frankly of the beachcombing fraternity, who, if they had not the price of a drink, wheedled it out of someone, preying particularly on those whose senses had gone up in the fumes of the spirits they were imbibing. The women, loud voiced and vulgar, painted and powdered, it is unnecessary to comment upon. The type is to be found from Singapore to New York, San Francisco to Sydney, Brisbane to Bombay, growing fat on the decadent passions of men, like vultures gorging themselves on the rotting carcasses of what had once been creatures fine and vital.

Bleary-eyed and drink-sodden, outwardly as much a drunken wreck as any of the derelicts in that saloon, Cousins inwardly felt nauseated and revolted by this display of life at its lowest. Suddenly, imperceptibly, he stiffened. The man for whom he was waiting had entered the room, was gazing round him with a fat smile on his unpleasant face, a cigar stuck between his lips. It became apparent that he was searching for something or somebody. Presently his eyes turned in the direction of the table in the first alcove. He saw three empty bottles, one man sprawled over the table, occasionally raising a head which he was unable to control; the other, glass in hand, watching with fatuous, leering smile, the people round him.

Tavares, soft-footed, despite his bulk, crossed quietly to the table. With a peremptory gesture, he sent away the boy who was about to attend to them.

'I hope your requirements are being properly looked after, gentlemen,' he purred.

They both attempted to look up at him, their eyelids

drooping, despite strenuous efforts to keep them raised. Kenton presently gave up the task, his head sinking back on to his arms; the man known as Collins propped up his by placing a fist under his chin and the elbow on the table.

'Wha' d'you want?' he demanded. 'Lemme tell you that if you're goin' turn me an' my friend out, I'm goin' to do lil bit pig-sticking.'

In his hand appeared again the knife that had caused Tavares such tremors in the dance hall. At once one of the retired prize-fighters hurried up and laid heavy hands on Cousins' shoulders. For his pains, he received a prick that made him start back with a curse, as though he had touched something red hot. His eyes glared fiercely, his teeth came together with a click; it looked for a moment as if Cousins was in for a rough time, but Tavares frowned, and held up a peremptory hand.

'Did I tell you come here?' he demanded harshly. 'Go away, and mind your business! This gentleman my friend.'

The other looked astounded. He glanced from Tavares to Cousins and back again, his mouth wide open. Presently he shrugged his shoulders, glared balefully at the little man eyeing him with a drunken leer, and wandered away rubbing his hand. Tavares turned to Cousins.

'Listen, my friend,' he remarked, 'it is not good that you are so quick with that knife here. People look, and they think. Put it away!'

Cousins shook his head with slow solemnity.

'Nothin' doin',' he replied. 'I tol' you wha' I do to people 'noy me. How d'I know you not goin' 'noy me?'

'I am your friend. In the dance hall I made the joke – you

think I am serious, but it is not so. I have come here to make myself certain that you do not misunderstand me. You are, what you call, up against it, I know; life is not good for you just now. I am sorry for you; it is my wish to help you.'

'I don' know wha' you're talkin' 'bout,' hiccoughed Cousins, 'an tha's truth, abs'lutely the truth. My life's all ri', his life's all ri'.' He waved a hand vaguely in Kenton's direction. 'Plen'y drink, plen'y money buy it. Tha's all tha' matters. You go 'way, let gennelmen 'lone.'

Kenton raised his head jerkily.

'You're 'ntirely ri', George,' he approved. He attempted to gesture Tavares away in lordly fashion, but only succeeded in performing some quaint inebriate movements with his hand. 'Go 'way an' leave gennelmen 'lone.' He appeared to be struck by some great thought, for, holding on to the table, he succeeded in raising himself to a more or less perpendicular position, and focused his blinking eyes on the Macanese. 'Dago!' he pronounced; 'dirty dago!'

Cousins nodded his head in slow but complete agreement.

'Jimmy,' he declared, 'you've hit it – hit it ri' on th' head. He's dirty dago.'

How long they would have gone on agreeing with each other it is difficult to say. Tavares, who seemed to have no objection to being called a dirty dago, cut them short. He leant down until his coarse mouth was very close to Cousins' ear.

'You do not always have plenty to drink and plenty of money to buy it,' he observed in low tones. 'Am I not correct?'

Cousins' head continued the nodding process, very much like a figure in a toy shop.

'Quite c'rect,' he assented. 'But money comes – always seem able t' get it anyhow.'

'But sometime no money comes,' persisted Tavares; 'then it is good to have a friend – no?'

With a great effort Cousins again fixed his eyes on the fellow.

'D'you know,' he remarked with the air of one who had discovered a remarkable fact, 'Now I look't you 'gain you don' lookserbad.' He tapped the lolling Kenton on the arm. The latter raised his head, and stared owlishly at him. 'Jimmy,' he pronounced, 'I was wrong. Thish man's dago, yes, but dirty dago, no!'

'Abs'lutely not dirty,' agreed Kenton, subsiding into his former position.

'You hear tha', Mister Wha'syername?' asked Cousins. 'The two of ush are perf'ly unan-unan-unan'moush you're not dirty. Shtand shtill, can't you? When you move 'bout like tha' there sheems two, three o' you. One'sh not so bad, but can't shtand three.'

Tavares, who had not moved, smiled in what was meant to be full and sympathetic understanding.

'You then realise that I wish to be your friend I think,' he stated rather than asked. 'When everything is gloomy to you, and you have no money; when the clouds seem all round, you come to me – yes?'

Cousins laughed thickly.

'I know,' he chuckled, 'you want be lil silver lining.' Then with solemn attempt to pronounce his words clearly, and beating time on the table with unsteady forefinger, he quoted: '"Though outwardly a gloomy sh-shroud, th' inner half o' ev'ry cloud is'h bright an' sh-shining; I therefore turn my cloudsh 'bout, an al-alwaysh wear 'em inshide out to sh-show the linin'." D'you know who wrote tha'?' he demanded.

'Was it you?' asked Tavares ingratiatingly.

'Course not,' returned Cousins with contempt. 'Was written by Ellen Thorn'croft Fowler – very clever woman. So you're my silver lining?' He laughed again. 'Wha' for?' he demanded suddenly and suspiciously.

'Because I like you,' returned the Macanese in silky tones. 'I think you are very nice and clever man. I am sorry things not too good for you. Never mind, when your money gone, perhaps I give you drinks. José Tavares has a good heart.'

'An' wha' d'you expect in return?' asked Cousins, leering at him cunningly.

Tavares shrugged his shoulders.

'Maybe sometime I ask you to do one or two little jobs,' he returned, 'nothing much.'

Kenton raised his head once more, a look of anxiety in his bleary eyes.

'Wha' bout tha' bottle brandy?' he asked. 'Must have brandy.'

'Yes,' agreed Cousins, bringing down his hand with a resounding thump on the table. 'I ordered 'nother bottle. Where is it?'

Tavares called a boy to him.

'Why you do not attend to these gentlemen?' he asked in angry tones. The Chinese waiter was about to reply that he had been stopped by Tavares himself, but the latter gave him no chance to speak. 'Go at once, and bring a bottle of brandy,' he ordered, 'and see that it is charged to me.'

Cousins, who had allowed nothing to escape him, since the advent of the proprietor, staggered to his feet, and held out a very unsteady hand.

'Shake!' he said with drunken enthusiasm, 'Musht 'pologise for thinking you a dirty dago. You're a goo' fellow, wha'syername, a very goo' fellow 'ndeed. Jim,' he added to Kenton, who was watching the performance with owlish gravity, 'shake hands with the gennelman. He's goo' fellow. We've mish-mishjudged him.'

Kenton found it quite impossible to rise, but he succeeded in holding out his hand to Tavares.

'Take y'r word for it, George,' he observed. 'If you say he's goo' fellow, he musht be goo' fellow.'

Solemnly he shook Tavares' hand until the latter drew away. The bottle of brandy with fresh glasses was placed on the table. Cousins and his friend insisted on their host drinking with them. He took very little and, after expressing the hope that they would patronise his establishment regularly, and obtaining their address, he left them. As he walked away, a gleam in his eye that seemed to express satisfaction, Cousins started to sing, 'For he's a jolly good fellow', but his efforts to express his appreciation of Tavares in song ended in a succession of loud hiccoughs much to the amusement of people near by.

As soon as Tavares had disappeared, two or three 'ladies', their predatory instincts roused by the apparent friendship Tavares had shown for the dilapidated men in the alcove, and the obvious fact that they had money to burn, judging from the number of empty brandy bottles on the table, strove to inflict their over-scented persons on the two. Kenton was too far gone to resist, but his companion showed such fierce though inebriate opposition to their presence, that they retreated in alarm.

Day after day went by, each a repetition of the one before. Kenton was never sober, and it soon became evident to Cousins that unless something was done very soon, his queer friend would sink into a drunken coma from which he would never recover. Cousins, though generally appearing almost as drunk as his companion, allowed himself to have occasional sober periods, when he would express disgust of drunkenness, and swear that he would never touch another drop of drink. These declarations, of course, were made in the presence of Tavares, and with a purpose. He did not wish the Macanese to think that he was an utterly hopeless dipsomaniac like his friend. Obviously a man who never had a sober period would be of little use to Tavares, if the latter really had intentions of using him for his own purposes, while one who was unable to resist drink, whose character was debased and weakened by indulgence, but who, nevertheless, was at times sober, was the type of man he would feel he could bend to his will; the only sort of tool, in fact, that a man like Tavares would use.

One day about a week after their arrival in Victoria, Kenton became very bad indeed. They had spent all the previous night as usual in Tavares' unholy establishment and, although Cousins had taken to carrying a flask full of water about with him, with which he diluted Kenton's brandy whenever he could do so without being seen, the ex-engineer rapidly got into a state of utter delirium. Towards morning, Tavares, fearful of what action might be taken by the police, if Kenton died on his premises from alcoholic poisoning, had ordered Cousins and his companion to be conveyed to their apartments. Rickshas were procured, and the two were taken to their unsavoury hotel; dumped unceremoniously outside the door. It was not that Tavares was a very particular kind of person, but he avoided trouble as far as possible. Men had died on his premises before, generally as the result of brawls. In their cases their bodies had been spirited away, and all trace of them eradicated, but that meant endless bother. If he suspected that a man was about to get himself killed in a quarrel or die a horrible death from over-indulgence in liquor, Tavares preferred the tragedy to happen elsewhere. He made up his mind. Kenton was approaching the gates of eternity; the ex-engineer was conveyed, therefore, to his hotel in order that his demise could have no possible legal repercussion on the house which the Macanese knew was regarded with disfavour by the police. Cousins was sent with him lest, when he awoke from the drunken sleep in which he was apparently submerged, he would become obstreperous on discovering that his friend was missing. Tavares had formed the opinion, which Cousins took pains to strengthen, that the little man was a hot-headed fire-eater, liable at any moment to become a thorough desperado.

Dawn was breaking as the rickshas departed with the men who had been given the task of seeing the two drunkards to their temporary home. Cousins, having assured himself that he was unobserved, sat up, and yawned prodigiously. He had had very little proper sleep since arriving in the colony, most of it having been uncomfortably taken sprawled across a table or on a hard floor, and he felt weary. However, there was no time then to consider himself; he knew Kenton was in a bad way, and must have attention as soon as possible, if he were to have a chance of recovery. Cousins looked down at the restless, muttering man for whom he had conceived a deep liking, and was filled with pity. He felt very guilty at the thought that he had accompanied him on the drinking bouts that had ended so disastrously, even though he realised quite well that Kenton would have drunk himself into his present condition sooner or later in any case. It was the fact that his money had chiefly paid for the brandy, with which Kenton had saturated himself, that upset Cousins. However, it was no use looking down at his companion, and doing nothing. At any moment he might give vent to the horrible fits of screaming and struggling that had so unnerved Tavares. Cousins looked round, his wrinkled face looking more grotesque than ever in the perplexity that troubled him. Could he arrange for Kenton to be conveyed to hospital, receive the utmost attention, and still continue successfully to sustain his character of a drunken, worthless, almost penniless reprobate? On no account must Tavares suspect that he was not quite the waster he appeared to be, but he felt that what he intended doing for Kenton was hardly in keeping with the personality he had assumed. Yet it had to be done; the one-time builder of bridges was too good a man to allow to die one of the most horrible deaths imaginable. His mind made up, Cousins rose to his feet; went in search of Ho Fang Ho. As he went, a horrible, long-drawn cry, scarcely human in its terrible note of agonised fear, ascended into the still air. He shuddered. Kenton was once again fighting the devils arrayed in his disordered imagination against him.

CHAPTER EIGHT

'Too Muchee Big Pilate'

By the time Cousins had found the Chinese boy who had insisted upon attaching himself to him as servant, and had returned to the unpretentious front door of the little hotel, the neighbourhood had been roused by the inhuman cries of the man grovelling on the ground. People on the terrace above, and the houses on both sides, hung out of their windows, most of them jabbering in excited Portuguese. Mrs Gutteriez, the landlady, did not appear, however, somewhat to Cousins' relief. Her slumbers were apparently proof against any noise, no matter how fearsome or shrill it might be. With the help of his master, Ho Fang Ho succeeded, after a desperate struggle, in binding and gagging the dipsomaniac. Once the cries ceased, the heads of the curious disappeared. It had not been light enough to see much of what was taking place, but the sound had been so inhuman that nobody had ventured to descend and investigate. Holy Church forbade any kind of intercourse with devils, and surely, thought these pious Catholics, only devils could shriek in such a manner. It behoved them to keep away for fear of dreadful consequences. Cousins breathed a prayer of thanksgiving and wiped his streaming face. It struck him as rather curious that a policeman had not heard the outcry – there was generally one somewhere in the neighbourhood. Perhaps, he, too, had thought of devils and, being a Chinaman, had departed elsewhere hurriedly, his reason not being so dissimilar from that which had kept the Christians from leaving their houses.

Ho Fang Ho was sent to procure a sedan chair. He was away some time; then returned with one carried by two sleepy-looking coolies. Kenton was lifted in, the coolies appearing to regard a bound and gagged passenger as nothing out of the ordinary. With Cousins walking on one side, Ho Fang Ho on the other, the ex-engineer was carried to hospital. There he was left in charge of the Chinese boy, while Cousins sought an interview with the senior house physician. The latter was in bed, and it took all the Secret Service man's powers of persuasion to get anybody to rouse him. Eventually it was done, however, and a sleepy-eyed, tousled-haired Irishman, arrayed in a somewhat startling kimono, appeared on the scene. He regarded Cousins with disfavour, which increased almost to exploding point when he had taken full stock of the seedy-looking individual before him. Without selecting his words, he launched into a blunt and graphic expression of his opinion of people who disturbed him in the early hours of the morning, especially those of the low order of society to which the interrupter of his slumbers obviously belonged. Cousins quickly decided that, despite his choleric outburst, the doctor was a good fellow, and let him continue until he could think of nothing else to say.

'Well, what is it you want now?' he concluded in exasperation, as though aggrieved that his tirade had failed to cause the little man before him to sink to the floor in terror or, at least, dismay.

Cousins proceeded to tell him of the very grave condition of his friend, adding that he had brought him to the hospital in the hope that there might still be a chance of saving his life, perhaps even of curing him of his craving for brandy. When he realised that he had been called from his bed by the insistence of one beachcomber, who had brought another, suffering from DT's, to the hospital, the doctor almost became apoplectic with rage. But, as Cousins went on, he gradually calmed down, and began to look interested, especially when the little man added that no expense was to be spared, and that he himself would bear all the cost.

'Well,' he declared, 'it's used I am to surprises, but, faith this is a new one! Here are you, a self-confessed waster, and a drunkard yourself, no doubt, pleading with me to save your friend from the drink. What is behind all this now?'

'Nothing except that he was once a man of position and ability. I like him, and I want to help him get back to respectability, if it's possible.' He pushed a bundle of notes into the doctor's hands. 'Take these,' he begged eagerly. 'They're part of a remittance I recently had. If that is not enough, let me know, and I'll get it for you.'

In order to cloak the fact that he was more interested and touched than he wished to appear, rather than from any desire to know how much money had been handed to him, the doctor counted the bundle. It comprised two hundred dollars.

'It will not cost all this,' he protested, and attempted to hand back some of the notes.

Cousins insisted on his retaining them, telling him that he wished Kenton to have a private room and secrecy.

'I don't want you to allow anybody but me to see him,' he pleaded. 'He only knows those who would have a bad influence on him and play on his weakness, and that would undo all the good I hope you will succeed in doing.'

'It's a good heart you have,' rejoined the doctor in somewhat husky tones, 'but why the devil is it that you – Bedad! And it's none of my business.' He pushed the notes into his pocket. 'Make your mind easy now. He'll be in very good hands and, if we can cure him, it's cured he'll be. He'll have a private room – in any case his trouble would necessitate that, you see. And if he's in the condition you describe, I doubt if yourself will be allowed to see him for some considerable time, let alone anybody else. Come along now, and let me have a look at him.'

He called a nurse and two Chinese orderlies with a stretcher, and they proceeded to the place where Ho Fang Ho kept guard over the sedan chair. The doctor smiled when he observed that his patient was bound and gagged, but made no comment. Kenton was placed on the stretcher, and conveyed to a distant part of the building, where he was put in a small room more or less isolated from other wards. Another doctor and two more nurses were sent for. The gag and ropes that bound him were removed, and a careful examination at once made. In the midst of it, he began to scream and struggle again. Cousins walked away, hating to stop and listen to him. Half an hour went by; then the Irish doctor appeared.

'It's in a bad way, he is,' he pronounced, 'and it's going to be a long job, but I think we'll pull him through.'

Cousins' haggard face creased into one of his illimitable smiles, and the doctor, unable to resist the spell of those laughing puckers, smiled broadly also.

'I'm jolly pleased to hear you say that, doctor,' said the former. 'Do you think you'll be able to cure him of his craving for brandy?'

'Ah! That is hard to say. But you can rely upon us to do our best.' He shook his head regretfully. 'It's a fine figure of a man he must have been before the drink took hold of him. And now is there anything about yourself you'd be after liking to tell me.'

'Not now, doctor,' smiled Cousins; 'sometime perhaps. If anybody asks about him, I'll be obliged if you say that the police brought him here. Is that too much to ask?'

The doctor eyed him thoughtfully for some moments.

'Perhaps it's not so dense I am after all,' he observed at length. 'Well, well, it shall be the police that brought him here.'

Cousins was about to express his gratitude, when a nurse came hurrying towards them.

'Is your name Collins – George Collins?' she asked. Cousins nodded. 'The gentleman in number three is asking for you,' she went on; adding to the doctor: 'He is quite rational for the moment, and seems very anxious to speak to Mr Collins.'

'You can go to him,' agreed the Irishman, 'but don't stay long now. We've given him an injection, so it's all right he'll be.' He held out his hand which Cousins grasped warmly. 'You can come and be after inquiring about him every day, but I cannot promise that you will be allowed to see him.'

He walked away, and Cousins followed the nurse. He found Kenton lying strapped in bed. The skin of his face looked curiously transparent with a little spot of hectic colouring burning on either cheek. His bloodshot eyes regarded Cousins with intense eagerness.

'Think I must have been dreaming it,' he commenced in a low, thick utterance, which was otherwise quite free from any suggestion of intoxication, 'but I felt I had to tell you.'

He paused for some time. They were quite alone, the nurses having tactfully stepped out into the corridor.

'What is it?' asked Cousins at length.

'Tavares wants to get you in his power for some reason,' whispered Kenton. 'He is going to stage a fake murder. It seems to me that I was lying asleep in our alcove – dunno where you were – and Tavares thought I was dead to the world. Anyhow he arranged that you were to be riled, until you saw red; then you were expected to fling your knife at your tormentor. He'd drop, and you would be told he was dead. After that you'd have to do whatever Tavares told you, or he'd threaten to hand you over to the police.'

Cousins smiled, but behind his merry eyes grim thoughts were racing through his brain. He certainly found Kenton's story most interesting. There was no belief in his mind that it was a figment of a disordered mind.

'You dreamt it, old chap,' he remarked lightly. 'No man is

likely to offer himself up as a sacrifice of that nature, even if he is certain he'll be wounded and not killed outright.'

'He wouldn't even be wounded,' Kenton assured him. 'Tavares was going to substitute a dummy for your knife; then, when you'd thrown it, the real one was to be brought to you covered with blood.'

The ingenuity of the idea almost took Cousins' breath away. He guessed at once what was behind it, and if indeed the plot was genuine and not a chimera of his friend's diseased mind, he resolved to be caught in the trap prepared for him. It is certain that, if Tavares had him, or felt he had him in his power, Cousins would be able to learn things which otherwise would be religiously kept from him. Men of the type of the Macanese dance hall proprietor are apt to be careless in their remarks to those they imagine are firmly planted under their thumbs. The Secret Service man chuckled.

'A nice plot for a thriller, Jim,' he commented. 'You certainly imagined it. What possible reason could Tavares have for staging such an elaborate snare for an insignificant bloke like me?'

'You're damn clever with a knife, George, and Tavares is the sort of devil who would find you a useful man to have in his power. But I suppose you're right,' he added wearily; 'must have imagined it.' His voice died away into incoherent mutterings, but presently he fixed his eyes on Cousins again. 'What am I here for?' he demanded. 'And why can't I move? What have they done to me?'

'You're all right, Jim; don't worry!' came in soothing accents from Cousins. 'You're ill; you'll be well looked after.'

'I'm not ill,' broke from the other. The little flame-like

spots in his cheeks appeared to be burning brighter; the light of madness returned to his eyes. 'Damn it all! Let me get away, do you hear me? George, be a pal, help me to get up. Come on! Don't stand there like a fool! Bring me brandy! Hurry up! I want brandy and plenty of it. God how my throat aches for it! The want of it's burning me away.' Once again his voice died away into unintelligible mumbling.

Cousins felt a touch on his arm. One of the nurses stood by his side.

'I think you'd better go,' she whispered.

He nodded, and with a last pitying look at his friend, turned, and left the room.

He had paid off the coolies with the sedan chair, and told Ho Fang Ho to return to the lodging house, but he found, on emerging from the hospital, that the latter had waited for him.

'Didn't I tell you to go home?' he demanded.

The Chinaman grinned.

'Me belong waitee for master. Ho Fang Ho velly good boy.'

'A very good boy should do what he is told,' retorted Cousins.

'Me tinkee master too muchee tired. Me helpee.'

'I suppose you think I might be too drunk to walk straight.'

Ho Fang Ho shook his head.

'Master no gettee dlunk,' he returned surprisingly. 'Allo time master pletend gettee too muchee dlunk, but no dlunk. Ho Fang Ho no undelstand, but not him pidgin. Me belong plenty good boy.'

Cousins stood still, and stared at the grinning Chinaman.

'Well, I'll be damned,' he ejaculated with emphasis.

Ho Fang Ho shook his head.

'No,' he declared with conviction; 'master him no belong gettee damn. Bad mans gettee too muchee damn, good mans no gettee damn.'

'So I am a good man, am I?' commented Cousins.

Ho Fang Ho positively beamed.

'Plenty too muchee good man,' he asserted, as though he would like to meet the man who dared contradict him.

Cousins walked on thoughtfully. He was not exactly pleased at the discovery that Ho Fang Ho knew that his masquerade as a confirmed drunkard was in very fact pretence. He wondered what it was that had undeceived the Chinaman and resolved to find out. He turned, and waited for the boy, who had been following him at a respectful distance.

'Why do you think that I only pretend to be drunk, Ho Fang?' he demanded.

The cheerful grin, never very far away, came into the other's surprisingly expressive Chinese face.

'One time me velly solly too muchee dlunk, master,' he explained. 'Me puttee you to bed, and you tinkee me walkee away, but I sittee by door on velandah because me tinkee you belong velly sick bimeby. But when me looksee into loom you no dlunk. You sittee up in bed, smokee pipe, and leading too muchee paper.'

Cousins grunted. That was a bad lapse on his part. Such a mistake must never be made again.

'Anything else?' he asked.

'Today, morning time,' declared Ho Fang Ho, 'you came

back with other master. Him plenty too muchee dlunk, but when you come catchee me you no dlunk – too muchee wolly. Bimeby when you walkee with chair coolies, you pletend dlunk. In hospital you no dlunk, now no dlunk.'

'You're too observant, Ho Fang,' grumbled Cousins.

Ho Fang Ho beamed more than ever. His face positively shone with delight. He looked as though a great compliment had been paid to him.

'Me belong too muchee obselvant master,' he agreed.

'Where did you learn to speak English so well?' asked the curious Cousins.

'My fader him cook, my mudder him amah,' explained Ho Fang Ho. 'Allo time bose workee for Englishmans. Me Chlistian,' he added, as though that were an additional and incontestable reason for his knowledge of the language.

'Well, look here. You forget that I ever pretended to be drunk. When I'm drunk, I'm drunk – really and horribly drunk, savvy?'

The boy nodded his head.

'Me plenty undelstand, master,' he assured Cousins. 'Any mans talkee my, me tellum you velly too muchee no good – allo time dlink too muchee.'

'Ho Fang Ho,' declared Cousins with conviction, 'I am beginning to believe that you're a treasure.'

The Chinaman's eyes danced with rapture.

'Velly good tleasure,' he agreed forcefully, with an artless and entire lack of anything in the way of mock modesty.

Cousins walked on with a smile. The early morning sun was shining now in a cloudless sky, giving promise of a very hot day to come. Back in his sordid lodging house, which in itself was surely an insult to the very name of hotel, Cousins undressed, and went to bed. There was a great deal to occupy his mind but he felt that, before considering his problems, he needed rest – he had had so very little since arriving in the colony. For once in a way the grubby sheets did not repel him, neither did the unclean pillow cause him to shudder with abhorrence. He threw himself down, and, within the space of a few minutes, was sleeping the sleep of the utterly weary.

A loud knock on the door awakened him. At once, with all his faculties about him, he opened his eyes cautiously. A glance at the cheap watch on the broken-down chair by the bedside showed him that the time was past noon. He had slept for nearly six hours, and felt wonderfully refreshed. But he did not show it. The person knocking on the door was not Ho Fang Ho – the Chinaman always walked in without bothering to announce his coming. Cousins decided that it was necessary, therefore, to give the appearance of a man roused from a drunken slumber. Again came a knock, louder if possible than before; the whole room shook.

'Who's there, and what do you want?' he demanded thickly and ungraciously.

The door opened, revealing the landlady standing on the threshold, an ingratiating and entirely incongruous simper on her fleshy and acquisitive countenance.

'I've come myself to tell you that you are honoured, Mr Collins,' she announced.

'How? By whom?' yawned Cousins, regarding her through half-closed eyes.

'Who is it? You think,' she challenged, her affected girlish tones sending a feeling of repugnance through him.

'Oh, can't be bothered,' he grunted. 'I don't want to see anybody.'

'You will want to see this gentleman,' she persisted, advancing closer to the bed until her garlic-laden breath seemed to strike Cousins like a wave, and cause him an unpleasant feeling of nausea. 'You men drink so much,' she rallied, 'that you sleep like the hogs. Never you have breakfast. This morning I was telling your boy to take you some, but he says you too drunk, want to sleep.'

'He was quite right,' murmured Cousins. 'I'm not drunk now – not much, anyway – but I still want to sleep.'

Her cloak of arch-girlishness began to drop from her.

'You can't,' she almost snapped. 'A well-known gentleman wish to see you. He was great friends with my husband, and is important man, so you must go to him.'

'Who is he?' asked Cousins wearily.

She shrugged her shoulders regretfully.

'Well, if you will not guess, I must tell you. He is,' she spoke with great impressiveness, 'Mr José Tavares.'

Cousins disappointed her. He showed no signs whatever of being overcome with wonderment that the great man should deign to call on him. Inwardly he was decidedly interested.

'What the hell does he want?' he growled.

She opened her mouth wide with dismayed surprise, showing two rows of uneven ugly teeth. His reception of her news gave her a shock from which she found some difficulty in recovering. Obviously she regarded Mr José Tavares with a great deal of respect.

'Of course it is drink that makes you dull,' she remarked at length. 'But remember, Mr Tavares is a man of much importance. He is very rich.'

'I don't doubt it,' mumbled Cousins, suppressing another yawn. 'Anyhow, I'm not going to get out of bed. If he wants to see me he can come up.'

'You are not polite, Mr Collins,' she complained. 'He will not like it.'

'If he doesn't like it, he can do the other thing. By the way, you might as well know that Mr Kenton won't be here any more, at least not for some time. He's in hospital.'

'In hospital!' she gasped. 'Why?'

'Because he's ill. The police took him there.'

Her flabby face turned a sickly yellow.

'The police!' she repeated. Apparently she had no more liking for the police than had her friend Mr Tavares. Then, remembering the loss of a tenant and the empty room, she almost shrieked: 'My rent! What about my rent?'

'You've had it,' returned Cousins coldly. 'At any rate, you've had most of it. If there is anything owing, I'll pay it. Now get out.'

She got out.

Cousins lay on his back staring at the ceiling, his mind very much alert to the significance of this unexpected call. There were several reasons which might have prompted Tavares to visit him, and it was as well to be prepared. Taking Kenton to the hospital, arranging for special treatment, and handing over a sum of money in advance for that treatment was a risk, Cousins fully realised. If Tavares got to hear what he had done, the fellow's suspicions might very likely be roused, for neither the action nor the possession of so much money was typical of the down-at-heels, drunken wastrel that the Macanese believed him to be. It was for that reason that Cousins had sworn the doctor to secrecy as far as possible, and had persuaded him to promise to tell anybody who might inquire that the police had taken Kenton to hospital. There was no doubt at all but that Tavares kept as far aloof from the police as he could. Cousins had long since discovered that he had a very intense hatred and fear of them. In that certainty lay security. Tavares was not likely to interfere, if he heard the police had taken possession of Kenton. In any case the man's interest was obviously in the desperado Collins with his knife throwing propensities, not in the mild and maudlin dipsomaniac, Kenton.

Perhaps Tavares had come to prepare the way for the setting of the trap in which, if Kenton's tale had any basis of actuality, and was not merely the drunken dream of a warped mentality, Cousins was to be inveigled. The face of a hundred wrinkles creased into one of its all-enveloping, attractive smiles, as Cousins reflected that the plot would have badly miscarried, if he had not been warned by Kenton, for the simple reason that the knife-throwing desperado was, in reality, no desperado at all, and his oft-repeated threats of flinging knives about indiscriminately, at all and sundry who offended him, nothing but bluff.

Above the little man's head hung a punka, frayed and battered, its rope hanging dejectedly in a long loop. Cobwebs, showing signs of a completely undisturbed existence, were festooned in almost every fold of the dilapidated material. Altogether the punka looked as though it had never been used, certainly it had not during the week of Cousins' residence in the Hotel Paris. But it gave him an idea, an idea that depended for its fulfilment on whether a similar punka hung in Tavares' office, or whether the Macanese was modern enough to have electric fans installed there. He was still studying the contraption when Ho Fang Ho crept quietly into the room.

'Master,' he whispered, a tinge of excitement in his tone, 'one welly bad man come looksee you. You plenty take care. One time before me belong see him. Him one too muchee big pilate.'

'Pilate is he?' commented Cousins with a smile. 'Say rather, Iscariot, and you'll probably be nearer the mark.'

With a finger to his lips, Ho Fang Ho slipped through the window on to the veranda as the sound of heavy, determined footsteps, approaching the door, reached their ears. It was then that the true meaning of his servant's words and their significance dawned on Cousins. He gave vent to a long, noiseless whistle.

CHAPTER NINE

The Sliding Panel

Tavares entered the room to find the man, on whom he had taken the trouble to call, lying flat on his back with his eyes closed. He gave no sign that he had heard the entry of the visitor, appeared in fact to be asleep. The black eyebrows of the dance hall proprietor met in a frown, his bulbous nose sniffed at the atmosphere disdainfully, his coarse sensual lips curled in contempt. Watching him from under his eyelashes – a trick which he could perform to perfection without others being aware that he was observing them – Cousins was secretly amused. He noted the over-dressed appearance of the man, the carved blackwood stick, spotless white suit, fancy waistcoat, ornate gold pin stuck rakishly in his pale green tie, the startlingly brown shoes. Tavares cleared his throat loudly, whereupon Cousins opened his eyes, and regarded him with bleary interest.

'Hullo!' he greeted him. 'Sit down, if you can find a chair to sit on.'

Tavares, after one glance at the only two chairs the room contained, selected the bed, though with an air of supercilious distaste. The ancient article of furniture groaned under his weight, but gave no other sign of disruption.

'What is this I hear about the police?' he asked somewhat anxiously, without preamble.

'What have they been doing now?' counter-questioned Cousins, not without a certain amount of inward misgiving.

'Mrs Gutteriez tells me that they have taken your friend to hospital,' explained the other.

Cousins experienced a sense of relief. He nodded.

'They have,' he returned, 'and it's no thanks to you.' He sat up in bed, leant on his elbow, and glared at the Macanese. 'What d'you mean,' he demanded, 'by giving orders for me and Kenton to be brought here, and dumped on the doorstep like a couple of sacks of potatoes?'

Tavares' face gave a fairly good imitation of a friendly smile.

'It is for that reason I come to you,' he explained. 'I thought perhaps you might misunderstand and be offended with me. I have no wish that the friendship which I feel for you should be interrupted by a misconception on your part.'

Cousins gave no sign of the satisfaction he felt at the knowledge that Tavares' journey to Robinson Road had been inspired by a motive so harmless; on the contrary he began to look decidedly aggressive.

'Don't talk to me of friendship,' he snapped. 'I was drunk last night, and didn't know what was happening. I'm not drunk now. Kenton was damn bad, and you had him carted away and, for all you cared, left to die.'

'Listen to me, my friend,' pleaded Tavares urgently. 'It was necessary that he should not be found so ill in my house. The police they do not like me now. If he had died of drinking too much, and they had found out, there would have been much trouble for me. It was necessary that he should be removed. Today I came to see what could be done for him, and explain to you.'

'Why was I carted away as well then?' demanded Cousins. 'I might have been drunk, but I wasn't ill.'

'No; but I think when you wake from your sleep you will miss him, and make trouble. It would not have been possible to explain perhaps to you then – you do not see reason very much, when you are not sober.'

Cousins grinned. The other went on speaking, pleading his case, and he allowed himself to be conciliated.

'Oh, well,' he agreed at length, 'I suppose you're right. I am apt to get a bit peeved at times.'

Tavares showed relief that his explanation, typically selfish though it undoubtedly was, had been accepted, but almost at once the look of anxiety returned to his small, pig-like eyes.

'Tell me what happened?' he begged.

'Damned if I know,' returned Cousins. 'As far as I can recollect, I woke up to hear an infernal shrieking going on. Kenton seemed to be rolling about the middle of the road, and I was pulling myself up – had some hazy idea of going to him I suppose – when a fellow ran up. He looked like a Chinese policeman, so I daresay he was one. He started to drag Kenton into the doorway where I was standing, so I hopped it. I've no fancy for getting mixed up with the police any more than you have. I can't remember everything, it's too darned blurred, but, while I was watching, some other police wallahs arrived, one of 'em was a European sergeant I guess. Anyhow they put poor old Jim into a chair, and I heard the bloke in charge tell them to take him to hospital. That's all there is to it. People in the houses round about heard the row, and looked out, but nobody came down, and I kept well out of the way.'

'You have not come into contact with the police at all?'

'Bet your life I haven't.'

Tavares' face broke into a satisfied, expansive smile.

'My friend, I am glad,' he declared heartily. 'When Mrs Gutteriez told me about the police, I confess I am much worried. I did not wish the police to regard you with the eye of suspicion. So far it is certain they do not know of you, but once they begin to take interest in you, they will find out your past unhappy record, and that would be bad – for you.'

'What do you care?' grunted Cousins.

'I care very much. Perhaps some day you and I do together work of great profit to us both. I have thought, I will help my friend much. That I cannot do, if you are under watch by the police.'

'Look here!' growled Cousins, purposely imbuing the tone of his voice with suspicion. 'What are you hinting at? I'm not fool enough to imagine that you are showing all this friendliness because you like my face. What's behind it all?'

'You are not a fool, no! But you are mistaken. I feel a great friendship for you really, strange though it may seem to you. If perhaps I ask you to do something for me some time, it will only be what you call' – he made an impatient sound with his tongue – 'I have forgotten the word in English.'

'Do you mean "incidental"?'

'Ah! That it is, I mean, that is it – incidental.'

'All this friendship,' remarked Cousins deliberately, 'commenced when you found out that I know how to throw a knife.'

Tavares looked nonplussed. He did not reply for a few moments; then:

'Sometimes, my friend,' he observed slowly. 'I think I like you better when you are drunk.'

'I daresay you do,' retorted the little man coolly. 'I'm liable to be taken in by you then more easily. But I shan't be drunk again. Believe me, I've had a sickener of liquor, and after what I saw last night I'm not drinking any more. I'm for the water wagon for the future; I've sworn it.'

Tavares smiled unpleasantly.

'What is the good of talking like that? You know you cannot resist it. You think now you will drink no more, but presently the craving will come, it will eat into you and again you will drink. Why try to resist? It is waste of time, and besides it would not be good for you to stop.'

'Well, I'm going to, see?' returned Cousins, with a show of the weak obstinacy of a confirmed drunkard. 'I don't want to get like Kenton. Look what's happened to him.'

'Bah! You will not get like that. To him brandy was poison – to you it is medicine.'

'Medicine be damned!'

Tavares rose to his feet, flicking a gaudy silk handkerchief ostentatiously over his person, presumably to remove any microbes that may have attached themselves to him.

Deliberately he ignored Cousins' reiterated assertions that he had sworn off drink.

'Tonight,' he proclaimed, 'when you come to my little place, I will introduce you to one of my friends. You will like him. He, too, likes the brandy. But of one thing I must warn you. When he drinks, he sometimes talks in a very rash and foolish manner. He does not mean harm, but he says insulting things, especially to people of your unfortunate position. I ask you to bear with him, if he by accident will insult you.'

So the trap was laid for that night! Kenton's tale had not been a dream after all. Cousins felt inclined to laugh at the manner in which Tavares, while appearing to warn him, was attempting to rouse his antagonism against an unknown man in the hope that he would be ripe for mischief when goaded to fever point by a string of carefully prepared insults. He shook his head.

'You needn't worry,' he stated with an attempt at emphasis that yet sounded weak and undecided. 'I am not coming to your joint tonight or any other night. I'm through.'

Tavares walked airily to the door, turned, and looked at the again recumbent figure on the bed.

'My friend, I know you better than you know yourself. You will not deprive me of the company I have grown to find so welcome and so amusing.'

He went out, but, in a moment, was back again.

'Hullo!' murmured Cousins, 'have you thought of something else to say?'

'It has occurred to me,' was the reply, 'that you may be short of money. Is that so?'

'I am,' nodded Cousins, 'but that is not an unusual state of affairs with me.'

'Why did you not tell me? I am angry with myself that I did not think to ask before.' He once again approached the bed, and handed a couple of notes to Cousins, each for fifty dollars. 'If you owe anything to Mrs Gutteriez you can pay her from that, and let me know.'

'Thanks,' said Cousins clutching the notes eagerly. 'It's darned good of you.'

'Not at all,' purred Tavares, 'the money will find its way back to me.'

'Are you going to see Kenton?' asked the little man innocently.

Tavares appeared startled.

'No, no,' he declared emphatically. 'What is he to me? Besides he is under police care. Perhaps even there is a policeman guarding him. Who can tell? If I go to the hospital they may say: "Ah in the bed lies a man dying of too much brandy, comes to see him José Tavares who owns a saloon which we do not like. Perhaps between them there is a connection. We will investigate." No; decidedly, my friend, I will not go to the hospital.'

'That's a good thing,' Cousins muttered under his breath.

'And,' continued Tavares impressively, 'it would be wise if you also avoided that place. Your friend Kenton will die, there is no doubt of that; there is nothing you can do, and you do not wish the police to know anything about you. Therefore, I say to you, keep away.'

With a nod he turned, and once more left the room. Cousins waited until his footsteps had receded in the distance;

then gave full vent to the laughter that had been inwardly consuming him for some time. He held up the notes, and looked at them.

'The first instalment of blood money,' he chuckled. 'Ho Fang Ho, you scoundrel,' he called, 'come here!'

The Chinaman appeared from the veranda, looking no whit abashed by this indication that his master had known of his presence there during the conversation with Tavares.

'Ho Fang Ho no belong scoundlel, master,' he protested.

'Then what do you mean by staying on the veranda listening to my confabulation – ah! That's beaten you – with the gentleman who has just left?'

A look of sheer disgust appeared on the Chinaman's face.

'Him no belong gentlemans, master,' he asserted, 'him belong velly bad mans.'

'Well, gentleman or not, you had no right to hang about listening to our conversation.'

'Me belong plenty too muchee aflaid for you, master. Me tinkee him pelhaps wantchee hurtee you.'

Cousins gazed at the unique individual before him with a look very much like affection in his eyes. He was deeply touched, for there was no doubting the sincerity of Ho Fang Ho's profound attachment for him. He put one of the fifty dollar notes into the boy's hand.

'That's your wages for the first month in advance, Ho Fang,' he said.

The Chinaman attempted to push it away.

'Me no wantchee,' he declared. 'Master alleady give me money. What for give me more? Master got money, give Ho Fang Ho; no got, no give.'

'You said words to that effect before,' observed Cousins. 'We quite understand each other. Put it in your pocket, and don't argue. You won't get any more for a month.' Ho Fang Ho reluctantly put the note away in the mysterious inner folds of his garments. 'Now,' went on Cousins, first ascertaining that there was nobody within hearing, 'tell me what it is about Mr José Tavares you dislike so intensely.'

'Him velly bad man, velly bad pilate.'

'Oh, yes; so you remarked before. Tell me how you know he is a pirate. I find myself vastly intrigued.'

Ho Fang Ho's story took some time in the telling, not so much because it was lengthy as that he insisted upon giving such a wealth of detail, and Cousins, at times, had to demand several repetitions in order thoroughly to understand him. Shorn of all embellishment and pidgin English, it appeared that a year or so previously Ho Fang Ho had been cook's mate on a river boat. Macao had been the intermediate port, and on one voyage, a short time after leaving the Portuguese colony, the ship had been attacked by pirates, captured, and looted. Ho Fang Ho had secreted himself in a hiding place that had been overlooked when the vessel was searched, and thus evaded capture. It was close to the bridge, and he had quite a good view of the men thereon. To his surprise, he saw that the occupants were not all Chinese, one of them being a stout Macanese individual whom he had previously noticed as a passenger, and who seemed to be regarded with a great deal of respect by the other pirates. When Ho Fang Ho first saw him, he appeared to be giving orders, afterwards drinking with the pirate captain. At nightfall the boat was run close inshore, and Ho Fang Ho succeeded in slipping over the side, and escaping in a sampan which had been tied to the gangway. On arrival back in Hong Kong, he had gone secretly to the police who had taken his depositions and description of the Macanese, but had seemed to place little credence on that part of his story relating to the evident authority of the latter among the pirates. Since then he had not seen anything of the man until he recognised him as Cousins' visitor.

'You are quite certain he is the same individual?' questioned the Secret Service man. 'A lot of these Macanese look very much alike.'

'Me plenty too muchee sure, master,' the Chinaman insisted. 'Him samee nose, samee eyes, samee mouse' – this was obviously intended for mouth – 'samee plenty big belly. Allo samee. Me tinkee him number one big pilate.'

'Well, I'm not surprised, but don't tell anybody else this, Ho Fang, until I give you permission. Someday between us we'll land this Mr José Tavares in gaol – perhaps.'

Ho Fang Ho smiled a trifle slyly.

'Me tinkee master belong pliceemans,' he asserted.

'The devil you do! Well, you're wrong, my lad. But if you get ideas like that, keep them in that head of yours – they're dangerous.'

'Ho Fang Ho no talkee,' the boy protested with simple dignity. 'Him belong master's slave, give him lifee for master.'

'I begin to believe,' decided Cousins, 'that I did a very good job when I jumped into the sea after you.'

'Plenty velly good job,' nodded Ho Fang Ho in hearty agreement. 'Master savee my lifee.'

After the greasy, garlic-ridden meal that was honoured by the name of tiffin, Cousins went out. Mrs Gutteriez made an attempt to detain him in conversation, but he eluded her adroitly. The intense heat of the afternoon kept all, except those who were out on business, within doors, and nobody took much notice of the shabby, badly-shaved little man with the dilapidated topee pulled down low over his eyes. He walked a considerable distance, and was in a bath of perspiration when he eventually entered the Shauk Ki Wan post office. From there he telephoned to the hospital, and had the satisfaction of speaking to the Irish doctor who had admitted Kenton. He learnt that the latter was desperately ill, and suffering the torments of the damned, but the medical man was still confident of pulling him through, possibly even of curing him of his terrible craving. He told Cousins that nobody would be allowed to see the invalid for a considerable time.

Satisfied that Kenton was in excellent hands, Cousins left the post office, and returned home. This time he travelled to Queen's Road in a tram, and had himself carried up the steep slope of Conduit Road to Robinson Road in a sedan chair. A fat Chinese room boy sat on his haunches in the untidy little entrance hall of the hotel fanning his bared abdomen. He watched Cousins pass with expressionless eyes, but made no attempt at salutation. With an involuntary shiver of disgust, the Secret Service man made his way up the stairs to his own apartment. Ho Fang Ho was squatting outside the door, a book covered with Chinese characters in his hand, softly chanting to himself. He sprang alertly to his feet when he saw his master, and followed him into the room.

'Too muchee hot,' he observed. 'You likee me catchee punka coolie?'

Cousins looked up at the contrivance overhead, and considered the matter.

'No,' he decided at last. 'If that's swung about, the dust of ages will fall on my devoted head. And, between you and me, Ho Fang, I'd rather be roasted by the heat than smothered by microbe-laden dust.'

The Chinaman looked puzzled.

'Me no savvy,' he complained.

'Good,' chuckled Cousins. 'It's quite a treat to find something you don't savvy. Now run away, and fly a kite or something. I am going to rest.'

Ho Fang Ho grinned.

'Allo samee plenty sleepee,' he remarked, 'get leady become dlunk mans.'

Cousins in pretended anger ordered him from the room; then called him back.

'You told me you were a Christian,' he observed. 'Didn't they give you a Christian name when you were baptised?'

The boy wrinkled up his nose in disgust.

'My Clistian namee Tom,' he replied in disparaging tones. 'Not good namee. Me no likee.'

'It's the first time I've heard of a Chinaman called Tom,' commented Cousins. 'It's generally John, though goodness knows why. So you don't like it? Well, I'll call you by it when I'm angry with you.'

'Master get angly with Ho Fang Ho, him die,' came the earnest reply.

'Well,' declared Cousins callously, 'if you don't want to die, don't make me angry.'

'My fader tellee me when him master get angly him talkee ABC.'

Cousins laughed.

'He must have been present when Athenodorus the Stoic told Augustus that the best way to restrain anger was to repeat the alphabet. "The sacred line he did but once repeat. And laid the storm, and cooled the raging heat".'

Ho Fang Ho eyed his master as though he thought he had suddenly taken leave of his senses.

'No savvy,' he repeated in awed tones.

'Sorry, Ho Fang, must give someone the backwash of my natural inclinations, you know.'

When the Chinaman had once again taken up his position outside the door, book in hand, Cousins threw himself on the unsavoury bed, and gave himself up to reflections. Sir Leonard Wallace was due in the colony in a few days, and there was little of note to report to him. It was absurd, of course, to expect that a problem that had baffled the Government and entire police force of Hong Kong could be solved in a few hours, but Cousins was not satisfied with himself. It is true that he had found Tavares, had become familiar with the man, and had been marked out by him for some sinister work, which he fondly believed was connected with the conspiracy. But it was all conjecture and, though there was little doubt but that Tavares had grown rich through his connection with or knowledge of the organisation which had well-nigh wrecked the Hong Kong treasury, and could be a fountain of information if he could be made to talk, there was no proof against the man. He had already undergone intensive questioning at the hands of the police, and had emerged triumphant, his oft-repeated parrot cry that he knew nothing, had not been in the confidence of his master, having beaten his cross-examiners. The men who had recently been sentenced to various terms of imprisonment had been merely understrappers of the Government, scapegoats who had feathered their own nests in the general state of financial disruption, and either did not know or would not reveal the names of the actual men behind the conspiracy.

Cousins consoled himself for his failure up to that date to discover anything tangible by the reflection that there was, after all, no hurry. He had not wasted his time. Ever since the day he had landed in Victoria with Kenton, he had quietly but systematically been investigating. At Tavares', though always appearing in a state of hopeless intoxication, he had been all the time watchful, storing up in that receptive mind of his anything that appeared out of the ordinary. He had become convinced that there was some connection between the establishment of Tavares and the houses on either side, but what that connection was he had so far been unable to ascertain. The building on the right was owned or rented by a retired official of the electric light company named Sales, an obvious compatriot of Tavares, and frequently to be seen in his company; that on the left was let off in flats, all but the ground floor, which was devoted to a Turkish bath concern.

Cousins was certain that between the houses of Sales and Tavares was a communication door. One evening, when he and Kenton were approaching the place, he had caught a glimpse of Tavares' unmistakable figure on the second floor veranda of Sales' house, yet, when they had entered the saloon, he had been strolling down the staircase towards them. It would have been utterly impossible for him to have left Sales' residence, entered his own establishment, ascended to the upper regions, and be on his way down again in the time, even if he had run, and Tavares was not built for violent exercises. As the first floor flat of the house on the left was his abode, it was not unlikely that there was a communicating door into that building also. Communicating doors between adjoining houses, especially when their existence is kept more or less a secret, are apt to give rise to conjecture in inquiring minds. Cousins had resolved to investigate, if and when an opportunity occurred.

He partook of the unappetising dinner which Mrs Gutteriez's underpaid cook served up, after which he set off for his usual nightly carouse. Tavares was right. It would appear that, despite his assertion that he had determined to give up drinking, he was too weak to resist the craving. Tavares did not know that he had had no intention of deserting the saloon; that his statement, to be followed by its evident repudiation, was only made with the intention of giving the Macanese a further proof of the instability of his character. Things would be a little more difficult now, however, that Kenton would not be present. The latter had drunk so much of the brandy that it had been unnecessary to throw much away. Now, being compelled to drink on his own, the question arose; what was he to do with the superfluous liquor? He certainly had no intention of drinking it, and spittoons were unfortunately not bottomless. He decided that circumstances would have to solve the problem for him.

Purposely later than usual he entered the saloon, and was making his shuffling way towards the alcove he and Kenton had constituted their own corner of the room, when the curtain, hanging between the saloon and the dance hall, was drawn aside, and Tavares entered, a frown upon his swarthy face. The frown quickly gave place to an all-enveloping, greasy smile, however, when he caught sight of Cousins. He strode towards him with that peculiar cat-like tread of his, which made Cousins think of a leopard stalking its prey.

'So you have come!' he remarked, making no attempt to keep the disdainfully triumphant note out of his voice. 'I knew it. It is impossible for you to resist, my friend.'

'Well, didn't you say it wouldn't be good for me to stop drinking,' muttered Cousins sheepishly. 'You said brandy was medicine to me, didn't you?'

'But, of course. No, do not sit in the alcove. Tonight you will be my guest. Come! You shall find I have secrets which only my friends share with me.'

He led the way behind the bar, and up the staircase. At the top he turned sharply to the right, and walked along a corridor lined with stained teak wood, which ended in a window overlooking a street at the rear of the premises. There he stopped. Cousins looked at him blankly, his expression appearing to amuse the Macanese, who laughed.

'You will be surprised,' he chuckled throatily. 'I will now show you something which only those I can trust know of.'

Making certain there was nobody about to observe them,

Tavares turned to the right hand wall. He pressed one of several ornamental knobs in the woodwork, and immediately a panel slid softly to one side, revealing a small opening. Through this Tavares stepped, beckoning Cousins to follow him; the panel moved quietly back into place.

'You are now in the next door house,' explained Tavares. 'Follow me!'

Reflecting that the Macanese must feel very sure of him to have disclosed such a well-guarded secret, a feeling of triumph pervaded Cousins.

'Tavares,' he murmured to himself, 'you think you are a clever man, I know, but you are, after all, nothing but a damn fool.'

CHAPTER TEN

A Tale of Two Knives

Traversing a corridor similar to the one in the adjoining
house, they presently came to a staircase, but, instead of
descending, Tavares walked a little farther on, stopping by
a curtain of beads hanging before an open doorway. These
he held aside, at the same time signing to Cousins to enter.
The latter did so, his escort following him closely in. They
were in a large room, lavishly and exotically furnished. The
highly polished floor was almost entirely covered by several
valuable-looking rugs. Two wonderfully carved Chinese
blackwood cabinets, packed with curios, stood on either side
of the window; shelves of the same wood, crammed full with
books, hid the whole of the opposite wall. Several carved
blackwood chairs and small tables were placed at almost
mathematically exact distances apart, while three divans
covered in deep yellow silk, marvellously embroidered with
blue dragons, relieved the hardness suggested by the chairs,

and gave a restfulness to the room. An incongruous note was struck by a great overmantel framed in gilt and an ornate clock which stood on the mantelpiece. On the fourth wall on either side of the door, through which they had entered, hung pictures painted on glass. A second door, also curtained by a portière of beads, was on the left of the open fireplace. Cousins gazed round him with mixed feelings, while Tavares stood by, apparently expecting him to break forth into cries of delighted admiration. When none came he frowned impatiently.

'Is it not all most beautiful?' he demanded. 'My friend Sales has good taste – no?'

Cousins nodded.

'Very nice,' he mumbled. 'So this is Sales' house, is it?'

'It is, and it is not,' returned Tavares cryptically. 'There are some things, my friend Collins, which it would not be judicious to explain to you.'

Cousins looked round him eagerly.

'What about a drink?' he asked hoarsely, not forgetting to live up to his character.

Tavares' face was the picture of contempt.

'Ah, bah!' he snarled, 'that is all you can think of – drink! Drink! Drink! What will you have – whisky?'

'Whisky!' echoed Cousins in tones of disgust. 'Why I'd never taste it. If there isn't any brandy here, I'm going back to the saloon.'

Tavares laughed.

'There is plenty of brandy,' he informed his guest. 'Sit down.'

Cousins chose one of the divans, and sank into its soft

depths with a sigh of contentment. Tavares watched him as though he feared for the silk embroidery, but made no objection. He clapped his hands thrice, and presently a Chinese servant appeared, clothed in a long, close-fitting silk garment reaching almost to his feet. He bowed low before Tavares who spoke to him rapidly in his own language. As quietly as he had entered, he departed, to return after a few minutes wheeling in a tray on which were several decanters, siphons, bottles, and an array of glasses. This was placed in front of Cousins who was told by Tavares to help himself. His eyes gleaming feverishly, the little man selected a bottle of brandy, poured out a liberal dose, and drank it off at once. The raw liquor burnt his throat, but he succeeded in suppressing the cough which yearned to come, and hid the tears in his eyes from the Macanese who was watching him with a sneering smile. At a signal from Tavares, the servant departed, and the two were again alone.

'You feel better now, eh?' asked the dance hall proprietor. 'Without the brandy, life is not good – no?'

'You're right,' nodded Cousins, helping himself to another liberal quantity of the fiery spirit. 'Aren't you going to have a drink?'

Tavares shook his head.

'Not yet. When my friends come, we will all make merry. But you could not wait, and I do not like people who are my guests, and are thirsty, to suffer. Drink, my friend. For a little while I will leave you alone. Presently I will return with those others. You will, I hope, not mind being left – I have business to attend to.'

'Don't mind me!' Cousins waved his hand expansively. 'I'll be all right.'

'You have all you require, I hope?' was said in a tone of sarcasm.

Cousins pretended not to notice it. He looked critically at the wine carriage.

'Yes,' he declared after a pause; 'I think there's enough here to carry on with. If there's not, I'll clap my hands like you did – three times, wasn't it?'

Tavares' mouth and eyes opened wide with amazement; apparently he was too astonished to speak, for on the trolley were four bottles of brandy, two of gin, two of vermouth, and three decanters containing whisky. It never occurred to him that Cousins was pulling his leg, but, like all his breed, he entirely lacked any sense of humour. He merely nodded dumbly and, without another word, left the room by the door close to the fireplace.

Cousins chuckled softly to himself. Inwardly, however, he was a trifle perturbed. He had chosen the particular divan on which he was sitting, because behind it was a large palm in an ornamental pot – an ideal depository for the brandy, if it were possible to pour it away without being seen. Tavares' exit gave him just the opportunity he needed, but he felt it behoved him to be very careful. It was quite likely that eyes were watching his every movement. He may have been brought to that room for the purpose of being watched, not because he was under suspicion, but to make certain that he was actually and really the type of man Tavares required for his sinister designs, whatever they were. On the other hand, and this Cousins thought more probable, he had been left to himself in order to have time to get thoroughly drunk before the curtain rose on the spoof tragedy which was expected to place him firmly and irrevocably under the evil thumb of Mr José Tavares. Still, he intended taking no risks; so much depended, he was convinced, on his worming his way into the confidence of the Macanese.

Barely suppressing a shudder, he drank off the brandy in his glass, and filled it again. Then, with bottle in one hand, and glass in the other, he commenced a tour of the room with the inquisitive but casual air of a man unused to such luxurious furnishing who thought he would like a closer view of everything. He wandered round the room, stopping here and there, pretending every now and then to take a drink. All the time he was searching for a spy hole, his sharp eyes missing nothing. He poked his head round the beaded curtain of first one doorway; then the other, but there was nobody outside either. He felt a keen desire to explore the house, but that, of course, was out of the question. It was an expedition he hoped he would be able to undertake at some future date.

At length he had entirely encircled the room, and was convinced that nobody was spying on him. In order to make certain, he passed through the open window on to the well-lit veranda. It was not likely, he reflected, that either Tavares or Sales would care for a man of his disreputable type to be seen on the veranda of the house by people passing below, who would naturally comment on it. The hidden watcher, if there were indeed one, would quickly give warning, and Tavares or somebody else would appear and call him in. However, nobody came, although he stood there, well within view of all who looked up from the road, for quite ten minutes. Then, feeling satisfied, he re-entered the room. He had been left to himself to get properly drunk and, as that was a process Tavares would expect to take some time, he could count on remaining undisturbed for an hour or so at least. He crossed to the palm; found that it had been recently watered. That was in his favour. Had the earth in the pot been dry, and it was known that the plant had not received attention, it would certainly give rise to comment, if it were noticed to have become moist apparently of its own accord. Cousins emptied his bottle into it, watching the liquid sink in. It disappeared quickly, proving that the plant had not been watered sufficiently, which was another favourable fact. The contents of a second bottle quickly followed; then a third, the earth continuing to absorb the fiery spirit.

'This palm seems to have as much liking for brandy as Kenton had,' Cousins murmured to himself, and wondered what effect the liquor would have on it.

He poured half the contents of the remaining bottle of brandy away, and replaced it on the trolley. Then he looked reflectively at the gin. Tavares would expect him to be very intoxicated; that was evident. Well, he would not be disappointed; would be given ample proof that the man he knew as Collins had employed his time well. The earth in the palm pot could hardly be expected to absorb any more fluid; it already looked badly soaked. He poured the gin on to the thick rug under the divan. It would be some time before it was absorbed, but that did not matter. It was hardly likely to be noticed, and by the time the room was cleaned out by the servants, there would only be a large patch, which would never be taken to represent the contents of a whole bottle of gin. No doubt the rug would be ruined, and Cousins thought of as a clumsy drunkard, but that was a mere detail.

When Tavares returned, accompanied by two other men, an hour and a half after leaving the room, his eyes almost goggled from his head. Cousins lay sprawled on the divan singing to himself in tipsy incoherence. He kept time with the glass in his hand. But what riveted Tavares' attention was the sight of four empty brandy bottles, and an empty gin bottle, all of which he had known to be full ninety minutes before. He turned significantly to his companions, his face creasing in a smile of cynical triumph, while his hands swept round in an expressive gesture towards the empty bottles.

Cousins, while apparently not aware of the entrance of the three, was studying the newcomers intently. One, old and bent, his lined face the colour of mahogany, had rather a benevolent appearance, though his eyes, sharp and roving as those of a bird, suggested craftiness. The other, a comparatively young man, was tall and lean, well-dressed, and prosperous-looking in an aggressive kind of way. Everything about him seemed somehow to indicate wealth with an entire lack of breeding. Yet it would have been difficult to indicate, without reflection, an article of his apparel that was not in good taste. His face was long and narrow; a small moustache adorned his upper lip; while his eyes, slightly almond-shaped and very dark, glinted cunningly and with a look of cruelty in them which caused Cousins to take an instant dislike to him. Although his hair was black, his complexion was fairer than that of either of his companions having more of a yellowish tinge than theirs. He was the first to speak.

'He has certainly done as you expected,' he remarked to Tavares in Portuguese, one of the numerous languages Cousins understood well. 'But do you not think he has become too drunk for our purpose?'

Tavares frowned a warning, and looked a trifle apprehensively at the recumbent man on the divan.

'I do not think he understands our language,' he muttered, 'but it is well not to take risks.'

'Bah!' sneered the other. 'He is too far gone to understand any language.'

'I agree,' put in the old man. 'No one could drink all he has swallowed, and remain sane. I am afraid, José, he is, at present, useless for your purpose.'

Tavares looked distinctly annoyed. He strode up to the divan, and looked down at the singing Cousins.

''Lo,' greeted the latter, blinking up at him. 'How're you, old filer. Glad to see y'r back.' He chuckled thickly. 'Tha's joke. D'you see it?'

'Get up!' commanded Tavares. 'I have brought friends to meet you.'

Cousins struggled into a sitting position; sat swaying as he blinked inquiringly at the other two.

'How'd you do,' he hiccoughed. 'Sorry I was lyin' down when you entered th'room. Must 'pologise for b'haviour un'coming gennelman.'

'I think it would be more polite if you stood up,' observed Tavares in Portuguese, eyeing him narrowly as he spoke.

Cousins turned to him, and strove to focus his flickering eyes on him. An expression of vacuous incomprehension was on his face.

'Wha's tha'?' he demanded. 'Me no savvy. Wha's the goo' speakin' t'me in Chinese? Tell me tha', Mister Wha'sy'r-name!'

Tavares showed his relief in a smile.

'It was thoughtless of me,' he apologised. 'I said that, if you will arise, I will have much pleasure in introducing you to my friends.'

'Oh!'

Cousins staggered to his feet. He stood unsteadily where he was, as though uncertain of what his legs might do, if he attempted to advance towards the others. Tavares put his arm round him ostensibly to help him along, but Cousins felt the fellow's other hand slip under his jacket to the place where the knife reposed in a sheath fastened to his braces. At once he pushed the Macanese away.

'Don' you touch tha',' he snarled. 'I 'low no one touch tha' knife, no one 't all.'

'I am most sorry,' Tavares hastened to assure him, at the same time casting a significant and triumphant look at the other two. 'I had no intention of interfering with your precious knife – I was but helping you along.' Cousins grunted. 'You see,' went on Tavares rapidly in Portuguese to his compatriots, 'he is not, as you think, Miguel, insane. He is very drunk, it is true, but not incapable.'

'In the correct state of mind for our purpose, in other words,' smiled the old man, speaking in the same language.

Cousins stopped dead. His eyes wandered from one to the other, appearing to be full of suspicion; that is, when the apparently heavy eyelids were intermittently raised.

'Wha's all thish?' he demanded. 'Why're you speakin' in

tha' out-lan'ish lingo? I'm beginnin' think surnmun wrong. Wha's marrer?'

'Nothing is the matter,' Tavares told him. 'We are merely speaking in our own language. That is but natural is it not? You would hardly speak to another Englishman in French, would you?'

'Can't speak French,' mumbled Cousins. 'But I didn' know y'r lang-langwish was Chinese.'

'That was Portuguese.'

'Oh! Now I understan'. Goo' ole Porchgese.'

Tavares smiled, if the sinister contortions his face underwent from time to time could truthfully be called smiles.

'This,' he indicated the old man, 'is my very good friend, Mr Miguel Sales.'

After several abortive attempts, Cousins managed to grasp the hand extended to him.

'It is a pleasure to meet you,' politely lied Mr Miguel Sales.

'Same here, ole cock,' responded Cousins emphatically, but not so politely.

'This,' went on Tavares, nodding towards the younger man, 'is Mr Manuel Garcia.'

Garcia bowed stiffly, ignoring completely the unsteady hand held out to him.

'I do not think I can truthfully reciprocate the sentiments of my friend Sales,' he observed in perfect, though somewhat stilted English, and with pointed rudeness. 'Further it is a puzzle to me why Mr Tavares should cultivate the society of a man of your obvious position.'

Cousins regarded him as though he were not quite certain he had heard aright. He turned to Tavares.

'It seems to me,' he remarked with drunken conviction, 'tha' y'r friend's tryin' be rude. You'd better tell'm from me tha' I don' stand f'rudeness from 'nybody.'

The perturbed expressions on the faces of Sales and Tavares made Cousins want to laugh. They were just a little overdone. The old man spoke severely to Garcia, Tavares soothingly to Cousins. The young man shrugged his shoulders and, without another word, strolled across to the wine carriage, and helped himself to a glass of gin, which he diluted very sparingly with soda from one of the siphons.

Now that the comedy had commenced in real earnest, Cousins wondered how he was to be deprived of his knife and a dummy substituted. True, Tavares had already made a very clumsy, or what seemed like a very clumsy attempt to obtain possession of it. But perhaps that had been done more to prove to his friends that the supposedly intoxicated man had not entirely lost all his senses, as they appeared to think. If Kenton had been correct, his knife was to be taken from him, replaced by a harmless substitute; then, when the fake murder had taken place, it would be shown to him covered with blood. Yet Garcia had commenced the performance by attempting to anger him while he still retained possession of his weapon. An involuntary smile almost crossed his face as he thought of the consternation he would create if, without further ado, he flung the knife at the sneering Garcia. He knew he could cause it to transfix any object within a quarter of an inch of where he aimed, within reasonable distance of course. He had practised the art in his youth after watching, fascinated, the skill of a knife-thrower at a circus. It would certainly be a salutary lesson to Mr Manuel Garcia, if the knife were sent through the fleshy part of one of his arms or legs.

He returned to the divan, Tavares and Sales walking closely behind. With deliberate insolence, Garcia moved away as he approached, taking pains to make it appear that it was distasteful to him to remain in the proximity of the disreputable little man. Cousins picked up the remaining bottle of gin, pulled off the stopper, and took a drink, without bothering about the formality of a glass.

'Don' like y'r friend,' he observed to Tavares. 'He makes me thirsty.'

Garcia gave a little laugh.

'Our feelings of dislike are mutual,' he sneered; 'but while I look upon you with contempt as a drunken waster, your dislike of me is no doubt engendered by envy.'

'Envy!' echoed Cousins. 'Fanshy env'ing you! You gotta goo' pinion o' y'rself, haven' you? It strikes me you been drinkin'. Tha's wha't is, you're 'toxicated.'

Sales and Tavares pretended again to pour oil on the troubled waters, without effect. Garcia continued his insults. Purposely Cousins refrained from showing any signs of violence for some time, and it amused him immensely when he caught from the corner of his eye a look of exasperation, probably due to his unexpected tardiness, pass between the two by his side. The little man, it must be confessed, was thoroughly enjoying himself.

'Let us sit down,' suggested Tavares at length, 'and speak together like friends.'

Then Garcia made a supreme attempt to rouse the victim of their plot to a pitch of madness.

'I would not demean myself by sitting in the same room as a drink-sodden waster like that man,' he asserted in biting tones, pointing melodramatically at Cousins. 'I am surprised at you, Tavares, making a friend of such a creature. He is lower than the beasts – a despicable worm! A rat! A skunk!'

Cousins decided it was time he acted. He suddenly burst forth into a string of profanity, his hand shot beneath his coat, emerged clasping the knife. At once Tavares and Sales were upon him, wrestling for possession of the weapon, which they presently succeeded in twisting from his grasp. He was pushed on to the divan, and held there, while he continued to give voice to the most bloodcurdling threats of what he intended to do to Garcia. The latter watched the scene silently, sipping his gin with an air calculated to retain his enemy's ire at fever point. Tavares bent down to pick up the knife, his back towards Cousins. A moment later he straightened up, and handed a weapon to him, but the Secret Service man knew it was not his own. It was about the same size, shape, and weight, but it was blunt. It is doubtful if it would have pierced the softest substance.

'Put it away!' ordered Tavares, 'and do not act like a fool.'

'Your concern,' sneered Garcia, 'is most flattering, my dear Tavares, but that rat of a drunken Englishman could not hit the side of a house at ten paces with a knife or anything else.'

'Couldn' I!' roared Cousins. 'Take tha', you perishin' dago.'

He swayed to his feet, and this time no attempt was made to restrain him. Like lightning the dummy knife sped across the room and, before Garcia could have moved hand or foot, if he had wished to do so, it had caught him in the throat. With a choking gasp, he collapsed to the floor, and lay still. The fall was very well done, but the cry had been genuine enough. Cousins, bent on obtaining a certain amount of satisfaction from the comedy, had deliberately aimed at the man's throat, and knew that he had damaged him enough to cause him a fair amount of pain and inconvenience for three or four days. With well simulated cries of horror and dismay, Tavares and Sales hurried across to their fallen compatriot, and dropped on their knees by his side.

Cousins sank back on to the divan, and watched them. He decided to let it appear that the calamity had considerably sobered him. There is no doubt that a really intoxicated man would have been thoroughly taken in. The plot had been somewhat elaborately staged, and had depended entirely on the supposedly fiery temper and knife-throwing tendencies of the Englishman. Probably, lest the expected did not materialise, an alternative scheme had been prepared to enable Tavares to obtain the hold he desired. Cousins watched very closely, but, as both Sales and Tavares were kneeling with their backs to him, it was impossible to see what they were doing. Before long, however, the latter rose to his feet, and stood staring at the little man on the divan. An expression of exaggerated horror was on his face but, by some trick of the electric light, he really appeared drawn and haggard, his small eyes enlarged and luminous.

'You have killed him,' he told Cousins, in little more than a whisper. 'He is dead.'

Cousins shook his head doubtfully.

'I tell you,' he snarled in a voice that suggested fear, 'I

never kill. I always throw to wound, but – but not kill.' His inflection rose a little hysterically. 'I'm not a – a killer, I tell you. You've made a mistake – must have made a mistake.'

Tavares came towards him slowly. In his hand was a knife – Cousins' knife. The latter recognised it at once. As the Macanese held it up for his inspection, he saw that the blade, right up to the hilt, was red – apparently wet with blood. A bottle of red ink had no doubt been brought into requisition. It looked realistic enough. Cousins rose from the divan, his eyes staring as though in fascinated horror.

He proceeded to give a very fine performance of a murderer stricken with fear and remorse. The shock, it seemed, had quite cleared away from his brain the fumes of the spirits he had drunk and, except that his voice was still thick, and at times he found a difficulty in pronouncing his words, he appeared entirely sober. But the terror in his demeanour was pitiful to behold. Again and again he reiterated, sometimes in a hoarse, sobbing mumble, that Garcia was not dead, could not be dead. He seemed to be in a terrible state, and Tavares, taking his cue from this display of abject terror, played on his feelings until he appeared to be losing his reason. Sales helped by talking of the necessity of calling in the police at one moment, and heaping curses on Cousins the next. But he was not nearly as convincing as Tavares. Nobody but a child – or a terror-stricken murderer – would have been deceived by his acting. They took Cousins to look at the 'corpse', taking care that he did not approach too close. Garcia was lying on his face, his legs screwed up in an unnatural position that certainly suggested death, but must have given him a good deal of discomfort. Cousins regretted that he was unable to see the bruise that the knife must have made on his throat. He felt it would have given him a good deal of satisfaction to have feasted his eyes on it. Underneath the body was a pool of very realistic-looking 'blood'. Garcia's spotless white suit was spotless no longer. The valuable rug on which he lay was also ruined. Cousins admitted to himself that, in order to obtain artistic perfection, they had certainly not hesitated to make sacrifices.

When Tavares had conducted the shivering, shrinking wretch of an Englishman back to the divan, and ordered him to sit down, he and Sales had a long and heated discussion in English anent the urgent necessity of sending for the police. Sales reiterated that they would themselves get into trouble for delaying such an important matter; Tavares appeared reluctant, although admitting that in a case of murder one's own dislike of the law should be subordinated to one's duty. Cousins decided that he was expected to grovel for mercy, whereupon he promptly grovelled. There was more heated discussion, Tavares apparently being inclined to save him, Sales calling dramatically for the full penalty of the law. At last the latter began to give way, though with an air of great reluctance. Tavares turned to Cousins.

'We will do what we can for you,' he declared, 'but it will be difficult and dangerous. Come, Miguel, we must carry the poor Garcia from this room.'

'Poor' was the right word, reflected Cousins. The fellow very likely had cramp by then, and would probably have a few words of complaint to say concerning the time he had been left in his unnatural attitude on the floor. With touching reverence, his compatriots lifted him, and carried him from the room, Tavares first ordering Cousins to make no attempt to leave before he returned. An apparently horror-stricken wretch, whose trembling and general comportment were nauseating to behold, watched them go, but, directly the beaded curtain had dropped into place behind them, he sat upright. A genial smile spread slowly over his features until the hundreds of little creases seemed somehow to contain each an individual grin. His eyes sought the spot where Garcia had been lying; then he laughed outright. On the floor was the dummy knife. It had been overlooked by Sales and Garcia a piece of carelessness that, in other circumstances, would have meant that their well-conceived plans and histrionic performances had gone for nought. Cousins would have liked to have taken possession of the weapon, if only as a reminder, in years to come, of an amusing and enjoyable interlude in Hong Kong. But it would be missed, and he suspected of finding it. He had no intention of raising any doubts in Tavares' mind now that the Macanese was so entirely convinced he was all he purported to be.

CHAPTER ELEVEN

In the Trap and Liking it

Cousins was left to himself for nearly an hour; then Tavares entered the room so quietly that he was almost caught napping. The rustle of the beads over the door warned him just in time to resume a hang-dog air, and eradicate the natural cheerfulness of his countenance. Crossing towards him, Tavares' eye caught sight of the dummy knife. A dull flush overspread his face; he muttered something angrily to himself. Quickly he stooped, and retrieved this eloquent piece of evidence against him, shooting a searching glance in Cousins' direction as he did so. But the dejected-looking creature on the divan looked as though he had not moved since they had carried Garcia from the room. Tavares drew up a chair, and sat down.

'It is settled,' he told Cousins. 'You are safe; at least for the present. It depends on yourself a lot – quite a lot,' he repeated significantly, 'whether it is ever discovered that you murdered the poor Garcia.'

'But I didn't mean to kill him,' Cousins shuddered. 'I tell you I have never killed a man before – can't think how it happened.'

'My friend, your aim was, for once, bad. Your boasted skill failed you. But you should never have thrown the knife – it was very wrong of you. It is only because I feel that it was Garcia's own fault that I am helping you. But I warned you, did I not, that he is a man who says insulting things? He had drunk much before he met you, and was rash.'

'Can't think what happened.' Cousins brushed a hand wearily across his forehead. 'It's all – all blurred to me.'

'Of course. You were mad drunk. Now listen to me, my friend: you will return to the house of Mrs Gutteriez, and will conduct yourself in your normal way. If you are careful, you will be safe. If you let people see that you are in terror, because of what you have done, there will be suspicion; then will come danger. Only Sales and I know what has happened, and he will not speak. With him I had great difficulty, because he had much love for Manuel Garcia, and also he has great respect for the law.'

'Are you sure he will keep quiet?' asked Cousins doubtfully.

'As certain as I am of myself. So long as you are careful, and do what I tell you always, you will have nothing to fear.'

'What are – are you going to do with the body?'

Tavares rose to his feet.

'That, my friend,' he declared, 'is my business. Be thankful that you have good friends to save you from the result of your hot head.'

'You are very good to me, Mr Tavares,' murmured

Cousins in broken tones. 'You will never regret it.'

'No,' returned the other complacently, 'I think that I will not.'

'I can't understand why you are doing all this for me, when – when he was your friend.'

'You will know – quite soon. Come! I will show you out.'

'Wouldn't it be better if I stayed here a few days,' Cousins asked, 'until – until there is no danger?'

'Of what are you frightened now? Have I not told you there will only be danger if you give yourself away. Come! You are too much a big coward.'

Cousins followed him without another word. He had hoped that Tavares would have fallen in with his suggestion, and agreed to his staying in the house. It would have given him the opportunity of conducting an investigation which he badly desired to make. However, it would not do to be too importunate – an opportunity would come, no doubt.

They left the room by way of the door near the fireplace, and Cousins found himself in a corridor. Exactly opposite was another apartment, the door of which was wide open. He glanced within, and was interested to notice that it had the appearance of a boardroom. A long table was placed in the centre with chairs grouped round it. On it were blotting pads, inkwells, and pens. Cousins wondered what body was in the habit of meeting there. Tavares led him down a softly-carpeted staircase to the hall below. Instead of making for the front entrance, which could be seen a little way farther on, however, he turned down a narrow passage to the right, descended a further short flight of stairs, and opened a small door that had a neglected appearance about it.

'Now go,' he ordered. 'I will see you tomorrow. Remember not to show that you are frightened about anything.'

Cousins stepped out into the moonlight, and found himself in an alleyway. Choosing the left he walked along, and presently recognised the street running behind the compounds of the block. Without further ado, he set off for his dingy hotel in Robinson Road. If Tavares could have read the mind of the man he fondly believed he had made his victim, he would have been astonished and dismayed. Cousins felt he had had a very satisfactory night. He had discovered that the apparently respectable abode of Miguel Sales, the retired electric light company official, was in some way connected with the enterprises of José Tavares. Furthermore, he had been shown the secret means of communication between the two houses, and would know how to manipulate the sliding panel when he desired to pass secretly from one house to the other. In addition, Tavares, now convinced that he had the little man completely in his power, would, before long, reveal why he had worked for that end, a revelation which Cousins felt assured would tell him quite a lot of things he wanted to know. He felt that he had made progress, and walked along with a jauntiness that ill became a man who had so recently committed murder.

Ho Fang Ho was asleep on the veranda when Cousins entered his room, but though the latter undressed quietly, and refrained from lighting the oil lamp standing on the mantelpiece, he awoke, and looked in. The moonlight streaming in gloriously behind him showed him his master surprisingly sober.

'Master plenty early,' he observed, 'and no pletend dlunk. What for?'

'Ho Fang,' returned Cousins, 'you have an inquiring turn of mind that will get you into trouble one of these days. However, I may as well tell you that I was drunk, but alas a terrible fear made me sober again. I was too frightened to be drunk, Ho Fang.'

'Master no gettee flightened,' scoffed the Chinaman. 'Him velly blave mans.'

'Many thanks for the compliment. All the same I do get frightened, very frightened sometimes. Your "pilate" friend, Mr José Tavares, if you care to interview that inestimable gentleman, will bear me out in my assertion that I was hopelessly drunk tonight, but fear, stark, naked, horrible fear, cured me with remarkable celerity. Fear is a wonderful cure of inebriety, Ho Fang. To quote *Ingoldsby Legends*: "What the vulgar call 'sucking the monkey' | Has much less effect on a man when he's funky".'

Ho Fang Ho's face could not be seen, but he was obviously impressed by the verbosity of his master.

'Master plenty too muchee clebber talkee,' he commented in tones of admiration. 'Ho Fang Ho no clebber, no undelstand.'

'I wish you wouldn't say "undelstand" – you slobber most horribly. Savvy is much easier you know. And, by the way, what are you doing here? Why aren't you sleeping in your own quarters?'

'Me wantchee plotect master,' explained Ho Fang. 'Too muchee flaid pilate mans come looksee night times.'

'Oh!' was Cousins' only comment. There did not seem anything else to say. The loyalty and devotion of Ho Fang Ho was more than impressive – it was distinctly affecting.

Cousins realised that, in saving the Chinaman's life, he had made a friend who would count it an honour to give that life for him.

The next day a typhoon hit Hong Kong with terrific force. Cousins found the power of the elements awe-inspiring. The rain fell as he had never seen it fall before, the wind thundered with appalling ferocity. Hong Kong was plunged into a darkness that was intermittently and brilliantly expelled by intensely dazzling flashes of lightning. Great trees were uprooted as though they were mere saplings plucked by a giant hand; chimney pots, roofs, anything the least unstable were carried away; people who were unfortunate enough to be out were lifted off their feet, many of them carried to death. The typhoon had arrived with such devastating suddenness that only the warning signal that it was on its way was flying from the guardship in the harbour when it actually struck the colony.

The water population suffered terribly. Junks and sampans were swept to disaster, men and women aboard them crying out in their piteous terror, some holding up their babies to the crews aboard the liners and warships in dumb entreaty for them to be saved. Sailors on the men-of-war performed heroic work that day. Hanging precariously over the sides of their ships by ropes bound round them they clutched at the sampans that came within reach, succeeding in that manner in rescuing quite a number of Chinese who otherwise would have been doomed. Two torpedo destroyers and a Japanese liner were torn from their anchorages and driven ashore, a river boat sank at her moorings. The barque which Cousins had admired on his first evening in Victoria was piled up, an irreparable wreck, on the Kowloon shore. The Praya, both east and west, was flooded and, for some time afterwards, people traversing it were conveyed in boats. The beautiful Botanical Gardens were laid waste, one of Victoria's most popular beauty spots a lamentable ruin. During the comparatively short time that the typhoon lasted, over two thousand of the Chinese water population alone lost their lives. It was the worst storm Hong Kong had experienced for many years.

Cousins saw nothing of Tavares that day, which was not to be wondered at. The block of houses, in the centre of which was his establishment, had become an island. The chairs and tables outside had been swept away, the floors of the dance hall and saloon were underwater, a considerable amount of damage having been done. Inhabitants of the three houses, like all others on that level, and in that neighbourhood, were marooned for some hours before boats were procured to enable them to pass to and from their homes. It was only in the evening that Cousins learnt of this when, as a matter of fact, he was debating with himself whether it would be judicious to turn up in the saloon or not. As the place was, of necessity, closed there was no sense in his going there. Instead he went for a walk, and viewed with a sense of utter amazement the devastation that had been wrought.

He returned to his lodgings when it was too dark to see anything more. Black, low-lying clouds hung like a pall overhead, but there was not a breath of wind, a startling contrast to the fury with which the gale had lashed the colony a few short hours before. It almost seemed as though an air of fearful expectancy was pervading the atmosphere, and Cousins wondered if the typhoon had circled round, as they often do, and was on its way back. He was met by Mrs Gutteriez, who handed him a cablegram. She informed him that it had been delivered shortly after he had gone out, and she had been waiting for him with it ever since. Apparently the arrival of a cablegram was an unusual event at the Hotel Paris. She stood by while he tore it open and perused the contents, watching him eagerly the while. An expression of disgust crossed his face, and he swore.

'It is not good news then?' she asked.

'Good news! No. I hoped that it would have been. Read it for yourself!'

She took it readily enough, and learnt that Mr Collins' mother was not in a position to send him a further remittance; that all her spare money had been spent in the autumn sales. She made a grimace.

'It is like a woman – that,' she nodded, handing back the form. 'I am the same when God is good, and there is money in the house. I like to go to the shops in Victoria when the sales are on, and buy. It does not mean that you will not be able to pay my rent this week?' she asked sharply and suspiciously.

'Don't worry about that!' he returned. 'You'll be paid, never fear.'

'It is good. I am a poor woman, and my life is hard. I cannot afford to lose money. Goodnight, Mr Collins.'

She shuffled away, and Cousins climbed to his room to find the ever-faithful Ho Fang Ho squatting on the mat as usual. Inside he received a surprise. The lamp, chimney cleaned and polished until it shone, threw a bright glow round an apartment that had undergone quite a transformation. Not a speck of dust lay anywhere, and, although nothing much could be done with the dilapidated furniture and matting, everything was orderly and clean. Fresh sheets and pillow slips were on the bed, a new mosquito curtain hung over it, even the punka above had undergone a thorough cleansing. Cousins turned to Ho Fang Ho, who stood beaming behind him.

'Have you done all this?' he asked.

The Chinaman nodded eagerly.

'Master give me plenty too muchee money,' he related, 'Me go piecee shop catchee mosquito net and sheets; then me clean loom. Velly good clean?' he asked anxiously.

'Very good indeed,' smiled Cousins. 'You have done well, Ho Fang. I am delighted. All the same I didn't intend you to use that money to buy things for me.'

'Me no wantchee. Buy tings for master makee Ho Fang Ho welly glad.'

He retired, well pleased with the praise he had received. It had taken a week for it to dawn on him that, if he did not clean the room, nobody else would bother, but once the idea had occurred to him he had made a thorough job of it. In some subtle way also the heavy, musty odours had been eradicated, and Cousins undressed, for once, without a sense of repugnance. In bed he proceeded to decode the innocent-sounding cablegram in which Mrs Gutteriez had shown such an interest, chuckling to himself at the recollection of her comments about women and sales. He knew that actually it meant something very different to what she had read, but the word 'Sales' puzzled him. Not for long, however. By means of a little book, taken from a belt round his waist against his flesh, he quickly had the message deciphered.

Find out where and what Sales is.
Meeting of conspirators to be held there on sixteenth
at seven.

Softly he whistled to himself. Sir Leonard Wallace had discovered something while at sea which he, Cousins, could hardly have found out. Undoubtedly there was someone travelling aboard the *Rawalpindi* who was connected with the conspirators, and a message to him had been intercepted. The P&O Mail boat was due in Hong Kong harbour on the fifteenth, the day before the meeting. It appeared that the latter had been arranged in order to enable the man on the liner, whoever he was, to be present. Sales of course referred to the house of Sales – Cousins pictured Sir Leonard Wallace puzzling over the word, not having the knowledge which he possessed, which enabled him to give it its rightful pronunciation, and thus know that it referred to the name of a person. The house of Sales was used as a meeting place, was it? Cousins understood now why there was a secret means of communication between the establishment owned by Tavares and the apparently innocent residence of the latter's friend. Here was proof indeed that both of them were actively connected with the men behind the Hong Kong scandal. There would, after all, be quite a lot of interest to relate to Sir Leonard Wallace on his arrival in Hong Kong and, unless the Chief had other plans, Cousins decided that, if it were at all possible, he would be within hearing of the discussion that would take place at the meeting on the sixteenth of the month.

He had already made up his mind regarding the manner

in which he intended to get in touch with Sir Leonard. It would, of course, be impossible to approach him openly. Apart from the absurdity of a down-at-heel beachcomber calling at Government House, and asking to speak to the Governor, any course of an overt nature would be bound to rouse the suspicions of Tavares and company, and render his future endeavours utterly futile. Cousins smiled as he thought of the means he had resolved to adopt, means which, he firmly believed, would cause Tavares to regard him as a fool perhaps, but render him less liable to be suspected than ever. He returned the little code book to its hiding place, and tore up the cablegram, with his scribbled notes on it, into minute fragments. These he burnt to ashes in the fireplace after getting out of bed for that purpose. He was about to extinguish the lamp when Ho Fang Ho re-entered the room.

'Me tinkee tai fung come back,' he declared, crossing to the windows, which he shut and firmly bolted.

Cousins returned to bed, and watched him. It suddenly occurred to him that the Chinaman, who was proving his loyalty and devotion to him more every day, would make an ideal liaison officer between himself and Sir Leonard Wallace. His initial plan for communicating with his chief, or Carter as his representative, was only possible for the day of disembarkation. Thereafter it would be necessary to have some means of instant and secret communication. It had been left to Cousins to arrange this and, up to that moment, he had been unable to make any decision. The little man was an astute and unerring judge of character, a very necessary asset in anyone of his profession, and he felt certain that Ho Fang Ho was utterly reliable. However, where so much was at stake it would not do to make a hasty decision. He decided to watch the Chinaman very closely during the following few days, and act according to his ultimate decision regarding his trustworthiness.

Ho Fang Ho was correct. The typhoon, or rather the fringe of it, returned, the wind rising suddenly until it reached a crescendo of fury, when Cousins momentarily expected the house to collapse about him. But it passed swiftly, leaving in its wake a profound sense of the puniness of mankind, whose works, no matter how solidly they are built, are subject always to devastation and ruin from an attack by the elements.

Victoria presented a tragic spectacle when Cousins went out the next day. Huge trees lay uprooted everywhere; roofless houses, wrecked verandas, in some cases the remains of buildings with all or most of the walls gone, gave an aspect of desolation to parts of a town that, a short time before, had looked almost immutable and entirely charming. He was astonished when he found the lower level completely under water. In places it had receded considerably, but round the establishment of Tavares it was still deep. He had the novel experience of being rowed across, and waded through the dance hall with his trousers rolled above his knees. Sitting halfway up the stairs was the proprietor, shouting orders to an army of coolies engaged in bailing operations. He greeted Cousins without any particular appearance of pleasure. In fact he scowled at him darkly, and asked in irritable tones what he wanted.

Cousins had decided to dispense with his terror-stricken attitude on the grounds that a man of his presumed character would quickly recover from his first reactions. He maintained a hangdog air, however, and gave Tavares the impression that he was, for the time being at any rate, thoroughly subdued. Meekly he told the Macanese that anxiety had caused him to return and seek information concerning the disposal of Garcia's body.

'Ah, bah!' snapped Tavares. 'Did I not tell you that would be arranged? The typhoon has made it easier.' He did not explain how. 'Go away! Do not come cringing to me. I have other things to think of. Perhaps tonight the saloon will be opened; then you can drink. But my beautiful dance hall will be closed for two or three days.'

He broke into a string of curses, and Cousins left him. The Secret Service man saw little of Tavares that night, but that little was illuminating. The Macanese showed, beyond any possibility of doubt, that he regarded himself as possessing power of life and death over Cousins. His previous affability was replaced by the manner of a master with a slave. The screw was adjusted, and was beginning to be turned, though not too fiercely at first. Cousins was given to understand quite clearly, if not in so many words, that henceforth he would be expected to carry out any orders that were given him, otherwise nemesis would strike without warning.

The Secret Service man refrained from appearing very much intoxicated until the night before Sir Leonard Wallace was due to arrive. Then he broke out completely. He invited all and sundry to drink with him. Bottle after bottle of brandy and gin appeared at the table, where he sat surrounded by men and women only too willing and eager to get drunk at his expense. Tavares kept a watchful eye on him, noting with a certain feeling of trepidation that he became more and more inebriated as time went on, until he was almost past speech altogether. He appeared to be pouring amazing quantities of the spirit down his throat, when really he was doing nothing of the sort. The companions he had invited to sit with him were actually doing all the drinking – that is why they were there.

The scene in the alcove, and overflowing from it, resembled bedlam by two o'clock in the morning. By four the uproar was terrific, and Tavares was constrained to give orders for the offenders to be evicted. They were thrown out willy-nilly, most of them being too far gone to resist. Cousins alone showed aggressiveness. Although for some time he had appeared to be unable to do anything but laugh and stutter, he suddenly recovered his voice as hands were laid on him.

'Leave me 'lone!' he screamed. 'If you don' take y'r hands off, I'll stick knife'n you; swear it. Don' care wha'ri do now. I'm killer I am. D'y'r hear – I'm killer.'

Tavares, listening, suddenly went pale.

'Take him to my office – quick!' he commanded the two men who were holding Cousins. 'Lock him in, and bring me the key.'

Shouting and kicking, Cousins was promptly and unceremoniously carried up the stairs, along a passage, into a room at the back of the house. There he was dumped on the floor. The two burly men who had conveyed him there retreated grinning, and locked him in. He sat up, and looked round him. The lights were on, which was fortunate, as he would have hesitated to have switched them on himself. He smiled with inward satisfaction. He had accomplished something else he had been anxious to do. He was in Tavares' private office. It was a fairly large room. A great desk, littered with papers, stood in the centre of the floor. One wall was covered with shelves full of ledgers and documents of all shapes and sizes; another was hidden by two tall cupboards, both apparently locked. A massive safe was the only piece of furniture against the third wall, directly opposite the double windows leading to the veranda; several chairs were placed round the desk. There was no fireplace, but a small electric stove, now standing neglected in a corner, obviously did duty in the cold weather. Cousins almost purred when his eyes fell on the safe. It was certainly substantial and strong-looking, but was of ancient make. He knew he would have little difficulty in opening it when the time came. What seemed to give him the greatest satisfaction, however, was the sight of a punka hanging above. Tavares had apparently not considered it worthwhile having an electric fan installed, even though the room was lighted and, when necessary, warmed by electricity. The idea which the punka in his bedroom had given him seemed more likely to materialise now. He wished he could have made a search of the room there and then, but, with the possibility of Tavares putting in an appearance at any moment, it would have been injudicious. He rose, and walked out on to the veranda. On both sides it was bricked up, thus making access impossible from either way. On returning to the room, his eye caught sight of a decanter of whisky, a soda water siphon, and a couple of glasses on a tray placed on the desk. Promptly he poured some whisky into a glass, and sat on the floor, his back against the desk, awaiting the coming of the Macanese. Ten minutes went by;

then the key was turned in the lock, the door flung open, and Tavares burst into the room, apparently in a towering rage.

'You fool! You dolt! You imbecile!' he roared, scowling down at Cousins, who had again become metamorphosed into a drunken, leering caricature of himself. 'What you think you do, eh? You want everything to spoil by you? Answer me – no? Yes?'

As usual in excitement his English had become a trifle mixed. Cousins blinked up amiably at him.

'Wha's th' marrer, ole cock?' he asked. 'Don' get 'cited – it's bad f'r nervesh. Have a drink?'

With an oath, Tavares stooped, and dashed the glass from his hand.

'Drink! Drink! Drink!' he barked. 'All you think of ever is drink. Mother of God! You will ruin my careful plans.'

Cousins pulled himself to his feet with the assistance of the desk, and stood swaying before the angry man.

'Th' tr-trouble with you, T'varish,' he remarked, 'is th' liver. Try Carrer's lil liver pills, m'boy.'

Tavares caught him by both shoulders, and shook him. Cousins' knees promptly gave away, and he fell gently forward to come to rest against the other's protuberant middle.

'This is sho nicsh,' he sighed drunkenly. 'C'n I go shleep here?'

Tavares held him out at arms' length.

'Do not realise you,' he stormed, 'that you have murdered a man, and if you get too much drunk, I am not able to save you?' All the time he spoke, Cousins' head nodded, as though it were on hinges. At last Tavares gave it up. 'Ah!' he yelled. 'Go to the devil!' and flung the little man from him.

Cousins staggered backwards until he hit one of the cupboards; then gently and softly he slid to the floor.

At that moment there came an interruption. The door was flung open, and into the room stepped a tall, well-groomed man.

'Tavares,' he said urgently, 'when Sir Leonard Wallace arrives today, there must be no . . .' He stopped and started back as he caught sight of the figure on the floor. At once he turned as though to hide his face. 'Who is this?' he demanded.

'Nobody of the importance,' returned Tavares, adding in assuring tones; 'Besides he is too much drunk for him to . . .'

'Get rid of him.'

The newcomer walked to the veranda, still keeping his face averted. But the glimpse he had obtained had left an indelible impression on Cousins' mind. As Tavares propelled his inert body down the stairs, and handed him over to his underlings to be ejected from the building, the Secret Service man's brain was very busy.

Had he been face-to-face with one of the leaders of the conspiracy?

CHAPTER TWELVE

The Queer Behaviour of Cousins

The RMS *Rawalpindi* glided slowly into Victoria Harbour, Hong Kong, her decks thronged with passengers, most of them gazing with rapt eyes on the magnificent panorama spread before them. The granite hills surrounding the harbour, rising to heights of two and three thousand feet, give it a striking appearance, which fascinates and attracts all who gaze upon its charm for the first time. The city of Victoria, extending for four miles at the base of the hills protecting the south side of the harbour, is more picturesque and conspicuous than any other city of the East. This is due to the fact that it is built on the slope and nestles among well-grown, beautiful trees, the luxuriance of which forms a great contrast to the barren aspect of the Peak towering above. On the northern side of the harbour beyond Kowloon the hills are even more rugged; in places look almost forbidding. The whole presents a notable picture which blends the classic beauty of Italy with the wild scenery typical of Scotland.

Hong Kong was *en fête*. One Governor was about to go on leave; another was arriving to replace him. Flags flew gaily from the large and handsome buildings on Praya West. Praya East, not to be outdone, looked every bit as festive and jaunty. The whole colony, in fact, as far as the reclaimed area at Kaitak on the northern end of Kowloon Bay, where the aerodrome stands, wore a carnival appearance. Every vessel in harbour, from the little river boats to the great liners and men-of-war were 'dressed', while the boom of guns at regular intervals from the guardship saluted the new governor, as the mail boat, on which he had travelled from Europe, drew to her anchorage. The crowds waiting near the landing stage to welcome him gave a special cheer to Sir Stanley Ferguson. The latter's car arrived from Government House at the identical moment that a naval pinnace shot from the towering hull of the *Rawalpindi*, and headed for the land. All eyes were on her as she was steered smartly alongside, and exclamations of admiration rose on every hand, when the beautiful Lady Wallace stepped ashore, to be followed immediately by her husband, looking exceedingly smart in the white tropical uniform of a full colonel. There was a sharp military command, the click of rifles brought to the salute, and the band of the Royal West Kent Regiment played 'Rule Britannia'.

Sir Stanley Ferguson was the first to greet the new arrivals, after which he presented them to various officials and important residents. He then accompanied Sir Leonard Wallace, as the latter inspected the guard of honour, while Lady Wallace was escorted to the car. A little later Sir Leonard walked with the man he was replacing to the pinnace which had brought him ashore. Sir Stanley Ferguson was to sail on the *Empress of Japan* to Vancouver, whence he would cross Canada on his way to England. The two representatives of the British throne shook hands, and saluted each other; after which Sir Leonard with his escort turned away.

It was then that a small individual in ducks that had once been white, a battered topee, and badly cracked shoes staggered from the crowd through the line of troops and, before anybody could stop him, confronted Sir Leonard Wallace. The latter eyed him with a frown, but without the least sign of recognition.

'Welc'me t' Hong Kong,' hiccoughed Cousins, shakily raising his hand in salute. 'On b'half shitizens o' thish glorioush country, I beg t' shalute th' new gov-gov'nor. It—'

His speech was rudely interrupted, several policemen having sprung to his side, and taken hold of him. He was dragged away, resisting violently, shouting that he had a lot more to say, and wanted to shake hands with the Governor, while the bystanders watched open-mouthed, startled but amused at this display of drunken effrontery. Mr José Tavares, standing in the midst of the crowd, viewed the scene with angry eyes, muttering fiercely to a man who stood by his side. Sir Leonard, smiling slightly, walked on to the car which, as soon as he had entered it, was driven away, followed by those containing members of the Executive Council and other officials and important people. Mr Gerald Cousins, alias George Collins, was conveyed to the central police station, and put in a cell. A bucket of water was thrown over his head, and he was left to get sober.

He languished in prison for some hours, most of the time being left severely to himself. He did not seem to mind; in fact, had there been anybody in a position to watch him during the period of his confinement, that individual would have been surprised at Cousins' genial unconcern. Further, he would have been struck by the fact that the little man only appeared in a state of intoxication when a policeman glanced into the cell. He looked more disreputable than ever now that his clothes were soaking wet and his hair lay dankly on his forehead.

A Government House car drew up outside the police station about six in the evening. The English sergeant on duty was at once informed, and hurried out. A tall, athletic young man on whose good-looking, bronzed face was a cheerful smile, nodded to him as he stepped from the car. He was followed by an assistant superintendent of police.

'This is Mr Carter, Sergeant,' the latter announced, 'his Excellency's private secretary.'

The sergeant saluted, and Carter held out his hand.

'The Governor was rather amused by the performance of that little drunkard this morning,' he explained, 'and sent me along to have a talk with him.'

A broad grin appeared on the face of the sergeant, which was reflected in the smiles of the others.

'I don't quite know what we can do with him,' chuckled the superintendent, a young man about Carter's own age. 'He's a perfectly harmless type really. He probably thought he was proving his loyalty and what not – there are crowds of his kind out East unfortunately. We hate having them landed on our hands, they're such a darn' nuisance. Has he sobered up at all, Sergeant?'

'A bit, I think, sir,' laughed his subordinate. 'Anyhow, he'll have plenty of time, as the magistrate will probably give him a month tomorrow – he's not likely to be able to pay a fine. A month without drink does the likes of him any amount of good.'

'I think the Governor will order his release,' put in Carter. 'May I see him?'

'This way, sir,' responded the sergeant, stepping aside to allow his visitor to enter the building.

Carter turned to the superintendent.

'Don't bother to wait, Williamson,' he said, 'you probably have something better to do than hang about here as you're not on duty.'

'Well, as a matter of fact, I am due at the club, but—'

'Don't let me keep you then. Take the car, and send it back for me.'

He entered the police station with the sergeant. The latter was about to send for the prisoner, when Carter suggested that it would be better if he interviewed the man in his cell; that is, if he were alone.

'Oh, he's alone all right,' was the reply. 'We are particularly free of European prisoners just now. In fact, he's the only one occupying a cell in his block.'

He removed a bunch of keys hanging with others on hooks behind his desk, led the way across a compound, and along a passage in which were several doors. One of these he unlocked, and threw open.

'There he is, sir,' he remarked cheerfully, indicating the bedraggled-looking object sitting somewhat disconsolately on a pallet.

Cousins looked up, and scowled.

'What d'you want?' he demanded thickly, but otherwise appearing to have attained a certain measure of sobriety. 'You're a nice lot, you are, to lock up a feller simply 'cause he wants to sh-shalute the new Governor. Next time I won't give him any welcome 't all so you can put that in y'r hip pocket an' sit on it.'

Carter and the sergeant laughed.

'Leave me alone with him,' ordered the former. 'I may be able to make a man of him.'

'Make a man of that type, sir!' scoffed the sergeant. 'You wouldn't be able to do that in a thousand years. I'm afraid I'll have to lock you in with him,' he added doubtfully, 'if you're going to be alone with him.'

'That's all right. Come back in about fifteen minutes for me.'

He advanced into the cell, and was locked in.

'Well, my man,' he began, 'you behaved like a—' the sergeant's footsteps died away in the distance, and his tone changed immediately. 'Jerry; you old reprobate!' he cried. 'What a scheme!'

'Yes,' agreed Cousins, as they shook hands warmly; 'it wasn't so dusty, was it? It occurred to me that a police cell was about the safest place in the colony in which to meet you. And, as I misbehaved myself before the Governor, what was more natural than that he should send his secretary to have a chat with me before releasing me as an act of – er – clemency! By Jove! It's good to see you again! I like you in tussores. How did you manage to get such a perfect cut? My experience is that even the best tailors make a sloppy mess of tropical gear.'

'Ah, it's the figure, my lad. I can't say that you look exactly a poem of elegance at the moment, though. Have they been trying to drown you?'

'More or less,' returned Cousins cheerfully, 'but much as I would like to exchange airy persiflage with you, there is no time. Yon sergeant will be back before long. I don't think there are any fellow sufferers in the adjoining cells, but—'

'No; there are not,' Carter assured him.

'Good! Then listen, Tommy—'

He plunged into an account of all he had discovered since arriving in Hong Kong, laying stress on the fact that he hoped, through his association with Tavares, to learn eventually who were actually the men behind the conspiracy. Carter took copious notes in a little book, laughing every now and again at Cousins' graphic description of his various adventures. When the latter spoke of Sales, the secret way of communication between the two houses, and the manner in which the fake murder had been arranged in order that Tavares could get him into his power, Carter's eyes gleamed.

'By Jove, Jerry!' he exclaimed, 'the Chief will be bucked. You certainly have accomplished a lot in the time you have been here.'

'Not as much as I had hoped,' was the reply. 'Still we're getting on. You'd better tell the Chief from me that I hope to be within hearing of the meeting tomorrow. By the way, how did he get hold of Sales' name?'

In his turn Carter related the events that had happened while on the voyage from Europe. He gave such a perfect pen picture of Wun Cheng Lo that Cousins was certain he would know the man anywhere, even in a place where the majority of the inhabitants were Chinese. The attempt on Sir Leonard at Singapore, frustrated so ably by Batty, caused the little man to whistle long and gravely.

'I did not realise before,' he commented, 'that they regarded the Chief with such fear. Why, he'll be in danger every moment he is on this island until we get the fellows we're after.'

Carter nodded.

'There's one thing in our favour,' he observed; 'when they strike, it will probably be through Wun Cheng Lo, who is supposed to be in Sir Leonard's entire confidence. As we shall be watching him carefully, we ought to be able to nullify any attempt made.'

'You're sure he's in the swim?'

'Positive. Hasn't it been proved, now we know all about the meaning of the word Sales in the wireless?'

'Oh, yes; of course.'

'That word puzzled the Chief and me. It never occurred to us that it was the name of a gent of the same breed as the fellow Tavares. By the way, Jerry, I can't quite make out why Tavares has taken such pains to get the drunken little waster you're supposed to be into his power.'

'My knife-play of course,' replied Cousins. 'That's impressed him tremendously, you must remember. I showed him what I could do with a knife in the first place to give him the idea that I was an unscrupulous, dangerous scoundrel who might be worth knowing, hoping thereby to get into his confidence a bit, and find out things. I never anticipated that he would take me up with such eagerness, and go out of his way to stage an elaborate plot that he anticipated would put me in his power.'

'But I can't think whom he might want you to stick your knife into. It's all rather perplexing, isn't it?'

Cousins sat very still for a moment then he looked at Carter with eyes puckered half-seriously, half in amusement.

'I believe I see through the game, Tommy,' he declared. 'It looks as though I am to be the instrument, at least in reserve if other means fail, to remove a certain individual.'

'And who is he?' demanded Carter.

'Sir Leonard Wallace.'

The young Secret Service man stared at his companion in amazement.

'Sir Leonard Wallace!' he repeated; then: 'Good Lord! What a notion! But how do they think you would be able to get in close enough touch to the Chief to stab him?' He shook his head. 'No, I think you're wrong, Jerry. Why not use a revolver or throw a bomb? Why leave such a deed to a man whom they know, or rather imagine, is nearly always in a state of intoxication? It doesn't make sense.'

'Listen, you boob, and brush up those wits of yours a bit. What the original idea was I don't know, but this is how I figure it out, now you have told me about the Chink on board the *Rawalpindi*. As Wun Cheng Lo has obtained the right of entry, at all hours, into Government House, he will smuggle me in. I will be hidden in some spot which Sir Leonard is bound to pass sooner or later, with orders to fling my knife into him when he does. It's quite an ingenious idea, you will admit. If they attempt to murder the Chief by throwing a bomb at him, or shooting him in the open, something is always likely to happen to frustrate the scheme. They won't attempt to have him poisoned, because it would probably mean bringing men into it who would blow the gaff under examination; besides they will anticipate that his food will be watched. But, in his own residence, where he is often bound to be alone, it should be the simplest thing in the world for a knife-throwing expert, carefully smuggled in by the Chinaman, to make a nice clean job of it.'

Carter shuddered.

'Then you would be smuggled out again, I suppose,' he murmured.

Cousins' face creased into a smile, rather grimmer than was usual with him.

'No,' he returned; 'I rather fancy Wun Cheng Lo would appear on the scene just as Sir Leonard fell and, in great indignation and horror, shoot me dead. He would be regarded as a splendid fellow who had attempted to save the Governor's life, and, like all dead men, I would be unable to tell tales.'

'But do they imagine that even you, as the drunken outcast you appear to them to be, would be willing to commit such a crime?'

'I wouldn't have any choice, my lad. If I refused, I'd be threatened with exposure for the murder of Garcia.'

'Good God!' exclaimed Carter. 'What a diabolical plot.'

'It's only conjecture, of course, but I feel certain I am right.'

'I'm sure you are,' agreed Carter, 'now you have put matters in that light. They would never have faked that murder unless there was something big behind it. They certainly seem to fear Sir Leonard.' He looked at his watch. 'Time's nearly up. How do you propose we keep in touch with you?'

Cousins proceeded rapidly to tell him of the manner in which he had rescued Ho Fang Ho, and of the latter's consequent devotion to him, adding that he had decided to rely upon the Chinaman as emissary.

'Originally,' he concluded, 'I had hoped to employ Kenton in that capacity, but that's out of the question now that he is in hospital. It would have been a horrible risk with a drunkard like Kenton, anyhow, though he's a good fellow.'

Carter looked doubtful.

'Are you absolutely certain you can rely on this Chinaman?' he asked. 'Wun Cheng Lo, remember, is supposed—'

'Wun Cheng Lo and Ho Fang Ho are two very different people,' interrupted Cousins. 'I'd trust Ho Fang Ho with anything anywhere.'

'Well, as you've been able to form an opinion of his character, you ought to know. What is your plan?'

'Every morning at ten he will go to look at the monkeys in their cages in the Botanical Gardens. If he has anything to give you, he will hold it in his right hand – you will brush past him and take it, at the same time handing to him any message you may have for me. If he has nothing, he will stand by a cage with his palms outspread on the wire; if you have nothing, you will brush your hands together as though wiping dust off them. Is that quite clear?'

'Quite,' grinned Carter. 'How am I to know him, and how is he to know me?'

'He is a young fellow – about twenty-two or three, I

should think – with extremely slant eyes, but far more expression on his face than most Chinamen. He will hold a white handkerchief in his left hand, which, you will agree, is an unusual enough proceeding to catch your eye. Chinamen of his class don't carry handkerchiefs. You will wear a red flower in your buttonhole, and stick a pipe in your face.'

'You certainly haven't left much to chance,' commented Carter. 'We're hardly likely to miss each other.'

'There's one thing,' observed Cousins. 'You will very likely be watched, so be careful. Don't let anyone see you enter the Gardens in the morning and meet Ho Fang Ho. That would be fatal.'

'And how do you propose that I should prevent it?'

Cousins gave vent to a sigh of pretended exasperation.

'If I didn't know you better, Tommy,' he growled, 'I'd imagine that you were expecting me to wet-nurse you.'

Carter laughed.

'It was only natural,' he contended, 'that, as you seem to have arranged for every contingency, you would have settled that matter as well. You are usually armed at all points.'

'So I am, but that happens to be your point, not mine,' retorted the little man severely. 'Take my advice, young man. Leave nothing to chance. "A figure like your Father, Arm'd at all points exactly, *Cap a Pe*." That's *Hamlet*, if you would like to know.'

'Good old Jerry is himself again,' chuckled Carter. 'Do you know, that is the first time you have given away to your prevailing passion since I arrived?'

'There is a time for everything,' replied Cousins sententiously; then, with a twinkle in his eye, quoted:

'"People may have too much of a good thing – Full as an egg of wisdom thus I sing." That, my boy, is from *The Gentleman and his Wife*. Methinks I hear the heavy tread of the sergeant. Get me out of here pretty pronto, Tommy; I have much to do tonight.'

'Right . . . A man like you should not have given in so easily. I'm interested in your story, of course, but keep off the drink, and then perhaps— Oh, hallo, sergeant, I thought you had forgotten me!'

He turned with a smile as the door opened, showing the police official standing on the threshold.

'It's only just fifteen minutes, sir,' came the reply. 'I suppose you couldn't get any sense out of him?'

'Oh, he told me his life story, and all that sort of thing, you know. I've offered to give him a leg up, if he'll keep off the drink.'

The sergeant guffawed loudly and sarcastically.

'You might as well ask a bee to keep away from honey, sir.'

'Well, we'll see. He's an ugly little shrimp,' remarked Carter, and winked at Cousins, as he caught sight of the basilisk glare the latter was bestowing on him, 'but I don't think he meant any harm. I'll recommend the Governor to let him go this time.'

'Do you hear that?' the sergeant asked Cousins. 'You don't deserve it, so you'd better show your gratitude by trying not to be such a fool in the future.'

'Go and suck eggs!' Cousins advised him inelegantly.

The little Secret Service man was set at liberty by order of the Governor about an hour after Carter had visited him.

He immediately returned to his lodgings in Robinson Road. Nobody there seemed to have heard anything about his adventure, or rather misadventure, which Cousins decided was a relief. It saved him from having to answer awkward questions. He had not been back at all since the previous evening, for he was nothing if not an artist. Having given the impression that he had broken out completely at Tavares' the previous night, it would have been manifestly absurd if he had returned to the Hotel Paris, gone to bed; then, when Sir Leonard Wallace arrived, appeared on the landing stage as intoxicated as before. Had Tavares made inquiries of Mrs Gutteriez, he would have learnt that her guest had not been back, and would have concluded that, after being thrown out of the establishment controlled by the Macanese, he had probably found some cronies, and gone on drinking until shortly before the episode on the pier. Cousins knew that Tavares had seen him. He had caught a glimpse of the scowling face of the Macanese as the police were dragging him away.

Having had a plain but substantial meal at the police station before being discharged, Cousins felt no desire to partake of the greasy, unwholesome repast, labelled by courtesy dinner, at the Hotel Paris. He went up to his room, where an exceedingly worried Ho Fang Ho greeted him with many manifestations of joy and relief. Cousins shaved, and changed his clothes. Then, making certain that there were no eavesdroppers about, he asked Ho Fang Ho if he could trust him in every way.

'I intend to put very great reliance in you,' he declared. 'If you fail me, it may mean great disaster. If I ask you to do something for me, will you always be faithful and never tell anybody what it is, or repeat anything I tell you?'

Ho Fang Ho did not understand completely what his master was saying, but he got the gist of it, and knew very well what he was driving at. Instead of making elaborate protestations of his loyalty, the Chinaman looked Cousins straight in the eyes.

'Master know he can tlust me,' he said simply.

Cousins nodded.

'I believe I can, Ho Fang Ho. Nevertheless, because this matter is so serious and means so much to me, I would like you to swear by your ancestors that you will never betray me in any way, that you will always do what I ask you without question, and never repeat what I tell you to anyone unless I say you can do so.'

He knew that a Chinaman has great reverence for his ancestors and, Christian or not, will seldom break an oath of such a nature. Ho Fang Ho took it seriously and without hesitation. Afterwards carefully, and in as simple words as he could find, Cousins told him that he wished him to meet secretly a tall young Englishman every morning by the monkey house in the Botanical Gardens. He described how he was to recognise him, and the manner in which messages were to be exchanged, also the signs to be used if there were no messages. When he had finished, he made Ho Fang Ho repeat his instructions, and illustrate the signs. The Chinaman had followed him with keen intelligence, and understood perfectly. Cousins was well satisfied. He decided to give some sort of explanation to Ho Fang Ho.

'There are a lot of very bad men in Hong Kong,' he

observed, 'and my friend and I are going to try and catch them. You can help a lot, if you are very careful, and do what I tell you.'

Ho Fang Ho grinned.

'Me tinkee allo timee master pliceemans pletend dlunk mans,' he remarked. 'P'laps Master wantchee catchee velly bad pilate mans.'

Cousins stood for a moment looking at him, and gradually a smile spread in twinkling creases over his face.

'Ho Fang,' he declared, 'you are plenty cute, but for goodness' sake get out of your head that I am a policeman because I am not. Savvy!'

'Me too muchee savvy,' returned the Chinaman, but he departed still smiling.

Cousins made his way to Tavares' drinking and dancing resort wondering what kind of reception he would receive from the Macanese. He guessed the man would be greatly annoyed by his performance of the morning, and not too polite in the expression of his opinion. He also expected that the screw would be turned a little tighter. If he were correct in his surmise that Tavares and his confederates intended using him as an instrument to remove Sir Leonard Wallace from their path, they would begin to let him see in no uncertain manner that he was marked out for some task, refusal to obey being threatened with exposure of his supposed crime to the police. If only Kenton had not been quite such a hopeless drunkard, how useful he might have been! When Cousins had first taken to him, and had discovered that behind his weakness was a lot to be admired, he had thought then that the ex-engineer might have been of service to him. Now, of course, that was out of the question. He had made enquiries every day by telephone – once he had surreptitiously called at the hospital. The latest news was to the effect that Kenton was improving, but was still fighting a desperate battle against the horrors that afflicted him.

He entered the saloon with the unsteady gait of a man who was still suffering from the effects of his libations, though not actually drunk. Tavares was standing by the curtain that hid the dancing hall from view, and appeared to have been waiting for him, for, as soon as he saw him, he strode across the room, his little pig-like eyes smouldering with suppressed passion. Cousins watched him come, a sheepish grin on his face.

'Follow me!' ordered the Macanese in low tones, directly he reached the other turned on his heels, as though he had no doubt he would be obeyed.

But Cousins had different ideas.

'What for?' he demanded.

Tavares swung back to him.

'I have something to say to you,' he snarled.

'Then say it here. I'm going to drink with my friends.'

'If you do not come, I will not answer for the consequences.' He looked meaningly at the little man.

'Oh, all right. Have your own way.'

The Macanese led him up the stairs, along the corridor leading to the secret door then, having ascertained that they were unobserved, slid the panel aside, and took him into Sales' house. They entered the room where Garcia was supposed to have been murdered. Cousins, adopting an air of rank aversion, went in with an appearance of the greatest reluctance. He edged round the spot where Garcia had fallen, noting that a new rug had replaced the one ruined by the 'blood'. Tavares watched his progress with a sneering smile on his thick lips. Cousins sank into a chair directly under the whirling fan, and mopped his brow. The other stood for a moment looking down at him.

'So they let you out,' he growled at length. 'I thought they would.' Suddenly his voice rose. 'Why the hell you did such a fool thing?' he cried. 'Why last night you want to get drunk worse than I ever saw you? You swine fool, you go letting the police get interested in you – now perhaps they watch you. You let the man see you, I don't want to see you.'

'Who?' asked Cousins.

'The Governor – that is the man. I did not want him put his eyes on you.'

'Why not?'

'That is our – my business. Tell me, dolt, why you do all this?'

'I dunno,' returned Cousins, sullenly.

'Well, you not do it again. From now you stop in this house, and not go out without I tell you, and one bottle brandy you will have every day, and no more. You will have bed, food, everything, but you will be watched so you don't go out. If you try, it will be very bad for you – very bad indeed. I will arrange everything with Mrs Gutteriez.'

Cousins looked up at him. His brain was working swiftly. To be detained thus did not at all accord with his plans, unless he could have Ho Fang Ho with him.

'Do you mean you're going to keep me a prisoner here?' he demanded.

Tavares shrugged his shoulders.

'Put it that way if you like it,' he returned.

'But I don't understand,' protested Cousins. 'Why should you keep me here?'

'Because, if you allowed to go on the same way you do now, soon you will be in hands of police, and I want to stop you from that. Presently you will be useful.' He walked across to the door through which they had entered, held the beaded curtain aside preparatory to passing out, but turned and looked back. 'Remember, if you try to get away, you will be stopped – orders have been given. If somehow you get out of this house then the police will truly have you, but the charge will not be drunk and disorderly. It will be murder!'

The beads fell into place with a rattle – he was gone.

CHAPTER THIRTEEN

A Change of Residence

Ho Fang Ho was not unduly perturbed by the absence of his master from the hotel that night. Had he not been away all the previous night and most of the day? However, as the hour of ten approached on the following morning, he felt a trifle puzzled. He had expected Cousins to turn up, and give him further instructions about meeting the Englishman in the Botanical Gardens, even if there was no message to be delivered to him. The Chinaman waited until a quarter to ten, then set off for the appointment he had been instructed to keep.

Carter left Government House soon after nine on horseback, accompanied by an Indian syce. The sentries at the gates sprang smartly to the salute, which was returned somewhat perfunctorily. Carter was more engaged in casting searching glances at the various loungers spread round than in acknowledging military formality. None of those in the immediate vicinity interested him a great deal. A vendor of sugar cane squatted close to the gates, several chattering women and children surrounding him. On the opposite side of the road were half a dozen coolies engaged in repairing a fence. A prosperous-looking Chinese gentleman, richly attired in shimmering silk, was passing by in a sedan chair carried by four coolies in white and blue livery, their steps falling in perfect unison, their free arms swinging away from their bodies with brisk concordance. The Chinaman bowed politely to Carter; the latter bowed back. There seemed no reason to suppose that there was anybody about who would be at all likely to be interested in his movements. As he turned into the road, however, and broke into a canter, he passed a small two-seater car in a clearing almost hidden by the surrounding trees. Three men were standing by and, without appearing to do so, he observed that they were surreptitiously studying him. A few minutes later he glanced casually round, addressing a remark to the syce behind. The car was following. A smile appeared on Carter's face. He did not bother to turn again.

Before long he came to the Roman Catholic Church of St Joseph. Dismounting, he handed the reins of his horse to the syce, who proceeded to walk it up and down. From the vantage point of the porch, Carter was able to look back without being seen himself. The car had arrived; had come to a standstill outside the gates. There were only two men in it, the third probably having remained behind to watch the gates of Government House. They were engaged in an earnest conversation, no doubt undecided whether to wait or go back. Presently the car was backed behind some trees on the opposite side of the road.

'I hope you enjoy your wait,' remarked Carter to himself.

Removing his topee, he reverently entered the church, and tiptoed to a door at the other end. Several worshippers were at prayer, and he was careful not to disturb them. He went out, bidding good morning to the bearded priest standing at the entrance to the sacristy, the latter returning the salutation courteously. Carter had noted the advantages the church offered when passing the previous evening. He had paid it a visit, afterwards strolling round the grounds. Remembering Cousins' injunction to be careful lest he were followed to his rendezvous with Ho Fang Ho, it had occurred to him then that he could very easily put trackers off the scent by visiting the church every morning, unless – and there was the snag – the men following him were of the same faith, when they would no doubt enter the church after him. However, they were Chinese, and apparently not Christians. Few Chinamen, unless of course they happen to be Christians, will enter the places of worship of the 'foreign devils'.

He made his way along a footpath behind the church, eventually reaching a road some distance above where his groom and the men in the little car were waiting. Assuring himself that he was not being observed, he then set off for his rendezvous. He arrived at the monkey house long before the hour appointed, and sat on a convenient seat, passing the time by smoking and watching with amusement the antics of the animals in the cages. There were few people about, a fact that would make it all the easier for him to recognise the emissary of Cousins. Just before ten he rose, and sauntered close up to the monkey house. Almost at once a young Chinaman appeared, carrying in his left hand a white handkerchief, and Carter gave a sigh of satisfaction. He put his pipe in his mouth, and adjusted the red flower in his buttonhole. The merest flicker of acknowledgement passed over the face of Ho Fang Ho, who went up to a cage, and stood for a moment with hands outspread on the wire, appearing to watch with great interest the antics of a pair of chimpanzees. But his eyes actually were studying the smartly-dressed Englishman. The sign which denoted that the latter had no message for him was not given, and presently Ho Fang Ho turned from the chimpanzees; strolled towards another cage. He passed Carter; for the merest fraction of a second their hands touched, and a folded slip of paper had passed into the Chinaman's keeping.

The Englishman wandered round for a few minutes longer; then departed. Ho Fang Ho had already gone. The lack of a communication from Cousins was not surprising. He had hardly expected the little man to have had any information to add to that which he had imparted in the central police station the evening before. Carter returned to St Joseph's Church by the same footpath he had used to leave it. The doors were still open, though now there was nobody either in the sacristy or elsewhere. A minute or two later the Englishman emerged from the church, strolled to the front gate, and remounted the horse waiting there for him. A glimmer of amusement showed in his eyes as he observed the two-seater still standing patiently where it had been stationed to await his return. He rode back to Government House with the almost pertain knowledge that his meeting with Ho Fang Ho had not been observed by anyone who might have felt an interest in it.

Ho Fang Ho waited patiently for his master to return, squatting outside the door of his room, his eyes seldom leaving the staircase up which he momentarily expected the little man to appear. Safely deposited inside his clothing was the note Carter had given him and, every now and again, he put his hand on it, as though to make certain it was there. As time went by, despite himself, he began to feel anxious. It seemed to him that, knowing there would very likely be a message from the Englishman, his master would have hastened back to find out. Of course he might be too drunk to remember anything about it, but Ho Fang Ho did not believe that. He had long since made up his mind that the little man who had saved his life was never really drunk at all.

Hour after hour went by, and still he sat where he was. His midday meal was long overdue, but he made no attempt to go and prepare it for fear of missing his benefactor. The heart of Ho Fang Ho sank more and more, until he began to feel that harm had overtaken the man whom he very nearly worshipped. He was casting about in his mind what steps he should take, if Cousins failed to return that night, when to his ears came the sound of a prolonged conversation carried on somewhere below. One of the voices belonged to Mrs Gutteriez; the other he did not recognise, but once the name Collins reached him. That he knew belonged to his master, and his interest was aroused. He moved nearer to the head of the staircase, but it was useless. They were speaking in Portuguese, a language he did not understand. At length came the heavy tread and asthmatical gasping of the landlady, as she ascended the stairs. Ho Fang Ho retreated to his former position. She arrived, and looked down at him coldly.

'Your master has gone away,' she announced in Chinese. 'His bag is to be sent after him. Pack it, and bring it to me.'

She was clutching a few banknotes in her hand, and Ho Fang Ho wondered if they had any connection with the extraordinary news which had just been conveyed to him. He rose to his feet, filled with a sense of foreboding.

'I will take the bag to him,' he observed. 'He will expect me to go to him.'

'He will expect nothing of the sort,' snapped the woman, whose knowledge of the Chinese language was perhaps even better than that of Portuguese and English. 'He has no need of you. After you have packed his bag, you can go. I do not want you in this house.'

'You will tell me where he is?' pleaded Ho Fang Ho.

She shook her head.

'Do what you are told. Nothing else concerns you.' She turned on her heel; went wheezily down the stairs.

Ho Fang Ho's heart was very heavy within him now. Some disaster, he felt sure, must have overtaken his master. Never, he declared to himself, would the man who had so recently put great trust in him, send a message that he no longer required him. Why had he not come back for his belongings himself? The memory of his fears that Tavares had evil designs on his benefactor recurred to the Chinaman's mind. Perhaps, after all, he had been right, and the man whom he had described to Cousins as 'a velly bad pilate' now had the Englishman in his power. Had not the latter told him that he and his friend were going to try and catch certain bad men, and that Ho Fang Ho would be required to help? Perhaps 'the pilate' was one of the people referred to, and, suspecting the little man's scheme, had captured or, even worse, killed him. Ho Fang Ho swore an oath to himself that he would not rest until he discovered his fears were groundless, or was able to save his master, if indeed he were alive to be saved.

He packed the shabby suitcase, not forgetting to stuff in the new bed linen and mosquito net he had so recently bought with such pride. After a final look round the room, he carried the bag downstairs, handing it with great reluctance to Mrs Gutteriez, who at once proceeded to open it and search among the articles inside.

'I suppose you have been robbing me,' she remarked by way of explanation for her action. 'Ah!' The sheets, pillow slip, and mosquito net were taken out, and placed on a chair. 'As I thought.'

'Those are not stolen,' protested Ho Fang Ho. 'My master gave me money to buy them.'

He made an attempt to rescue the things she had purloined, but she grabbed them in her hands, and held them behind her back.

'Go away, you thief,' she screamed. 'I will call the police.'

'Very well,' returned Ho Fang Ho, 'I will wait for the police to come.'

Thereupon she called out loudly in Portuguese. A young man, obviously of her own race, came running to her assistance, followed by a couple of Chinese servants. She told them that Ho Fang Ho had attempted to rob her by putting articles that belonged to her in the suitcase. Rough hands were promptly laid upon him, and he was thrown out of the house. He made no attempt at resistance. It had occurred to him that she might go to the length of having him searched, when his precious paper would have been discovered. He preferred her to keep the linen rather than risk a disaster of that nature by further attempts to recover the property of his master. But he felt extremely dejected as he picked himself up, and wandered away along the road. He had felt so proud of purchasing the things for the man he had decided to serve all his life.

Hidden a little distance away, he waited and watched. Scarcely ten minutes had passed when the young Macanese appeared from the misnamed Hotel Paris carrying Cousins' suitcase. He stepped into a sedan chair that was waiting, was immediately carried away, but Ho Fang Ho took care not to be far behind. He did not bother to seek his own meagre belongings from the servants' quarters, where they had been deposited. In fact it is likely he had forgotten all about them. His mind was too much occupied with other and far more serious matters. The man in the chair ahead of him changed into a tram in Queen's Road, but did not notice Ho Fang Ho in the second-class compartment. When he got out, Ho Fang Ho did likewise. The latter, with a sense of satisfaction, observed him enter a large house and, getting into conversation with the extremely fat but genial proprietor of an establishment containing succulent-looking pigs and ducks roasted whole, squatted down to watch.

There were three houses in the block on the other side of the road. The middle one, to judge from the tables and chairs spread outside under an awning and on the verandas above, was an eating house of some kind. That on the right appeared to be an ordinary residence. As it was into this that the young man had disappeared with the bag, all Ho Fang

Ho's attention was devoted to it. There were four storeys, the middle two containing verandas. These riveted the Chinaman's attention for some time. He was hoping that the gods would be good, and vouchsafe a glimpse of his master who, by this time he had become convinced, was being held a prisoner within. He argued that the latter's suitcase would hardly have been taken there if he had been dead. Ho Fang Ho had not been a Christian very long, a missionary having taken him in hand less than three years previously, and, in moments of stress, he was apt to forget, and pray to the deities of his youth. He suddenly realised what he was doing now and, with a muttered word of apology, transferred his appeals to the God of the Christians.

As though in answer to his prayer, two men appeared on the first floor veranda of the house. One was a stranger to him, but the other was the 'pilate' man. His fears had been justified. His master was in the power of the man whose visit to the Hotel Paris had so roused his anxiety. He wondered if it would be of any use his going to the police, and telling them that he had found the man he had seen in conversation with the pirate captain on the bridge of the looted steamer. Reflection decided him that such a course would be a waste of time. He could not prove his words, and they were not likely, in consequence, to take any notice of him. He was so much engaged in watching the two men that he failed to notice for some time that a window in the top storey of the house had opened; that a figure was craning its head out in an attempt to see below. Eventually, however, something caused him to glance up, and immediately a surge of joy went through him. It was his master.

Ho Fang Ho was greatly relieved to see him. At all events he appeared unharmed, and there was much satisfaction to be derived from that knowledge. The question now was; how would it be possible to rescue him? The first necessity was to acquaint him with the fact that he had found him, but he dared not make an endeavour to draw his attention. Any signals would be bound to rouse the suspicion of the two men on the veranda; there might possibly be observant eyes elsewhere as well. Ho Fang Ho grunted with a sense of aggravation. Presently his master's head would be withdrawn into the room, and he would remain ignorant that his servant was nearby, longing to communicate with him. It happened that Cousins himself resolved the difficulty by looking across the road. Immediately an idea occurred to Ho Fang Ho. He took out the white handkerchief, which Cousins had given him to carry in order that Carter would recognise him, and raised it to his lips. His ruse was entirely successful. The flutter of something white caught the Secret Service man's eye, whereupon the unusual sight of a Chinaman, of the class of the individual sitting in front of the roast pork shop, using a handkerchief caused him to stare. Almost at once he had recognised Ho Fang Ho, and gave ample evidence of that fact to the delighted Chinaman.

He proceeded to make signs that he was quite all right; that Ho Fang Ho was to go away, return at eight o'clock, and take up his stand directly under the window. It took the Chinaman some time to understand what was intended, but eight fingers held up, followed by the index finger of Cousins' right hand pointing directly downwards eventually caused it to dawn on him what his master wished him to do. Without making any gestures himself, he rose, and sauntered away.

At first Cousins had not been unduly perturbed by the announcement made by Tavares that he was to be kept a prisoner in Sales' house. In fact such an arrangement might, he thought, be of benefit to him. But, as time went by, and he discovered that a Chinese servant squatted on guard outside each door of the room in which he had been left, he decided that it was very much to his disadvantage. There was absolutely no chance of his roaming about at will, and thus making investigations. He was a prisoner in fact without liberty of any sort. Of course, if Tavares allowed him to have Ho Fang Ho with him it would not be so bad, but were he denied the Chinaman he would have no opportunities of communicating with Sir Leonard Wallace. He had certainly not anticipated a move of this kind from the Macanese, and he half regretted now that he had given an impression of such utter recklessness when apparently under the influence of drink. He was compelled to appear cowed by Tavares' threats, but he promised himself that, as soon as they brought him brandy, he would regain a measure of courage, and become obstreperous. Unfortunately, no brandy was brought to him that night, and he saw nothing further of Tavares. A Chinese servant entered the room, and made signs that he was to follow him. To his demands for brandy the fellow made no response, merely continuing to indicate that he was to go with him. Cousins followed the man up two flights of stairs, and found that behind him walked two other servants. He was ushered into a small room; then, before he quite realised what was intended, the door was shut, and he was locked in. He decided that it would have been futile to have shown indignation or rage, and to have rained a storm of blows on the wood. Nobody would be likely to take any notice of him. He, therefore, sat down, and looked round him. A small bedstead covered by a couple of sheets, so worn that they had a gossamer look about them, a chair, a decrepit washstand with towel and soap, and a mirror hanging on the wall was all the furniture the room contained. A fairly large window let in a supply of fresh sea air from the harbour, which was something to be grateful for, because the apartment was neither provided with a fan nor a punka. Cousins sat where he was for a time; then, with a shrug of his shoulders, went to bed.

He lay awake most of the night attempting to discover a method whereby he could communicate with Carter, if Ho Fang Ho were denied him, but was unable to think of anything. He hardly anticipated that Tavares would agree to his having the Chinaman with him. The Macanese was not likely to countenance the presence of a stranger at liberty to come and go in a house of so many secrets. Cousins began to feel, as the dreary hours of the night passed slowly by, that he was in a very difficult position. All he could do was to wait and see what the next day would bring forth. On one point he was absolutely decided; if it were at all possible, he must find means of listening to the meeting due to take place the next day, or, failing that, of at least catching a glimpse of those who attended it.

Breakfast was brought to him by the Chinaman who had conducted him to his room on the previous night. Try as he would, however, he could get nothing out of the man. He either could not, or would not, speak English, and eventually

Cousins gave up the attempt. He washed and dressed; then sat down to await the coming of Tavares, expecting him every moment. But the morning passed wearily by without the Macanese putting in an appearance. Cousins began to feel extremely worried. Was it the intention of those in whose hands he was to keep him shut up in that little room? If so, his hopes of seeing or hearing anything of the meeting that evening were doomed to disappointment. It was extremely hot, and he perspired so freely that before long his clothing was saturated. He shut the window, and drew the curtains in an effort to keep out as much of the heat as possible, for there was no breeze to temper it, but without experiencing much relief. Twelve o'clock came, and he was beginning to suspect there was a more sinister design behind his incarceration than he had surmised, when the door was unlocked. The same Chinaman entered, and beckoned to him. He followed the man down the stairs to the room which by now was very familiar to him. He assumed an appearance of sullen resentment and, when he found Tavares and Sales awaiting him, broke into a bitter denunciation of the manner in which he had been treated, demanding to know why he was being kept a prisoner in the house.

Tavares was more suave than on the previous night. He had apparently recovered from his anger and, in consequence, his English had recovered also. He took pains to point out that that which was being done was to save Mr Collins from himself or, at least, from the risk of giving his dreadful secret away when in the grip of brandy and kindred spirits. He turned a deaf ear on Cousins demanding to know why he had been locked in, and observed that it was his desire and the desire of his friend Sales that their 'guest' should be as comfortable as possible. For that reason he would send to the Hotel Paris for his belongings, at the same time recompensing Mrs Gutteriez for the loss of her boarder. Cousins proceeded to tell him what he thought of him, demanding to be allowed to go his own way. This, he was informed, was impossible, Tavares, with an appearance of great patience, again endeavouring to point out to him that they were keeping him there for his own good.

'We have a service which we will ask you to perform one of these days,' he concluded, 'and for that purpose it is necessary that you remain here under our care.'

'I'm damned if I'll do anything for you,' retorted Cousins violently.

'Oh, yes, you will,' came the softly spoken reply. 'It is easy, and you will be recompensed. If you refuse, you will simply be handed over to the police.'

'He is not worth saving,' put in Sales. 'Take my advice, and give him to the police now.'

Cousins, behaving as was no doubt expected of him, cringed back in his chair.

'All right,' he muttered, 'I'll stay.'

Tavares laughed.

'That is exceedingly kind of you,' he returned sarcastically. 'You seem to have forgotten that you have no choice, my friend.'

'What about the brandy you told me you'd let me have?' came in hoarse tones from the Englishman. 'I suffered the tortures of the damned all last night.'

'You shall have it – presently. Tell me first if there is

anything you want brought to you, apart from the things at the house of Mrs Gutteriez.'

Cousins told him about Ho Fang Ho, explaining why the Chinaman had become so attached to him, and asked that he should also be sent for. Tavares laughed.

'It is very touching that a Chinese should feel so great a devotion,' he sneered, 'especially for a man like you. But I regret you will have to dispense with his services. You will find other Chinamen in this house who will do anything you require – in reason.'

To all Cousins' entreaties he shook his head, and the Englishman was forced to abandon the idea. It would not do, he felt, to make the others suspicious by appearing too insistent upon having Ho Fang Ho, but his spirits fell considerably. He now had to face the fact that he was in an extremely difficult, not to say delicate, position. Tavares informed him that it would be necessary to keep him locked up for the rest of that day – Cousins had no difficulty in guessing the reason why. Afterwards, if he behaved himself, he would be allowed more liberty.

Still demanding brandy, he was sent back to his room. Quite a respectable luncheon – probably from the restaurant next door – was brought to him, and he was again locked in. His thoughts were very gloomy, as he sat sweltering in the heat of the little chamber and, try as he would, he could work out no solution to his difficulties. During the afternoon his battered suitcase was handed in to him. A little later the promised bottle of brandy arrived. Cousins eyed it with distaste. It would not be of much use to him now there was no object in appearing drunk any longer, and, in any case, a bottle of brandy would hardly be sufficient to intoxicate the hardened drinker he was thought to be. But it would be sufficient to restore to him a certain amount of his aggressiveness and courage! To Cousins came the germ of an idea. If he could succeed in getting out of the room, perhaps he might yet hear something of the discussion at the meeting, catch a glimpse of those present. If he were caught, and the chances were that he would be, he would give the impression that he was simply attempting to get away; that the brandy had clouded his brain sufficiently to rouse his courage, and give him nerve to do what he would have done, for Cousins had come to the conclusion that his only means of escape lay in climbing out of the window, and descending to the floor below. He had already glanced down. It was likely to be a dangerous and difficult task, but not impossible. He went to the window, drew the curtain aside, and opened it. A breeze had risen, and blew gently into the room like a breath of new and invigorating life.

He looked at the roof of the veranda below, and estimated his chances of reaching it, or, with a grim smile, of crashing down to his death. There was no foothold or fingerhold whatever between the windowsill and the top of the veranda, a distance of quite ten feet. Cousins was only five feet in height and, at the full extent of his arms, did not measure more than six and a half feet. Add to that the fact that the veranda roof sloped abruptly, and a pretty problem presented itself. There was only one thing for it, he decided; that was to trust himself to the flimsy sheets of his bed tied to the shaky, unsubstantial washstand – the bed, a cane affair of a type he had never seen before, was out of the question;

it looked as though it would fall to pieces if any strain were put upon it. The meeting was to be held at seven, but he would have to wait until after that hour before making his attempt. It would be too light then. But the discussion would undoubtedly last for some time. If he could hear half of it, he would be satisfied, while the more important thing was to catch a glimpse of the people present. As he raised his head, his eye caught the gleam of something white across the road. He looked, and saw a Chinaman squatting there with a handkerchief in his hand. Strange sight, he mused; a Chinaman, apparently of the servant class, looked queer with a white handkerchief. That was one of the reasons why— Suddenly he stiffened, and looked hard. A feeling of delight permeated his whole being. It was Ho Fang Ho.

CHAPTER FOURTEEN

So Near and Yet—

The presence of Ho Fang Ho in the vicinity gave Cousins a great sense of relief. It not only proved once again how loyal the Chinaman was to him, but reopened the possibility of his being able to communicate with Sir Leonard Wallace. If he succeeded in getting out of the room, and heard something of the conversation at the meeting, Cousins felt that he might, after all, be able to send very important information to his chief. He made signs to Ho Fang Ho to return at eight, and take up his stand directly under the window at which he now saw his master. By that time Cousins hoped to be on the first floor veranda, and able easily to drop a note to him. Ho Fang Ho gave no sign that he understood but, as he presently wandered away, Cousins felt satisfied that he had.

The little man cast an anxious look up and down the road to ascertain whether his gesturing had been observed, but nobody below appeared to be taking any interest in the house. He went back to the bed and, taking a diary and pencil from his pockets, sank on to the crazy contraption, and proceeded to write with great rapidity. Afterwards he removed the little book which reposed in the belt round his waist, and wrote again, putting his message into code. That done, he tore both sheets of paper from the notebook – the first was reduced to minute pieces, which he burnt and crumbled into ash, the second was folded up and put in a pocket with the diary and pencil. The precious little code book was returned to its secret receptacle. He had written to Sir Leonard Wallace telling him of the manner in which he was being detained in the house of the Macanese, Miguel Sales, and why. As there was a possibility that his activities might for the future be very much hampered, if not entirely curtailed, he gave a description of both houses and the secret means of communication between them. He also wrote about Tavares' office, the safe and cupboards therein, and spoke of his idea – which he still hoped to carry out – of searching the place thoroughly, though his original scheme of disguising himself as a punka coolie seemed likely now to be impossible of accomplishment. He again gave a description of the man who had entered the office when he was there with Tavares – he had already done so to Carter in the gaol, but repeated it, because he felt the individual in question was an important member of the band of conspirators, if not the actual leader. The unconcluded remark of the man in which the name of Sir Leonard Wallace had been mentioned, as well as his air of authority, had been sufficient to convince Cousins of that. Finally he had written that he hoped to hear a good deal of the discussion arranged for that night and, if at all possible, see the conspirators. Ho Fang Ho was to be told to return on the following night. If Cousins had succeeded, there would then be vital information for the Chief. He made no mention of what he thought would happen were he to fail. He hardly considered that necessary; besides, if Ho Fang Ho returned to report that he had neither been entrusted with a message nor seen his master, it would be fairly obvious to Sir Leonard that something had gone wrong.

A meal was brought to Cousins about half past six. He showed the Chinese servant the bottle of brandy, now empty, and demanded more. His tone was somewhat thick, and decidedly offensive; sullen resentment, tempered by fear, having apparently given way to a kind of resolute aggressiveness under the influence of the brandy. The boy looked slightly alarmed, but shook his head, whereupon Cousins, bottle in hand, made for him as though bent on mischief. The fellow dashed from the room, slamming the door behind him, and locking it. Cousins sat on the bed, and chuckled. Tavares would, no doubt, be informed of what had happened; he would probably visit his prisoner to reprimand him, and thus see for himself that the latter was in a state of militancy. Cousins hoped that would go a long way towards explaining his behaviour, and consequently lull suspicion, if he were caught during the subsequent operations.

Tavares came as expected, and found the dishevelled little man in a decidedly combative state of mind. His threats on this occasion had no effect, Cousins declaring that, if he did not send up more brandy, he would smash up the room, and throw the remains of his destructive efforts out of the window. That brought sneering references to the police making enquiries and the murderer Collins being taken away to stand his trial. Tavares was dismayed to find that the captive laughed at him; even told him to fetch the police, as he was tired of living like an animal in a cage. The Macanese eventually promised to send up another bottle of brandy at once, rather to Cousins' surprise – he now felt he would have more excuse than ever for breaking out. Tavares departed with a look on his face that seemed to imply that his 'guest' was not quite so easy to handle as he had expected. He had probably determined that once the little man had recovered from the effects of the spirits, he would deny him further supplies, and thus keep him in a state of apathetic and shrinking irresolution for the future.

The brandy came, and Cousins ate his dinner. When the servant returned to remove the empty plates, he noticed that three parts of the second bottle had gone, and that the Englishman, now well under the influence of the liquor, was singing drunkenly to himself. The Chinaman hastened to clear away, expecting momentarily to be attacked, but Cousins took no notice of him. The latter was anxious to be left to himself, and sighed his relief when the man, at last, shut and locked the door on him.

It seemed to be a long time before the light went that evening, but at last darkness fell with its usual suddenness. Cousins knotted his two sheets together, and tied one end securely to a leg of the washstand which he had previously moved across the room to the window. He looked dubiously at the rickety piece of furniture to which he was about to entrust his weight, but, without hesitation, climbed out on the windowsill, and let his improvised rope cautiously down. A searchlight on a warship in the harbour swept its brilliant ray inquisitively not many yards above his head, and he muttered something uncomplimentary about searchlight practice and naval routine. If the beam fell any lower, it would expose him to the full view of anyone who looked up, and people have a habit of watching the movements of searchlights. However, he decided to risk that. It was already after half past seven – perhaps the meeting was nearly over. The thought caused him to hurry.

He swung himself over the sill and, with a muttered prayer, gripped the sheet, gradually letting it take his weight. There was an ominous creak from within the room, but the washstand held, and gently he let himself down. The searchlight was at the moment stationary, its beam being focused on some object away to his right. His feet touched the roof of the veranda below, and he grew more cautious than ever. It would be distinctly unfortunate, if someone were sitting on the balcony. However, he went on and, before long, was hanging from the roof, his feet resting on the balustrade. The veranda was in darkness, as was the room within. Cousins gave vent to a deep sigh of satisfaction, swung the end of the sheet on to the roof in order that it would not be discovered by anyone who might later on chance walk on to the veranda, and dropped lightly to the stone floor. He found that the doors opposite were bolted on the inside, but farther along one leading into the next room stood open. He crept quietly through to find himself in a bedroom. No time was wasted there. He tiptoed quickly out into a corridor beyond, and came to a flight of stairs. These he recognised. They would take him to the floor where was the room in which he was supposed to have killed Manuel Garcia and, what was more important, the apartment furnished like a boardroom, in which he firmly believed the meeting was being held. Now came the most ticklish part of his task. He had to descend the stairs and, at any moment, someone might appear either from one of the rooms adjacent, or from above or below, and discover him. He crept to the banisters as the murmur of voices reached his ears, looked down with the greatest care; then quickly drew back. One of the servants was squatting at the foot of the stairs; a little way along was another. The conspirators were very well guarded from intrusion.

Cousins returned to the room through which he had come, and remained there while he considered what course to pursue. Having succeeded in getting so far, he was determined not to be balked. His eyes were quite used to the darkness, and he became aware that he was in a lady's bedchamber. The dim outlines of various articles, which only a member of the opposite sex would use, could be seen on the dressing table and in other places in the room. Suddenly he remembered Ho Fang Ho. The boy was probably waiting below by now. It would be as well if he handed over the note intended for Sir Leonard Wallace before attempting to do anything else. He would feel a good deal easier in his mind once that was accomplished. But how was it to be done? Of course, once he had ascertained that Ho Fang Ho was there, and by some means had made him aware of his presence above, he could throw the paper to him. But that would not solve the difficulty of receiving any message the Chinaman might have for him. An idea occurred to him. In a lady's bedroom might very likely be a workbox, and in a workbox would be cotton. Silently he searched and, before long, had the gratification of finding the object for which he was seeking. It was made of some sort of basket work, liberally decked with bows in silk ribbon and other trifles dear to the female heart. Very pretty, no doubt, but quite without interest to Cousins just then. He opened the lid, and plunged in his hand, giving a muttered exclamation as a needle ran into his finger. His hand quickly closed on a reel of cotton, however, which he withdrew from the basket, forgetting the injury in his delight.

He stepped quickly and silently on to the veranda, making for the end overlooking the spot where he expected Ho Fang Ho to be standing. He climbed on to the balustrade, and looked down. By leaning over precariously he was able to see part of the balcony underneath. It was in darkness, indicating fairly certainly that it was unoccupied. Luck, which he felt had deserted him when he had observed the two Chinese on watch at the bottom of the stairs, seemed to have returned to his aid. He could easily slip down the corner pillar which extended as a support from one veranda to the other. He would then be directly over Ho Fang Ho and outside the room in which the conference was being held. Only one consideration gave him pause. That was the possibility that another watcher was stationed there. The chance of being seen by any of the men within, he decided, was negligible. They were in a lighted room, the veranda was in darkness. The windows were obviously closed, otherwise he would have been able to have heard the murmur of voices. As he could see no reflection of light at all, he came to the conclusion that the windows were also shuttered or curtained. He made up his mind to make the descent, and risk the chance of a man being on guard there. It was a fortunate circumstance that this side of the house was farthest from Tavares' establishment, otherwise the lights thrown from the gaudily-lit building, and the people dining on the veranda at the same level, would have entirely prevented his working unobserved.

Hardly making a sound, he lowered himself from the balustrade, gripped the pillar with his knees and, putting first one arm, then the other round it, slid softly to the veranda below. A rapid glance assured him that there was nobody on watch there, and he breathed his relief. As he had surmised, the windows of the all-important room were closed and shuttered, the smallest crack of light at one corner being the only indication of life within. Not a sound could be heard, and Cousins made a grimace. The chances of his being able to hear anything began to appear rather remote. However, he had first to give the missive intended for Sir Leonard Wallace to Ho Fang Ho. Looking down, he endeavoured to pierce the darkness, which at that corner was more opaque than elsewhere. It did not take him long to make certain that someone was standing almost directly below. Whether it was his Chinese servant or not, however, there was no means of telling. He coughed, not loudly, but with sufficient force he thought to be heard. A moment or two passed; then the individual standing underneath coughed. That seemed to suggest that he was Ho Fang Ho, but certainly did not prove it. Cousins was casting about in his mind for another and more definite way of making sure, when a match flared into life, and the man applied the flame to a cigarette. Cousins nodded his head with keen approval. The light showed him

Ho Fang Ho's face beyond any question of doubt and, once again, he reflected that the Chinaman certainly had all his wits about him.

The note was quickly tied to the cotton, and lowered. The glow of the cigarette was almost directly beneath Cousins, and he had no fear of missing Ho Fang Ho. Even if he did, it would not matter, as he could swing the missive to and fro until it touched the boy, who would thus become aware of it. He dared not light a match himself in the manner the Chinaman had done to show his face, but after all it was hardly necessary. Ho Fang Ho would know that nobody but his master would be lowering notes to him. It was an extremely fortunate circumstance, reflected Cousins, that that side of the road was almost entirely deserted. Only people entering Tavares' dance hall and restaurant seemed to approach there at all, and they mostly came from the other direction. Ho Fang Ho more or less had the corner to himself.

Apparently expecting that a letter would be dropped to him, the Chinaman quickly took hold of the cotton, and released the missive, tying another in its place. Cousins drew it up, and detached it, slipping it with the cotton into an inside pocket of his jacket. He then turned away, dropping lightly from the balustrade to the stone floor of the veranda.

He crept quietly to the shuttered windows, and applied his ear to the tiny opening through which showed the little ray of light. All he could hear was a dull murmur – not a single word was distinguishable. He wandered along the veranda to find that all other doors were bolted and shuttered, not that it would have helped him much had they been open, for the Chinese servants on duty in the corridor made it quite out of the question for him to approach the all-important room from that direction. Listening by the wall dividing the veranda of Tavares' house from that of Sales, he could hear the clatter of plates and the voices of diners. He decided that he would climb round the barrier later on, when he was sure there was nobody about, and, if possible, make his way to Tavares' office. Perhaps, after all, he might find an opportunity of searching it. First, however, he must endeavour to discover some means of listening to what was going on at the meeting. It was distinctly tantalising to be so close, and unable to hear a thing.

Softly he walked back to the other end of the veranda. This was not bricked up, and he was able to lean out over the balustrade, and look along the side of the house. He noticed a window a little way along. It was open, the illumination within throwing a shaft of light into the darkness. A narrow ledge not more than a few inches wide ran along, a yard or so beneath, from the front veranda to the back of the house. Cousins wondered if he could possibly walk along it – there was nothing, as far as he could see, to which his hands could cling. It would be an extremely risky endeavour, but as there was no other means of hearing or seeing what was going on, he determined to make the attempt.

He climbed over the railing and, keeping his body and hands pressed against the wall in order that his weight would not, in the slightest degree, be thrown the other way, he started on his perilous journey. Inch by inch he edged his way along, every movement threatening to plunge him to death or very serious injury below. For a long time it appeared that he was making no headway, that the window was just as far off as ever. When he eventually reached it, he felt that he had taken hours. He was in a bath of perspiration, and for some reason or other his limbs were trembling. With a great sense of relief he clutched at the window ledge; drew himself as near as he dared, listening hard to distinguish what was being said by a voice that he was now able to hear quite plainly. It gave him something of a shock to realise that it was speaking English with cultured, well-bred accents. He had expected that the language spoken would have been Portuguese, why, he hardly knew; possibly because Sales and Tavares, the only men he had met connected with the plot, and Mathos the financier, who had engineered it, were of that race, or, rather, partially, of that race.

'In my opinion, therefore,' the voice was saying, 'and I am sure in the opinion of most, if not all of you here, it would be unwise to attempt anything of that nature unless circumstances drive us to it.' Cousins wondered to what he was referring, but soon received enlightenment. 'I don't agree with Wun Cheng Lo that the attempt at Singapore was a mistake. If those fools hadn't blundered, we should not now have Wallace in this colony, with the constant fear hanging over our heads that he may discover something vital. We know he is the head of the British Secret Service, and we know that he is not acting as Governor simply to relieve Ferguson for a few months. He is here for a definite object, and unless we are careful he will succeed. If our plans had not miscarried in Singapore, we should not have had the present anxiety to face. Whatever Wun Cheng Lo may think to the contrary, I contend that, had he been removed in Singapore, Hong Kong would never have been thought of in connection with the deed. It was to keep Hong Kong and the so-called conspiracy here from any apparent concern that we arranged for the venture in Singapore. However, it failed, and we are compelled to face the fact that, in our midst, is the very man we fear most in the world.'

'Why should we fear him?' snapped a harsh voice. 'He may be clever, but other clever men have not succeeded in unmasking us over a period of several years, and now that our activities have by force of circumstances been suspended, I do not think—'

'Not all your activities I hope,' put in a voice in perfect English which, nevertheless, had a trace of some foreign accent about it. 'You are not forgetting, I trust, that my country, for services rendered, is making up the deficiency caused by the unfortunate – er – suspension of your other operations.'

'No; we are not forgetting that,' returned the first voice. 'You must realise, though, that even there our difficulties are vastly increased. But we will carry out our contract with the Japanese Government.'

Ah! Cousins had definitely learnt one thing. It was that the Hong Kong scandal and the leakage of confidential schemes and information of a military nature were connected, the conspirators being responsible for both.

'To reply to your question,' went on the same speaker, apparently addressing the man with the harsh voice; 'I would like to remind you that the British Secret Service is the most efficient in the world, and Sir Leonard Wallace is said never to fail when he undertakes anything.'

'Bah!' growled the other, 'That is ridiculous. Anyhow, he'll fail this time.'

Other voices clamoured in with remarks, all of which in various ways echoed the first speaker's vehement: 'He must!'

'I dare not consider the consequences, if once he begins to find out who we are,' he continued.

'I still think it would be better to have him killed at once,' declared another voice. 'It will save us a great deal of anxiety.'

'My dear fellow, I contend that, if possible, we must avoid anything of that nature in Hong Kong. His assassination here would cause such an upheaval that it is likely our security would be greatly endangered. Now that the man Baxter is dead, nobody knows who we are except those in our own circle. Unless Wallace does begin to look dangerous, and Wun Cheng Lo will quickly tell us if he does, I propose nothing be done at present against his life. Every obstacle must be put in his way, of course, and we rely on Wun Cheng Lo to do a great deal to put him on the wrong scent. Later on we will consider if it is possible to offer up a few victims to him as substitute villains of the piece. Actors have understudies – why not we? There are quite a number of people in Hong Kong, eligibly important, against whom it should not be difficult to manufacture evidence. I should hate Sir Leonard Wallace to be disappointed in his endeavours, besides which he might remain in the colony if, at the end of his six months of office, he has found no victims to offer up to the British Government.'

His remarks caused a good deal of amusement and applause. The proposal was generally voted a good one, and the names of various prominent people mentioned as individuals they would like to see under accusation. The leader, however, pointed out that they could not discuss such a scheme at the present time. There would be ample opportunity later on. Cramp in both his legs and arms was beginning to attack Cousins, and he felt that, if he did not soon return along the ledge to safety, all power would desert his limbs, with the result that he would crash to the ground below. But still he lingered, hopeful that a name would be mentioned to give him a clue to the identity of one at least of those present, or that he might presently be able to steal a glance into the room.

'We are decided then, I take it,' the spokesman was concluding, 'to make no attempt upon the life of Wallace unless, and until, we have reason to believe that he is getting on the track. Then he must die. The suggestion by Tavares that this knife-throwing beachcomber friend of his be made to do the deed in Government House itself seems as sound an idea as any other that has been mentioned, and certainly less likely to cause upheaval than most. Wun Cheng Lo should have no difficulty in smuggling him in. You are sure that your fake murder has put the fear of the Lord into the little ruffian, Tavares?'

Cousins smiled to himself. It gave him a great deal of satisfaction to know that he had guessed right. He frowned with an air of puzzlement as he heard Tavares reply to the question addressed to him.

'Yes, your Excellency, I can assure you that he is full of a great terror lest the police arrest him. I can make him do whatever I want – never fear.'

'Liar,' muttered Cousins.

He was very puzzled by that 'Your Excellency'. Was it simply the courtesy title of respect usually accorded by a man of Tavares' race and breeding to one of higher circumstances, or was the man entitled by his official position to the designation? He decided that the time had come for him to cast a look into the room. Slowly, and by cautious degrees, he moved his head forward until his eyes were on the point of glancing in. But the movement put the final touch to the triumph of the cramp, which seemed now to have taken entire possession of him. His legs suddenly gave way, his feet slipping off the narrow ledge on which he had been standing. Frantically his fingers caught and gripped the edge of the window; at the same time he choked back the cry that rose involuntarily to his throat. For an agonising moment he hung there, subconsciously noting that the voices went on speaking; no alarm had been roused; then, unable to hold on any longer, he crashed to the ground below. The shock, of course, shook him up tremendously, and he lay for a few moments dazed but not unconscious. Nobody appeared at the window above and, as though in a dream, he realised that nothing could have been heard of his accident.

He pulled himself together, and began to congratulate himself on the fact that apparently no bones were broken, as he had feared. He felt himself all over; then commenced to struggle to his feet. At once a most excruciating pain shot through him and, with a pang of sheer dismay, he realised that his left leg was broken. A groan escaped him, not on account of the pain, but because his usefulness to the Chief was absolutely gone for a couple of months. He brushed the perspiration from his forehead, and gritted his teeth. It was no use lamenting, but it was hard luck. Success had seemed within his grasp. The words he had heard spoken proved beyond all possibility of doubt that the men in the room above were actually the conspirators whose identity had so cleverly been kept secret. No names had been mentioned, but in another moment or two he would have succeeded in catching a glimpse of the faces of, at least, some of them. All he had to help him now was the memory of one voice – the others were nondescript, might have belonged to anybody; there were thousands like them – but this voice was different. He would recognise it anywhere. But where would he be likely to hear it again, especially during the next two months when he would be cooped up in hospital? 'Damn the cramp!' muttered Cousins feelingly, and with bitter emphasis.

The sight of the light streaming from the window above prompted him to move. If he were found where he then lay, it would not take a very cute mind to guess what he had been attempting to do when the accident occurred. Agonisingly, every moment biting his lips to refrain from groaning, he dragged himself along to the front of the house. There it would appear to Tavares and Sales, after they had discovered the sheets knotted to the washstand, that in attempting to get out he had slipped, probably due to the state of drunkenness he was in, and fallen to the ground. Why he had not been killed after dropping from such a height would be regarded as a mystery, but then drunken men have often been known to fall with impunity from heights that to others would have been fatal. Cousins reflected, with a faint smile, that there would be no doubt regarding his condition. Before leaving the little room, he had gargled his mouth with brandy and sprinkled some on his clothes; besides, the two empty bottles should be eloquent enough testimony. He reached the corner where Ho Fang Ho had been standing, and propped himself up against the wall feeling sick and dizzy. The exquisite agony caused by dragging his broken leg over uneven paving stones was almost as much as he could bear. He sat in a state of semi-stupor, longing for a cigarette.

From the dance hall appeared a short, stout man accompanied by two girls. He seemed to be rebuking them.

'I'm surprised at trim, tidy little craft like you, clean fore and aft if you take after your mamma, piloting me to a place like that.'

He was walking past Sales' house as he was speaking, both girls appearing much amused.

'In your indignation,' replied one in a very pretty voice, 'you are going in the wrong direction.'

'Well, why—' began the man, and stopped abruptly. He had trodden on the leg of someone half-sitting, half-lying on the pavement. The latter groaned, and fainted dead away. 'Sorry, mate,' apologised the stout man, and looked down, 'but if you will come to anchor – seems to me there's something wrong here.' He lit a match and, holding it cupped in his hand, bent over the silent figure. He gave a great start. 'Why, it's—' he cried; interrupted himself with a cough. He turned to the girls. 'Go and knock on the door of that house,' he directed, 'and tell them there's a man 'ere wot's fainted.' Batty gazed down at the man he knew as one of Sir Leonard's most brilliant assistants. 'Poor little cove!' he muttered *sotto voce*, 'I wonder wot they've been doing to you?'

CHAPTER FIFTEEN

Momentous Discussions

Late that night Sir Leonard Wallace sat in his study in Government House in conversation with his private secretary, Tommy Carter. His first full day in Victoria had been exceedingly busy. The morning had been spent with the Colonial Secretary, and in taking over the reins of government. During the afternoon he had held his first meeting of the Executive Council, followed by a garden party at which he and Lady Wallace had met the members of the Legislative Council, naval and military officers, and prominent citizens with their wives. At night he and Molly had attended a dinner given in their honour by the Executive Council. He lounged in his chair now in an attitude of pleasant relaxation, but, though he gave an impression of languid ease, his brain was working busily. Carter had been speaking and, for some seconds after he had ceased, there was silence. Sir Leonard sat gazing at the carpet, his chin sunk on his breast. Suddenly he looked up.

'What I want to find out,' he observed, 'is whether Cousins' usefulness out here is merely suspended temporarily or definitely ended. In other words, has this accident roused the suspicions of the people he is watching or not? From what Batty told you, it seems likely that he fell from some precarious position. The inferences are that, as the secret meeting would be on about that time, he was endeavouring to listen to what was being said or get a glimpse of the conspirators. Now, if they have guessed that, I shall not be able to use him out here again. In fact, I am afraid his life will be hardly worth a moment's purchase. On the other hand, they may think he fell from a veranda while under the influence of drink – you say Batty reported that he smelt strongly of spirits?' Carter nodded with a smile. 'Well,' went on Sir Leonard, 'we'll hope for his sake and ours that their suspicions are not roused. It's very annoying to be so much in the dark though. You're sure Batty couldn't add anything to what you've told me?'

'No, sir. I questioned him very closely. But perhaps you'd like to speak to him yourself. I told him to stand by.'

'Yes,' agreed Sir Leonard; 'tell him to come in. Make sure none of Wun Cheng Lo's myrmidons are about. How many men did he introduce on the staff – was it three or only two?'

'Three, sir, and I'm keeping a fatherly eye on them all. By the way, I also had Sergeant Herrington's report concerning the Philippino Feodoro. He tracked him to a ramshackle house in Chai Wan. There appears to be an enormous family of Philippinos living there.'

'And their name?' shot out Sir Leonard.

'Feodoro, sir,' grinned Carter.

Wallace grunted.

'Gochuico, of course,' he commented, 'may have been the alias, and Feodoro the right name. Tell Herrington to put somebody, on whom he can rely, to keep an eye on the place, and watch for the appearance of the other two. They're probably on their way out on another boat – may arrive at any moment. Impress on him that the watchers must not be members of the police force.'

'Not!' repeated Carter in tones of surprise.

'I said "not",' nodded Wallace. 'The police are probably known to a man. Now call Batty.'

The ex-sailor entered the room with rather a sheepish air. Wallace smiled at him.

'I hear you went gay tonight, Batty,' he remarked.

'Well, no, sir,' replied the valet; 'not exactly, sir. You see it was like this, sir' – he leant confidentially towards his master – 'when I was stationed out 'ere way back in nineteen-ten, sir, I was very friendly like with a Chinese cove – beg pardon, sir, I mean gent – wot 'ad two daughters – fine pair of craft they was too, sir, both built for speed and grace as you might say, sir. I almost got married to 'em.'

'What both of them?' demanded Wallace in mock scandalised tones.

'Shouldn't 'ave been surprised, sir,' admitted Batty. 'You see they was as like as two peas, and I knew the old man would 'ave liked to 'ave 'ad me as a son-in-law. Anyhow I was sent 'ome before things got too 'ot, as you might say, sir—'

'I certainly would not say anything of the sort,' objected Sir Leonard, 'but come to the point. What I actually want to know is how you came upon Mr Cousins, and what happened to him.'

'Aye, aye, sir. I'll go full speed a'ead, sir. When you gives me shore leave tonight, sir, I thinks I'll go along and look up me old friends, if they're still living down Shauk Ki Wan way – that's where the old man used to 'ave 'is 'ouse, sir. Sure enough he was still there an' didn't look much older neither. One of 'is daughters is living with 'im – 'er 'usband died a year or two back. They was very glad to see me, and I was made very welcome, sir. The daughter has two daughters of her own now, sir, an' they're both as pretty as paint, sir. They've been in Europe, an' wear European clothes a darn sight better than some of our womenfolk – beggin' your pardon, sir – an' they talk English as well as I do.'

'The same problem appears to be repeating itself after twenty years,' murmured Sir Leonard to the grinning Carter. 'Come on, Batty! Much as I would like to dwell with you on the charms of your fair friends I—'

'They're not fair, sir,' Batty hastened to assure him. 'Their 'air's black like – black like—'

'You want Mr Cousins here to find an appropriate quotation for you,' interposed Wallace. 'Do get on!'

'Aye, aye, sir. Well, to cut a long story short, sir—'

'Thank goodness,' muttered his employer.

'The girls wanted to take me dancing,' continued Batty, not noticing the interruption. 'I 'aven't done anythin' in that line for a few years, but I didn't want to disappoint 'em like, so I went. We 'ove to in a dive near Chinatown, an' I soon saw it was no place for young gals, sir, full of dagoes and other craft sailing under queer colours. Soon's we 'ad dinner,

I up anchor an' took the gals in tow. As it 'appened, I took the wrong turning—'

'It seems to me you'd already done that,' commented the patient Wallace.

'I turned to the left instead o' the right, an' trod on a cove wot was lying on the pavement. I lit a match an' looked at 'im – it was Mr Cousins, sir, an' 'e smelt like a brandy cask, sir. 'E seemed to be in a dead faint, so I sent the gals to get 'elp from the 'ouse. When the Chinese servants wot came out saw Mr Cousins they got 'orribly excited, sir. One went in an' fetched out an old Portuguese cove, beggin' your pardon, sir, who called 'imself Sales. 'E also seemed to get in a fluster when 'e saw Mr Cousins. 'E said something to me about fallin' from a winder, but whether 'e meant Mr Cousins or someone else I don't rightly know – I s'pose it was Mr Cousins. 'E told the Chinks to carry 'im inside, and then 'e turned to me and said, "Thank you. Now you go", which seemed to me pretty cool cheek. But just then an English policeman came along. He asked a lot of questions; then started to help to carry Mr Cousins inside, and discovered that his leg was broken, an' pretty bad too from wot 'e said.'

Wallace smiled at Carter.

'The arrival of that police officer must have been a very bad blow to friend Sales,' he remarked. 'The last thing they desire, I imagine, is for the police to become interested in Cousins. Go on, Batty, what happened then?'

'When the copper – beg pardon, sir, police officer, sir – noticed the leg, he asked Sales if Mr Cousins was a friend or relation of 'is. The old cove said no – seemed a bit 'urt at the idea, 'e did too – and the bobby said 'e'd 'ave Mr Cousins removed to 'orspital. Old Sales said 'e'd 'ave 'im looked after there, an' seemed mighty upset at the notion of 'is being took away. But it wasn't no use – an ambulance was sent for, Mr Cousins was 'oisted aboard, an' the police officer went with 'im to the 'orspital.'

Sir Leonard looked straight at him.

'You didn't, by any chance, mention Mr Cousins' name or that you had any knowledge of him, did you?' he asked sharply.

'No, sir,' replied Batty promptly, ''ad too much to do with the service, sir, to foul 'is cables like that. Guessed 'e must be on a job o' some sort, sir.'

Sir Leonard smiled slightly.

'Well, listen, Batty,' he observed. 'You don't know him from Adam. His name happens to be George Collins, and he's merely a beachcomber or on the way to becoming one. Do you understand?'

Batty grinned.

'Aye, aye, sir.'

'From what Batty has told us,' Sir Leonard turned to Carter, 'it is impossible to know what that fellow Sales was thinking. You say he was very much perturbed?' he asked, eyeing the valet.

'Yes, sir. 'E was in a regular stew, sir.'

'Did he seem angry? You did not see him casting vindictive looks at Mr Cousins?'

The ex-sailor shook his head.

'Nothing like that, sir,' he declared with conviction. ''E was just upset at the occurrence as you might say, sir, though I don't rightly know wot it 'ad to do—'

'No; of course you don't.' Wallace cut him short.

'All right, Batty that'll do. It is a good thing you were on the spot. You have brought us information that we might not have heard for days, perhaps weeks.'

The ex-sailor's round face beamed with pleasure.

'Glad to 'ave been o' service, sir,' he remarked. 'It's a lucky thing the gals set a course to that there restaurong, sir.'

'It is indeed,' agreed Wallace. A thought occurred to him, and he stopped Batty as the latter was about to leave the room. 'Tell me,' he demanded: 'Did you mention your name or connection with Government House at all?'

'No, sir,' Batty assured him.

'The police officer did not know you?'

'No, sir.'

'I suppose the Chinese girls know of your connection with me?'

'Yes, sir, but they didn't say a word, sir; never opened their mouths.'

'You're sure of that?'

'Take me oath, sir.'

Sir Leonard sat in thought for a few minutes.

'Do you think Sales or the Chinese servants knew them?' he asked presently.

'Didn't seem to, sir. Come to think of it, one o' them asked me arterwards who 'e was.'

'Good. That seems satisfactory, anyway. All right, Batty. I'll be coming to bed in about half an hour.'

'Aye, aye, sir.'

The ex-sailor quietly left the room. Sir Leonard vacated his chair, and began to pace to and fro.

'It is most unfortunate that this should have happened,' he observed to Carter, 'just when Cousins seemed to have been getting a grip on things. Poor fellow, he'll be thoroughly fed up. I wonder if he saw anything of the conspirators or heard the discussion. Somehow we must find out, Carter, but how is it to be done?'

The two men spent several minutes in deep reflection. Wallace continued to walk backwards and forwards; his assistant stood thoughtfully by the desk.

'How about sending Batty to talk to him, sir?' asked the latter at length. 'It would seem a natural sort of thing for the man who had found him to go to the hospital, and visit him, wouldn't it?'

Sir Leonard stopped; looked at him for a moment; then shook his head.

'It would not be wise;' he decided. 'Sales and Tavares are sure to keep a watch on Cousins and, if Batty turned up to visit him, they would find out who he is.'

'Would that matter, sir?'

'Of course,' returned Wallace a trifle sharply. 'Don't you think it would strike them as curious that on two occasions, innocent though they may appear, someone connected with me visited him? Cousins' behaviour on the pier when we arrived, and your subsequent visit to him in his cell at the police station is natural enough when it stands as a solitary incident, but if Batty, who they would quickly discover was my manservant, went to him in hospital, their suspicions might very easily be roused. Men in their position are certain to be on the *qui vive* all the time, ready to put a construction, to suit their own fears, on anything that has the slightest appearance of being in the least strange. It was a pure coincidence that Batty should come upon Cousins when he was lying there with a broken leg. But they are hardly likely to regard it as coincidence, if they discover who he is. Oh, well, we'd better sleep on it.'

'Perhaps Cousins' Chinese servant will have a message, sir.'

'That's not very likely. He may, of course, have a note given to him by Cousins before the accident, but that will not throw any light on what I want to discover. In any case you'll meet him in the morning. If possible, find out if he knows anything of what has befallen his master. There is no reason why he should not go to the hospital. But you'll have to be very careful. On no account must you be seen by any of the spies of this organisation talking to him, and I'm beginning to feel that they are everywhere. Cousins may still be able to continue playing the same role when he leaves hospital. That will not be for six weeks or two months, I'm afraid. I had hoped to have finished the whole business in less than that time.' He sighed. 'It looks very much as though you and I will have to start all over again. Poor Cousins! Goodnight.'

He went off abruptly to bed.

On the following morning Carter took the same precautions as before to put the men watching him off the scent. They again used the small car, which Carter decided showed a lack of wisdom on their part. When he entered St Joseph's Church, however, they turned back, apparently satisfied that his expedition was the perfectly harmless act of a religious man. He redoubled his precautions on the way to the Botanical Gardens, though he had no reason to believe that they would have set a watch for him elsewhere. Carter, as a matter of fact, had begun to feel a sense of contempt for the men spying on Government House, but nobody realised more than he that it never does to underrate one's opponents. In the gardens he took elaborate precautions, making his way to the monkey house by devious and unfrequented paths, often doubling on his tracks. As a consequence, he found Ho Fang Ho already at the rendezvous when he arrived.

He rubbed his hands together to show that he had no message, but the Chinaman made no gesture. Carter concluded, therefore, that Cousins had, after all, given the man a letter for him. They brushed by each other, and a missive, folded into as small a size as possible, was thrust into his hand. At the same time the Englishman stole a quick glance at the other's face, and noticed that the slant eyes held a look in which perplexity and anxiety seemed equally blended.

'Follow me,' muttered Carter. 'I want to talk with you.'

He walked on, not troubling to look back. In a very quiet part of the gardens, a place he had previously noted, where it was impossible for anybody to approach without being observed, he sank on to a seat. Nearly a minute went by; then Ho Fang Ho came quietly along, to stand a few yards away looking inquiringly at the Englishman.

'Sit at the other end,' directed the latter, 'and pretend that you have nothing to do with me.' Ho Fang Ho obeyed, and sat looking ahead of him, an expression of bland unconcern on his face – a little too bland, perhaps, Carter thought. 'Your name is Ho Fang Ho, I believe,' he began, 'and your master tells me you are very loyal and faithful to him. Do you understand me?'

'Me plenty undelstand,' came from the Chinaman, whose lips hardly seemed to move. 'My master too muchee good master; Ho Fang Ho belong allo time tlue to him – allo lifee him boy.'

Carter was a little bothered by the pidgin English at first, but became used to it as the conversation proceeded. He learnt from Ho Fang Ho about the disappearance of Cousins from the Hotel Paris, and that the Chinese boy had been ordered to pack his bag, afterwards being told he was no longer required. Carter gave him a word of congratulation, when he was told how he had tracked the man with the suitcase to Sales' house and subsequently established communication with his master.

'Me tinkee him plisoner,' declared the Chinaman, and Carter was inclined to agree with him.

Ho Fang Ho went on to describe how Cousins had made signs for him to return at eight, and the manner in which the letter was lowered to him from the balcony.

'I see,' commented Carter thoughtfully, when the boy had finished. 'It looks very much as though the poor old chap overbalanced somehow, and fell from the veranda.'

An exclamation from the Chinaman caused him to turn towards the other. He had almost forgotten the boy's existence for the moment; had been speaking more or less to himself.

'You talkee master fallee?' demanded Ho Fang Ho, his eyes eagerly and anxiously searching his companion's face.

Carter nodded.

'It must have been after you left him,' he replied. 'He was found with a broken leg, and taken to hospital.'

At once Ho Fang Ho was all concern. He declared his intention of visiting the hospital immediately. Carter smiled sympathetically, but pointed out to him that there were certain hours set for visitors, and hospital rules were generally enforced except under special circumstances.

'When you go,' he warned the other, 'be careful to make no mention of me. Other ears may be listening – ears belonging to men who would harm our master.'

Ho Fang Ho nodded.

'Me too muchee savvy,' he asserted. 'Me go looksee master, because me belong him boy.'

'I am beginning to understand,' smiled Carter, 'why Mr Collins likes you and trusts you. You are a good fellow, Ho Fang Ho.'

The Chinaman beamed; then grew serious again.

'Master velly bad hurt?' he inquired.

'His leg is badly broken, I believe. I have no reason, though, to fear that there were any other injuries. You will be able to find out. By the way, Ho Fang Ho, how will you explain your knowledge that your master is in hospital. You may be asked by someone, and you must not say I told you.'

A broad smile appeared on the Chinaman's face. His slant eyes screwed up until they appeared nothing but slits.

'Ho Fang Ho go plesently talkee man belong house where me tinkee master plisoner. Me tellee him master talkee me him fliend. Me wantchee looksee. Him tellee me master blokee leg – go catchee hospital.'

Carter looked puzzled, but, when the boy's meaning dawned on him, he laughed.

'You certainly have a full share of commonsense, Ho Fang

Ho,' he approved. 'Meet me tomorrow as usual. Perhaps your master will give you a message for me.'

He strode away. Ho Fang Ho remained where he was for a little while then went off in the opposite direction.

Carter had to wait some time before he had an opportunity of relating to Sir Leonard Wallace what he had been told. Until lunch time the Governor was kept fully occupied with affairs of administration. Directly tiffin was over, however, he and Carter retired to the study and, behind locked doors, the latter told his story. Cousins' note was decoded, and read carefully by the two. Certain parts of it they both took care to memorise. Afterwards Sir Leonard sat back in his chair thinking deeply, while his assistant destroyed every trace of the message they had received.

'Well, we are not quite so much in the dark now,' remarked the former at length. 'It seems fairly obvious that in attempting to listen to the discussion Cousins fell and was injured. It is absolutely necessary to find out as soon as possible whether he is under suspicion. He will probably be able to tell us that himself.'

'No doubt he will give Ho Fang Ho a note to give me,' put in Carter, 'so we ought to know tomorrow.'

Sir Leonard shook his head.

'His chances of writing notes in a hospital ward, where he is constantly under observation from patients in other beds, nurses, and doctors are not very great. No; I'm afraid we can't depend on the Chinaman as an intermediary now – not to the same extent at all events. Either you or I must have a talk with Cousins. That is essential before we can decide on our future plans.'

'How will that be possible, sir?' asked Carter.

'I have not quite made up my mind yet. We'll return to the matter presently. I am wondering what Tavares and company will do, now that Cousins is laid up. If his idea is correct, that he was to be the instrument to remove me out of the way, and it certainly appears so to judge from the lengths they seem to have gone to get him into their power, they will probably be greatly angered by the accident. It will mean that their plans will have to be altered.'

'It will also mean,' put in Carter significantly, 'that we no longer know from which direction the attack will come.'

Sir Leonard smiled.

'I think we can be fairly certain,' he replied, 'that it will be engineered by Wun Cheng Lo and, since we are not blind to his part in the scheme of things, I am confident that I shall not be caught napping. There is the possibility that, having taken such elaborate steps to obtain a hold over Cousins, they will wait until he is about again. If that is their intention, it will depend, of course, on what I do in the meantime.'

'They will expect you to commence operations at once, sir.'

'Exactly. Unless we are unlucky, however, they won't know what those operations are. Until we have some sort of proof in our hands concerning the identity of the ringleaders, we shall have to work very quietly and secretly. This is a case in which somebody in high authority is concerned and, for that reason, Carter, we must trust nobody.'

'Nobody, sir?'

'Nobody at all,' replied Sir Leonard firmly. 'Whatever steps you or I take must be taken without the knowledge of a soul in this colony. You understand?'

'I understand, sir.'

'The description Cousins has given us of the two houses run by Tavares and Sales, and the private way of communication between them, may turn out to be very useful. Later on one or both of us will find a way in, and make a thorough examination. It is likely that in the office of which Cousins speaks, or elsewhere in the buildings, there may be a vital clue, and we must find it.'

'Is the description of the man who entered the office, when he was there with Tavares, likely to help, do you think?'

Wallace shrugged his shoulders.

'Not much I am afraid,' he replied. 'It might apply to so many men. Once we are in a position to narrow down the suspects it will be helpful but not before.'

Carter eyed him curiously.

'Do you already suspect some people then, sir?' he asked eagerly.

Sir Leonard looked straight at him.

'I suspect everybody who has held an official position in Hong Kong during the last eight or ten years.'

Carter whistled softly to himself. He watched curiously as Sir Leonard rose suddenly from his chair, and walked round the room, stopping now and again to examine an article. The Governor opened all the drawers of the desk one by one, looked within, and closed them again. Presently he turned to his assistant; there was a strange glint in his steel-like grey eyes.

'What time did you get back from the gardens?' he asked.

'About eleven sir,' was the reply.

Wallace nodded.

'I left for the secretariat at ten,' he observed; 'that would give him ample time.'

Carter looked puzzled.

'Who, sir?' he asked, 'and what—'

'Wun Cheng Lo I suppose. He is taking full advantage of his right to come and go as he wishes. This room has been systematically searched, and by a man who understands the job. It may not actually have been done by Wun Cheng Lo himself – possibly one of the men he has added to the staff is an expert at that sort of thing.'

'Shall I—'

'You won't do anything at all. Nothing will ever be left about to give a clue to the steps our investigations are taking. They can search, therefore, until they are black in the face with their exertions, if they like – so long as they continue to tidy up after them. I hate untidiness.'

He continued to wander round the room. Suddenly he approached the door, took hold of the handle, and pulled it open. Into the room stumbled a servant attired in the livery of Government House. Sir Leonard caught him by the collar; jerked him to his feet. The fellow stood with bowed head while his captor sternly surveyed him.

'What were you doing?' asked the latter sternly.

'Excellency, me polishee door handle,' began the servant.

'Don't lie!' He turned to Carter. 'Take him to the butler,' he ordered, 'with instructions to see that he is discharged immediately.'

The Chinaman commenced to protest, but Carter took him by the arm, and ran him from the room. While his assistant was away, Sir Leonard continued to pace to and fro, his eyes glancing from one place to another without cessation. He was quietly making certain that nothing of an inimical nature had been placed in the room. It was not that he suspected an attempt so crude would be made on his life, but he left nothing to chance. After about five minutes, Carter returned.

'It was one of the new men, sir,' he informed his chief. Wallace nodded.

'Exactly as I thought. Do you know if Wun Cheng Lo is anywhere in the house?'

'I don't think so, sir. Do you want him?'

'No; but I thought he would be interested to know that one of his men had blundered. I'm afraid the poor fellow will have a bad time of it. They are not likely to be mild in their treatment of blunderers.'

'How did you guess he was there, sir?'

'While I was looking round I noticed that a shaft of sunlight was shining through the keyhole, probably from the window across the corridor. It suddenly disappeared. Yet the sun continued to shine in here through that window over there. I cannot congratulate Wun Cheng Lo on the perspicacity of his henchmen.'

'Do you think he heard anything, sir?' asked the young man anxiously.

'I thought I had told you this room is practically soundproof.' He looked round at the rather ornate, heavy furniture. 'That is the only reason I like it,' he added. He returned to his seat, a smile chasing away the sternness on his face. 'I have made up my mind to visit Cousins myself,' he announced. 'Lady Wallace is the guest of the Chinese

Women's Association, and will not miss me, therefore. Everybody else will think I am busy in here with affairs of administration.'

'But how—' began his curious secretary.

'Do you think you can obtain for me the complete habit of a Capuchin priest from the Catholic Cathedral or St Joseph's Church, Carter, without causing a lot of inquisitiveness?'

The young man grinned.

'I think so, sir. I'll try, anyhow.'

'Go then, and be as quick as you can. Take a car, so that you can hide your bundle, and bring it to me by way of one of the side doors. Be careful that nobody sees what you have with you.'

'I shall probably be followed, sir. I always am.'

Sir Leonard nodded.

'Just think, Carter,' he murmured, 'what a saintly reputation I am helping you to obtain. The Chinese will soon be giving you a name which translated will mean, "the young man who lives in Church".'

CHAPTER SIXTEEN

A Friar Visits the Hospital

Less than two hours later a benevolent-looking friar of the Capuchin Order of Franciscans passed through the main gates of Government House. His tropical habit fitted his rotund figure unusually well, the girdle and beads swung rhythmically as he walked, his hands were enclosed in his flowing sleeves, from an unsuspected pocket peeped the top of a breviary. His bushy grey eyebrows, rosy cheeks, and long flowing grey beard gave him a patriarchal aspect, but a pair of piercing grey eyes, partially hidden by his *pince-nez*, stole searching glances at the many loungers squatting or reclining in the vicinity. Few took any notice of him. Were there not many priests like him at the Catholic Cathedral or the Church of St Joseph? There may have been some there who casually reflected that they had not seen him go in, but there is more than one way of entrance to the grounds of Government House. A sedan chair was standing by the side of the road, its coolies squatting close by. At his signal they sprang to their feet. In excellent Chinese – learnt that afternoon from a book entitled *Conversational Chinese* – he directed them to convey him to the civil hospital. He took his seat, was lifted from the ground, and his two bearers went swinging along the road. No attempt was made to follow, in fact it is unlikely that anybody who had seen him emerge from the grounds of Government House gave a second thought to him. Those who had looked up quickly resumed their attitudes of complete relaxation, for the afternoon was very hot and the shade of the trees most welcome.

The Capuchin, his white topee pulled well forward to shade his eyes, read his breviary as he was carried along. He seemed to have no eyes for the life round him. Not that there was a great deal, for nobody ventures out in the heat of the day, if he or she can possibly avoid it, and his way lay mainly through residential districts. They came at last to the hospital, the coolies let him down, and stood by mopping their perspiring faces, while he sought for and found money for them. Inside he made his way to the office, and a Chinese clerk politely inquired his business.

'I am not ze regular veesitor 'ere,' he explained in somewhat laboured English, 'but I 'ave been ask to veesit a poor man wiz broken legs. There will, I 'ope, be no deeficulty.'

The clerk shook his head with a smile.

'Clergymen,' he explained in perfect English, 'have no restrictions imposed on them.'

'Zo. Eet is vat I sought – can I go to heem?'

'What is his name, sir?'

'Ah! Zo stupid am I. Hees name are George Collins.'

'Just a minute please.'

The clerk studied a register; then called an attendant whom he directed to show the reverend gentleman to the ward where the patient, George Collins, lay. The priest thanked him, and went off in the wake of the barefooted native. Outside the ward he was met by a sister, who smiled brightly at him. He removed his topee, and bowed, showing a mop of grey hair, thin on top, but that may, of course, have been the tonsure. To her he again laboriously explained his mission.

'Oh, yes,' she nodded, 'Collins is in bed number five. The poor fellow broke his leg last night. I am afraid he is rather down and out, Father; the type of man who has let himself go to—' She blushed a little, and hesitated.

'Ah, yes, I know,' he supplied for her. 'You mean, he go to ze devil?'

She laughed.

'More or less, Father – a drunkard I am afraid. But one can't help liking him – he has such a jolly face. I am glad you came to see him. It will cheer him up.'

'Yes, I 'ope zo. He has no friends I zink?'

'No real friends, I believe, except a man who is in a private ward suffering from DT's.'

'Vat is zat?'

'A disease brought on by drink.'

'Ah! Zey are vat you call birds of a fezzar; no? Zere are no ozzer friends?'

She smiled and shook her head.

'A Portuguese gentleman came to see him this afternoon – the accident took place outside his house. Will you come with me, Father?'

She piloted him to bed five, where Cousins lay a little wan and haggard, but otherwise cheerful. A cradle kept the bedclothes from his leg, which had been set, and was now encased in plaster of Paris.

'This reverend gentleman has called to see you, Collins,' she announced, and turned to the priest. 'Would you like a screen placed round the bed, Father?'

'Yes, zank you. I zink eet a leetle more private will be – no? You are zo much kind.'

'Not at all.'

The nurse gave orders accordingly, after which she left the two alone. Cousins was looking a trifle puzzled. He could not understand why a priest should visit him, unless Sales or Tavares had sent him, but why should they do that? He looked inquiringly at the bearded friar, who was contemplating him with a genial smile.

'Ve are now all alone,' observed the latter, 'and will 'ave a leetle talk. First I must tell you zat I am zo zorry ze leg are broke. Eet is much pain – no?'

'Not so bad now, thank you,' replied Cousins, the look of perplexity still on his face.

'Eet is broke much?'

'Compound fracture of the tibia,' he was informed.

'Poor old chap,' came the sympathetic tones of Sir Leonard Wallace, 'what rank bad luck!'

It says a lot for Cousins' power of self-control that he showed none of his amazement in his face. His hands, however, involuntarily clutched at the bedclothes.

'We shall have to talk in whispers,' went on Wallace, giving an approving nod, as though in acknowledgement of the other's self-restraint. 'The screens were a happy idea – save too much acting.'

'By Jove, sir!' murmured Cousins, 'it is good to see you, but aren't you taking a risk?'

Wallace shook his head.

'Not much risk in this,' he declared. 'What more natural than that a clergyman should come to see you? I chose the Franciscan habit because it is fairly common here, and makes a much better disguise than just an alpaca suit and a Roman collar, besides it enabled me to wear a beard.'

'I should never have known you,' admitted Cousins in tones of admiration, and quoted softly, '"For he was of that stubborn crew | Of errant saints, whom all men grant | To be the true Church Militant". Did you have the things with you, sir?' he asked.

'The beard is one of a collection, so is the wig – you'd be surprised what I possess in that way. Carter obtained the habit – I rather suspect he stole it, temporarily that is. Now tell me what happened to you.'

Cousins quietly but graphically related the whole story, from the time of his escape from the room in which he had been locked up to the moment that someone had trodden on his leg and caused him to faint. Sir Leonard listened with careful attention, making no attempt to interrupt him. The only time his mouth opened at all, during the recital, was to murmur his approval when Cousins described how, he had crawled to the corner of the house, dragging his broken leg behind him, in order that he would not be suspected of having fallen from the vicinity of the window at which he had been listening. He was astonished to hear that Batty was the man who had stepped on him.

'How extraordinary!' he exclaimed. 'That explains how you knew I was here – I was wondering.'

'Do you think the suspicions of your Macanese friends will have been roused by what has happened?' asked Wallace.

'I'm positive they haven't,' returned Cousins. 'In fact I have proof. Sales came to see me this afternoon,' he smiled at the recollection, 'and subjected me to a tirade on the evils of too much brandy. He and Tavares are convinced that, in my drunken foolishness, I tried to climb down the side of the house, and fell. He told me I had had a miraculous escape – anybody but a drunken waster would have been certain to have been killed. On the whole, now that they have grown used to the idea, I am rather inclined to think they are of the opinion that my being in hospital is about the best thing that could have happened. It would have been rather a problem keeping the fellow they believe me to be shut up indefinitely.'

'Why indefinitely?'

'Because I am marked out as your assassin, sir, and the conspirators have decided to make no attempt on your life until they find that you are becoming too hot on their track.'

'Is that just conjecture?'

'No; it's fact.'

'But suppose I get hot on their track while you are in hospital?'

'Then they'll be forced to make other arrangements I daresay. But you'll want to know how I discovered this, sir.'

He plunged into an account of what he had heard, when standing in his precarious position outside the window. Again Sir Leonard listened without interruption, and he was so interested that, when the injured man stopped talking, he asked him to repeat the greater part of the conversation he had heard. His grey eyes were gleaming almost with triumph when, at last, Cousins concluded.

'You have done well, Jerry,' he whispered, 'very well indeed.' The little man felt a glow of pleasure at his words; even the broken leg did not seem so bad. 'We know now that the theft of the plans of fortification,' went on Sir Leonard, 'and the other scandal were engineered by the same people. That means that we actually have only to deal with one issue, which is all to the good, and will make things less complicated. We also have a clue to the identity of at least one of the conspirators. It's only a voice, true, but the cultured, well-bred voice of an educated Englishman should be recognisable.'

'That's what I felt, sir,' nodded Cousins, 'I'd know that voice again anywhere.' A rueful smile crossed his face. 'Unfortunately I'm not likely to hear it here.'

'Don't worry about that. You can search for the voice when you're able to get about again. In the meantime, Carter and I will carry on the job you've begun so well.'

'In your position you're badly handicapped though,' commented Cousins, adding with a groan: 'What a fool I was to get laid aside like this! I'll never forgive myself – never!'

'You're a fool to talk like that,' rebuked Sir Leonard, 'not for breaking your leg. That was sheer bad luck – few would have dared what you did.'

Cousins smiled. He felt he knew better. It was very decent of Sir Leonard, but—! The Chief was talking again, and he listened.

'Do you think the man you saw in Tavares' office the night before I landed is the fellow with the extra special voice?'

'No, sir,' replied Cousins. 'His was quite different – very ordinary in fact.'

'He appeared to have authority?'

'Undoubtedly. I should certainly say he was one of the leaders, but the other man is unquestionably the big noise.'

'Well, you have accomplished a great deal more than I expected in the time you have been here. You've seen one man; the voice of another – probably the ringleader – is impressed on your mind; you have discovered that the Japanese plot and Hong Kong conspiracy are bound up in each other, and—'

'And I have ascertained that no attempt will be made on your life, sir, until you show signs that you are getting on their track.'

Wallace waved his hand as though that were a matter of small moment.

'Altogether, Cousins,' he observed, 'you can rest easy. You deserve it and, although I am sorry in more ways than one that you have broken your leg, you deserve a rest. I might come to see you again in this garb, but don't expect me – it is better not to take too many risks. If you hear anything from Sales or Tavares – I suppose they'll make periodical visits to remind you that you are a murderer, and in their power – send along Ho Fang Ho to the gardens. Carter will go there daily just in case. By the way, I must congratulate you on that boy of yours. He certainly seems to be one in a thousand.'

'One in a million, sir. Can you get word to him that I am here? It won't do any harm, and he'll keep me amused.'

'Carter told him this morning. He'll be along as soon as they let him in. I don't think there is anything else at present. You'd better keep up the impression that you are craving for brandy. By the way, how's your friend?'

'I hear he is improving, sir. It would be great if he got over the craze.'

'Taken a fancy to him, haven't you?'

'He's a good sort, Sir Leonard. I can't say that we're exactly in the Pylades and Orestes class yet, but I certainly like him. I thought at one time I might be able to use him – I didn't know then that he was in such a bad way. Would you mind taking these? They'll be safer with you.' He fumbled in the belt round his waist, presently producing the tiny code book, and certain other papers. Wallace nodded, and slipped them under his habit into a pocket. 'The note I received from you last night is there also,' Cousins told him. 'I haven't had a chance of decoding it.'

'It doesn't matter now. It only urged on you the necessity of listening in to that meeting if you could, and of keeping yourself on the alert for an opportunity to search Tavares' office and the room where they hold their meetings.' He rose to his feet, shook Cousins warmly by the hand, and smiled. 'Zo,' he observed, 'eet is time now zat I go – yes? You become tired, is eet not zo?'

Cousins smiled a trifle wistfully.

'God!' he whispered, 'how I wish I could go with you. Give my salaams to Tommy, sir.'

Wallace nodded, pushed aside one of the screens, and stepped through the gap. He cast an eye at the neighbouring beds, and assured himself that they contained serious cases.

It was out of the question that he and Cousins could have been heard; the conversation had all along been conducted in whispers. The same sister whom he had seen before hurried up to him.

'I am sure your visit has done him a lot of good, Father,' she observed. 'It was nice of you to come.'

''E is a goot man gone wrong,' came the reply. ''E vant the brandy all zee time – eet is ver' sad.'

She accompanied him to the door of the ward, and was about to bid him farewell, when a young Chinaman hurried up to her. His slant eyes were full of trouble.

'Please, missisy,' he pleaded, 'you lettee me go talkee my master. Him blokee leg. Me too muchee wully. Waitee plenty long time.'

The priest pinched his ear.

'Zuch devotion is goot,' he commented. 'Your master told me you vas a ver' goot poy. You vill led him go?' he asked, turning to the sister.

She smiled.

'Very well,' she agreed, 'you can go, but don't stop too long.'

Ho Fang Ho beamed his gratitude. He bent down and kissed first the sister's hands; then those of the priest.

'Tank you, Fader,' he murmured; 'tank you, missisy. Ho Fang Ho belong too muchee happy now.'

He hurried away. Sir Leonard walked thoughtfully down the stone steps, and out of the building. There was a slight mistiness in his eyes – it might, of course, have been caused by the glare, as he emerged into the open. He called a ricksha, and was conveyed as far as the barracks. There he dismissed the conveyance, and toiled up the hill, eventually reaching a different entrance to Government House from that by which he had gone out. A sentry eyed him curiously but made no objection to his entry. Inside stood an English police sergeant who approached him questioningly.

'I 'ave ze appointment viz ze Governor's private zecretary,' announced the priest.

'You have come in the wrong gate, sir,' smiled the other. 'Never mind, I'll – why, there is Mr Carter.'

He escorted the friar to the tall, athletic-looking young man, who was apparently taking a pre-dinner constitutional.

'This gentleman tells me he has an appointment with you, sir,' answered the sergeant saluting.

'Ah, yes,' exclaimed Carter. 'You are Father Augustine, are you not? The Polish priest on a visit to Hong Kong?'

Wallace bowed, and took the hand extended to him.

''Eet is ver' goot of you to receive me at zis hour,' he remarked.

'Not at all. Come this way, will you?'

He conducted the supposed visitor through a private doorway, up stairs very little used. A little later they entered Sir Leonard's dressing room without having been seen by a soul. Wallace was in excellent spirits.

'You'll have to help me out of these things, as you helped me into them, Carter,' he observed. 'Then you can take the habit back to the place where you obtained it, and I hope you escape being arrested for theft.'

Carter laughed.

'It's a marvellous get-up, sir,' he declared. 'It would take in anyone.'

'It has – even Cousins,' returned his chief.

While disrobing, he repeated the conversation he had had with the invalid, and they were deep in the discussion of their future plans when Batty entered to help dress his employer for dinner. By then the beard and wig were locked away, and the friar's habit packed up in a small suitcase. Carter went off to return the garments he had purloined, not too certain in his own mind that he would be able to replace them with the same ease and safety that he had taken them. However, he succeeded. Secret Service agents are, of necessity, experts at many things.

During the days that followed, Sir Leonard was kept extremely busy. From morning till night his engagements crowded on him so thickly that he was allowed practically no time to himself. The ill health of Sir Stanley Ferguson seemed to have left tremendous arrears of administrative work to be made up. Every day official business compelled his attendance at the Secretariat or at Government House in consultation with the heads of one department or another. The state of chaos into which affairs had been plunged by systematic mismanagement over a period of several years compelled complete reorganisation. Many officials, some of fairly high standing, had been broken in the scandal caused by the disclosures. A number were now in prison undergoing various terms of imprisonment, but the cunning and resource with which the whole affair had been managed had enabled those really responsible to escape scot-free. Every department in the colony, almost without exception, had been involved in some way or other, and Sir Leonard was forced to admit before very long that a man of superior brain must have controlled it all. He soon had evidence to prove that that brain was still at work. Day after day his engagement book was crammed full with obligations and functions it was impossible to avoid. Never was a governor so unremittingly occupied or so completely tied, and he became convinced that behind this was someone whose intention was to keep him so busy that there was no time left for him to devote to the secret investigations he had planned. Yet it was difficult to fathom how it was done, impossible to point to any official or any department responsible. It merely appeared to be the accumulation of work caused partially by the impotence of a man, who could not carry out his duties on account of ill health, and the tremendous confusion in administration, consequent upon the criminal and almost complete depletion of the Treasury.

Carter, as the private secretary of the Governor, was kept as busy as his chief, and was equally puzzled by the manner in which work almost mysteriously accrued whenever there promised a breathing space. It became apparent, as time went on, that deprived of outside aid, Sir Leonard was hopelessly handicapped. He felt as though a cordon were drawn round the office of Governor, both materially and abstractly, through which he could not pass. Not only was he kept constantly occupied with administrative work, and with what he regarded as a thoroughly irksome series of at-homes, garden parties, soirées, dinners and luncheons, but he knew his every movement was spied on, noted, and reported. Carter, to a lesser extent, felt the same. He continued his apparent churchgoing, but, before long, the men who had followed him were replaced by one or two others, and these entered the church behind him, rendering it impossible for him to continue on his way to the Botanical Gardens. He was thus prevented from meeting Ho Fang Ho, with the result that he and Sir Leonard had no means of telling whether Cousins had obtained news. Their lines of communication, so to speak, were entirely severed, and all the time the work of reconstruction continued to pile up before the Governor – masses of documents that required his immediate and careful consideration before sanction. He could not protest, or demand to know why it was deemed necessary that every detail of administration should be brought to him, without giving himself away to some extent; he was not willing to proclaim openly his real purpose in acting for Sir Stanley Ferguson. Besides, there would be a simple and convincing reply to such a demand; namely that, in the present state to which affairs in Hong Kong had been brought, responsibility for reorganisation must rest entirely with the head of the Government. It was clever – damnably clever.

All the time, quietly but thoroughly, he delved deeply into the ramifications of the conspiracy, searching ever for a clue that would give him a hint concerning the identity of the men he was determined to expose. But though he obtained a fairly complete comprehension of the magnitude of the plot, as he painstakingly went back step by step through the revelations, he was forced to admit failure. With amazing forethought, not a single incident, during the years that the conspirators had been engaged in their nefarious work, had been allowed to point even vaguely in any particular direction. Of course, there had been numerous arrests of clerks in the Treasury, Audit, and other departments, but they, Sir Leonard was convinced, had been catspaws. The Colonial Treasurer, at the time of the disclosures, had been a well-known official called Sanderson, whose reputation was practically unassailable. He, with the Chief Auditor, Whiteside, had immediately resigned, demanding an investigation into their affairs. Nothing in any way prejudicial to their characters was found. There had been negligence, that was all.

Over the whole affair loomed the sinister shadow of the Macanese banker Mathos. Originally a contractor who made money during the War, principally by grossly overcharging on work of inferior quality, he became interested in various small native banks in Canton, Macao, and Hong Kong. Later he formed a banking corporation of his own, which grew to be a very large concern. It was then that he began dabbling in Government securities, and, from a nightmare of contradictory evidence, emerged the appalling fact that bonds had been forged for enormous amounts, fictitious loans floated, and expenditure made to appear far in excess of that which it actually was. Mathos could not have engineered all that himself. He may have been the forger, but otherwise he could only have been the instrument through which the organisation behind him worked. That organisation, it was clear, must have been formed, at least partially, by men able to direct government finances, yet, though the finger of suspicion pointed unerringly at two or three individuals, who held high ministerial posts, not a shred of evidence against them could be produced. They had welcomed investigation and cross-examination, to emerge triumphant from both. With revelation came the fall of Mathos. Police were immediately sent to arrest him, but arrived too late. He had committed suicide. Proofs of his own guilt were found, but nothing at all involving others.

'And that,' remarked Sir Leonard Wallace to Carter, referring to the suicide of the Macanese banker, 'is the only little bit of hope I can find in the whole report that success will ultimately reward us.'

Carter looked puzzled.

'I'm afraid I don't understand, sir,' he murmured.

They were in the Governor's study one morning about three weeks after their arrival in Hong Kong and, for once in a way, were able to devote their attention exclusively to the matter which was uppermost in their minds, without being continually interrupted by officials importuning for interviews, or Government messengers carrying files of documents marked 'urgent'.

'I don't believe that Mathos did commit suicide,' declared Sir Leonard with conviction.

'You mean you think he was murdered?'

'Exactly. When you come to consider the type of man he was, and the records give a pretty fair estimate of his character, it is inconceivable that, at the first sign of danger, he should shoot himself. True, the police statement says that he was found sitting at a desk clasping a revolver in his hand, and the wound in his temple gave every indication of being self-inflicted. But why should he do it? He was immensely wealthy, he could have sought sanctuary in a number of places, where men fleeing from justice are known to take up their abode, and remained there for the rest of his life in ease and safety. Only a certain portion of his property was in this colony. The greater part of it was in Canton and Macao and, if he was afraid of settling down in either of those places for fear of the extradition laws, there was nothing to prevent his realising on his belongings, and directing that the proceeds be sent to him. But what strikes me as the most significant fact in favour of murder is that, although after his death various papers were found to prove his guilt, a systematic search failed to bring to light anything whatever implicating those who had intrigued with him against the government.'

'I thought a document was discovered which proved that certain members of the Legislative Council were involved, sir.'

'Yes; but the reference was, after all, only vague. No names were mentioned and, even without it, it was perfectly obvious to anybody that certain individuals, closely connected with administration, must have been deeply concerned in the plot. Is it likely that an unscrupulous blackguard, as Mathos undoubtedly was, would not have taken measures to protect himself in the event of exposure? Those measures would naturally take the form of undeniable proofs of the guilt of his colleagues. You may be sure that those proofs were in existence, but where are they now? He was murdered in order that they could be destroyed, Carter, and his mouth shut for ever. I think it likely that he made no secret of their existence, thinking that knowledge of that kind would be a deterrent against any notions of treachery in the minds of others. But he was not equal to them. They killed him, as they killed the Shanghai magistrate and the Chinese banker, to preserve inviolate their own connection with the conspiracy.'

Carter was very thoughtful for some minutes. Then he asked:

'Do you think a search of his residence and any concern

in which he was interested might, after all this time, reveal anything to us, sir?'

Wallace shook his head.

'No,' he decided; 'but I feel certain that a search of Tavares' premises would and, at the first opportunity, we shall go there.'

'Why Tavares'?' asked the other in surprise.

'Because he was Mathos' servant, and he is deeply concerned in the conspiracy. He knows the others; is working for them. For their own ends, I imagine, they have let him live. But Tavares, like Mathos, will have taken steps to protect himself. I shall not be satisfied, Carter, until I have ransacked that office of his.'

CHAPTER SEVENTEEN

Sir Leonard Becomes a Dictator

Several weeks went by, however, before Sir Leonard was able to put his project into action. He was kept as constantly occupied as ever. Any move he made to relieve himself of the manifold duties that continued to come his way was countered very adroitly. Everything had such an appearance of complete innocence all the time that, despite himself, he grew to admire the cleverness of those opposed to him. They had, of course, one great advantage over him. They must have been aware that he realised that obstacles were continually being put in his way to prevent his taking any private steps at investigation but, whereas they knew the two men whose presence in Hong Kong threatened danger to them, their own identities were screened. On the other hand, Sir Leonard knew that a good deal of the restraint imposed on his actions was due to the Chinese merchant Wun Cheng Lo.

Blissfully unconscious that his association with the conspirators was known, the latter appeared daily at Government House, always obsequious, always taking pains to give the impression that he was doing his utmost to assist, sometimes imparting false information which appeared significant but meant nothing. All the time he was doing everything in his power to tighten the girdle which was constraining the man he pretended to serve. At times Sir Leonard longed to give vent to his feelings by kicking him, but he consoled himself with anticipations of the very painful shock he would one day give the Chinaman by ordering his arrest.

It is quite certain that, during the weeks when his activities were so closely confined, Wallace was greatly worried. For once in his career, he felt baulked, and the possibility of failure occurred more than once to his mind. He even began to regret that he had accepted the appointment of governor; wished that he had insisted on carrying out investigations in his own way without being hampered by an office which he certainly had not desired. He had accepted it only because with it went full executive power, and he had thought in an emergency that might be of great value. He had not anticipated that the opposition would have proved so infernally clever. His belief that the three Phillipino brothers – who had called themselves Gochuico – were being employed by one of the ringleaders of the conspiracy, and would inevitably lead him to their master had not been fulfilled. Except that he knew that the man he believed to be one of them was in Hong Kong, he had heard nothing of them since. Sergeant Herrington – Batty's police officer friend, who had travelled out on the *Rawalpindi*, and who had been so useful in Singapore – was no longer available. He had been posted to Lan Tau island. He was the only man, apart from his own people, Sir Leonard had been disposed to trust. The scandal had caused a cloud of suspicion to hang over anybody who held an official position in Hong Kong and, until, as he put it himself, he saw daylight, he was unwilling to place reliance in a single soul. It began to look very much as though Wallace would have to await Cousins' recovery before he could continue his investigations on the lines he had mapped out. Through the instrumentality of Batty, who kept in touch with the hospital by means of cautious telephone inquiries from the house of his Chinese friends, it was learnt that Cousins' leg was proving most obstinate. The fracture had been a bad one, and two months went by before the little man was even able to hobble about the ward.

Lady Wallace had no inkling of the sinister force that hemmed in her husband. She often expressed herself as profoundly surprised that the governor of a colony should be kept so tremendously busy, but, on the whole, she was happier than she had been for a long time. For once she felt that her husband's duties were being performed in an atmosphere free from danger; besides, was she not always with him, or at least near him? It was no wonder, therefore, that she was enjoying every moment of her stay in Hong Kong. She entered into her social duties with zest, and revelled in the numerous entertainments and receptions she was called upon to attend. I do not think she will ever realise, unless she reads this narrative, that she was watched with almost the same care as that which noted every movement of

Sir Leonard's. It was wasted labour, however; it would never have occurred to her husband to use her to further any of his designs. One day she opened a new wing of the civil hospital and, during her inspection, actually passed through the ward in which Cousins lay. The Secret Service man nearly covered his head with the sheet, and pretended to be asleep. He knew Sir Leonard would not like her anxieties to be aroused by observing him there.

She became tremendously popular. Her beauty and charm won the hearts of everybody, and many there were who sighed regretfully at the thought that she would be in the colony for so short a time. Sir Stanley Ferguson was a bachelor and, though the wife of the Colonial Secretary had acted as his hostess, a married governor was an asset, especially when his wife had the character, personality, and gentleness of Lady Wallace. A keen motorist, she discovered, to her surprise, that Hong Kong possessed a beautiful motor road entirely encircling the island. Thenceforth, she spent as much time as she could on it, glorying in the unrivalled views to be obtained, especially from the windswept hill districts. She motored, too, through Kowloon and the New Territory, finding a never-ending source of enjoyment in the continually varying panorama of fascinating scenery over a run of several miles to Fanling by way of Tsuen Wan, Castle Peak, and Ping Shan, thence back by Tai Po and Lok Lo Ha on the shores of Tolo Harbour. She also made several trips in the large Government House launch, with her friends, to the many attractive spots which the seaboard had to offer her, steaming into the inlets of Mirs Bay, skirting the islands between Fung Bay and Fu Tau Mun, or bathing by moonlight in the placid stillness of the water under the shelter of Devils Peak. The only jarring note to her wholehearted enjoyment was the fact that her husband was so rarely able to accompany her. But, as he often said to her, once he had disposed of the business which occupied most of his time, he would be at liberty to go about with her more, and share in her pleasures. The trouble was that the business in question showed little signs of being disposed of during his term as Governor.

November had nearly gone, when occurred the incident that changed the whole tenor of events, and brought matters to a climax. The Legislative Council was sitting, and a heated debate took place one day on the subject of a loan required by Victoria Municipality for a new drainage scheme they proposed to put in hand. Although most of the members were in favour, there came violent opposition from others. One of those holding an unofficial seat, a wealthy English merchant noted for his bluntness, caused a profound sensation in the colony by some of his remarks.

'For thirty years I have lived in the east,' he declared, 'and during that time have seen many strange things, met strange people, and witnessed strange happenings. Unsavoury events have taken place, men and places, which previously could point to good reputations, have fallen into disrepute. But never, during all that time, has anything happened to equal, in its strange, unsavoury, scandalous, and altogether reprehensible character, the scandal which has come upon this colony, and dragged its good name into the mud. The affair has been hushed up, the press given no details, proper steps have not been taken to purify and purge the stench of dishonour that overhangs us. The time has come, I say, for that to be done without fear and without favour. Before making any grants for unnecessary schemes, let us put our house in order, restore our finances to their proper state of healthy solvency. This can only be done by rigid economy. I believe the Treasury is considering a new system of taxation in an effort to make good the loss of a hundred million dollars – a hundred million dollars that were stolen. Why should the inhabitants be made to stand the brunt of the sins of a few? I call upon his Excellency the Governor to put an end to the shilly-shallying which is going on under the name of an investigation. I ask him to sift to the bottom the scandal, clear from over our heads the heavy cloud of suspicion and distrust, and restore to Hong Kong the good reputation it hitherto enjoyed, irrespective of name or fame. Until that is done, I contend that there should be no grants, no loans whatever made for any fresh projects. It is high time we started afresh to build up what has wantonly been wrecked by trickery and crime of the most despicable and abhorrent nature. I, for one, am ready and eager to place at his Excellency's disposal every ounce of my brain and every bit of energy I can call upon to help him in a task he will not shirk. I admit publicly that I possess knowledge which should be of the utmost value. Hitherto I have remained silent, as I felt expediency required it. I demand that a debate shall take place on this point at tomorrow's session. I will then put before the house the information I possess.'

Sir Leonard was about to dress for dinner when the report of this remarkable speech was brought to him by Carter. The latter's eyes were dancing with excitement as he turned over the typescript sheets recording the afternoon's proceedings.

Sir Leonard read without comment but, when he came to the last sentence, he turned abruptly to his assistant. For once in a way he allowed his feelings to show in his face.

'Why was I not informed of this man's speech before?' he thundered.

'The first I knew of it, sir,' returned Carter, surprised by the unwonted vehemence in his chief's tone, 'was when I read it here.'

'More of their dastardly tricks,' snapped Wallace. He did not mention to whom he referred, but Carter knew. 'Get me the Inspector-General of Police on the telephone – hurry!'

The young Secret Service man hastened to obey. Sir Leonard took the receiver in his hand.

'Is that you, Winstanley?' he demanded and, without waiting for the other's reply, went on: 'Were you at the meeting of the Legislative Council today?'

'Yes, I was there, sir,' came the reply.

'Then how is it you did not immediately inform me of the speech made by Mr Burrows?'

'I hardly thought it necessary, sir. I knew you would receive a verbatim report in due course.'

'In due course!' echoed Sir Leonard acidly. 'Due course is correct. It is about four hours since that speech was made. What steps have you taken?'

'I'm afraid I don't understand, sir. Steps with reference to what?'

'Protecting Mr Burrows from possible assassins, of course.'

'Assassins, sir!'

'For Heaven's sake, man, don't repeat what I say like a parrot. Don't you realise that, after the remarks he has made, his life is very likely in grave danger?'

The Inspector-General pooh-poohed the idea.

'That was only a lot of hot air I think, sir,' he observed.

'Either you're a fool or you're asleep,' snapped Sir Leonard, and the I.G. removed the receiver from his ear, and looked at it as though it were distorting utterances in the most amazing manner. 'You know very well,' went on the Governor, 'what happened to the Shanghai magistrate and the Chinese banker who reported that they could give information regarding the conspiracy. If Burrows is murdered, I'll hold you responsible. Put your most reliable men on to guard him at once, and instruct them that they are not to let him out of their sight, even if they have to sleep with him. Report to me in the morning.' He replaced the receiver, cutting off an attempt by the aggrieved Chief of Police to justify his inaction. 'Even now it may be too late,' observed Sir Leonard to Carter, as though he took it for granted that the latter had heard both ends of the conversation. 'Hot air indeed! Burrows may or may not have valuable information to impart, but, if I am any judge, his life is now not worth an instant's purchase. He was courageous and honest, but damnably injudicious. I wish to God he had come to me. See if you can get him on the telephone, Carter.'

There was an expression in the steel-grey eyes which had not been there for some time. It almost looked, mused Carter, as though Sir Leonard had decided that the period of forced inactivity was due to end. The young man knew the signs – that glint, the manner in which the lips were pressed together, the firm jaw clenched, spoke of imminent activity. A feeling of elation began to take possession of him. He anticipated that Sir Leonard intended no longer to submit to the irksome shackles that bound him. He had hitherto resigned himself to them because it suited his plans, because he did not desire to rouse suspicion until he had something tangible to assist him in his operations, and because Cousins' accident had necessitated his waiting, if he were to rely on outside help. But now! Carter felt that, if he were any judge, the event of the afternoon had decided the Chief to wait no longer; in other words, he would emerge into the open, and show his hand. A thrill of excitement ran through the man who acted as the Governor's private secretary. It took him some time to get through to Burrow's house at the Peak. He then learnt that the man responsible for the commotion had left about half an hour previously with some friends bound on a moonlight launch picnic. Their destination, it was thought, was somewhere in the vicinity of Stonecutters Island. When this information was imparted to Sir Leonard, he laughed.

'Either he doesn't care,' he remarked, 'or he does not realise the danger he is in. A moonlight picnic! Could anything be more suitable to the purposes of men who desired to remove him? Let me see, what is the nearest police post to Stonecutters Island?'

That point was quickly settled, as a result of which Carter again went to the telephone, and rang up the police station at Sham Shui Po. He conveyed the Governor's orders to the officer in charge that the boat containing Mr Burrows and his friends was to be searched for, and a careful guard kept on the member of the Legislative Council by armed police. If he objected, he was to be told that the action was a protective measure expressly ordered by the Governor himself. When the picnic was over, the party was to be escorted to Victoria, where arrangements would be made for it to be met, and Mr Burrows to be accompanied to his home. The Inspector-General of Police was informed of the orders given to the officer in charge of Sham Shui Po police station, and asked to take the necessary steps for the picnic party to be met on arrival back in Victoria.

The head of the police was a disgruntled man that night. He felt that the Governor had interfered with his authority, and was making a large mountain out of a very small molehill. When it later transpired that the precautions taken by the latter had been the means of saving Mr Burrows' life, the IG changed his tone, and felt properly humbled. While the picnic party was disporting itself on Stonecutters Island a fast motor launch had suddenly appeared. On being challenged by the police boat it had made off again. It reappeared during the return journey to Hong Kong, and, in a desperate effort to kill Burrows apparently, had swept a hail of machine gun bullets along the deck of his launch. Orders had previously been given for everyone on board to lie down, however, and no one was hit. On fire being opened by the police boat the dastardly intruder made off, and disappeared. A chastened and apologetic Chief of Police rang up the Governor in the morning, and informed him of what had occurred.

'I will refrain from saying, "I told you so",' remarked Sir Leonard unkindly, 'but you can take it from me that I am thinking it. I suppose you have taken steps to trace the motor boat?'

'Yes, sir,' came the reply, 'but the chances are not very

great. No name or number, by which it would be identified, was seen. It was like many others here. It appeared to be manned by half a dozen Chinese.'

Wallace grunted.

'Is Burrows quite safe now?' he demanded.

'Perfectly. Two men are in the house with him, and others are in the grounds. I spoke to him on the telephone a few minutes ago. He seemed to be a badly scared man. I think, for his own safety, he should be advised to make a public announcement that he has changed his mind about the information he declared he would give to the Legislative Council today. Don't you agree with me, sir?'

'No,' snapped Wallace, 'if your men protect him adequately, there is no reason why he should not make his statement in perfect security. Once it is over, there is hardly likely to be much danger to him. His mistake was in standing up in the council chamber and making such a declaration publicly. He should have come to me, but since he has taken this course, he can hardly withdraw now.'

Nevertheless, he decided that it would be as well if he had an interview with Burrows prior to the latter attending the afternoon session of the Council. Carter was instructed to invite the merchant to lunch privately at Government House – there would be no other guests that day – and to go himself to see that the visitor was adequately guarded from the Peak to the Governor's residence. Every precaution he could devise for the safety of Burrows was taken by Wallace. Yet he did not feel satisfied. He knew very well that the men, whose liberty the merchant was threatening, would shrink from nothing to prevent him from making the statement they feared either before the Legislative Council or to the Governor.

Sir Leonard, as usual, spent a very busy morning. As half past twelve approached, however, he dismissed the officials who were then closeted with him, and gave instructions that nobody but Mr Carter and the gentleman who was expected to arrive with him were to be admitted to his study. He had directed Carter to time his arrival for half an hour or so before luncheon in order that he could have a conversation with Burrows before the meal. Sitting alone in his study, Sir Leonard glanced every few minutes at the clock, as the seconds ticked slowly by, making no attempt to suppress the anxiety he was feeling. The half hour came and went; slowly and inexorably the minute hand drew closer to the three quarters, reached it, and passed by. Then the telephone bell rang loudly, startlingly. With a hand that showed not a tremor, though his lips were pressed tightly together, he took up the receiver.

'This is Carter, sir,' came in a hoarse, unnatural voice, which Sir Leonard had difficulty in recognising as that of his secretary. 'Mr Burrows has – has been killed, sir.' Except for an involuntary clenching of his teeth, Wallace gave no sign of the horror Carter's announcement caused him.

'How did it happen?' he asked in quiet, almost matter-of-fact tones.

'The house was blown up by dynamite. It is an absolute wreck, and what is left of it is blazing fiercely.'

'When did it occur?'

'Not more than ten minutes before I arrived, sir.'

'Ah!' Sir Leonard's exclamation was eloquent. 'You are all right then?'

'I? Oh yes, sir. It had all happened before I reached here.'

'You're quite sure Burrows is dead?'

There was a pregnant little silence at the other end for a few seconds; then:

'I saw part of the remains myself. A policeman and a Chinese servant were killed also.'

'I see. You'd better come back at once. I'll be awaiting you in the study.'

Feeling sick at heart, Sir Leonard left the telephone. He resorted to his habit of pacing to and fro when deeply thoughtful or in a disturbed frame of mind. A servant came to announce luncheon, was told to convey his regrets to Lady Wallace, and inform her that he would be delayed for some time. He was still walking about when Carter entered the room. The young man's face was white; in his eyes was the recollection of dreadful things. He could add little to the information he had given over the telephone. By some means a large amount of dynamite had been smuggled into the house, the police were of the opinion that every room on the ground floor must have contained a quantity. Under the library was a kind of cellar, to which admittance could be obtained by means of a door leading from the garden. In this it was thought the greater portion of the dynamite had been placed, and a train lit leading to it. The merchant was working at his desk in the library when the first explosion occurred, followed immediately by several others. The house was practically blown to bits, the little that remained catching fire. Mr Burrows, a police officer who was on duty outside the library, and a Chinese servant were killed instantly, their bodies being practically torn to shreds. Carter shuddered at the recollection. Several other servants and one or two policemen who had been in the vicinity at the time had been badly injured. It was quite certain that, if there had been any documents in the house, relative to the information which Mr Burrows had threatened to divulge to the Legislative Council, they had been utterly destroyed. Carter had heard the explosions when approaching the house and, anxious with a sense of foreboding, had urged on the chair coolies, who were carrying him from the cable car station, arriving to view a scene of desolation and death that was horribly reminiscent of the War.

'Can you explain?' asked Sir Leonard in ominous tones, 'how it is the police allowed anyone to enter the house and place sticks of dynamite in the rooms in broad daylight, also to permit an individual to light a train in a cellar where another stack of dynamite had been placed?'

'I thought it probable that the dynamite was put in position last night, sir,' ventured Carter, 'when Burrows was out.'

'It may have been, of course,' admitted Sir Leonard. 'But if so, why should there have been such a determined attempt made on his life last night? In any case the scoundrel who lit the train must have entered the cellar in broad daylight.'

'He could have approached the house by means of a nullah, sir, which offered ample opportunities of concealment. Then from the nullah to the cellar door there is a mass of thick undergrowth.'

'The police should have watched the nullah and examined

every inch of the cellar,' snapped Wallace. 'Come along to tiffin.'

Lady Wallace had waited, preferring to have a late luncheon with her husband rather than an earlier one alone. She expressed surprise at the absence of the guest she had been told was expected. There was no point in keeping news of the tragedy from her. She would be bound to hear it. Sir Leonard told her, dwelling a little on the reason that had caused it. She caught a look in his eyes that spoke of the cold, unemotional fury that was consuming him, and shivered a little. For the first time, since arriving in Hong Kong, she sensed danger threatening her husband and, hardly knowing why, began to fear for him.

It was extraordinary how long the news of the tragedy took to spread through Hong Kong and Kowloon. Once it was known what had happened, it circulated like wildfire, of course, but few people knew that anything out of the ordinary had occurred before the deputy president of the Legislative Council made his announcement. The Council Chamber was full, the visitors gallery packed to suffocation, when the session began. Necks were craned and eyes strained by the curious to catch a glimpse of the man who had demanded a debate on the Hong Kong scandal, and had promised to impart publicly information that was generally expected to be of a most sensational character. An air of expectancy seemed to hang over the men taking their places in the hall and the crowded gallery above. When nothing could be seen of Mr Burrows, tongues began to wag, people turned questioningly to each other, one or two there were who spoke sneeringly about cold feet. All eyes were fastened on the deputy president as he took his place on the rostrum. He was a small, slight man, bent and rather wizened, who seemed somehow a pathetic figure as he stood there. He made no attempt to seat himself. Instead he remained looking round him, his fingers beating an agitated tattoo on the table before him.

'It is my very sad and painful duty,' he remarked at last in a thin, weedy voice, 'to announce that our honourable and very esteemed colleague, Mr Cedric Burrows, an unofficial member of this Council, is dead. He was killed shortly after noon today.'

A gasp of incredulous horror came involuntarily from the people assembled in the building. The deputy president sank into rather than sat in his chair, and one by one the others took their seats as though fearful of making a noise. The Colonial Secretary rose slowly to his feet again.

'In rising to move that this house be adjourned,' he began, 'out of respect for the memory of one whom—'

There came a dramatic interruption. Into the hall stalked Sir Leonard Wallace, closely followed by Captain Barker, his aide-de-camp, and Carter, his secretary. As the members of the Council rose to their feet, he looked grimly from one to another. The deputy president slid unobtrusively from the dais as though anxious to be relieved of his duties, now that the Governor had arrived on the scene. Sir Leonard quietly took his place. He continued to eye the faces raised rather interrogatively to his, and there were many present who began to wonder what had previously given them the impression that the Governor was a mild type of man. They felt suddenly compelled to revise their opinions. There was something in his expression that caused an uneasy feeling to run coldly down their spines. At last he spoke, and his tone was bitter, unemotional, and relentless, as though every vestige of human feeling had been drained from it.

'Today,' he declared, 'a cold-blooded murder has been committed. A member of this Legislative Council has been cruelly done to death in a most dastardly manner, undoubtedly in order to prevent him from giving information likely to bring certain malefactors to justice. I refer to the men responsible for the conspiracy that has cast a blot on the administration of this colony and thrown the finances into a state of chaos. This is not the first murder. A magistrate stationed in Shanghai and a banker living here in Victoria both lost their lives, because they declared they could supply intelligence regarding the plot. Yesterday Mr Cedric Burrows publicly asserted that he could do the same. He is dead. He demanded a debate, and called upon me to put an end, to use his own words, to "the shilly-shallying which is going on under the name of an investigation". He has not called upon me in vain. He asked me, and again I quote his words, "to sift the scandal to the bottom, irrespective of name and fame", and clear away the heavy cloud of suspicion and distrust that is overhanging this Legislative Council. I am here to declare my intentions. I will not rest until the conspirators are exposed, and the administration of the colony restored to the state of healthy purity usual under the British flag. While the finger of suspicion continues to be pointed at every member of the Executive and Legislative Councils, they cannot continue to function. For the present I will delegate to myself the duties of all official members, with the single exception of that of the General Officer commanding troops, who has recently taken up his appointment, and cannot be involved. Until the conspirators stand unmasked, the members of the Executive and Legislative Councils, official and non-official, are suspended with effect from today. *This house is adjourned sine die.*'

The gloves were off with a vengeance. Every man there stood dumbfounded as though rooted to the spot. In the midst of an amazed silence, Sir Leonard Wallace walked out.

CHAPTER EIGHTEEN

The Man Who Killed Himself

To state that Sir Leonard's drastic action caused a sensation is to put it mildly. From one end of the British Empire to the other intense surprise was expressed, but with it, in most cases, admiration and approval. There were one or two expressions of opinion antagonistic to his coup, a few newspapers spoke vaguely of the danger which would accrue if other governors of colonies or provinces took it as a precedent. The Secretary of State for the Colonies cabled suggesting that his action had been rather too forcible. Wallace cabled back a reminder that he had been given *carte blanche*. He also mentioned that he would return to England at once if the British Government was dissatisfied. He heard nothing more from that quarter. It is significant that none of the suspended officials raised any protest. Carter expressed his surprise that they did not.

'Those who are guilty dare not,' Wallace told him drily;

'the others welcome my action, as it will end in clearing their characters.'

Lady Wallace was naturally very worried. She fully realised now that Sir Leonard was more or less sitting on a mine, liable at any moment to explode. She indignantly refused to leave the colony on the yachting cruise he tentatively suggested. She was not often, she declared, given the opportunity of standing by him when danger threatened and, now that the chance had come, had no intention of deserting him. A great many social engagements were cancelled. There was little time for that sort of thing now. Sir Leonard was surprised, however, to find with what facility it was possible to conduct administrative affairs without the assistance of the heads of departments. He decided that the reason was that he dispensed with red tape. He became in very truth, for the time being, a dictator, and it amused him to reflect how easy such a role could be.

Two or three days went by without the opposition showing the slightest sign of taking action of any sort against him. He knew, however, that he was being watched, if possible, more closely than ever. Wun Cheng Lo and his satellites were very busy indeed. Wherever he went, whatever he did, his actions were being observed unobtrusively by sharp-eyed men, some of whom were Chinese, some Macanese. They would have been extremely surprised had they known that they were more or less under observation themselves, if not by Wallace, then by Carter or Batty, who quietly but cleverly was taking quite a large share in this game of hide-and-seek.

On the day following the murder of Mr Burrows, the Inspector-General of Police had spent a bad quarter of an hour with the Governor, who had blamed him bitterly for the slackness which had made such a crime possible. A hue and cry throughout the colony had been raised in an effort to apprehend the assassins, but there seemed little hope of success, as not a clue to their identity had been found. Everything was suspicion, nothing tangible could be discovered anywhere. The Governor himself attended the funeral of the man who had lost his life for an ideal. Crowds lined the route to the Happy Valley, where the body was laid to rest, and the cortège was spoken of as one of the longest the colony had ever known.

Once affairs were running smoothly under his direct control, Sir Leonard sent for the official members of the Legislative Council, and had a heart to heart talk with them. As most of them were also members of the Executive Council – the Inspector-General of Police, the Director of Medical Services, and the Harbour Master being the only three who did not have seats on the senior body – there was no necessity to invite the members of the Executive Council separately. Wallace reiterated his intention not to rest until he had brought his investigations to a satisfactory conclusion. He pointed out that affairs had reached such a state that he had had no alternative but to suspend them all, and called upon them to do everything in their power to assist him, if only for their own sakes. One by one they assured him of their desire to help in every way possible, though each of them expressed himself differently. Levinson, the Colonial Secretary, was rather on his dignity; Owen-Wendover, the Attorney-General, was openly incensed at what he described as the manner in which they had been treated like a pack of naughty schoolboys; the Secretary for Chinese Affairs, Sydney Hurst, did not seem to mind much whether he continued to hold office or not; Paul Vassinger, the swarthy, Hebraic-looking Director of Public Works was full of a nervous eagerness to impress the Governor with his keen desire to be of assistance. The Harbour Master, Captain Allan Gatacre, R. N., Dr Ferdinand Saville, the Director of Medical Services, and Sir Masterson Winstanley, the Inspector-General of Police, were resentful, but each declared he would back Sir Leonard to the utmost of his ability in the Governor's efforts to rid the colony of the menace which overhung it.

Of them all, Meredith Collinson, the Colonial Treasurer, who, as Senior Assistant Treasurer, had first discovered that the finances were being defrauded, had inspired the most confidence. He was entirely genial and expressed himself as whole-heartedly with the Governor in the action he had taken. It was due to Collinson that so much of the plot had been brought to light, through him that the machinations of Mathos had been fully investigated. On the resignation of Sanderson, he had stepped into his place, receiving the CMG in the birthday honours for the work he had accomplished. Ever since his appointment, he had spared no efforts to restore the finances of the colony to a more satisfactory level. It had been a difficult task, but gradually, under his assiduous care, they were recovering. It may be thought that of all officials he, at least, should have been spared the humiliation of suspension, but Sir Leonard probably recognised that he could hardly make a distinction in his favour. At any rate, it is certain that Meredith Collinson himself was in no manner aggrieved. He remained with Sir Leonard for some time after his colleagues had departed, giving, as far as he was able, suggestions which he hoped would help the Governor to progress in the right direction.

'It is all rather hopeless, though, I am afraid, sir,' he remarked, as he was about to take his leave. 'These people have proved so infernally clever. As far as we know, none of them may be connected with administration at all, though it is hard to see how things could have been so manipulated otherwise. You are more handicapped than Sir Stanley, for he, at least, had an intimate knowledge of people and conditions, due to the fact that he has been in the Colonial Service for years, most of them spent in Hong Kong.'

'That is true,' agreed Wallace. 'Sir Stanley was Colonial Secretary here before he was appointed Governor, was he not?'

'Yes. Rather a rare occurrence and a great tribute to him. It's a pity this infernal business has impaired his health, but it's enough to destroy the health of anyone. However, we have checkmated the conspirators now. They dare not carry on their operations, and I suppose, if we drop further investigations, the whole thing will die a natural death.'

'That would mean allowing the scoundrels to go scot-free. I tell you, Collinson, I will not rest until I bring everyone of them to justice.'

'And I am absolutely with you to the last ditch, sir,' the Colonial Treasurer assured him earnestly. 'I only pray that no harm will overtake you in your endeavours. I wish there was something tangible I could place before you to help, but everything is so wrapped in mystery. Have you succeeded in finding out anything at all, sir?'

'Nothing much,' Wallace told him. 'Of one thing I am certain, however, and that is that the same organisation is in negotiation with Japan for the sale of military and naval secrets. I suppose, as one of their sources of revenue has been blocked, they are now trying another. The theft of those plans of fortification, which we know reached Japanese hands, was undoubtedly contrived by them.'

'I never thought of that,' murmured Collinson thoughtfully. 'I believe you are right, sir.'

'I am positive of it.'

'I suppose you found out through the Japanese agent who is in league with them?'

Sir Leonard smiled.

'That is one of the secrets I do not intend to divulge even to you until I am on the road to complete success.'

Collinson laughed without a trace of umbrage.

'I forgot,' he commented; 'I am at present one of the suspects, or at least under the cloud that is overhanging us all.'

It occurred to Wallace that the Colonial Treasurer might be a useful man to have at hand during an interview he intended arranging with José Tavares before many days had passed.

'You know Tavares,' he asked, 'the fellow who was a confidential servant to Mathos?'

'I can't exactly say that I know him, sir,' was the reply, 'but I know of him.'

'Well, I am going to have him up here in a day or two, and give him what the Americans would call a thorough grilling. I am convinced he could tell a lot if he wished. Will you come along and help?'

'Certainly,' was the prompt reply. 'I'm afraid we shall not learn much, though. The police cross-examined him very severely after Mathos committed suicide, and the result was practically nil.'

'Perhaps my methods will prove of a more persuasive nature,' smiled Wallace. 'I have a feeling they will.'

Collinson laughed as they shook hands.

'I hope so, sir. I shall rather look forward to seeing you handle him. I certainly believe he knows something.'

'I am convinced he does. I will inform you when I intend having him here. Good day.'

Carter had been present during the Chief's interview with the officials, and had studied them all closely. It seemed to him absurd to imagine that any of them could possibly have been associated with a plot that not only had the wholesale embezzlement of public funds as its object, but had included murder and treason as concomitants. He said as much to Sir Leonard. The latter smiled a trifle grimly, but made no comment.

That evening they learnt through Batty that Cousins had been discharged from hospital, now apparently quite fit. It was not known where he had gone. That, however, did not worry Sir Leonard. There were only two places where he was likely to have taken up his abode and, as his long stay in hospital would have been considered by Tavares and his associates to have cured him, at least temporarily, of his craving for intoxicating liquor, it was probable that he had returned to the lodging house which had been given the high-sounding title of Hotel Paris. Once, during recent weeks, Carter had managed to shake off his trailers, and had gone to the monkey house in the Botanical Gardens, but Ho Fang Ho had not appeared, and he and Sir Leonard were forced to rely subsequently entirely on the news that Batty was able to procure.

It transpired, however, that Cousins had gone to neither of the places which Wallace had in mind. Late on the night of the little man's discharge from hospital, Carter was returning from a concert, when close to the main gates of Government House he was involved in an accident. He was driving the car himself, the driver, the only other occupant, being seated in the back. A man appeared suddenly and seemed to walk deliberately in front of the motor. Carter swerved violently, felt a bump, and stopped. Hurriedly jumping out, he found a Chinaman lying face downwards on the road. His heart was beating quite strongly, but he appeared to be unconscious. A careful examination failed to reveal that there were any bones broken, but it was impossible to make certain there. Carter decided to take the fellow into Government House, and ring up for a doctor. As he bade the driver help him to lift the man into the tonneau, he noticed that another car had drawn up a few yards away, from which three Chinamen were watching. They were his indefatigable followers, the men who trailed him wherever he went, sometimes in one car, sometimes in another, sometimes on foot, but invariably the same individuals. Carter had long thought that the opposition would have shown more intelligence had the watchers been changed occasionally. The accident had apparently interested them so much that they had overlooked caution. Some seconds passed before they noticed that Carter was studying them. 'Nice choice collection of cut-throats,' was his mental summing-up. They made hasty preparations to move on, while one shouted across something in Chinese!

'What did he say?' Carter asked the driver.

'Him asking master wantchee help.'

'Tell them to go to the devil,' replied Carter crossly.

Apparently the driver did so to judge from the chorus of fearsome-sounding words that burst from the occupants of the car as it drove off. Carter conveyed his unconscious victim to Government House, and had him carried to a small room adjoining the entrance hall. Under the brilliant illumination of the electric lights, he went to examine the man, and received a shock. It was Ho Fang Ho. Carter knew him well enough to be certain. He gave no sign of surprise, however, but continued his search for the injuries which he now guessed were non-existent. The driver was dismissed, and the two other servants who had appeared on the scene sent for water and bandages. As soon as they had gone, Ho Fang Ho opened first one eye; then the other. He grinned cheerfully at Carter.

'Plenty safe talkee in this piecee loom, master?' he inquired.

As it happened, it was as safe as practically any room in the house. Carter went to the door; made certain there was nobody in the passage.

'Yes,' he assured the Chinaman, 'it is quite safe, but you'll have to hurry. Now tell me—'

'Me talkee,' interrupted Ho Fang Ho. 'No time two piecee mens talkee.' Carter smiled, and made no objection. 'Me no gettee hurt, master,' Ho Fang Ho began by assuring him. 'Me looksee you go big house with fliends; then come back waitee by tlees – no mans can see. Bimeby you come, me pletend fall down allo samee my master tellee me.'

'I see. Your master told you to do that, did he?'

Ho Fang Ho nodded.

'Him velly clebber mans,' he declared. 'Him talkee me his fliend belong secletaly Governor. Tellee me go looksee you, no lettee ozzer mens see – velly bad.'

The servants were heard to be coming, and Ho Fang Ho promptly lapsed into 'unconsciousness' again, Carter took the water and bandages from them, and got rid of them on some pretext or other. As soon as they were gone, and he had again assured himself that he and Ho Fang Ho could not be overheard, the latter continued his story.

'Master no can give letter. Him talkee me – me talkee you. Savvy?'

Carter nodded.

'You have a message for me?'

Ho Fang Ho beamed.

'Him wantchee me tellee you, number one topside velly bad mans takee him Macao side. Two, thlee days come back killee Governor.'

Carter frowned momentarily then it dawned on him what Ho Fang Ho intended to convey.

'You are telling me,' he said, determined to get the message right, 'that my friend Collins has been taken to Macao. In two or three days' time he is to be brought back to kill the Governor.'

Ho Fang Ho nodded emphatically.

'But master no belong killee Governor leally,' he impressed upon his hearer in earnest tones.

'No, I know,' admitted Carter with a smile, 'but he wants the Governor to know, and be prepared.'

Again the Chinaman nodded.

'Velly bad pilate mans takee him Macao side,' he remarked.

Carter was as puzzled as Cousins had once been.

'Pilate mans!' he repeated in somewhat stupefied tones.

Ho Fang Ho looked worried.

'Him namee too muchee hard me speakee,' he explained. 'Plentee mens go him house dancee, eatee, and dlinkee.'

'Oh!' exclaimed Carter. 'You mean Tavares, do you?'

An expression of relief showed in Ho Fang Ho's face.

'Master velly clebber,' he commented. 'You velly fightee tinkee pilate mans names.'

The Secret Service man did not bother to ask the Chinaman why he referred to Tavares as 'pilate mans'.

'Can you tell me,' he asked, 'why he has gone to Macao?'

'My master say he tinkee him velly flightened.'

'Oh! Why?'

Ho Fang Ho shook his head.

'Me no savvy.'

'Is there anything else you want to tell me, Ho Fang Ho?'

'One 'noder ting. Master talkee me, you tellee my fliend velly good go looksee pilate man's office tomollow night times. Sunday allo shutee, no mans come, pilate mans Macao side.'

'I see,' nodded Carter with great satisfaction. 'You're a splendid fellow, Ho Fang Ho.'

'Me likee makee plenty tings for master,' replied the Chinaman simply. 'My master velly good master.' He slipped from the couch on which he had been lying. 'Me go now, not good too long stopee. Tomollow you go looksee office?'

'Very likely,' Carter assured him.

'You no lettee ozzer mens follow allo time watchee you,' the Chinaman warned him. 'Ho Fang Ho waitee for you with ozzer fliend belong master, plenty good helpee.'

'What other friend?'

Ho Fang Ho smiled broadly.

'One time him catchee too muchee blandy,' he explained, 'now no catchee.'

'Is his name Kenton?' asked Carter.

The boy nodded eagerly; then, pointing to the watch on Carter's wrist, gave the latter to understand quite clearly that, on the following night, he and Kenton would be waiting near Tavares' establishment from midnight until two or three in the morning. Afterwards Carter called a servant; somewhat ostentatiously he gave Ho Fang Ho a few currency notes.

'You don't deserve this,' he remarked severely. 'The accident was your own fault, you must have been asleep.'

Turning to the servant, he directed him to see Ho Fang Ho off the premises; then went to ascertain if Sir Leonard Wallace was still up. Late as the hour was, he found the latter working in his study. Before him were various sheets of paper covered with pencilled notes, some underlined, some marked by asterisks. He appeared to be very engrossed, and did not look up.

'Well, Carter,' he asked, 'what is it?'

The young Secret Service man did not appear surprised

by the fact that, though Sir Leonard's back was towards him, the Chief knew it was he. Cunningly arranged on the desk was a mirror in which the figure of anyone entering the room was reflected. It was so placed that it was barely noticeable unless one knew it was there. Carter smiled slightly.

'I have just been talking to Ho Fang Ho, sir,' he announced.

If he had expected Sir Leonard to show elation or surprise he would have been disappointed. But Carter knew the other too well to anticipate a display of the ordinary emotions from him. Wallace took up a pipe and tobacco pouch; swung his chair round until he was facing his secretary. He proceeded to fill the briar, making use of the artificial arm with an adroitness which the young man never failed to admire. The latter refrained from offering to help. He knew from experience that the Chief was very sensitive – one of his few weaknesses, if it could be called such – on the subject of his missing arm, and preferred to do things for himself. Sir Leonard applied a match to the tobacco. Only when it was burning to his satisfaction did he make any comment.

'Well?' he encouraged the other.

Carter told him about the fake accident, and repeated Ho Fang Ho's message. Wallace listened thoughtfully, giving no indication that he was in any way interested, but the sigh he permitted himself at the end was quite eloquent for him.

'Cousins has certainly trained that young Chinaman well,' he observed. 'We owe a lot to Ho Fang Ho – a very great deal indeed.' He swung back to his desk, wrote rapidly on one of the sheets of paper, underlined the words, and connected them with a line to other notes. He then stood up, and turned with a smile to Carter.

'I think you have provided me with the link I was wanting,' he remarked. 'I believe we are on the track at last.'

Carter's eyes showed his intense interest.

'May I know what it is I have told you, sir,' he asked, 'that has caused you to come to that conclusion?'

'You may. It is the fact that Tavares has gone to Macao.'

He smiled again at the astonished expression that crept into his assistant's face.

'I don't think I quite understand,' confessed Carter.

'No, perhaps not, but you soon will. So Cousins suggests,' he added briskly, 'that, as tomorrow is Sunday, and Tavares is away, it would be a good plan to search that office. I quite agree. We are hardly likely to obtain a better opportunity. The question is, can we shake off our watchers completely enough to get there unobserved?'

'I think I can manage it, sir,' returned Carter confidently. 'I doubt if we both could. Besides, wouldn't it be better if I went alone? There may be trouble, and—'

'We shall both go,' interrupted Sir Leonard firmly. 'Two of us will do the job more quickly. Apart from that there may be something there that, with the best intentions in the world, you may overlook. As for shaking off trackers, has any member of the service ever failed to do that when he really wished to do it? It will not take long to think of some subterfuge.'

Carter knew better than to argue the point. He felt a trifle hurt, however, at the suggestion that he might overlook something. Wallace apparently sensed the thoughts that were passing through his secretary's mind, for he placed his hand kindly on the other's shoulder.

'You have not been following the line of investigation that I have recently been taking, Carter,' he observed, 'therefore a document, which to you may not seem of importance, may to me be of the utmost value. You see – it is necessary that I go.'

Carter smiled.

'I understand, of course, sir,' he returned cheerfully. 'I hate to think of the risk you might be running, though.'

Sir Leonard's eyes flashed.

'Since when have I started to lead a cotton wool kind of existence?' he snapped. 'Everything is risk in the big game, but don't we expect it?'

'I was only thinking, sir,' came the humble reply, 'that they'd murder you without the slightest hesitation or compunction if—'

'That's been tried before, Carter, but I'm still alive.' He turned to the desk, and gathered up his papers, which he folded and put carefully away in the inside pocket of his dress coat. 'I wish you would remember that in this service we all more or less carry our lives in our hands. It's part of the price we pay for the privilege we enjoy of being trusted above our countrymen, of often having the welfare of Great Britain and the rest of the Empire in our keeping. And not one of us has any right to be shielded from danger more than another, whether he happens to be the head of the department or a man trusted with his first job who has still to win his spurs. Are you coming to bed?'

'Not just yet, sir. I have some letters to read.'

Wallace nodded, and turned away. By the door he stood thoughtfully tapping his pipe on his teeth for a few moments; then looked back at Carter.

'Did you say that Cousins' drunken friend Kenton would be in waiting with Ho Fang Ho to help us, if necessary, tomorrow night?' he asked.

'So the Chinaman told me, sir,' replied Carter; 'he has apparently recovered from his weakness.'

'I wonder. A man who has once nearly gone west with DT's is hardly the type I am eager to trust. Well, we'll see. Goodnight.'

Carter was left alone, and sank into the chair his chief had recently vacated. For some time he remained lost in deep thought; then pulled several letters from his pocket – recent arrivals by the English mail – and commenced to read. All at once his eye caught sight of a slight movement beneath a long, low couch standing close to one wall. He went on apparently reading, but was watching intently. Nothing human, he reflected, could possibly squeeze beneath the couch, the space between the bottom of the seat and the floor being little more than four inches in height. He must have seen a mouse, or perhaps it was the cat which sometimes visited the study. Then suddenly he saw the tip of a finger, a finger adorned with a long cruel-looking nail. What sort of a creature, he wondered, could have worked its way into such a cramped space. Only a very small thin boy – but the finger was not that of a boy. Abruptly he had pushed the letters into his pocket; was on his feet, standing with the poise of a rugby player prepared to make a tackle.

'Come out!' he ordered in low, vibrant tones. There was no response. 'You under the couch,' again called Carter, 'come out at once!'

Whatever was there either did not understand, or preferred to remain where it was. Carter waited a few moments; then, with a sudden, rapid movement lifted the heavy couch, and pulled it aside. At once something long and incredibly emaciated sprang to its feet; launched itself at him. In its hand he caught the gleam of a knife. He fought frantically to release the octopus-like grip which enfolded him, but made little impression. Long, spidery legs entwined his body, an arm amazingly thin, but as strong as steel, was round his neck. He saw the knife uplifted, about to strike downwards; then, exerting every ounce of his strength, he succeeded in tearing loose the other's hold, and flinging him away. The creature went to the floor with a crash; there was a choking sob, the body seemed to crumple up, twitch a little, and lie still.

'He has fallen on his own knife, I'm afraid,' remarked a quiet voice.

Carter turned to see Sir Leonard standing just inside the room, a revolver in his hand. Together they looked down at what was nothing but a travesty of a man. Of ordinary length, he was attenuated to the point of ludicrousness; wearing only a kind of loin cloth, he was a repugnant, nauseating sight.

'A contortionist, of course,' murmured Wallace. 'Otherwise he couldn't have crawled under that couch.'

'Then you knew, sir?' queried Carter.

'I thought I saw something move when I left the chair,' explained the Chief. 'I waited outside to see if there would be any developments – and there were,' he added drily.

He bent down, and turned the body over. There was no need to examine it further, the knife had gone in up to the hilt in the centre of the breast. Death must have been instantaneous. Sir Leonard rose again; put his revolver away.

'That throw of yours, Carter,' he commented, 'would have done credit to the world's champion wrestler. I thought I would have had to shoot him to save your life. It is just as well he is dead. He must have overheard our conversation – I suppose that is what he was there for. Do you notice anything significant?'

'He is a Philippino, isn't he, sir?'

Wallace nodded.

'Yes it appears that friend Wun Cheng Lo is after all the employer of Philippinos. He must have put this fellow in here, which rather suggests that he himself is somewhere about. You are certain your conversation with Ho Fang Ho was not overheard?'

'Positive, sir.'

'Good. Well, you'd better give orders to have that body removed hush up the business as much as possible.'

As he was speaking, they were walking out of the room. Sir Leonard's quick eye almost at once caught the flutter of a silken garment, as its wearer disappeared round a bend of the corridor.

'Is that you, Wun Cheng Lo?' he called loudly.

The Chinaman appeared; his expressionless face conveyed nothing to the two men eyeing him so intently. He bowed low.

'As ever, your illustrious Excellency,' he murmured, 'your

humble servant is at your honourable service.'

'A bit late, aren't you?' queried Sir Leonard. 'I should have expected you to be in your own home at this hour.'

'I could not rest. The lowly mind which inhabits this paltry body tonight felt a great unease. I but came, most distinguished sir, to assure myself that all was well, to see that those baseborn menials, whom I brought here to watch that no cloud of danger threatens to dim the sun of your brilliance, shall dare to close their vulgar eyes in sleep.'

'They haven't done that,' Wallace assured him drily. 'One in fact, has killed himself in an excess of zeal.'

Wun Cheng Lo's face remained bland, entirely expressionless.

'I humbly beg to confess to your highborn nobility,' he murmured, 'that my poverty-stricken brain fails to grasp your admirable meaning.'

Sir Leonard led him into the study, and pointed to the still figure on the floor.

'Do you recognise him?' he demanded.

Wun Cheng Lo shook his head.

'Can such a question come from such distinguished lips?' Despite the unchanging face, Wallace caught the slightest tremor in the voice. 'How could such a dog obtain access to this illustrious apartment?' asked the Chinaman.

'Perhaps your baseborn menials were not on watch,' observed Sir Leonard sarcastically. 'At all events, he was hiding under that couch. When discovered, he attempted to kill Mr Carter, but only succeeded in killing himself. Perhaps, since you are so eager to serve me, you will have the body removed and the carpet also; I have an antipathy to bloodstained furniture. It would be as well, I think, if nothing was said about this incident.'

He walked away, followed by Carter. Wun Cheng Lo watched them go. When they were out of sight and sound, the Chinaman kicked the emaciated body of the dead man, and broke into a torrent of Chinese profanity. This was the second of his agents who had blundered.

CHAPTER NINETEEN

Captain Ferrara Pays His Respects

Sir Leonard had not decided in what manner he would elude those who kept a watch on his movements when, during the evening of the following day, he was motoring back to Government House after a tour round the island with Lady Wallace. For once in a way they had had the day to themselves; and even partaken of a tête-à-tête tiffin, for both Carter and the ADC had obtained permission to lunch out. Days of that kind were very precious to Molly. Sir Leonard had entirely eschewed work, and, with the exception that their attendance at Divine Service in the Cathedral had been accompanied by the usual formality, they had been alone. During the afternoon they had driven out, under a sky of radiant blue, to the Shek O Club on the other side of the island. There amidst the magnolia-perfumed atmosphere, overlooking the sparkling wavelets tumbling playfully on the sand below, a soft breeze blowing gently round them, they had been served with tea.

Molly thought, as she gracefully reclined in a comfortable wicker chair, that there could be few more beautiful spots on earth. On the way back to Victoria, the chauffeur had been ordered to drive slowly in order that they could enjoy to the full the lovely scenery through which they passed, the softly green hillsides, leafy glades, translucent bathing pools which, in their ordered luxuriance, were irresistibly reminiscent of a well-kept country seat in far-off Britain. Night, with its tropical suddenness, had fallen long before they arrived back at Government House, and the harbour had become a scene of fairy enchantment, myriads of lights from numberless mastheads and port holes, appearing like gleaming gems on beds of the softest velvet. Waves, brightly shimmering in the reflected glow, danced their way from shore far out to sea. There was something deliciously serene, ineffably peaceful about the scene. Sir Leonard sighed.

'Lovely, isn't it?' he murmured.

For reply Molly pressed his hand. Her heart was much too full for mere words. Entry into the grounds of Government House seemed to break the spell. She felt a sad little throb, as she stepped from the car. Duty, she knew, beckoned to her husband with peremptory finger, but she was left with the memory of a wonderful day, made more perfect by its rarity. They entered the building by one of the side doors, passing by the little anteroom where the visitors' book was kept. Sir Leonard glanced in; observed the thickset figure of a fair-haired man laboriously inscribing his name in the volume kept for that purpose. The latter turned as he heard footsteps, disclosing a round, jolly face, smiling blue eyes, and a closely-clipped, fair moustache. Sir Leonard stopped in his stride. He had only seen the visitor once before, and that a mere glimpse through a pair of binoculars, but he never forgot a face. Lady Wallace had gone on, and he stepped into the room.

'You are Captain Ferrara of the steamship *Genova*, are you not?' he asked.

The other bowed.

'That my name,' he admitted, 'but not now of *Genova*. Today I arrive in Hong Kong on motorship *Arabia*. You, sare, are—?' he stopped enquiringly.

'I am Sir Leonard Wallace,' was the reply.

Captain Ferrara looked confused. He bowed very low indeed.

'This are – is a verra great hon – hon – pardon me, I do not spik Engleesh to my satisfaction yet.'

He took the hand held out to him, rather as though it were something brittle that might break, if he were not very careful.

'I am very glad to meet you, Captain Ferrara,' said Wallace. 'Captain Taylor of the *Rawalpindi* spoke highly of you. Our ships passed in the Straits of Messina – perhaps you remember?'

'I remember well,' replied Ferrara, his eyes dancing with pleasure. 'I was then on *Genova*, since on *Arabia*. Again I am meeting *Rawalpindi* in Colombo to my satisfaction. I see Captain Taylor in Club. We verra good friends over long years. He tell me of new Hong Kong Governor. Today *Arabia* arrive; I hurry pay my respect in book.'

'That was very prompt of you,' approved the Governor.

'It were my duty, sare.'

In his left hand he held a tin of some kind at which he glanced rather longingly, Sir Leonard thought. Noticing the Governor's eyes on it, he proceeded to explain, in his careful, deliberate English, that it contained prickly heat powder.

'All the time I get it too bad,' he added. 'On my neck, on my back, on my –' he stopped for loss of the word; patted his chest – 'on my this. So I carry powder to on put.'

'But surely, now that the weather is cooler, prickly heat does not trouble you?'

'I bring it, sare, all way with me from Suez. Always it is the same.' His eyes twinkled. 'That is why I carry in my hand the powder. What is it you Engleesh say, Excellency? "Birds in hands worse two in bushes"?'

Sir Leonard laughed. His preconceived notion that Captain Ferrara was a thoroughly good fellow had been borne out. An almost infallible judge of men, he knew that here was an utterly trustworthy individual, simple-minded and sincere, homely and entirely honest. An idea had come to him, and he resolved to carry it out.

'If you have no other engagement for tonight, Captain Ferrara,' he observed, 'I shall be very pleased if you will dine with my wife and myself. There will be no formality, as no one else will be present but my aide-de-camp and my secretary.'

Captain Ferrara's blue eyes almost goggled from his head. This indeed was an honour. He also had conceived an instant liking for the slim, keen-eyed Governor. He proceeded to express his pleasure in a jumble of words in which he managed to insert his favourite expression, 'to my satisfaction,' several times. Sir Leonard listened with an air of smiling approval then, reminding him that dinner was at eight-thirty, nodded and strolled away. Captain Ferrara stuck out his chest, dabbed his neck with the powder, and beamed.

'What is it my English passengers sing to me?' he murmured to himself. 'Ah! I know!' He walked down the steps to a sedan chair, which he had kept waiting, singing softly to himself, and very much out of tune: '"For he's sholly good fell-o-ow, He's sholly good fell-o-ow. And so us say of all-l-l."'

Dinner at Government House that night was an exceedingly cheerful meal. There was not an atom of formality in the composition of Captain Ferrara; he treated anybody he liked with the same easy *bonhomie* he was wont to show to his bosom pals. As he quickly grew to feel quite an affection for Sir Leonard, Carter, and Captain Barker, he forgot that he was dining at Government House; all feeling of embarrassment quickly wore off, and he became the life and soul of a very jolly party. Of Lady Wallace he was lost in admiration. He was utterly charmed with her sweetness and beauty, and treated her all the time with the courtesy of a very gallant gentleman. What a tale he would have to tell to the wife and bambinos he adored, when he returned to his beloved Italy. The evening turned out very much to 'the satisfaction' of Captain Giuseppe Ferrara. His host and hostess, and their two attendants, did their utmost to make him happy, and entered fully into his spirit of camaraderie. When, half way through dinner, he found that, with the exception of Captain Barker, they all spoke Italian – Sir Leonard very fluently – his delight knew no bounds. Thereafter the conversation was carried on partly in that language, partly in English.

Later on in the drawing room he admitted that he sang, and was persuaded to perform – not that he took much persuading. There was no mock modesty about Ferrara, besides which, he regarded a request from Lady Wallace very much in the nature of a command. With Molly at the piano accompanying him with skill and great feeling, he sang gloriously various excerpts from Verdi. He possessed a voice that would have made him famous on the concert platform, but thought little of it himself.

'I am sailor not singer,' he declared. 'The sea I lof her. *E del mio cuore la carina.*'

He had a passion for English proverbs and idioms, which he laboriously wrote down from time to time, according to the manner in which the sounds of the words struck his ear, in a little book he always carried with him. In the latter respect Sir Leonard reflected that he resembled Cousins. Unfortunately, not knowing English very well, this phonetic way of writing was apt sometimes to cause him to become rather mixed. Carter spent an amusing ten minutes trying to point out that a stitch in time had nothing to do with gathering moss.

When, at last, he rose reluctantly to go, Wallace told him that he would like to have a talk with him first in the study. He bowed low over Molly's hand, assuring her in tones, the sincerity of which there was no doubting, that he had spent one of the most pleasant evenings of his life. Barker shook hands with him heartily, gladly accepting an invitation to visit the *Arabia*. Carter, at Sir Leonard's request, accompanied them to the study. Once there, Captain Ferrara was somewhat surprised to observe his host and the private secretary make a careful search of the room. He was further amazed, when the door was locked, and a heavy curtain drawn before it. Carter mixed him a whisky and soda, and held out to him a box of choice cigars from which he accepted one.

'I have asked you here, Captain Ferrara,' began Sir Leonard in low tones, as soon as he had quite assured himself that this time there was no spy in the apartment, 'because I am perfectly certain that I can rely entirely on your discretion. I am going to ask you to help me in a certain matter.'

He spoke Italian in order that there could be no possibility of misunderstanding. Ferrara beamed with delight.

'There are few things, Excellency,' he replied simply in the same language, 'that could give me greater pleasure than to serve you.'

'Thank you,' acknowledged Wallace.

Continuing to speak Italian, he told the captain that he was engaged in a very serious investigation, but was badly handicapped by the fact that he was hemmed in by spies, who watched every movement he made. Ferrara was intensely indignant. He wanted to know why the Governor did not at once order the arrest of all the scoundrels. Sir Leonard smiled.

'It is not so easy,' he told him. 'I could, of course, have those who watch arrested, but that would not help me to apprehend the principals, whose identity at present I only suspect.' Carter looked up quickly at that, but made no comment. 'If I gave evidence,' went on Sir Leonard, 'that I knew I was being spied on, I should be in a worse position than ever. In fact, attempts would immediately be made to assassinate me. One might succeed; then,' he smiled, 'I certainly should fail in my endeavours.'

'This is terrible!' exclaimed the startled Ferrara. 'I did not think such things could happen in British colonies.'

'It is a trifle unusual,' returned Wallace drily. 'Of course, I rely on your discretion, though I am afraid it is out of the question now to keep affairs secret. There is bound to be a sensation. Already papers, both British and foreign, have commented upon what is known as "the Hong Kong scandal". Nevertheless, I hope you will not divulge anything I am telling you or ask you to do until I give you permission.'

Ferrara assured him that he would regard whatever was said as sacred.

'In what manner can I help?' he asked eagerly.

Sir Leonard bent forward.

'Tonight,' he stated. 'I wish to visit a house where I hope I may obtain some valuable information. In order to succeed, it is necessary that I am not followed when I leave here – it would be fatal to my plans, if my movements were spied upon, you understand?'

'Certainly. That is quite clear, Excellency.'

'Very well, to make such a thing possible, I am going to ask you to lend me your identity.'

Captain Ferrara looked puzzled.

'My identity!' he repeated.

'Yes,' smiled Wallace. 'It is certainly known that you are my guest. When you leave, nobody will follow you. But it will not be you who will go; it will be I.'

'Still I do not understand,' murmured the perplexed captain.

I ask your permission to disguise myself as you – that is all.'

'Oh, I see. But can you do that, Excellency? We are much of a height, otherwise so different.'

'You will see how it is done, if you agree.'

'Most certainly I agree,' came at once from the other.

'Thank you. You will not mind staying here with the door locked until I come back? It is necessary that it should be thought that I remain here working. Please tell me if you would rather not assist me in this thing. It is a lot to ask, and I will naturally understand, if you have objections. I can make other arrangements.'

'It will give me the utmost happiness to do what you ask,' protested Ferrara. He shrugged his shoulders, his hands outspread. 'It is little I am asked to do. I just stay here. And what of Signor Carter? Can he not accompany you? It would mean less danger to you.'

'Carter will leave the house separately, disguised as one of my Indian orderlies. I do not think they will consider it worthwhile to follow an orderly. If they do, he will have no alternative but to return, and leave me to work alone. We have already arranged that.'

'It is a pity,' regretted Ferrara, 'that I cannot come and help also.'

'I appreciate the thought,' smiled Sir Leonard. He turned to Carter. 'You'd better go, and make your preparations at once,' he suggested. 'Your greatest danger, of course, is the house. On no account must you let yourself be seen. An orderly walking about inside at this time of the night would give rise to suspicion at once.'

Carter shook hands with Ferrara, and departed. Wallace took care to lock the door behind him, and draw the curtain once more. The captain rubbed his hands softly together.

'Now,' he declared, 'I am full of eagerness to see your Excellency become me. Perhaps I can help.'

'You certainly can,' was the reply. 'As you will have noticed, I am a little handicapped.'

From a drawer in which they had been locked in readiness came a large make-up cabinet, a box full of wigs and rolls of crêpe hair, and an evening suit several sizes too large for Sir Leonard. Two or three cushions followed, and a large three-sided mirror which folded into quite a small compass. He pushed all the papers on his desk to one side, and placed the mirror in such a position that every advantage of light was obtained. Ferrara watched curiously, as he opened the make-up cabinet, and took from there some sticks of grease paint, nose paste, and various strange-looking rubber articles of different shapes and sizes. That done he turned his attention to the wig box, and searched among the large number that appeared to be inside. It took him some time to reach a decision; he did not seem to be able to find quite what he required. At last, however, he brought one to light which satisfied him. With a glance at the wiry fair hair of his guest, he set to work on the wig with a comb. After ten minutes he tried it on; looked at himself critically in the mirror from all angles.

'It will do,' he murmured. 'Not quite the same perhaps, but nobody is likely to have taken particular stock of your hair.'

Rapidly he divested himself of his own clothing, and put on the other suit, Ferrara helping him, and chuckling the while at the misfit. Cushions, scientifically placed, quickly repaired that drawback, however, with the result that when

Sir Leonard had finished, and stood by the Italian, their figures looked identical. The Governor then carefully fixed the wig into position again, sticking it down with spirit gum, in order, as he explained to Ferrara, that it would not become displaced, if there happened to be a rough and tumble. The most interesting part of the transformation process now took place. Wallace sat at the desk, having previously asked Ferrara to take a seat exactly opposite him. After studying the configuration of his guest's face, he fixed some of the small rubber objects on to his own with adhesive tape. That done, quickly and dexterously he moulded the nose paste over the top until it appeared to merge into his flesh. Then, to the amazement of the captain, a metamorphosis took place. He had never seen a past-master in the art of make-up at work before, and he found the experience of absorbing interest. Under those painstaking, skilful fingers, Ferrara saw his own face appear, exact in shape and colouring, every line – and there were many – absolutely accurate. The moustache and eyebrows were fixed almost hair by hair; then, after a prolonged scrutiny, Sir Leonard stood up, fastened a collar round a neck enlarged three sizes at least, and smiled at the astonished captain, who hastened to tie his bow for him.

'It is extraordinary,' Ferrara repeated several times.

'The eyes I cannot change, I'm afraid,' remarked Wallace. 'The shape, yes, but not the colour. Still, I do not think anybody is likely to notice that.'

'My own crew would be deceived,' declared Ferrara. 'It is wonderful.'

The process had taken well over an hour, but it was a triumph of art. Sir Leonard transferred various articles to his pockets, including a case containing a strange assortment of steel instruments, and a wicked-looking automatic; then announced that he was ready to depart. He took care to see that his guest had everything he required; warned him to keep the door locked and the curtain drawn over it until he returned, when he would knock three times, and cough loudly to assure Ferrara that it was he. The door was then opened. Wallace stood on the threshold and, in a clever imitation of the captain's English, bade goodnight to the Governor presumably within, thanking him for a very pleasant evening. As he walked away, he heard the sound of the key turning in the lock.

A servant, squatting a little way along the corridor, rose to his feet as he passed. Sir Leonard looked back, as he was about to descend the stairs. The man had resumed his previous attitude; appeared in no way interested in him. Ferrara had retained his sedan chair; the coolies were lying by it fast asleep, when Wallace walked up. At his touch they sprang to their feet; held the conveyance at the requisite angle for him to get in. He directed them to take him to Queen's Road. A smile flickered across his lips, as certain figures loomed out of the darkness, and peered at him as he was being carried to the gates. There, as though by accident, a powerful torch was flashed in his face. In Ferrara's voice he gave vent to an annoyed protest in Italian. Someone muttered apologetically, and the light was switched off. After that no further interest was taken in him.

On arrival in Queen's Road, he vacated the chair, paying the coolies generously in recompense for their long wait. He had not been followed; he was quite certain of that.

Nevertheless, he took strict precautions during the second part of his journey. A ricksha conveyed him to within a couple of hundred yards of his destination; he walked the rest of the way. He wondered whether Carter had managed to get through. If he were not already in waiting, he decided he would give him fifteen minutes. Wallace had passed Tavares' establishment several times, and, therefore, knew exactly where it was situated. It was in complete darkness, but lights showed on the second floor of the house on the right, which he knew was occupied by Miguel Sales and his family. That, he reflected, was a pity. It was his intention to pay a visit to the room where he knew at least one meeting of the conspirators had been held. The house on the other side also interested him. Cousins had informed him that Tavares possessed a flat there, above the floor devoted to the Turkish bath business. He had not the slightest doubt that, though the baths might be run as a genuine concern, they actually were there as a blind. Open at all hours of the day and night, they were a great convenience to people who wished to come and go without being particularly noticed. Sir Leonard also felt convinced that between Tavares' flat and the restaurant there must be a private communication, very likely similar to that which enabled Tavares to get into the house of his friend Sales. He intended to find it.

Strolling along on the opposite side of the road, he stopped and lit a cigarette, a signal agreed upon between himself and Carter. For a moment he allowed the match to illumine his face; then threw it away. Almost at once a hand touched his arm, and he swung round. Standing close by, he could dimly make out the form of a tall Indian attired in the uniform of a sepoy.

'Carter, sir,' whispered the newcomer. 'Everything seems perfectly quiet. Ho Fang Ho is round at the back. I had the devil's own job to convince him it was really me. Kenton is with him, eager to do all he can to help – and absolutely sober.'

'Glad to hear it,' grunted Wallace. 'Have any difficulty in getting away from Government House?'

Carter chuckled softly.

'I was tracked, sir,' he returned, 'and by two of them. They probably thought I was on some mission from you. I led them to a street which I know has rather an unsavoury reputation, and where the police usually go about in pairs. I was lucky. I came upon three – all Chinese, too – if they had been Indians, I wouldn't have dared speak to them, not knowing the language sufficiently to support my disguise. I told them that I suspected I was being followed by two men who were probably bent on robbery. In their anxiety not to lose me, I suppose, the two approached quite close while I was talking. I pointed them out, and the policemen promptly fell on them. In the confusion I slipped away. I haven't been followed since.'

'Good,' commented Sir Leonard. 'Let us get round to the back.'

There was hardly a soul about, which made their task of accomplishment easier than it would otherwise have been. As a matter of fact, it would have been impossible on any other night but Sunday. Apart from Tavares' establishment, there were no recognised night clubs in Hong Kong, and all bars and dancing halls closed at midnight. Nobody quite knew how he alone had succeeded in obtaining the necessary permission to keep open as long as he liked. The only prohibition he suffered under was that his premises could not be opened at all on Sundays, while other, better class, bars were.

The compound at the back was in absolute darkness, not a single reflection from the dim lights in the street beyond straying in to diminish the gloom. Not far away a Chinese wedding was being celebrated, to judge from the din. With scarcely a pause, crackers were exploding with noisy reverberation. Carter led his companion past the servants' quarters, both of them treading very softly for fear of disturbing any of the sleeping people within. Presently they came to two men, one tall and straight, the other small.

'My friend has arrived,' Carter told them – Wallace had previously warned him that it would be as well not to let even Ho Fang Ho know that he was accompanied by the Governor. 'Did Collins give you any idea what we should be doing here?' he asked the tall man.

'No; but, when he told me in hospital that there were certain things he and others wanted to find out about Tavares and company, I guessed he was not quite all he had pretended to be, and I was naturally keen to do all I could. I owe him – rather a lot, you see,' he added simply, 'and Tavares is a swine.'

'We're going to start by searching Tavares' office.' Wallace took command. 'You and Ho Fang Ho can greatly assist by keeping watch. Follow me, and for the Lord's sake, don't make a sound.'

Like most houses of more than one storey in China, wooden staircases, for the use of servants, connected with the verandas at the back of the premises. It was not very difficult to discover which belonged to Tavares' establishment. There were only three, and Wallace knew it must be the one in the middle. He led the way, followed by Carter, with Kenton close behind. Ho Fang Ho, as noiseless as a cat, brought up the rear. Sir Leonard had been able to form a mental picture of the place from the excellent description given to him by Cousins. Arriving on the first veranda, he examined his surroundings, not a very easy task in the darkness, though it was lighter there than below. Both ends were walled up, but whereas he knew that that to his left, as he faced inwards, must divide the veranda of Sales' house from the one on which he was standing, the wall on his right, very much nearer, must be the one erected to keep private that part of the balcony adjacent to Tavares' office. He walked up to this, leant over the balustrade, and craned his neck round the partition. Easy enough to climb round, he decided, and returned to the others.

'You stay here with Ho Fang Ho, Kenton,' he ordered. 'and keep a sharp lookout. If you have any reason to suspect that all is not well – anybody approaching, movement below, or anything like that – send Ho Fang Ho to warn us.'

'Right-ho,' returned the ex-engineer, wondering dimly who the thick-set man was who had taken charge, and how he had learnt his name.

Ho Fang Ho having assured Sir Leonard that he could climb round the partition if necessary, the two Secret Service men scaled the balustrade, wormed their way to the other side of the wall, and dropped lightly down. Carter, as he had often done before, marvelled at the agility of the Chief who only had one hand to use. He was an athletic young man, but even he had not found the operation easy, as the wall extended out in an ornamental curve quite two feet beyond the railing. The French windows were strongly bolted, but that did not perturb Sir Leonard. Out from his pocket came the case he had placed there. From it he took a strangely-shaped instrument, exceedingly fine at one end, and curving to a knob at the other. He worked silently at the bottom of one of the windows for a few minutes, after which came a slight sliding sound; the process was repeated at the top, with the same result. Still the window would not open, and it was evident that another bolt was in place halfway up. A few more minutes' work, and they stepped into the room. A powerful beam of light from a torch no bigger than a fountain pen swept inquisitively round, and was extinguished. Carter was directed to close the window, and draw the curtain, in order that no ray of light could possibly show outside. When that was done, Sir Leonard sought for and found the electric light switch. In a moment the room was brightly illuminated.

The two men gazed round them. Wallace smiled a little. The place was exactly as he had pictured it, surely a tribute to Cousins' descriptive powers. His eyes even sought the punka hanging above, as he remembered the little man's statement that it had been his intention to disguise himself as a punka coolie, and bribe or force the existing fellow to let him take his place.

'Search the books and papers on those shelves, Carter,' directed Sir Leonard, nodding in the direction indicated. 'I will open the safe.'

Carter immediately set to work, while Wallace knelt down, and examined the massive-looking article from which he hoped to obtain something of great value to him in his investigations. A smile of satisfaction quickly lit up his face or, perhaps it would be more correct to say, the face of Captain Ferrara. Although the safe was substantial, the lock was of an out-of-date pattern that presented little difficulty to a man who had studied safe-breaking with the same assiduous concentration that he brought to bear on most things. He had opened his case of instruments, and was about to select one, when he distinctly heard a click. At once he was on his feet; moved swiftly to the electric light switch, and the place was in darkness. Carter felt a clutch on his arm; was hurried on to the veranda. The window was gently closed behind them, but Sir Leonard took care to leave the curtains open sufficiently to enable him to watch what went on inside. Nothing seemed to be happening for some time; then suddenly the light was switched on. Two men stood looking round them, and the door of one of the two cupboards stood open.

'So that is the secret way into Tavares' flat,' murmured Wallace to himself.

'Good God!' came in a low gasp from Carter. 'Why they're—'

'S'sh!' breathed Sir Leonard in his ear, 'they'll hear you.'

CHAPTER TWENTY

An Eventful Night

Apparently it did not occur to the men in the room that the light might be seen outside and betray their presence, for neither of them approached to make certain that the windows were shut, or draw the curtains. They behaved as though they had a perfect right to be there; yet at the same time there was something nefarious about their demeanour. They spoke in whispers which made it impossible for the watchers to hear what was said, but presently one pointed to the safe, and nodded his head vigorously. The other took two keys from his pocket which they both examined. Sir Leonard managed to obtain a view, and came to the conclusion, from the crudeness of construction, that they had been made from a wax impression by someone not very expert at the job. The two knelt down before the safe. As their backs were turned to the windows it was impossible to follow their movements, but it was not hard to guess what they were doing, or rather attempting to do, for they appeared to be experiencing a great deal of difficulty. Eventually one rose to his feet, and stood in an attitude of chagrin, but his companion persisted in his attempts to open the safe, at last succeeding, much to their united delight. Directly the ponderous door had swung open, they searched eagerly within, scattering papers and books all over the floor. They were apparently looking for some definite object, and knew the form it was in. As time went by, and they failed to find it, their search became more feverish; then one pulled open a drawer, a glance seemed enough, for they both dived their hands in, which immediately emerged clutching a bundle of papers, kept in place by several elastic bands. For some minutes they knelt examining their find, after which they smiled at each other with great satisfaction. Eventually one stuffed the papers into a pocket. They hastily threw back into the safe the articles they had pulled out, closing the door, but not bothering to lock it. Sir Leonard decided that it was high time he and Carter took a hand. Once those papers were taken away, the chances were that they would be destroyed, and he felt a great desire to examine them. Drawing his automatic, he touched Carter on the arm, whispering to him to stay where he was, and remain hidden until called. Then, flinging wide the window, he stepped into the room. At the sound of his entry, the two men swung round with cries of consternation.

'Give me those papers that I have seen put in your pocket!' ordered Wallace in the halting English of Ferrara, waving his automatic at them threateningly.

They exchanged quick glances.

'Who are you?' demanded one.

'That is not matter. I have papers stolen from me, and I know brought here. I have see you put in your pocket. Give me, or I shoot!'

The second man laughed – his voice sounded full of relief.

'It seems,' he observed, 'that there is a misunderstanding. You, whoever you happen to be, are in a position similar to the one that caused us to come here. Papers were stolen from us also – very important papers, which would have meant our being blackmailed. We came to recover them. I can assure you they are certainly not yours. The safe is open – no doubt you will find your property there, if you search.'

'I not believe you,' persisted Wallace. 'I tell you I have see—'

'How did you get here?' interrupted the first man suspiciously.

'That not matter to you. My papers it is I want now at immediately.'

'Oh, go to the devil!' was the response.

'I tell you, if not you give I will shoot at both. Birds in hands worse two in bushes.' For the life of him Wallace could not refrain from repeating Ferrara's favourite proverb.

Carter, on the veranda, felt an inclination to laugh.

'Look here,' put in the second man, who appeared to possess more patience than his companion, 'would you know your papers if you saw them?'

'Of course I know.'

The fellow turned to his companion.

'Show them to him,' he suggested; 'he'll soon recognise that they are not his. Obviously Tavares has been doing a little dirty work on his own.'

The other reluctantly drew the roll from his pocket, which was exactly what Wallace had been playing for. He held it out.

'It is not yours, you see,' he grunted irritably.

'How can I see when you hold it so covered? It looks like mine.'

'Oh, be damned to you! Take a good look, if that's the only way you'll be satisfied.'

He approached closer, and held it not more than eighteen inches from Sir Leonard's eyes. With a sudden downward sweep of his automatic, the latter struck it out of the fellow's hand and, as it struck the floor, backheeled it through the open window behind him in a manner that was suggestive of Alex James's manipulation of a football. With cries of rage the two men darted forward, only to be brought up abruptly at sight of the wicked-looking automatic pointed steadily at them.

'Outside I have one friend who will take away it to places of safety.' That was a hint to Carter. 'When it is certain he is gone, and no tricks can be done by you; then I put away gun and go also.'

They stormed at him, threatened, cursed, but it was of no avail; they tried pleading, cajolery, with the same effect. Finally, in a desperate effort to get the better of him, they launched themselves at him. Without hesitation he fired twice, the second shot following so rapidly on the first that they almost sounded as one. Both men went to the floor hit in identically the same place just above their right knees. Sir Leonard contemplated them.

'I tell you I would shoot,' he remarked. 'Now for your foolishnesses you both with broke legs.'

He looked thoughtfully round the room, wondering if it were worthwhile to continue his search; decided that he had obtained all that he required. If there had been anything else relative to the conspiracy, the men now groaning on the floor would have been sure to have taken it.

'Let us get out of here,' suggested one to the other through clenched teeth, 'the noise of those shots will have been heard, and—'

'Do not fear, gentlemen,' put in Wallace; 'there is too other noises I think of wedding crackers. Nobody can heard my practice of targets.' He smiled down at them almost benevolently. 'You take rest down there; it so good for you. Tomorrow police come perhaps – you make it the explanation.'

'Curse you,' cried one. 'Who are you?'

'Someday it may be you know,' returned Wallace. 'Now it not matter.'

He bowed ironically, and backed on to the veranda. Standing there in the dark, he presently made out the tall figure of Kenton. There was no sign of Carter. He had taken the hint, and obeyed the veiled order. Wallace smiled his approval. He knew what it must have cost the young man to leave him in a position of grave danger, but discipline, that stern discipline of the Secret Service, which takes no account of personal or individual safety, had been too much for him to ignore.

'I didn't come in,' whispered Kenton. 'I thought you might have objected. You had brought the two of them down by the time I had succeeded in climbing round. The other man – Carter isn't it – asked me to stand by to help. He told me to tell you he has taken the bundle of papers to your home.'

'Good!' approved Wallace. 'I intended to search this block of buildings thoroughly,' he added more to himself than to Kenton, 'but since events have taken such a turn, I'm afraid I'll have to leave it. Are you game?' he asked Kenton, 'to accompany me on another burgling expedition?'

'Rather,' came the immediate response. 'If anything I can do to help you in your mysterious schemes has the sign, seal, and approval of old Collins, you can count me in all the time.'

They climbed round the brick barrier on to the other part of the veranda; found Ho Fang Ho anxiously awaiting them. He did not understand what was happening, but since these people, who did such strange things, were friends of his master, and the latter had told him to place himself at their disposal, he was determined to leave no stone unturned in their service whatever the consequences might be. If Ho Fang Ho had ever heard of Tennyson's poem on the charge of the Light Brigade at Balaclava, he might easily, and with truth, have adapted to himself the immortal lines: 'Theirs not to reason why; Theirs but to do or die.' They were his sentiments exactly. He had heard the two rapid shots, even though the din of the crackers seemed to have become louder and more prolonged than ever, and hoped sincerely that the round man, as he had dubbed the Ferrara-disguised Wallace, had not been wounded or killed. The Governor's 'secletaly', wondrously made-up to look like an Indian soldier, had passed him by, telling him to wait for the other, and had gone down the stairs, so he knew Carter was all right. Besides, had not the shots come after he had seen him. His relief was great when Kenton climbed back, followed by the 'round man'.

As Wallace had anticipated, no alarm had been created in the adjacent houses, or in the servants' quarters below, by the shots. All was as dark and as peaceful as before. He wasted no time, but led the way down the stairs. There was a lot to be done before daylight. Ferrara would have a long wait, but it could not be helped. Sir Leonard sincerely hoped that no ill consequences would fall on the Italian captain because of what had happened in Tavares' office. It had been necessary for him to continue to sustain the role he had adopted in the presence of the two men he had left there wounded, for no suspicion of his real identity must be allowed to leak out until he was prepared to act definitely and completely. If they had guessed who he was, his plans would have been ruined. No doubt they would be extremely puzzled, as well as perturbed by the loss of the papers for which they had gone to such lengths. It was hardly likely they would continue to believe the story the pseudo-Ferrara had told them. The manner in which he had kicked them out to someone in waiting on the veranda suggested that there was more behind his appearance than they had first been led to suppose. Consequently they would do all they could, through their confederates, to discover who the intruder was. They were not in a position to do anything actually themselves. Sir Leonard smiled grimly at the reflection that they would have a good deal of difficulty in explaining their wounds. He felt no regrets. Men who had abused their official positions, condoned, perhaps even committed murder, deserved neither pity nor mercy. Unfortunately, it was possible that Captain Ferrara's life had been endangered. His ship was remaining ten days in Hong Kong and, during that time, it was hardly conceivable that he would escape recognition by one or more of the conspirators, or their emissaries, who would have been furnished with a description of the man who had appeared in Tavares' office. It was partly for that reason that Wallace had determined on another enterprise that night. It might be possible to find the last links in the evidence he required, and act without further delay.

They got away from that neighbourhood without incident, driving in rickshas to the cable car station. Cars were still running, but Sir Leonard reflected that by the time he desired to return from his destination, they would have missed the last one down. However, that could not be helped. They ascended to the Peak and, in the lighted interior of the compartment, Sir Leonard took stock of the man for whom Cousins had conceived such a warm affection. Well over six feet in height, he was almost painfully thin, his crumpled blue suit hanging on him in shapeless fashion. His face, drawn and haggard, with its hooked nose, thin lips, and sunken eyes suggested a death's head. Yet, though so deep-set, the eyes were large and fine; shone with an expression of triumph that implied that their owner had suffered and conquered. Kenton had been down to the very depths of hell, but, with the assistance of the Irish doctor, and the sympathetic attention of the nurses, he had won through, and regained his manhood. Wallace began to understand why Cousins had been attracted to this man. There was something intensely appealing and magnetic about him; his weakness had not destroyed his predominating sincerity and honesty. If, and indications pointed that way, he had succeeded in eliminating his craving for drink, he was a man to be trusted, to be relied upon to the last ditch.

It was a happy omen, reflected Wallace, that in one day he had become acquainted with two such men as Ferrara and Kenton.

On arrival at the Peak, they set off as silently as before, little Ho Fang Ho still bringing up the rear. Up there, nearly two thousand feet above the harbour, which appeared more fascinating than ever from that height, everything seemed wrapt in slumber. Like a lot of the buildings in the city below, the houses had a somewhat grim, mid-Victorian aspect, though night had softened what could be seen of their heavy grey walls and sombre windows. They are specially built to withstand the climate, for in the rainy season everything is apt to become mildewy; even clothes and footwear suffering. Windows are fitted with double glass, a precaution also necessary to protect pictures. Sir Leonard knew the strength of the buildings; realised that he would have more difficulty in getting inside the one he intended to burgle than the ordinary dwelling.

Before long they came to it and crept softly into the grounds. Like all the others in the neighbourhood, it was in absolute darkness, not a suggestion of light showing anywhere. Ho Fang Ho was left at a vantage point from where he could keep watch both on the house and the drive leading to it. Wallace took Kenton with him. They stole on to the veranda, and made their way to one of the French windows. Sir Leonard had been there twice before as a guest, and knew exactly where he wanted to go. Wasting no time, he set to work with one of the instruments taken from his case. It took him longer to force an entry than it had done into Tavares' office, but, at last, the window was open. Kenton followed him into the house with rather mixed feelings. This sort of thing went against the grain, but he knew the man he was with was not actuated by motives of larceny. There was something deeper behind his rather doubtful actions, something of which Kenton's friend Collins approved, something, in fact, which he guessed had the approbation of Government House itself. During the conversation between Ho Fang Ho and the supposed Indian sepoy, at which he had been present, he had learnt that the latter, as the Chinaman had put it, was the Governor's 'secletaly'.

A ray of light flashed out, showing him the configuration of the room. Sir Leonard took him by the arm, and led him to a door, where he whispered to him to stand and listen and, if he heard the slightest sound, to warn him, immediately. Thereafter he had the rather weird experience of watching what could easily be described as a will-o'-the-wisp dancing about the room, becoming stationary for prolonged periods; then off inquisitively in another direction. Wallace dared not switch on the lights, the curtains were not thick enough to prevent all illumination from showing outside. Of course the windows were provided with storm shutters, but they would probably have made a noise if closed; contrivances of that kind generally did.

A small safe in the corner of the room was the first to receive his attention. He opened it in less than five minutes. Everything inside underwent the most careful scrutiny, but he found nothing of the least interest to him. Each article was replaced exactly as it had been before, and the door closed, and locked. Sir Leonard then turned his attention to the desk standing in the centre of the room. Drawers, whether locked or not, were opened and their contents examined. Several packets of letters tied with ribbon were unfastened, every letter being read. Not a single thing in or on that desk escaped the sharp eyes of the man who was searching for evidence against the owner of the house. He even went over the woodwork inch by inch in an effort to discover if it contained any secret receptacle, but all his endeavours proved in vain. Leaving the desk as he had found it, he crossed to the bookshelves, examined the books, opened a locked cupboard. It contained nothing but masses of stationery. Kenton watched operations, as far as he could see them, with a sense of fascination. It had quickly become obvious that he was observing the movements of a man expert in the task he was performing. He had heard something of the scandal in which Hong Kong was involved, knew that the secretary of the Governor was working hand in glove with this man, and it was not difficult to put two and two together, and make a fairly reasonable four of it. Kenton became convinced that his companion was acting for the British Government, was perhaps a man sent out from Scotland Yard. The only thing that did not quite accord with that theory was that he remembered vaguely to have heard that police officers' hands were badly tied, that they could not search houses without warrants. But he guessed that sometimes they dispensed with such a formality. Perhaps the man with the tiny flash lamp possessed a warrant, though, if that were so, it was rather surprising that he should burgle the house instead of going through his search in a more direct manner.

Sir Leonard came to the conclusion that there was nothing to help him in that room. He softly opened the door at which

Kenton had been on guard, and drew the latter outside. A quick flash of light from the torch showed that they were in a broad hall.

'Stay here,' whispered Wallace, 'and don't move whatever happens, unless I call to you. Understand?'

He moved away into the darkness without the slightest sound, and Kenton was left alone wondering where he had gone. As a matter of fact, Sir Leonard entered room after room, searching diligently everywhere. On the upper storey he was compelled to exercise the utmost caution, for the doors of the two occupied bedrooms stood partially open. One, at least, he intended to enter; it was the last hope he had of finding anything tangible. Without hesitation, he slid into the room nearest him. The ray of his torch shot on to the floor, was immediately extinguished, but the light had been sufficient to enable him to observe that the occupant of the bed was a woman. Not much likelihood of finding anything there, he decided. He would return, if he failed in the other room. Slipping into the passage again, he made his way to the door of the other bedchamber; crept quietly within. Again came a momentary flash from the lamp. Lying on the bed, breathing deeply and regularly, was a man – *the man*! Sir Leonard had observed also that a door at the opposite side of the apartment stood open. Undoubtedly a dressing room, his quarry's clothes would be there. Two minutes later he was inside with the door closed, going carefully through the suit lying neatly folded on a chair. Nothing again, apparently, of any interest – a pocket-book well stocked with bank notes, a case of visiting cards, one or two uninteresting letters. Almost casually Sir Leonard's hand slid into one of the trousers' pockets; there was hardly likely to be – but there was! An unusual place to put a letter. It was crumpled up, as though it had been stuffed there quickly, out of sight of eyes that the reader did not wish to see it. Wallace drew it out, unfolded it, and removed the several sheets of notepaper from the envelope. Intermittently switching on his torch, he read scraps here and there, and a feeling of elation took possession of him. At last! In his hand he held all the evidence he needed. By sheer good luck, as he regarded it, he had come upon a document perfectly damning to the man in whose pocket he had found it. It was dated that day, had, therefore, only recently been delivered. Judging from the few extracts he had read, Wallace was able to imagine the consternation of the recipient. It had not been destroyed, because it would be necessary for others to see it first. Obviously there had been no time yet. Sir Leonard glanced at the signature at the end, smiled, and stuffed the precious letter carefully into his own pocket.

There was no longer any need for him to remain there. His quest had been successful, far more successful than he had dared to hope. The sooner he was outside now, and on his way to Government House, the better he would be pleased. He looked at the luminous dial of his wristwatch. The time was close on half past three. There was no other way out of the dressing room except that by which he had entered it. He was compelled, therefore, to creep once more through the room in which lay the sleeping man. All went well until he was in the passage beyond, and passing the door of the woman's bedchamber; then suddenly came the sharp yap peculiar to those toy dogs dear to certain feminine hearts. A little animal ran out, and snuffled loudly round Sir Leonard's legs. With a muttered curse, he hastened towards the top of the stairs, wondering how he had missed noticing it before or how, which was more surprising, it had not previously been aware of his presence. It must have been very soundly asleep in the lady's bedroom. Its mistress, it appeared, was a very alert woman. He had nearly reached the head of the stairs, when a shrill feminine voice behind commanded him to stop.

'I can hear you,' she cried unnecessarily, 'so you needn't pretend there's nobody there.'

'Switch on the lights, and you'll see me as well,' muttered Wallace, as he dived down the stairs.

Abruptly came the spiteful and rapid bark of a small automatic; he heard bullets droning by; something seemed to sting him viciously in the calf of the leg, and he almost lost his balance. He scrambled rather than ran down the remainder of the steps. As he reached the bottom, the lights above were switched on, and he heard a man's deep voice. Kenton was standing where he had left him, and came eagerly forward. His face grew anxious when he noticed, in the illumination thrown from above, that his companion was hopping rather than running.

'Here, take this!' muttered the latter urgently, endeavouring to thrust something into Kenton's hand. 'Get it to Government House – to Carter. I'm lamed – can't run fast enough to get away.'

'Take it yourself!' promptly snapped Kenton. 'I'll keep 'em back, while you get away – doesn't matter about me – only a tramp. Go on – get out – fightee!'

There was no time for argument. Sir Leonard went; first pushing his revolver into Kenton's hand. Hopping along as best he could, he hurried through the room he had first searched, on to the veranda, and down the steps. He found Ho Fang Ho, and took the Chinaman with him, not stopping for explanations. There were people in the grounds now; he could see lights obviously being carried by running men approaching the house from the servants' quarters and other buildings in the neighbourhood. No doubt they had been roused by the hysterical shooting bout indulged in by the lady. Wallace grimaced ruefully – his leg was beastly painful. Strange how a little thing like that hurt more sometimes than a bad wound. Then he smiled and, if anyone could have observed his eyes at that moment, he would have been surprised at the gentleness and softness in them. He was thinking of Kenton. Never during his career had he been spoken to as the ex-engineer had spoken to him. But he liked it. Kenton had done something fine; he would not forget. 'Great fellow!' murmured Wallace, and hurried on.

He and Ho Fang Ho escaped from the grounds without incident; then he bent down and, with the assistance of the Chinaman, tied his handkerchief tightly round the wound. After that he found he was able to walk better. The cable cars had long since ceased running for the night, and it looked as though he would be compelled to walk all the way down to Government House. However, they eventually came across a sedan chair on a bridge over a nullah, its two coolies being spread out at full length beside it fast asleep. Ho Fang Ho kicked them into wakefulness and, though they did not seem keen to carry a passenger at that time of the morning, and such a distance, the promise of much *cumsha* was too acceptable to be refused.

Near Government House, Sir Leonard dismissed Ho Fang

Ho, telling him to look out for Carter in the Botanical Gardens in the morning and, if he did not appear, to lounge outside Government House like all the other idlers who congregated there, and wait until means was found of communicating with him. Whether it was that they were confident that neither the Governor nor anyone connected with him would be likely to leave Government House at that hour in the morning, or weariness had made them slack, it is difficult to say, but the men placed on watch by the opposition were lying together in a heap on a grassy bank on the other side of the road fast asleep. Sir Leonard smiled. All the better, he thought. If he could enter the grounds unobserved, there would be no surprised speculation concerning the return of a man, known to have been a guest the previous evening, at that extraordinary hour in the morning. The sentry was very wide awake, however; was exceedingly dubious about letting the stranger in. Having sent his chair coolies jubilantly away with more money than they had seen for a considerable time, Wallace told the smart-looking Indian soldier in his own language that he had news of the greatest urgency for the secretary of the Governor, which must be delivered at once. Perhaps the sound of his own tongue acted as a charm. At any rate, Sir Leonard was admitted, and a man called from the orderly room, who conducted him to a side door.

Carter had been awaiting him with the greatest anxiety for nearly three hours, and knew which door he would approach. He admitted him, and dismissed the sepoy. Without meeting a soul, they reached Sir Leonard's dressing room. There an exceedingly worried Batty was only prevented, with great difficulty, from giving vent to his relief in loud shouts of joy;

that is, when he was really convinced that behind the face and figure of Captain Ferrara was his master. With the help of the valet and Carter, Wallace quickly removed the clothes and makeup and, clad in pyjamas and a dressing gown, puffed placidly and contentedly at the pipe Batty filled and lit for him. Both men had expressed concern at the wound in the calf of Sir Leonard's leg, but the latter made little of it. He permitted Batty to clean and bandage it, however. He satisfied their curiosity by relating what had occurred, without mentioning the name of the man to whom the house he had burgled belonged. They were both full of admiration for the manner in which Kenton had stepped in, and covered Sir Leonard's retreat. Then the latter demanded to know if Carter had examined the bundle of papers he had brought away with him from Tavares' office. In response Carter's eyes gleamed. He took from his pocket a paper on which he had written a list of names.

'They were papers,' he informed the Chief, 'that had originally belonged to Mathos, and they involve these men in the conspiracy without shadow of doubt.'

Wallace read the list, and smiled.

'All there,' he commented, 'except the names of the two ringleaders, and I have evidence against them here.' He held up the letter he had taken from the house on the Peak. 'Tomorrow, or rather today, Carter, I commence to clear up Hong Kong. Now I must go and apologise to Ferrara.'

They found difficulty in gaining admittance to the study. Ferrara was asleep. When eventually they had succeeded in rousing him, they also awoke a man who had been lying asleep on a divan in an alcove hidden by a curtain. Captain

Ferrara accepted Wallace's apologies with great good humour. Carter and Batty conducted him to a bedroom, and the latter provided pyjamas. Ferrara had accepted an invitation to spend two or three days at Government House as the guest of Sir Leonard and Lady Wallace. The former felt that thus he would be able to intercept any danger that might threaten the genial captain, as a result of the impersonation. Wallace was the last to leave the study. When he had gone to his bedroom, Wun Cheng Lo appeared from the alcove. For once in a way the Chinaman's face was not expressionless. He looked thoroughly perturbed. He could not understand the locked study and the presence inside of a stranger in evening dress. Something had occurred which spelt danger to those he served. Of that he felt certain. As the result of what he had seen, he communicated very early by telephone with a certain individual. On hearing Wun Cheng Lo's report, the latter also grew anxious, especially as something had happened in his house during the night which had mystified and alarmed him. An urgent telephone call was put through to Macao, and, without delay, a certain diminutive individual, who went under the name of George Collins, but whose proper name was Gerald Cousins, was sent back to Hong Kong in a fast motor cruiser.

CHAPTER TWENTY-ONE

Kenton Returns to Hospital

Kenton sighed his relief as Wallace left him. A man of sense that, he reflected; prepared himself for what was to come. The hall was suddenly brilliantly illuminated, and down the stairs came running a tall, dark man in a dressing gown, followed a few seconds later by a woman even taller. Both were flourishing revolvers, but they pulled up dead as they saw the intruder calmly awaiting them, one hand holding an automatic levelled steadily in their direction, the other stuck in the pocket of his shabby jacket.

'I hardly anticipated being discovered,' he drawled, 'especially before I had had an opportunity of purloining a few articles I am sure you could have dispensed with.'

The dark man looked him up and down contemptuously.

'A white man,' he sneered. 'A white thief!'

'Not yet,' Kenton returned. 'I have not had an opportunity so far of earning the title of thief. That exceedingly wide awake poodle of yours rather cramped my style.'

The dog in question, having followed its mistress down the stairs, now ran up to him wagging its tail as though to show that no harm had been intended.

'It's all very well, old fellow,' commented Kenton, 'you gave me away, you know. You can hardly expect me to want to be friends after that. No; don't move, please!' The order was directed at the woman who had taken a step forward. 'It would give me a great deal of pain to be compelled to shoot a female, but you must admit that I am in a somewhat sticky position.'

'I don't think even you would shoot a woman,' she snapped in hard, metallic tones.

Her voice was exactly the kind he would have expected from a woman of her type. Not only was she tall and rather boney, but, although possessing fairly good looks, her mouth was thin-lipped and petulant, her eyes hard and pitiless.

'That is where you are mistaken,' he told her, and there was something in the manner in which he spoke that caused her to raise her eyebrows slightly. 'I should have more compunction in shooting a man than a woman as it happens.'

'Oh,' she sneered, 'a broken romance has embittered you, I suppose. A girl jilted you, and you let yourself sink to – this.'

'No; a wife left me with a young baby who was ill,' he replied, and the bitterness in his voice could almost be felt. 'I worshipped the child – he died. Now perhaps you understand,' he added with a snarl, 'why I would have no objection to shooting a woman.'

'Very tragic!' she laughed disdainfully. 'Quite a pitiful little story.'

'Enough of this,' growled the man. 'How did you get in?'

'Just walked,' returned Kenton, resuming his unconcerned manner; 'and I am about to walk out. Under the circumstances, it would be ridiculous to go on with my search for articles of value here, don't you agree?'

'You're an unmitigated scoundrel,' snarled the other, 'and, if you get away, I'll have the island searched from end to end for you.'

'I suppose you will,' came the cool retort, 'but I doubt if you will find me. Madam,' he turned again to the woman, 'I think it would be as well if you returned to your bed. The night air is chilly, and—'

'Address your remarks to me,' interrupted the man vehemently, 'and leave this lady out of it.'

Kenton shrugged his shoulders.

'I am glad you have told me she is a lady,' he retorted with calm insolence. 'I should have thought that a lady would have thrown a wrap, at least, over such exceedingly – er – scanty night attire.'

At that they both let their anger have full play in loud-voiced and threatening denunciations. He took no notice of them. By that time, he thought, the man whose retreat he was covering, should be well away. It was time he made a move himself. He began to walk backwards, continuing to keep the couple well covered with his automatic. At that moment came a thunderous knocking on the front door, and a few seconds later appeared two Chinese servants at the back of the hall. Kenton realised that his own retreat had been cut off, but not a tremor of fear or consternation troubled him. He even smiled at the expressions of triumph on the faces of the two he was holding up. At once he made up his mind.

'Upstairs, both of you,' he snapped, 'and you, too,' he added to the servants.

The latter, too frightened to advance, were only too willing to obey his command. They ran up the stairs, as though they expected momentarily to be riddled with bullets. The man and woman seemed inclined to defy him, but, as he began to advance towards them, their resolution was not proof against the menace of the weapon he held pointed so steadily at them. Reluctantly they retreated up the stairs. To his delight they presently reached an open door. Inside was in darkness, but the electric light in the corridor threw in enough illumination to show him a bathroom without any other exit. The servants had gone farther along. He called them back and, when they had approached in fear and trembling, herded the four into the bathroom. He quickly and adroitly removed the key from the inner side of the lock, and slipped it in the outside. For the fraction of a second his attention was off his prisoners and, in that infinitesimal space of time, both the man and woman fired hastily at him. He felt what seemed like two blows from a hammer, one on the side of his head, one in his left shoulder. He reeled drunkenly, but, with a great effort, pulled himself together, closed the door, as hands were about to grasp it, and turned the key.

He was compelled to lean against the wall in an effort to recover fully his faculties. Blood was streaming down his face, and his head was beginning to ache fiendishly, while his shoulder was already throbbing agonisingly. He felt in a daze and, despite his efforts, feared that his senses would leave him. He could still hear the hammering on the door below, and now, to add to the clamour, came the shouts of the people he had imprisoned. With a great struggle, he succeeded in getting full possession of his wits; staggered down the stairs to the hall below. Another manservant and an ayah stood fearfully there, attracted by the shooting, too terrified by the din to dare open the front door. The woman screamed, when she saw his blood-covered face. Kenton wondered vaguely why the people knocking had not found that one of the veranda windows was open.

'Half-witted lot it seems,' he muttered; 'plenty of other doors. Anyhow, there's a chance I'll be able to get away after all.'

He waved his hand uncertainly at the two servants, forgetful that in it he held the revolver. With squeals of terror they both dived under a blackwood table, their heads coming together with a crash. For a moment Kenton forgot his peril, and stood laughing at them. He pushed the automatic into a pocket; then made his way into the room Wallace had searched so thoroughly, bumped from one piece of furniture to another, eventually reaching the window. He pulled it open, and looked cautiously out. The knocking had now ceased, and he could dimly discern three men apparently engaged in a consultation.

'You try all the veranda windows, Thurston,' he heard one say. 'I'll go round to the back. You stay here, Fielder. By Jove! Listen to the shouting! There's something damnably wrong here.'

He ran down the veranda steps; one of the others came towards the window at which Kenton was standing. The latter immediately stepped out.

'Quick!' he cried loudly, though somewhat incoherently. 'There's been dirty work in here – I'm going for a doctor.'

In the darkness they could not see him distinctly, therefore failed to notice his shabby appearance and the blood on his face. Before they could speak, he had passed them, had staggered down the steps, and was making his erratic way towards the gates. For a couple of seconds they stared after him; then simultaneously dashed in the open window. Kenton gave a weak little chuckle. They were fooled, but for how long? There was not much chance of getting away, was there? He was stupidly weak; seemed unable to conquer that dizzy feeling; his feet did not appear to be treading on earth at all. He stumbled on to his hands and knees, and an excruciating pain shot through his shoulder. He felt that he would like to let himself go lie there where he had fallen. Impatiently he gave himself a shake, wincing at the pain that shot through his head. After what seemed ages, he was on his feet again. In the gloom the gates seemed a very long way off; he did not seem to be getting any nearer to them. Better not go that way, he decided; turned sharply to his left. From behind came a shout.

'There he is. Don't let him get away! He's a killer!'

'Killer, me!' laughed Kenton weakly to himself. 'Haven't fired a shot – not likely to.'

He made for a hedge and, at that moment, from behind came a regular fusillade. Something hummed by his ear like an angry bee; at the same time he felt a blow in the shoulder that had already been wounded. He made one last despairing effort to retain his senses; then all power of resistance to the blackness that seemed to be closing round deserted him, and he lost consciousness.

He opened his eyes to find, rather to his amazement, that he was lying in bed, apparently in a small whitewashed or distempered room. His left arm was strapped to his side; his shoulder appeared to be enveloped in bandages. A few minutes fumbling with his right hand convinced him that his head was similarly decorated.

'Must be in hospital again,' he muttered.

'Faith, and it's right you are first time, bad cess to you,' came a voice.

Kenton turned his head, and saw a man in a white jacket standing by his bed. He recognised him at once as the doctor who had had most to do with his rather wonderful recovery from his previous illness. A warm, though perhaps strange, friendship had been formed between these two during the weeks of the ex-engineer's convalescence. Perhaps not so strange after all, for, though Kenton was admittedly a man who had let himself sink to the depths, there was something very appealing about him to those who learnt to know him.

'Hullo, doc!' he greeted the medical man in a voice that sounded to his ears far away. 'How did I get here?'

'It's lucky you are to be under my tender care,' was the reply, 'and it's a puzzled man I am. I've watched over you, and nursed you like a baby, driven all the devils of hell away from you, and it's yourself repays me by being after committing a burglary. Outside the door at this very minute sits a policeman, and it's locked in you are, when the nurse and myself are away. Jimmy, me boy, is it mad you've become entirely?'

Kenton started to shake his head, found it a painful process, and desisted.

'I'll tell you all about it someday, doc,' he promised. 'I believe I'd be giving away secrets, if I told you now. But I'm not really a burglar.'

'Faith, I never believed you were. It's weak you are, or rather have been, for it's myself thinks you have recovered your manhood, but you're not a rogue. But 'tis said you were in a house shooting people in the early hours.'

'That's quite untrue. I was in the house, but I didn't do any shooting, and never intended to.'

'Then how are you after explainin' that in the automatic found on you two cartridges had been fired?'

Kenton laughed weakly. It was his companion who had done the shooting in Tavares' office – he remembered that now. But he could not say anything, could he? He had been concerned in some mysterious affair, but it had had the approbation of the Governor apparently, as his secretary had been there disguised as an Indian soldier. He had better say nothing, until he was able to get into communication with Carter.

'Things look black against me, don't they, doc?' he murmured.

The Irishman eyed him curiously.

'They do that,' he nodded; 'very black. But sure an' it's not my business at all, at all. My job is to be after getting you well.'

'Is there much wrong with me?'

'Well, it might be worse. You've had two bullets through your left shoulder, and it's passed within two inches of each other they have. The scapula's badly smashed, but it will mend with care and time. Another bullet was after grazing your skull just above the ear, but that will not take long to heal.' He frowned thoughtfully. 'It's myself is thinking,' he observed gently, 'that the more obstinate your wounds prove, the better it will be for you. When you are well, Jimmy, they'll be after putting you on trial, the devil take them. I'll keep you here as long as I can, me boy.'

Kenton smiled gratefully.

'You're a good sort, doc,' he declared. 'I already owe more to you than I can ever repay.'

'Ah, now none of your blarney! It's ashamed I ought to be letting you talk like this. Go to sleep for a little while, if you can. Nurse will be after bringing you some soup in half an hour.'

'What's the time?'

The doctor consulted his watch.

'Twenty to twelve,' he replied.

Kenton whistled.

'I've been unconscious quite a time,' he commented.

'A lot of it was forced unconsciousness,' retorted the medical man. 'Did we not put you under an anaesthetic to put that shoulder of yours right now?' He moved towards the door. 'I will be back this afternoon.'

'Just a minute, doc,' pleaded Kenton. 'This is a private room, isn't it? Who's paying for it?'

The Irishman snorted.

'There are bars on the windows, bedad! The door is strong, and has a lock. Faith, an' that's why you're here. Is it forgetting that it's a dangerous character you are?'

He snorted again. Kenton smiled.

'Doctor,' he whispered, 'I can rely on you, can't I?'

The Irishman eyed him thoughtfully.

'You can,' he asserted, also in low tones.

'Well, will you do me a favour, and keep it absolutely to yourself?'

'I will.'

'Thank you. Then, when you are perfectly certain no one can hear you, please ring up Government House, ask for the private secretary, Mr Carter, and say, "Kenton's in hospital". That's all. Will you do it?'

The doctor's eyebrows were raised, as he slowly nodded his head.

'Faith, and I will, and gladly. And it's not a soul will know anything about it.'

'You're a brick.'

Without another word, the Irishman left the room. Kenton heard the key turn in the lock.

It was close on noon when the telephone in Carter's office rang for perhaps the twentieth time that morning. He was busy, and exceedingly worried; it was, therefore, a trifle impatiently that he removed the receiver from its hook, and applied it to his ear.

'Hullo! Governor's secretary speaking,' he snapped.

'Mr Carter, is it now?' asked a voice, with a distinct suggestion in it that its owner hailed from the Emerald Isle.

'Of course. Who are you?'

'Sure I'm Connolly, senior HP at the hospital. Listen, Mr Carter, I've been asked in confidence to be after giving you this message – are you there?'

'Yes; go on!' urged Carter.

'This is it: Kenton's in hospital. Have you got it now?'

Carter suppressed a whistle, and frowned thoughtfully at the instrument. His mind was working rapidly.

'Yes,' he assured the other; 'I've got it all right. Let me see, Kenton is that drunkard you people were trying so hard to reclaim, isn't he? So he's lapsed? Bad luck! But I don't believe you can ever really hope to succeed with those fellows.'

Dr Connolly was about to launch out in defence of the man he had cured, and tell Carter that he was now lying wounded. But the memory of Kenton's words restrained him. There was something so mysterious about this affair that he felt the least said the better. With a curt goodbye, he rang off.

Carter heard the other replace his receiver, but continued listening for some moments. Presently there came a soft click and, with a grim smile, he hung up his own earpiece. He knew the line had been tapped; he had simply waited to make certain that someone had been listening in. His previous state of worry had been relieved by the news concerning Kenton, but another anxiety had arisen. He hurried out of the room; ran up the stairs to Sir Leonard's study. He found the latter closeted with the Inspector-General of Police, who had arrived a few minutes previously.

'May I speak to you privately for a moment, sir?' he begged.

At once the IG excused himself, and left the room. Wallace eyed his assistant questioningly.

'Well?' he prompted.

Carter told him about the telephone message, repeating practically word for word what he and the doctor had said. He concluded by mentioning that someone had been listening to the conversation, and confessed to a feeling of anxiety that the conspirators might thereby have gathered that Government House was concerned with the finding of Kenton in the house on the Peak. For some minutes Sir Leonard sat turning over in his mind what he had been told. Presently he shook his head.

'I don't think so,' he observed. 'You saved the situation, Carter, by your remark concerning Kenton being a drunkard the doctor was trying to reclaim. If you had shown any particular interest, there might have been danger of their growing suspicious. As a matter of fact, I don't suppose the name Kenton conveys anything to them at all. Whatever happened after I got away, it is hardly likely he told them his name. In any case it doesn't matter a great deal. I hope to have the whole bunch under lock and key by this time tomorrow. I'm glad you received news of Kenton – as you know, I was extremely anxious about him.'

'It looks as though he's been hurt, sir, since he is in hospital. Of course I was unable to ask for particulars.'

'Naturally,' nodded Sir Leonard. 'I would like you to go and find out, but it would not be judicious, and perhaps twenty-four hours more or less will not make any difference.' A sudden thought occurred to him. 'Look here; if Kenton was shot and overpowered, the police would know something about it. Call in Winstanley. By the way, you had better stay here; you might be interested.'

Sir Masterson Winstanley re-entered the room, and took the chair Wallace pushed forward.

'I was about to tell you, Winstanley,' commenced the latter, 'all I have discovered concerning what is known as the Hong Kong scandal, when Carter entered the room. Before going any further, it would be as well if I mentioned that the suspension which I imposed on the Legislative Council no longer applies to you. You will, from the time you leave this room, continue your duties as before.'

Winstanley gave vent to a sigh of relief. He did not look particularly gratified, however. That was, no doubt, due to the sense of grievance under which he was labouring, as his words indicated.

'I presume that means I am no longer among the suspected, sir,' he commented drily. 'Naturally I am glad, but I should like to say quite frankly that I consider your action was extremely high-handed. I have been tempted to offer my resignation. Perhaps you'll ask for it,' he added with a wry smile, 'since I have taken the liberty of being so outspoken.'

'You do me an injustice,' protested Wallace. 'I would never ask a man to resign simply because he was blunt in an expression of opinion. But I am going to show you that you and all the rest who thought I behaved in an arbitrary manner were wrong. I had no alternative. With regard to yourself I had no suspicions at all. My training has taught me to become a fairly sound judge of character, and yours stood the test. Also it may interest you to know that I have watched every man holding an official position on the Council since I arrived in Hong Kong. Keenly and searchingly I have studied their lives and their characters – I have imagined myself in their places, considered thoroughly the opportunities, the scope they had, if any, of being concerned in the conspiracy. For a long time I had little to help me, with the result that it was more or less a question of what I might describe as investigation by study. One by one, I eliminated certain officials, and you were among them. Mind you, I do not exonerate you and them from all blame. I think there has been a great deal of slackness in administration, but let that pass. When evidence, at last, fell into my hands, I found that I had not wasted my time. I was right.'

Winstanley, who had flushed at the rebuke, now leant eagerly forward.

'Do you mean to say, sir,' he cried, 'that you have actually discovered who the conspirators are?'

Sir Leonard looked up at Carter, who was standing near the desk.

'You are certain that door is fastened tightly?' he asked.

'Yes, sir,' replied Carter. Nevertheless, he tried it again.

'I have already made certain there are no creatures, deformed or otherwise, hidden in the room,' went on Wallace drily, and turned to the Chief of Police. 'Yes,' he nodded; 'I know who the conspirators are.'

Sir Masterson breathed deeply. His eyes were aglow with excitement.

'May I know—' he began.

'Just a minute,' Sir Leonard interrupted. 'There is an item of information I want from you which, for the moment, may appear irrelevant. Although you have been under suspension you have naturally kept in touch with police affairs. Do you happen to know if a man – an Englishman – was found in a house last night on the Peak and shot?'

'Why, yes,' returned the IG. 'It was a pretty sordid kind of affair. There hasn't been time for it to get into the papers yet, but one of those vagabonds, of whom we get such a number out East, broke in. When he was discovered, he held up the occupants at the point of a revolver, and locked them in a bathroom. He had fired at them apparently, for the sound of shots was heard, rousing people in of the neighbourhood, who ran to see what had happened. Afterwards, when searched, it was found that he had fired two shots. A pretty dangerous character altogether, I should think, from what I have been told. Anyhow, in attempting to get away he was brought down. He is now in hospital under police supervision.'

'Ah!' commented Wallace. 'Is he badly hurt?'

'His shoulder blade was smashed by a couple of bullets, and he has a scalp wound. But he'll recover all right. And,' he added sternly, 'I'll see that he is made an example of.'

Sir Leonard shook his head slowly.

'No, you won't, Winstanley,' he said quietly. 'You won't even prosecute.'

'But – I don't understand.'

'You will presently. What is his name, by the way?'

'It is not known yet. He had not recovered consciousness when I last heard about him, an hour or so ago.'

'Good!' commented Wallace, and the Chief of Police frowned his perplexity. 'Now to resume,' went on the Governor: 'A good deal of what I am about to tell you is conjecture, but it fits in. Once you have the conspirators in gaol, it should not be difficult to supply the missing links. I think you can be pretty certain that one, perhaps two, when they are sure they will be safe from vengeance, will gladly turn King's evidence.' He brushed his hand in a weary gesture across his forehead, and sighed. 'To do what I am about to do,' he confessed, 'will cause me to feel a very deep regret for the rest of my life, because it will cast a blot on the administration of British colonies, and the integrity of officials, which will require years to erase. But it must be done. It cannot be hushed up, or kept secret. Too much is involved.

'I came out here with full executive power, absolute *carte blanche* from the British Government. My term of office as Governor was to last for six months or longer if necessary, Sir Stanley Ferguson, as you know, being granted sick leave. I was handicapped from the first, because it was known to the conspirators that I was the Chief of the British Secret Service. They were, therefore, under no delusion concerning the real reason why I had accepted the appointment. A Chinaman in their service, a well-known merchant of Kowloon, accompanied us on the voyage from Marseilles. He set out to worm his way into my confidence, and I let him. He has the entry of Government House at any time, and has taken full advantage of this privilege. While apparently assiduous in his attentions and devotion to me, he has surrounded me with spies, and has succeeded in cramping my movements very badly.'

'How did you find out that he was in the pay of the conspirators, sir?' queried Winstanley.

'A little incident on board ship first roused my suspicions; then came his very flowery offer. Afterwards, two innocently worded wireless messages, one from the Chinaman to his own address in Kowloon, the other from Hong Kong, convinced me. Before leaving England, I had sent an agent of mine to Hong Kong. He travelled most of the way by air, and arrived some time before I did. His instructions were to get in touch with Tavares, who at one time was the confidential servant of Mathos, and find out all he could.'

'But we spent days in questioning Tavares,' objected the IG.

'I know you did, and he emerged triumphant from the ordeal. Nevertheless, Tavares knew practically everything. I should imagine he had been blackmailing Mathos for a considerable time prior to his death, or perhaps the banker confided in him for his own protection, and paid him a percentage of his profits. At all events, Tavares became a wealthy man, and has since been the confidant of the other conspirators. On one side of his establishment as you are aware, is a house in which the ground floor is devoted to a Turkish bath business; on the other side is the residence of a man called Sales. The conspirators are in the habit of holding their meetings in a room set apart for the purpose in Sales' house. No interest or curiosity has ever been caused by men of their type, and, I may as well add, high position, congregating in the house of a Macanese who is merely a retired minor official, because they do not enter by his doors. It is their habit to walk openly into the Turkish bath establishment – who would take the slightest notice of that? Many men of rank go there – but, once inside, they ascend to the floor above, where Tavares has a flat, enter the next house by a secret entrance that opens into his office, walk along a couple of passages, and through another secret door into the house that is supposed to belong to Sales. As a matter of fact, there is not the slightest doubt in my mind but that Tavares owns all three houses, and that Sales and the man who ostensibly manages the Turkish baths are in his pay.'

He went on to tell the astonished police official of the discoveries made by Cousins, and the latter's attempt to listen to the discussion at the meeting on the 16th September, which had resulted in his falling and breaking his leg. Sir Leonard then told of his own narrow escape at Singapore, and the decision of the conspirators to make no attempt on his life in Hong Kong until they were convinced that he was becoming dangerous to them. He further related how he had been present at the murder of Baxter in London, and of the significance he had attached to the discovery that three Phillipinos, apparently related, who called themselves Gochuico, but whose actual name, he believed, was Feodoro, had been sent on the track of Baxter, and had murdered him to prevent his revealing the identity of their employer. When the Inspector-General heard the name Feodoro, his face paled, and he clutched the arms of his chair.

'Good God!' he muttered. 'They were in the employ of—'

'Exactly,' interrupted Sir Leonard grimly. 'You are beginning to see daylight. It is only recently that I discovered who was their master. We'll leave that point for the moment, however. This is what I think led up to the disclosure of the conspiracy and the death of Mathos – we shall soon be in a position to verify it: the ringleaders found that it was becoming impossible any longer to prevent revelation. The affair had grown so gigantic that quite a number of minor officials were beginning to get suspicious, probably because documents that went through their hands roused their curiosity. Although, in the ordinary way, the rank and file of clerks deal with the work of their own particular department alone, and take no interest in that of others, the discrepancies, in time, were bound to be noticed. Possibly, in the course of conversation, statements were made by some which others knew must be incorrect. Thus inquisitiveness was engendered. At once action was taken, and very cleverly, by the principals. They pretended to suspect leakages, investigation was ordered, and the whole appalling situation became public knowledge. Initial inquiries pointed to Mathos. His arrest was ordered, but, when the police arrived, he was found to be dead. Apparently he had committed suicide to avoid the consequences of his actions. But he did not commit suicide. He was murdered.'

He raised his hand as Winstanley was about to speak.

'I know what you are going to say; the revolver in his hand, the wound, everything pointed to suicide! But the fact that nothing was found to incriminate his confederates caused me to think from the very start that he had been murdered, first to prevent his talking and, secondly, to obtain whatever he possessed, the revelation of which would undermine the security of those concerned in the conspiracy with him. Mathos was not the type of man to commit suicide. From what I have learnt about him, I believe it would have given him a warped sort of pleasure to have involved in his ruin those whose fall would be greater and far more cataclysmic than his. He was murdered, Winstanley, without a doubt, and his murderer was one of the most senior men of your own department. I refer to Wayne, the Divisional Superintendent of Police!'

CHAPTER TWENTY-TWO

Wun Cheng Lo is Shocked and Pained

Sir Masterson was now as pale as death. He sat rigid in his chair.

'I can't – I simply can't believe it,' he whispered at last.

'I'm afraid there is no possible shadow of doubt,' returned Sir Leonard quietly. 'I am convinced that he was also concerned in, if not actually responsible for, the deaths of the Shanghai magistrate, the Chinese banker, and Mr Burrows, all of whom had announced their intention of imparting information which had come into their possession concerning the plot. He travelled by the same boat from which the magistrate fell overboard and was drowned; the banker dined with him a few hours before he was found poisoned. Wayne was also in charge of the police whom you delegated to guard Burrows. All that could be coincidence, as also could be the fact that, when the other divisional superintendent, Ponsford, arrived to arrest Mathos, he met

Wayne near the house, who told him he had gone ahead
to prevent the Macanese escaping, in case he got wind of
what was intended. But these papers' – he tapped a roll of
documents on his desk – 'definitely state that Wayne killed
Mathos.'

'What are they?' asked Winstanley hoarsely.

'Most of them are the documents which Mathos kept as a
safeguard against betrayal by his confederates, the documents
which were known to be in existence, and which Wayne
expected to procure after killing him. But Tavares had stolen
a march on him, and has kept them ever since. They consist
of letters from members of the gang to Mathos of a most
incriminating nature, with a statement by Tavares – written, I
presume, to make certain that, if anything happened to him,
they would not escape justice. Among other things, he declares
that he actually saw Wayne kill Mathos. Obviously Tavares
was reaping a rich reward as the result of his possession of
the documents, and his house, or rather houses, became the
headquarters of the organisation. He had too much faith in
his safe, however, or in his ability to keep the keys in his
possession. Last night Carter and I went to search the office
in the hope of finding there the evidence we required. You
see, I felt certain all along that Tavares must have some hold
over the others. If he had not, it is certain that, possessing
the knowledge he did, they would have killed him as they
killed his master. While Carter and I were in the study,
two men entered and, with a key, obviously made from a
wax impression – Tavares must have been caught napping
at some time – they opened the safe, and took from it this
roll of papers. By a trick I obtained them, but was forced to

shoot the two men. You will find that Wayne is not on duty today. He was one of them. The other is Donald Waverley, cashier to the Treasury Department. I'm afraid they must be finding a great deal of difficulty in explaining away identical bullet wounds above the knee, while they and their fellow crooks are, no doubt, in a state of anxiety on account of the loss of those papers and another which I also have here. You had better glance through them, Winstanley.' He handed the packet to the IG. 'You will find that they prove the guilt of the First Assistant Auditor of the Audit Department, Percival Stevenson, the Treasury Cashier, Donald Waverley, Divisional Superintendent of Police, Henry Wayne, and the Postmaster-General, Gabriel Gomez.'

'Good Heavens! It sounds incredible!' muttered Winstanley, as he took the papers.

He read them slowly and carefully through, neither of the others interrupting him in any way during his perusal. At last he handed them back.

'It is appalling,' he commented. 'So this is the end of the conspiracy – my God! What an end!'

'As you say,' repeated Wallace, 'what an end! But the two ringleaders are not mentioned there. They were clever enough to avoid putting anything in writing. By a fortunate circumstance, a letter was delivered to one of them yesterday. It was in the nature of a threat from what I shall call the Japanese element. Having nothing but my suspicions to go on, I went to the Peak last night, or rather early this morning, after leaving Tavares' office, hoping, by committing a burglary, to obtain the evidence I required. I searched thoroughly, but for a long time feared I was doomed to failure. It was in one

of the pockets of a pair of folded trousers that I found this.'
He held up a crumpled letter. 'It turned out to be the last link
in the chain of evidence. A dog barked while I was passing
the bedrooms, and I was shot through the fleshy part of a leg.
No! Don't look startled; it's nothing really – a bit stiff and
sore today, but nothing of consequence. While I escaped, a
man, whom I shall henceforth be proud to number among
my friends, remained, and covered my retreat. It seems that
he was badly wounded, and is now in hospital under police
guard. Now you perhaps realise why I said that you will not
prosecute him.'

'Good Lord!' The Inspector-General's speech that
morning consisted mostly of exclamations of amazement.
'Then, do you mean to say that Collinson is the ringleader?'

Sir Leonard nodded.

'One of them,' he replied calmly. 'The other is Sir Stanley
Ferguson, recently Governor of Hong Kong.'

There was absolute silence while his hearers attempted to
assimilate his astounding declaration. Carter was as much
amazed as Winstanley, for Sir Leonard had not told him of
his suspicions, or of the contents of the letter he had found.
The Chief of the Secret Service held out the missive to them.

'Read it,' he suggested. 'It not only proves the guilt
of the two men, but shows the connection between the
misappropriation of the finances and the sale of confidential
military information to Japan. The writer, as you see, is Mr
Yumasaki, the Japanese Consul in Victoria.'

Winstanley took the letter and read it through, after
which he handed it to Carter without a word. It was dated
from the Japanese Consulate, and ran:

Dear Mr Collinson,

Your telephone message informing me of your determination to go no further with our agreement has caused me a great deal of pain. I say pain, because I shall be most reluctant to take the course I am instructed to take in the event of your failure to carry out the terms of our bargain. So far, all we have received from you are the plans of fortification which, though of great importance, are not paramount. There remain the chart showing the exact position of the minefields, lists of the number and calibre of the big guns, and a map in which all magazines and other military stores are located. These you promised would be in my possession shortly after our last meeting, and now you telephone to say you cannot do it. It is distasteful to be compelled to remind you of the consequences of default. But it is inevitable, if you persist in your determination, that the present Governor shall be but in full possession of facts relating to the conspiracy against the Treasury, which you and Sir Stanley Ferguson, and those who have assisted you, manipulated with such astounding, though I personally feel deplorable, success. It was perhaps an evil day for you when the agent of my country, while searching Government House for certain plans we believed to be hidden there, brought away a document concerning the plot in which appeared a full list of the members of the organisation. But, from our point of view, it was a fortuitous lever to help us attain our desires, and we cannot be blamed for using it. It is impossible that

*suspicion can be roused against Sir Stanley Ferguson
and Mr Meredith Collinson – gentlemen of such high
position and <u>integrity</u> unless it becomes my painful
duty to inform the British authorities of the manner
in which they have betrayed their trust, and, with
others, systematically robbed the Treasury. That I will
do only with the greatest reluctance, if compelled by
a continuation of your present attitude. On the other
hand, if you fulfil your contract, you need never fear
that your secret will be divulged.*

   I am, dear Mr Collinson,
   Very sincerely yours,
   Yumasaki

The Inspector-General made no comment. He was
altogether too surprised by the revelations. He sat there
bemused, perhaps hoping that he was dreaming it all. Sir
Masterson Winstanley, as it will probably be surmised, was
not a brilliant man, but he was intensely patriotic, and it
came upon him, with something in the nature of an icy
shock, what these disclosures would mean to his country.
It was terribly difficult to credit that men like Ferguson,
Collinson, Stevenson, Waverley, and Wayne, who had been
his friends, with whom he had lunched, dined, and generally
associated, had done these things of which he now had proof.
He regarded Gabriel Gomez in a different light. He was the
son of a Portuguese father and English mother, who had been
born and educated in Hong Kong, and had risen to his high
position as Postmaster-General by sheer ability. Nevertheless,
he was a half-caste. Carter, though equally appalled at the

realisation that Britons could thus betray their great trust, was thrilled by the knowledge that Sir Leonard, despite great obstacles, had succeeded in his task.

'What made you suspect Sir Stanley Ferguson and Mr Collinson, sir?' he asked.

A slight smile crossed Sir Leonard's face, but there was no mirth in it, rather it carried the suggestion of sadness.

'A combination of little circumstances caused me to wonder if Ferguson could possibly be involved,' he replied. 'To start with, it occurred to me that Wun Cheng Lo showed a remarkable knowledge of this building for a man who, presumably, had not had the run of it before. On being questioned, he stated that he had never been inside. Then I found that the staff of servants had been entirely changed a week or so before we arrived in the colony. I wondered why. To add to my mystification, I discovered that a new set of account books was in use; the old ones had mysteriously disappeared. You will remember that I asked you to make inquiries with a view to finding them. You were baulked at every point, and the books never appeared. I commenced to search the house in my leisure moments, not with any serious idea in my head, but because of the little circumstances that puzzled me. It seemed ridiculous then to associate Ferguson with the conspiracy, especially as the very fact that he had apparently welcomed sick leave would appear to point to his entire innocence. No guilty man would welcome the idea of being replaced by someone who would set out to pry into affairs.

'At last I obtained my first real clue. I came across one of the servant's children playing with an old torn prayer book. As I was determined to let nothing of an unusual nature

go by without investigation, I examined the book. On the
flyleaf was written the name "G. Feodoro". Immediately I
made inquiries of the child's father, and was informed that
the book had been found with a lot of lumber in a corner
of the servants' compound. After that, I continued my local
investigations, as I may as well call them, with renewed
energy. My great difficulty all the time has been that I
did not know whom I could sufficiently trust to question,
without Wun Cheng Lo and his satellites learning of the line
of investigation I was taking. However, Captain Barker got
in touch with his predecessor, from whom he gathered the
information that Ferguson had a liking for Phillipinos and,
at one time, had three brothers in service here. Their name
was Feodoro! I felt fairly certain once I knew that that he
was involved. Unlike the majority of colonial governors, he
was appointed while actually serving in Hong Kong. He had
thus been here during the whole course of the conspiracy.
I had instructed Batty to search, and to bring me anything
he found that might have been lying about for a long time.
He brought me several things from time to time, which
by no stretch of imagination could have been helpful.' He
smiled at the recollection. 'But one thing he found proved
highly significant. It was a demand for the payment of three
hundred dollars with interest, instalment due on a loan from
G. Mathos to S. Ferguson, Esquire, and was dated some
years back, when Ferguson was Colonial Secretary. It had
been rolled up with some other pieces of paper, and stuffed
into a small crack in the storm shutters of the dressing
room. Apparently Ferguson had carried it about for years,
and one night, perhaps during a storm, had used it with the

other scraps of paper to stop up the crack, and thus prevent a draught – a piece of rank carelessness for a criminal to commit. It is yellow with age and exposure, but perfectly legible. Here it is.'

He removed it carefully from his pocket-book, and showed it to them, afterwards placing it with the other documents on the desk.

'I think I suspected Collinson first,' he went on, 'when I had a talk with him here a few days ago after the other official members of the Legislative Council had left. Cousins described the voice of the man who spoke most at the meeting in September as exceedingly cultured and well bred. While I was talking to Collinson it occurred to me how well his voice fitted the description; then two remarks he made roused my suspicions. One was, "If we drop further investigation, the whole thing will die a natural death". Innocent enough, of course, but could not the wish be father to the thought, so to speak? The second was – "I only pray that no harm will overtake you in your endeavours". That also was very innocent-sounding – a kindly sentiment in fact – but I happened to be watching his hands at the time – hands can be very expressive, you know – and he was clenching them until the nails pierced the flesh. He really meant, "I pray that harm *will* overtake you". Finally, he made a bad bloomer, but I do not think he noticed it. I was speaking about the theft of the plans of the fortifications, and stated that I was positive the conspirators had been concerned in the transaction. Thereupon he said, "I suppose you found out through the Japanese agent who is in league with them". Now only a member of the organisation could possibly know that a Japanese *was* in league with them. When he made that remark I was convinced he was the man I wanted. If any further verification was necessary, it was supplied by the flight of Tavares to Macao. I told Collinson that I intended having the fellow here, and giving him a thorough grilling. Before that could be done, Tavares had gone, obviously to avoid being questioned. Only Collinson could have told him of my intentions.

'I think he has been the moving spirit in the conspiracy all along. The manner in which he, when Senior Assistant Treasurer, made, or rather pretended to make, the discovery that the finances were being defrauded, and the great zeal he showed in sifting the criminal activities of Mathos was exceedingly clever. I don't think he and Ferguson bothered much about the other men in the conspiracy with them. They did their utmost to protect themselves, taking care to avoid the traps into which the others had fallen. If it had not been for the Japanese Consul, and that letter, what proof would there be against them? The others might endeavour to involve them in their ruin, but I doubt if they would have succeeded. The idea would appear too fantastic. Collinson only made the disclosures when he knew things were bound to be found out; then both acted promptly and convincingly. Who would suspect the Governor or the man who had brought to light a great plot? Nobody. Ferguson was commiserated with on the strain which the investigations had caused him, and given sick leave. Collinson was promoted to Colonial Treasurer, and awarded the CMG; I believe that they were hopeful of laying the whole blame on the shoulders of Mathos. When it became evident that that could not be done; when everything indicated that a member or members of the legislature must be involved, Collinson showed greater zeal than ever. It was through him that certain clerks, who had taken advantage of the general slackness by attempting to feather their own nests, were arrested, tried, and sent to prison. But even that did not satisfy the public outcry and indignant demand for the fullest investigation. Certain people, of the type of Burrows, wanted the scandal sifted to the very bottom, and the good name and reputation of Hong Kong restored, no matter what it cost. Ferguson was forced to send a full report to the Colonial Office, with the result that I came out to take his place.'

'It seems to me strange,' mused the Inspector-General, 'that he should ask to be relieved at such a time. Surely, from his point of view, it was a most risky step to take. He may not have known that you would be appointed in his place, sir – in fact, I don't suppose such an idea occurred to him – but there was always the possibility that whoever came might find out something of danger to himself and Collinson.'

'He did not ask to be relieved,' smiled Wallace, 'and I am certain it was the last thing he desired. But, when he made his report, he committed the mistake, in his covering letter to the Secretary of State for the Colonies, of stating that the strain, caused by the appalling nature of the scandal, had brought him to the verge of a nervous breakdown. The Colonial Secretary immediately conceived the idea of giving him leave and suggesting to the Cabinet that I be asked to take his place. Ferguson's first notification of this was a cable informing him that six months' sick leave was granted him dating from September the fifteenth, on which day I would arrive in Hong Kong and take his place. He could not protest or refuse the leave, but, before I arrived, he and Collinson did everything in their power to make things difficult for me. Collinson has gone on doing that ever since.'

'What a shock that cable must have been!' commented the Chief of Police.

'I suppose it was. Well, now, Winstanley, it's up to you. I'm not going to rub it in, because I am sure that Collinson, with the assistance of Wayne, did everything to render police activities abortive; nevertheless, you have been slack, and must admit it. You can wipe that out, however, by making your arrangements to apprehend the conspirators foolproof. Remember to choose your men with care. It is quite likely – in fact, probable – that Wayne has corrupted some, particularly those of his own division. As far as possible, strike everywhere at the same time; that will prevent warning reaching any of them. Wayne and Waverley should prove easy to arrest, as they are wounded men. Stevenson shares a bungalow with Waverley, which is another helpful feature from your point of view. There remain Collinson, Gomez, Sales, Tavares and the Feodoro brothers. The Phillipinos will eventually have to be sent to England to stand their trial on the charge of committing and being concerned in the murder of Baxter. Before that happens, however, we'll see how much evidence we can get out of them for our own purposes. I only hope they are all in the colony by now – we know one is. It is a pity Tavares is in Macao. Perhaps Cousins will be able to trick him into returning, once the others are under lock and key, and cannot communicate with him. I want you to raid the three houses comprising the block in which Tavares lived and conducted his activities, and take everyone found there into custody. Sales is to be kept apart. I want him and Tavares as King's evidence. I think that is about all – I'll see to Wun Cheng Lo myself, and a cable in code will go to London this afternoon demanding the arrest of Ferguson. How long will it take you to make your preparations?'

Winstanley considered the matter.

'I think the best time to carry out the arrests, sir,' he replied at length, 'will be between six and seven tomorrow morning. They will all be in their homes then, and I shall have had ample time to make my plans and get my men into position.'

'Good. I'll prepare the warrants myself. Come and see me this evening, and I'll hand them to you. Be very careful of Collinson. He's likely to prove a slippery customer.'

'What do you propose to do about the Japanese Consul, sir?'

'That's a very ticklish matter. Of course a strongly-worded protest will be sent to Japan by the British Government concerning the espionage activities of their agents. Japan will naturally deny all knowledge and recall the consul. That is all that will happen on that point, I suppose. But we will subpoena the consul as witness against Ferguson and Collinson on the other charge, and keep him here, even if we have to place him under arrest.'

'He is privileged – we cannot arrest him, sir.'

'We can, as soon as Japan relieves him of his appointment, which she is bound to do on receipt of the British note.'

Winstanley smiled. There appeared to be nothing, he reflected, that the slight, grey-eyed Chief of the British Secret Service overlooked. He rose, and prepared to take his departure.

'Do you still consider my action in suspending the Legislative Council high-handed?' asked Wallace casually.

A dull flush overspread the stern features of the policeman.

'I certainly do not, sir,' he replied in exceedingly humble tones for him. 'I owe you a very sincere apology.'

Sir Leonard laughed, rose, and clapped him on the back.

'My dear Winstanley,' he confessed, 'if I had been in your place, I should certainly have felt exactly the same as you.'

After tiffin, Wallace handed Carter a sheaf of papers which he had taken from his pocket.

'Put that message in the DCO code,' he directed, 'and despatch it, but not before five. There will be no fear then of news reaching Hong Kong before tomorrow morning of Ferguson's arrest.'

He walked out, leaving Carter to his task, which took some time. When eventually it was done it was close on the hour for afternoon tea, which he had promised to take with Lady Wallace and Captain Ferrara. Carter verified his work, destroyed the original, and locked away the code book.

It had naturally been somewhat difficult to keep Captain Ferrara within the bounds of Government House, without causing the genial seaman to feel a sense of surprised inquisitiveness. However, it was managed; the Italian having no idea that he was under a close protective watch. The Governor did not think it likely that he would be recognised, as neither Wayne nor Waverley was about, but there was a possibility that their description of the man who had taken the papers from them and shot them might have caused some emissary, on the lookout, to apply the description to Ferrara, and thus place him in grave danger. Kenton had been badly wounded; Sir Leonard had no intention, if he could help it, of allowing another man who had been of service to him to suffer. A telephone message to the agents of the Maritima Italiana Company had resulted in the chief officer of the *Arabia* being informed that his captain was remaining at Government House as a guest for two or three days, and given the necessary orders to take temporary charge. A bag was packed, according to Ferrara's instructions, and sent to him, not the least important of the articles placed in it being a tin of prickly-heat powder. Lady Wallace had, of necessity, to be told something of the circumstances and, though her anxiety for her husband increased, it was she who arranged matters in such a way that the notion of going outside the grounds never occurred to the Italian.

Carter found them being served with tea under the shade of a group of banana trees. Ferrara had out his little book, and was jotting down, according to sound, a fresh list of proverbs dictated to him by the smiling Molly.

'Ah!' he exclaimed, as the secretary approached; 'comes for tea a hungry man. "A steetch in times safes ni-nine".'

'I am not hungry, my dear Ferrara,' laughed Carter, 'but I could not resist your company. Remember, "Birds of a feather flock together".'

The captain beamed.

'Anozzer!' he exclaimed triumphantly. 'Wait! I will write.' Laboriously he inscribed half a dozen strange-looking words in his book; then read: '"Birds of fezzers flock togezzer". To your satisfaction?'

'Quite,' they both agreed.

They had almost finished tea, when Sir Leonard joined

them. Carter thought he detected an unusual gleam in the Chief's eye. Something out of the ordinary had happened. It was not until an hour later, however, that his curiosity was satisfied.

'I had a telephone message from Cousins before tea,' announced Wallace quietly.

'From Cousins?' repeated Carter in great surprise.

'Yes; he is back in Hong Kong, and Tavares has returned with him. Apparently the conspirators have had their suspicions aroused. At all events, Cousins is to be smuggled in tonight by Wun Cheng Lo to do his knife-throwing act. The poor fellow seems to have had a pretty bad time since he left hospital. They've been at him all the time, worrying him, and doing their best to craze him by threats of the consequences, if he refuses to obey them. They even made a tiny gallows, and danced a figure about on it before his eyes. He thinks that a man, who had really committed a murder, would have been thoroughly unnerved, and made pliable by their behaviour, though he has been inwardly amused. They brought him back by fast motor cruiser today and, on the way, told him what they wanted him to do. At first he pretended to be horrified, and refused, but under compulsion reluctantly agreed to obey. A very significant fact is that the motor boat is manned by a crew of twenty pirates. Cousins found that out by listening to a conversation which he was not supposed to understand. Ho Fang Ho was quite right – Tavares is connected with a band of pirates. The plan is that, if Cousins fails with his knife, Wun Cheng Lo, who will have doubly gained my confidence by shooting him dead, will smuggle in the twenty cut-throats, and let them loose to massacre everyone in this building who is not in his pay. Great little scheme, isn't it?'

'How abominable!' cried Carter. 'Good Heavens! What fiends these people are! But how did Cousins manage to telephone, sir, and what about the listeners?'

'They shut him in a room with a half bottle of brandy to keep him company and, I presume, give him just enough, and not too much, courage for tonight's business. There happened to be a telephone in the room, and he took the risk. As he spoke Russian, the chances of a listener understanding were very remote. I had the utmost difficulty, for it is one of the languages with which I am not very well acquainted. However, he helped me out with words I did not understand by putting them in German – a combination, I should imagine, calculated to beat anyone.'

Carter's eyes shone.

'Good old Jerry!' he exclaimed. 'Did he tell you what time the play commences, sir?'

'He did not know. But that doesn't matter much. We'll expect him when we see him, so to speak. However, all preparations are made. Wun Cheng Lo and the pirates are due for a nasty surprise.'

A conversation Wallace had had with Sir Henry Dalkeith – the General in command of troops – during the afternoon had resulted in fatigue parties of Indian sepoys appearing in the grounds of Government House to sweep up the fallen leaves, and generally tidy up. As there was big dinner party that night for the naval and military element of Hong Kong, it was, perhaps, quite natural that the gardeners should receive the assistance of troops. Probably nobody noticed, however, that whereas half a dozen, sometimes ten, stalwart Sikhs accompanied the barrows that went in, only two or three went out with them, and that then they did not contain certain implements wrapped in canvas that had been borne in under shovels, rakes, and various other gardening utensils. The canvas-shrouded articles were later carried unostentatiously to the guardroom, and their coverings removed. They proved to be rifles. The men who had not departed with the barrows remained inconspicuously out of the way in a remote and thickly shrubby part of the grounds, ready to reinforce their comrades of the guard when called upon.

Captain Ferrara and Carter dined together in a small room adjoining the large dining hall. As neither was connected with the British Army or Navy, he was unable to take part in what was strictly a service affair, but they could observe the brilliant uniforms of the officers and dainty toilettes of the latter's wives. Ferrara was thrilled, while he went into ecstasies over the musical programme played splendidly by the band of the Royal West Kent Regiment, with all the precision of time and execution so typical of British military bands. When Carter sent a note to the bandmaster asking for a selection from *Rigoletto*, a request which was immediately complied with, Ferrara became so enthusiastic that the secretary had the greatest difficulty in preventing him from standing up, and lilting the opera through with all the power of his lungs. However, he contented himself with singing in a low voice to his companion, consequently neglecting his dinner.

Afterwards in the grounds, beautifully lit by hundreds of fairy lamps hanging from the trees, he was taken among the guests by Carter, and introduced to many of them, but it was the music that continued to appeal most. He stood at the right distance from the band to catch the quality of each instrument, beating time with his hands, occasionally humming a refrain. Ferrara was blissfully happy. When the visitors departed, and the band dispersed to partake of well-earned refreshment, he gave vent to a deep sigh expressive of regret. Sir Leonard shook hands with the last guest, and limped across the lawn to join him. In his mess dress of a full colonel, with its row of glittering decorations and war medals, the Governor certainly looked a striking figure, but hardly merited Ferrara's description.

'I look now,' the Italian declared, 'to my satisfaction at the greatest beautiful Governor.'

Sir Leonard took him to a small drawing room where Molly sat awaiting him. In her evening gown of gold tissue, she made a lovely picture, too lovely for any superlatives the entranced captain could think of in English, while he dared not say what he felt in Italian for fear that she would misunderstand his enthusiasm. While stirring events were happening elsewhere, she entertained him, and he never guessed that behind her glorious, smiling eyes lurked a fear lest something might go wrong with her husband's plans with which she had been made acquainted. When Ferrara quoted 'There is many slips 'twix cups of leeps,' she almost felt that his words were an evil omen, but still continued to smile and chat away to her guest.

Twenty minutes before midnight Sir Leonard left his study, and walked along the softly carpeted corridor. Suddenly, as he was approaching a corner, something glittering sped with lightning-like rapidity across the gallery in front of him.

There came a scream of pain, the noise of a heavy object falling to the floor, and Wun Cheng Lo emerged from an alcove, his left hand gripping his right wrist, just below which gleamed a knife. It had gone clean through from back to front, and blood was dropping in a steady stream to the carpet. Round the corner appeared Cousins, rather paler, perhaps even thinner than usual, but with his face creased in one of its illimitable smiles.

'I didn't like the look of that revolver in his hand,' he observed calmly, as he retrieved the fallen weapon, 'and, as he was so anxious for me to use the knife, I used it.'

Behind Sir Leonard appeared Carter and Captain Barker. From all directions came troops, some British – these had marched into Government House with the band – some Sikhs, until the corridor quickly became crowded.

'The game is up, Wun Cheng Lo,' Sir Leonard announced sternly, and, indicating Cousins, added: 'This gentleman whom you and your confederates thought to use as an instrument to encompass my death, and afterwards murder, is a member of the British Intelligence Service.'

CHAPTER TWENTY-THREE

The End of a Great Conspiracy

Wun Cheng Lo's face was no longer expressionless. It was distorted with pain and malevolence, as he looked unutterable things at Cousins. The latter stepped forward, and drew the knife from the wound; afterwards tying a handkerchief, given to him by Carter, round the hand.

'Let this be a lesson to you to lead a better life in future,' he enjoined with mock severity. 'It is no use scowling at me in that manner. Hatred doesn't kill. "Vice is a monster of so frightful mien | As, to be hated, needs but to be seen".'

The Chinaman, although he must have known it was useless, made an attempt, in loud protesting tones, to assure Sir Leonard that he was innocent. The Governor interrupted his protestations contemptuously.

'I have known of your duplicity since you came to me with your flowery lies on the *Rawalpindi*,' he told him in tones vibrating with scorn, and turned to Carter. 'Take him away,' he ordered. 'You'd better telephone for a doctor.'

Sir Leonard had made his arrangements with care. One by one the spies who had been placed in the house under the guise of servants were arrested, all of them being locked in a cellar, and a guard placed before the door. A cordon of troops surrounded the building, making it impossible for anyone to get in or out without being seen. Most of the illuminations had been extinguished, but a few lights remained, and Cousins, who was in high good humour, was constrained to quote: '"The troops exulting sat in order round, And beaming fires illumined all the ground". Pope must have anticipated this scene,' he added to Carter.

'The troops are not sitting,' came from that prosaic young man, 'neither are there any fires illumining the ground.'

'Pshaw!' exclaimed Cousins in deep disgust. 'What a creature! It grieves me to reflect that you lack a "Vital spark of heavenly flame". Ah, well! We cannot all be worshippers at the shrine of Calliope.'

Outside Government House waited the party of pirates that Tavares had brought with him from Macao. When Sir Leonard learnt from Cousins that the Macanese himself was there with them, he smiled.

'We shall have him sooner than I anticipated,' he commented. 'All the better.'

A plan had already been decided upon whereby it was hoped to take the pirates by surprise. Wallace wanted no bloodshed, if it could be avoided. He realised that when cornered, the ruffians would fight like fiends, if they were not overpowered before they could offer resistance, especially as they were led in person by Pei Wu Chow, known to be one of the most bloodthirsty scoundrels on the coast. The exact location of the place where they were congregated was known to Cousins, for they had already taken up position when he and Tavares had arrived on the scene. It was situated almost directly opposite one of the smaller pairs of gates, always kept locked at night, where, in the midst of some dense shrubbery, they were well hidden from view.

Forty soldiers were moved quietly to the vicinity of the gates; then Cousins climbed over them – the leg which had been broken seemed to give him no trouble. He disappeared from view, and Sir Leonard, Carter, Captain Barker, and the officers in charge of the troops waited anxiously. They knew well enough that, if the slightest suspicion was created, Cousins' life would pay the price.

The little Secret Service man felt no apprehension himself. As soon as he had reached the other side of the gates, he looked carefully about him, though it was too dark to see anything clearly; crept across to the shrubbery. A light was suddenly flashed in his face, while several hands roughly gripped his arms. He felt the point of a knife at his throat; then came the low voice of Tavares speaking in Chinese, apparently reassuring his companions. The light was extinguished, the knife removed, but still the hands held Cousins in a tight hold.

'What is it that has happened?' came anxiously from Tavares. 'Why are you here?'

Cousins smiled in the darkness. The Macanese was probably wondering why he was not dead, shot to death by Wun Cheng Lo in a fit of simulated indignation and horror at the murder of the Governor.

'It was no good,' explained Cousins in shaky tones. 'When the Governor passed along the corridor, he was walking with three other men and, as he was on the farther side, I couldn't fling the knife at him. He has now gone to bed.'

'Well, why did you not go in and stab him?' snarled Tavares.

'The doors were locked. We waited until all was quiet; then the Chink and I came to that gate over there. He told me to climb over – he's too fat to do it himself – and fetch you and these fellows. There's nobody about, and he's waiting there to lead you into the house.'

Tavares spoke rapidly to a man by his side. The latter grunted; then in the high-pitched accents of China, snapped a few phrases that sounded like commands. Men rose on all sides. For a moment Cousins was released, but almost immediately Tavares came to his side, and took hold of his arm.

'Listen!' he hissed. 'If you have played us false, you will be cut into a thousand pieces.'

'Why should I play you false?' growled Cousins. 'Look here,' he added in wheedling tones, 'don't let us go through with this, Mr Tavares. I hate murder, and—'

'Be quiet!' snapped Tavares. If he had had any doubt of the truth of Cousins' story, the latter's words convinced him now that all was as the little man had described it. 'You make me smile, you who have already murdered a man. Tonight, my friend Collins, you shall murder many. It was a pity our plans went wrong, but perhaps it will be more amusing this way. Six of these men will creep on the guard, and slay them then nothing can interfere with the good work. It will be a deed that will make Pei Wu Chow famous for ever.' He said something in Chinese to the diminutive figure by his side, who again grunted, but this time as though well pleased. 'There are I think,' went on Tavares, in a gloating voice to Cousins, 'two white women as well as the ayah and the wives of the servants. There will, therefore, be great amusement. It will be much interesting to see the so-beautiful Lady Wallace in the hands of Pei Wu Chow and his men.'

A tremor of abhorrence went through Cousins. His hands itched fiercely to get at the throat of the vile scoundrel by his side.

'You haven't a drink on you, have you?' was all he said.

Tavares laughed softly.

'Have patience, my friend,' he murmured. 'When our work is finished, you shall drink your fill in Government House. Come!'

Led by Tavares and Cousins, the pirates crept quietly across the road. The Macanese looked through the bars of the gates; could dimly make out the figure of a man.

'Is that you, Wun Cheng Lo?' he asked softly in fluent Cantonese.

'It is I,' came back the low reply at once. 'Come quickly! All is quiet.'

Sir Leonard's number one boy had been coached well in his part. Tavares had no suspicion that he was anybody but the Kowloon merchant.

Cousins climbed the gate first, followed by the others in twos and threes. Before long the whole party stood in a group inside the grounds. Tavares was the last to surmount the obstacle. He peered into the faces round him.

'Where are you, Wun Cheng Lo?' he called quietly, 'and where—?'

Suddenly a brilliant light illumined the scene from a tree close by and, before the startled pirates could move a hand, they found themselves surrounded by soldiers, whose fixed bayonets were held with ominous warning within an inch or two of each individual breast. Sir Leonard strolled into the circle of light, and contemplated the snarling faces of the prisoners, who had been so completely taken by surprise that they could do nothing but glare impotently at their captors.

'Quite a choice little collection of cut-throats,' he commented. 'I suppose you are José Tavares?' he added to the Macanese. 'I shall have a word or two with you before you are locked up.'

The pirate leader, a small wizened man, had been crouching in the centre of the circle, his eyes almost bulging from his head with the intensity of his hatred. Nobody noticed, however, that most of his looks were directed venomously at the shrinking, fear-stricken Tavares. Apparently he blamed the latter for the manner in which they had been trapped. As Sir Leonard turned to give orders to his men, the scoundrel launched himself at Tavares like a wild cat, a long, thin-bladed knife in his hand. Once, twice he stabbed. At the sound of the stricken man's choking cry, Wallace swung round. Like lightning a revolver appeared in his hand, and he fired, as two soldiers lunged at Pei Wu Chow with their bayonets. The man seemed to crumple up in mid-air; crashed to the ground with a bullet through his brain. Tavares was still alive, though unconscious. He was carried into the house, while the pirates were disarmed, manacled, and marched off to the cellar in which Wun Cheng Lo and the other prisoners were already incarcerated.

Everything possible was done for Tavares, but it quickly became evident that he was sinking fast. The doctor who had been summoned to attend to Wun Cheng Lo arrived while they were endeavouring to arrest the flow of blood. He quickly took charge and, under his ministrations, the Macanese recovered consciousness. When he realised that he was dying, he made a statement which was taken down by Carter, the wounded man just having strength enough left to sign it at the end.

The declaration filled in a number of the blanks that had puzzled Sir Leonard, though a good deal of it he already knew, or had conjectured. It asserted that Tavares had been more of a friend than a servant of the financier Mathos, and was entirely in his confidence. Mathos, Gomez, who became Postmaster-General, Sales, and Wun Cheng Lo were all graduates of Hong Kong University. Although their activities lay in different spheres, they joined together after the War to run privately, apart from their ordinary avocations, a money-lending business. Ferguson, who was at the time Secretary for Chinese Affairs, and Collinson, then Assistant Treasurer and Estate Duty Commissioner, got into their clutches and became deeply involved. Collinson it was, who in a desperate effort to think of a way out of his entanglements, hit upon the gigantic scheme of swindling the Treasury. He and Ferguson put the proposition before Mathos and Gomez and, as a result, the organisation came into existence. Wun Cheng Lo and Sales, who had only had small shares in the money-lending business, were employed in a more or less subsidiary capacity in the new association. To help the scheme, Stevenson and Waverley, one of whom was in the Audit department, and the other in the Treasury, were entrapped in an unsavoury kind of affair and, to avoid the risk of exposure and consequent loss of their posts, agreed to assist. They appeared to have been very pliable and willing victims, Sir Leonard thought. The next to be inveigled in was Wayne, it being thought useful, for various reasons, to have an officer of the police in the organisation. It was not a very difficult matter to persuade him to join. An overbearing, ambitious, and ruthless man, he already held a somewhat shady reputation.

Mathos and Gomez, who were exceedingly clever draughtsmen and engravers, executed a great number of forgeries, Tavares assisting in the process. Stevenson and Waverley passed them through, Collinson endorsed them. No other officials ever thought of questioning anything approved by men of their positions, and thus the swindling went on. Owing to his interest in so many banks, Mathos was able to flood the market with bonds, securities, and share certificates, all of which had received, through Collinson and his colleagues, the seal of Government, but were actually utterly valueless. Contracts were given out, and various schemes undertaken, all being charged up to the Treasury, sometimes as much as two hundred per cent above their actual cost. Post Office finances were manipulated by Gomez, first as Assistant Postmaster; then, through the influence of Ferguson, as Postmaster-General.

As time went on, and Mathos found that he was being pushed more and more into the background, he became alarmed. He cunningly succeeded in obtaining incriminating documents from Stevenson, Waverley, Wayne, and Gomez, but, although he tried many subterfuges, he failed to obtain anything of a similar nature from Ferguson or Collinson. Then came revelation, and Mathos was preparing for flight, when Wayne entered his house ostensibly to talk over affairs with him. From a recess, in which he had been tearing up papers, Tavares actually saw the policeman shoot Mathos, put the revolver in the dead man's hand, and arrange everything to give an appearance of suicide. Wayne then searched for the incriminating documents which Tavares, with thoughts of blackmail in his mind, had already purloined. The arrival of Superintendent Ponsford with the men to arrest Mathos had forced him to desist.

Tavares quickly made his intentions known to the others, and they were compelled to accept him as a confederate. The residence of Mathos had previously been their meeting place. They now had to find another, and he was asked to make the arrangements. He bought the block of three houses, one of which he already rented as a dance hall and restaurant, and had secret communications constructed between them. Sales, with whom he was very friendly, went to live in one house, the Turkish bath establishment was opened in the other. Thus an innocent way in and out was provided for the conspirators. About that time it was found that a man named Baxter, who held an important commercial post, had stumbled on an item of information concerning Sir Stanley Ferguson and Collinson, which, if published, would place them in grave danger of exposure. Attempts were made to kill Baxter, but he escaped, eventually becoming so alarmed that he sailed for England. Wun Cheng Lo, who had been acting in the capacity of watchdog for Ferguson, was sent after him with Sir Stanley's three Phillipino servants who, for some reason not stated, were devoted to their master. Baxter was murdered.

In the meantime, a magistrate in Shanghai told the police that he had information to impart. Wayne, as a senior officer, immediately became aware of this. He obtained leave, and travelled to Shanghai secretly. He told the magistrate he had come to escort him to Hong Kong. On the voyage he learnt what he had to divulge, stabbed him, and threw him overboard. Later a Chinese banker in Victoria sent in confidence to the police to say that he could give intelligence concerning the plot. Wayne invited him to a private dinner, ascertained that there was no documentary evidence to support his story, and put aconitine in his coffee. The Chinaman died in his own home two or three hours later, and nobody knew how he had been poisoned, or that he had dined with Wayne.

There followed a good deal concerning the arrangements made to kill Sir Leonard, and a statement that Wayne had also organised the blowing up of Burrows' house, after failing with a crew of Chinese pirates, which Tavares himself had supplied, to kill the merchant during the picnic. The dying man also corroborated the information, which Sir Leonard had obtained from the Japanese consul's letter to Collinson, concerning the reason why the conspirators had been compelled to sell military secrets to Japan. Finally he confessed that for some years he and Mathos had been hand in glove with the pirates of Bias Bay.

'A pretty scoundrel altogether,' reflected Wallace. 'He

is ending his life in a cleaner and better manner than he deserves.'

While Tavares was feebly making his dying depositions, the troops were engaged in apprehending every man found in the vicinity of Government House. Those who were unable to give an entirely satisfactory account of themselves were thrown into the cellar which, with the advent of the gang of pirates, had become uncomfortably crowded. Among those sent in to be examined was Ho Fang Ho. He had gone to the Botanical Gardens at the usual time and, as Carter had not appeared, had waited patiently outside Government House ever since in the expectation of being summoned. When he saw Cousins, he almost went hysterical with joy, an extraordinary thing for a Chinaman to do.

'Master,' he cried, 'my too muchee, too muchee happy you come back Hong Kong side. Pleasee you no go with velly bad pilate mans 'gain.'

'Velly bad pilate mans is dying, Ho Fang Ho,' Cousins told him. 'You can, therefore, be sure that I have no intention of accompanying him on his last journey.'

'My belong plenty glad him soon makee dead mans,' declared Ho Fang Ho callously. 'Him debbil go looksee odder debbils. Master no pletend dlunk allo time now.'

'Cheeky beggar!' grunted Cousins. 'I'll soon be going to England. What will you do then?'

'Ho Fang Ho go England side with master,' came the reply simply but with determination.

'Bless the boy! It seems that I can't get rid of you.' He turned to Carter who was standing by. 'What would you do in a case like this?'

'Take him with you,' suggested Carter with a smile.

It may as well be recorded here that, when Cousins went back to England, Ho Fang Ho, the faithful, did go with him.

Tavares died just as dawn was breaking, and his body was laid in a shed with that of the pirate leader who had killed him to await removal to the mortuary.

Sir Leonard did not go to bed that night. He simply changed into pyjamas and a dressing gown, and sat in his study writing a long and detailed report. At eight o'clock, as he was drinking tea brought to him by Batty, the telephone bell rang. It was a triumphant message from the Inspector-General of Police. The raids had been carried out without a hitch. The conspirators had all been taken by surprise, and were now under close arrest. Sir Leonard smiled, put down the receiver, and went to his room for an hour's rest. He felt he could afford to relax. His work was accomplished.

At eleven, as alert as ever, he met the members of the Executive Council, hastily summoned to Government House by Carter. There was one exception – the Colonial Treasurer, Meredith Collinson. They had already heard the news, and all looked like men who had received a terrible shock. First announcing that the suspension of both Councils was from that hour removed, the Governor went on quietly and gravely to take them step by step through his investigations, very much in the same manner that he had made his disclosures to Sir Masterson Winstanley. Afterwards, with a few graceful words of regret for the suspension he had been compelled by circumstances to impose, he dismissed them. Before departing, the two unofficial Chinese members, Sir T'so Lin Tao and Sir Peter Hing Kee, begged him to convey to the

British Government expressions of their profound horror and assurances of their unfailing loyalty. He thanked them; promised that he would not fail to do so.

It was shortly after half past twelve that, as the result of a telephone message, Dr Connolly entered Kenton's room at the hospital in a state of excitement. A nurse, who was engaged in making the patient comfortable, looked up at him curiously.

'Nurse darlin',' he cried, 'you're afther wastin' good time by doing that.'

'Why?' she asked in surprise. 'What do you mean, doctor?'

'Is he not to be removed to the best room in the hospital, and looked after as though he were the Lord Mayor of Dublin himself now?'

'Good gracious!' she exclaimed. 'Who gave orders for the change?'

Kenton was listening to the conversation with interest. The doctor's eyes sparkled; his brogue became broader than ever as his excitement seemed to grow.

'Who would they be from but the Governor himself,' he declared. 'The police guard has already been removed, bad cess to it. An' that is not all now. His Excellency himself and his lady will be afther visitin' this omadhaun at two pip emma. Faith, an' it's a flustered man I am this day.'

Kenton's pale face flushed slightly. A look crept into his eyes that seemed somehow to bring back youth and strength into his expression. The nurse looked at him; smiled almost proudly. She had attended him during his desperate fight with the devils of Delirium Tremens, and had learnt from his ravings a considerable amount of his history.

'I am so glad,' she murmured simply.

Kenton was removed to a large airy room on the ground floor, which he found had been turned into a bower of flowers sent specially from Government House. Promptly at two Sir Leonard and Lady Wallace arrived and, under the unaffected kindliness of their manner, Kenton regained all his old resolution. With it came the determination to blot out entirely the black period of his life when, through a woman's faithlessness and callousness, he had allowed himself to descend to the depths. From that hour life became worth living again. He was vastly astonished to learn that the man whom he had accompanied to Collinson's house on the Peak had been the Governor himself. Molly, who by that time knew everything, almost drew tears to his eyes by her gratitude for the act of manliness that had probably saved her husband's life. As they rose to go, Sir Leonard leant down, and grasped the invalid's hand.

'There must be no turning back,' he smiled. 'You are far too good a man to give way to despair. There are great schemes ahead, schemes which need the brains of the engineer whose work on the Indus and Sutlej remains as a monument to his skill.'

'Then you know my real name, sir?' whispered the man who called himself Kenton.

'My dear chap, I recognised you directly I saw you.'

After they had gone, Kenton lay for some time with a faraway, misty look in his eyes. A wonderful transformation had taken place in him. When, soon after three, Cousins entered the room, he was so lost in deep and pleasant meditation that he failed, for some time, to notice the little man, now his own spruce, well-groomed self, who stood quietly by his bedside.

'Dreaming, Jim?' asked Cousins at length.

Kenton turned his head abruptly; his right hand shot out to his friend to be warmly clasped.

'By Jove, George!' he cried. 'I can't tell you how glad I am to see you.' He looked the other up and down. 'So you're not a beachcomber after all,' he commented with a grin.

'No,' responded Cousins, 'and neither are you. What a couple of old frauds we were, weren't we? And, by the way, don't call me "George". By all accounts he's gone to "Lyonch". My name is Gerald Cousins – Jerry to you, old chap.'

At first with a trace of embarrassment, afterwards with enthusiasm, Kenton told his friend of his plans for the future, and Cousins, with a deep sense of gladness, knew there would be no sliding back.

'"How good is man's life, the mere living! How fit to employ",' he quoted, '"All the heart and the soul and the senses for ever in joy!"'

That was undoubtedly Kenton's busy day. In the early evening Batty arrived smiling and cheerful, carrying a basket of luscious fruit for the patient sent by Lady Wallace.

'Come aboard, sir,' he reported, touching his forelock in true nautical style. "Er Ladyship told me to tell you that you are commanded – I was to say "commanded" special-like – to tell the nurse if there's anythin' wot you fancies, and it'll be sent immediate.' Kenton murmured his gratitude. 'And,' went on Batty, 'as soon as you're able to up-anchor, sir, you're to stand out from this 'ere 'ospital, set your course for

Government House, an' take up your moorings there.'

The invalid smiled at the phraseology, but was a little troubled by the invitation. He was hardly in a position, he felt, to stay as a guest at Government House. Batty sensed his embarrassment. He had heard Kenton's story, knew what he had done for Sir Leonard and, in the ex-sailor's opinion, anyone who performed a service of such a nature for his master was worthy of the utmost deference and attention.

'O' course 'er Ladyship will send you a proper invitation, sir,' he asserted. 'I was only to tell you so's you wouldn't make no other arrangements.' And, in such a manner that there could be no possible hint of offence, he added: 'Comin' out of 'ospital, it's likely you'll be needin' a few extra duds, but don't you go boardin' shops an' layin' in stores, sir. You won't be fit enough for that. When you come to Government 'Ouse, just lay alongside o' me, an' I'll fit you out fore an' aft, below decks and above. An' now, if you'll 'scuse me, sir, I'll be settin' sail. I've got a date with two little craft wot are takin' me in tow to the pictures.'

Kenton held out his hand. Not for the first time that day, there was a suspicious moisture in his eyes. Batty gave him a hearty grip then moved away. At the door he turned, looking a trifle sheepish.

'I'd like to thank you for meself, sir,' he muttered almost inaudibly, 'for wot you did. You see Sir Leonard Wallace is – well, there ain't another cove in the world like 'im – beggin' yer pardon, sir.'

Batty was gone and, for a long time, Kenton gazed at the closed door.

At about the same time that the ex-naval man was at the

hospital, Sir Leonard and Lady Wallace were strolling round the grounds of Government House. Captain Ferrara had been with them, but had left his little book inside. As he disliked being without it, he had excused himself, and had gone to get it. They came to the large conservatory, and entered.

'The real work for which I came to Hong Kong, Molly,' Sir Leonard told her softly, 'is accomplished. There is no longer anything for you to fear. For the next three months, every moment that I can spare from the duties of administration is yours, dear.'

Her eyes shone. She took his arm with a little movement that was a caress in itself.

'Three months,' she murmured; 'three months of utter happiness!'

Ferrara came round the corner of the building, and noticed them inside. He chuckled.

'"People in glasses house",' he quoted, '"gazzer no moss".' He shook his head a little impatiently. 'It is wrong,' he muttered; 'not to my satisfaction. What says the book?'

But, as he started to open the little volume, something about the attitude of the two inside the conservatory warned him that, for once, he was *de trop*.

Captain Ferrara stole quietly back the way he had come.

To discover more great books and to
place an order visit our website at
allisonandbusby.com

Don't forget to sign up to our free newsletter at
allisonandbusby.com/newsletter
for latest releases, events and exclusive offers

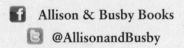 **Allison & Busby Books**
@AllisonandBusby

You can also call us on
020 7580 1080
for orders, queries
and reading recommendations